SCOTT SPENCER

and

PRESERVATION HALL

"PRESERVATION HALL was hard to put down. Written with great control and expert pacing, it is a compelling narrative....Spencer has written a powerful and intelligent novel about the discord between a father and son...gracefully written, with drama, irony, and insight skillfully interwoven, and it has about it the inevitability of a Greek tragedy."

Chicago Daily News

"Scott Spencer's...novel is a very good one indeed....PRESERVATION HALL...is... ambitious....The verb 'to entertain' is much abused; it means 'to hold together.' A novel is entertaining because it is engaging, compelling, affecting, because it is like PRESERVATION HALL."

The Philadelphia Inquirer

"The novel stings our age-old fears and makes the pain seem fresh and revelatory...."

Publishers Weekly

(more)

SCOTT SPENCER

"This is a novel that has everything—suspense both physical and psychic, characters well delineated and recognizable, lots of sex, and is written with grim humor. It is unputdownable...."

Hartford Courant

"A beautifully written story of a young man whose flight from his father and all that his father represents becomes, ultimately, a journey to 'the center of his own fear'...So powerfully does Spencer write these things, that the reader learns them afresh. Spencer handles his hero's spiritual journey in such a way that the novel's symbolism never overpowers the narrative. His descriptive passages have a sustained power, and his characters...have the substance of flesh and blood. Spencer is a truly fine novelist...."

St. Louis Post-Dispatch

"Spencer deserves a good deal of praise for having the imagination to know more about his characters than they do themselves."

The New York Times Book Review

PRESERVATION HALL

Also by Scott Spencer
Published by Ballantine Books:

WAKING THE DEAD

PRESERVATION HALL

Scott Spencer

BALLANTINE BOOKS • NEW YORK

Originally published in hardcover by Alfred A. Knopf, Inc. in 1976

Grateful acknowledgment is made to Famous Music Publishing
Companies for permission to reprint lyrics from "Thanks for the
Memories" by Leo Robin and Ralph Rainger (p. 43–44). Copyright
1937 by Paramount Music Corporation. Copyright renewed 1964 by
Paramount Music Corporation.

Library of Congress Catalog Card Number: 76-13681

ISBN 0-345-34478-2

Manufactured in the United States of America

First Ballantine Books Edition: August 1987

To my parents
and to Devorah Zeitlin

ONE

1

IN 1960, when Earl Morgan, my father, was forty-five and I, his only son, was twelve, we left Chicago to move to New York. Earl had decided to drop the mask of his obscurity and claim his place in the world of music. I didn't believe anything of the sort would happen—the man was cursed, I thought, doomed—but as we piled our belongings into our gangsterish black Pontiac and prepared for our assault on America's cultural capital, my father and I were almost as one, for though I could not believe that Earl was going to realize or even *cure* his chronic ambitions, one thing was certain: in New York we'd be unknown, unjudged, and I, at least, could begin again.

In Chicago, while he nursed the wounds of a failed career and then a failed marriage, my father taught music in the same public school I attended and this, in a childhood brocaded with real and imagined mortifications, was my central, ravishing woe. It was worse than living in a chaotic pisshole of a house, and worse than my mother running off the way men are supposed to—with a cheap, battered suitcase and a couple hundred bucks, marking her trail with increasingly far-flung postcards, from Nevada, California, Oregon, and British Columbia. She traveled with a man named Stewart, who was dying and wanted to see the world.

Earl was hated by our neighbors. We lived in a rabidly provincial lower middle-class neighborhood and his presence on the block was barely tolerated, even when he was a married man. Once Evelynn left him and he entered his second bachelorhood, he traveled downhill in their collective estimation from oddball to outcast. Once, coming home from the bus stop, someone threw stones at him. My father stoned! He talked about it for months, and though I never was certain who'd done it I dreaded that it was someone I knew.

If Earl had been hounded because he had an accent or because he limped, he might have held a firmer grip on my allegiance, but I could never rid myself of the suspicion that his position as pariah was somewhat willed. No one else in sight wore even a colored shirt or a mustache, but there was my vulnerable papa with his tusk-like goatee and the linty beret he wore even when he gave our tiny patch of lawn its annual mowing. Our neighbors might eventually have forgiven him his vaguely fruitcake job of teaching their children music at the Burnside Public School. They could have forgiven him his ignoble loss of spouse and the subsequently sporadic brand of parenthood that turned me, his only child, into a pest, one of those fast-talking kids who show up around dinnertime or when their favorite shows are on TV—Earl wouldn't have a set in the house. I think they could have arranged amnesty for his reading the *New York Times* on our tiny, three-step cement porch. But that beard and that beret—never! It was an affront, like a lewd remark. Of course they were silly and hysterical about Earl's democratic right to decorate himself as he pleased, but why in the world did he press it?

I waited for people to turn on me as well. I envisioned the day when sides for softball would be chosen and I would shuffle off, red-faced and unchosen. But no one blamed me, or the blame was not thrust in my face. It amazed me. In some soft, childish way, it frightened me that those who had contempt for Earl would welcome me. And knowing they felt as they did, there was no one on that block I could ever open my heart to. I had to live there and, by and large, I didn't press my luck.

The neighbors didn't know the half of it, of course. No one knew Earl stayed up past midnight writing long, unpunctuated letters to friends he hadn't seen in ten years, or that he spent a minimum of two hours every night slaving over a piano concerto he'd been pulling through the birth canal since the dawn of time. Not one of our stolid, intolerant neighbors knew that Mr. Morgan favored a little can of caviar for breakfast, which he would eat on soda crackers along with a demi-tasse of muddy coffee. And no one was privy to my most guarded secret about him: from the day my mother left, when I was seven years old, to the day we quit that house and moved to New York, when I was twelve, my father slept in his bed no more than twenty times. Every night he would lie on the couch with that garish flowered slipcover and pretend he was just going to read for a few minutes. Fifteen feet away, in the salmon-colored cubicle that held his double bed, the sheets were turned down, the alarm clock set, but he almost never slept there. Every school day I'd hear the alarm go off in his room, hear him groan, and then he'd pad through the living room, across the small kitchen, past my bedroom and into his own. There he would turn off the alarm, sigh as if it were execution day, and then come into my room and touch my shoulder gently to make certain I was awake.

But there was worse: for this was the period when we both left for the same destination. He knew better than to ever ask me to walk with him, assuming, of course, that he wanted to. The school was only five blocks away. I rode my bike. I didn't trust myself to refuse Earl should he suggest we walk together, so I pedaled my tomato-red Schwinn every day, through the rain, through those supernatural winds, even through the snow—the school's bike rack would be coated with a soft layer of snow interrupted only by my thick black lock and chain. Yet it was within that low-slung, modern schoolhouse that my immunity to Earl suffered its final devastation, for there I would be faced with him, and all the eyes that gazed upon him could turn and gaze upon me as well. Nothing could break my pink boy's heart quite so convulsively as watching Earl teach music to my friends. It was like madness to be sitting with him in that hot, honey-colored classroom while he swayed back and forth like a human metronome, his huge claws beating the keys, singing:

> Some say that life was made for fun and frolic
> And so do I
> And so do I
> Funiculi, funicula
> Funiculi
> FUNICULA!

Earl's aim was to take two-lane highways all the way from Chicago to New York. "This way," he explained, as we moved out into the hot July dawn, "we'll actually *see* where we're going. I hate those turnpikes, Virgil. They're inhuman and, just you wait, one day they'll take over the whole country. Everything will be concrete." There were other, less sentimental reasons for taking the back roads: no tolls to pay, cheaper gasoline stations, and a chance to price shop when we were hungry.

He had me laughing from the moment we left town. I'd never seen him in better spirits. He did redneck imitations in Indiana and told stories about hick stupidity and Ku Klux Klan mayors. In Ohio, our road sometimes moved right alongside the turnpike and we could see the new cars, with their outlandish fins, passing us as regularly as cards being dealt off the top of an endless deck. Earl urged the Pontiac on with whoops and slaps at the steering wheel, like a cowboy racing his horse to the death against a train. He made remarks to the waitresses in the little restaurants we'd stop in every three hours, coolly demanding boiling water for his imported tea bags and then lavishly complimenting their culinary skills. He even let me listen to the car radio and seemed to develop a taste for Elvis Presley singing "Won't You Wear My Ring Around Your Neck." We were like convicts escaping; every mile crossed testified to our incredible good fortune, our giddy peril.

Earl wanted to make it across the country in one sprint, without wasting money on a motel. He asked me to keep an eye out for hitchhikers, so he might have someone to share the driving. My father had, however, exacting tastes in freeloaders and though we passed perhaps a half dozen I had no luck in finding someone who met Earl's standards.

"No, I won't ride with servicemen," said my casually seditious father, as he slowed down and peered at a young soldier and then resumed his full cruising speed, while I, patriotically offended, watched the stunned defender of my freedoms kicking at his dufflebag and getting smaller and smaller as planet Pontiac continued its fuming orbit. We passed teenagers, we passed old men, we passed a man in a suit who held a gas can, and each time Earl had a different excuse for not stopping.

Finally, I felt the sullen rage of one whose suggestions have been systematically rejected and I exploded, "Why don't you ever stop? It's not fair to look at people and then not stop, goddammit."

Earl looked at my face. "I don't know, Virgil," he said. "I think the reason is that I don't want anyone in the car. We never have any time alone and I like it with just the two of us."

"But you're getting so tired." It was no use, though. My reply was a weak reflex and it could not control the surprise I felt at his unexpected tenderness nor could it conceal the tears in my eyes. He wanted us to be alone! How wonderful, yet how disturbing, and how unprepared I was to hear it.

We pulled in for the night some twelve hours after leaving Chicago and checked into a nameless motel. We stayed in a cabin that smelled like a brand new shoe. It had two double beds, soft as éclairs, pink walls, sanitized glasses, a tub the size of a child's casket, and a TV that received but one channel and even that rather ectoplasmically. It was in this motel that my father and I spent one of the best nights of our lives. He watched television with me for a while and then he cadged a deck of cards from the motel manager and did card tricks for me—a talent I had no idea he possessed. Then my father and I played casino and were so entertained and comforted by the game that we took the deck with us when we drove for a late night snack of ham and eggs. The sky was riddled with stars and before we went to bed we turned out all the lights in our room and looked out the window. I thought about my mother because I always imagined her beneath a sky bright and thick with stars, planets, comets, and moons. Earl had a soft, distant expression on his face and I was certain his thoughts moved in the same direction as mine, and for that moment our loss combined with our blood, and he was my friend. We whispered to each other in bed, like boys who fear they might be overheard. He told me what he remembered of New York, a city which, in his mind, held hope itself in its huge electronic fist. I don't remember what I said, but I was sure he was listening, and certain that, perhaps for the very first time, I truly interested him.

* * *

Since that night, I have stayed in at least a hundred hotels and maybe, without my even knowing it, I was all the while listening for Earl's whisper—but really this is just mockery because the fact is that years went by when the memory of that night was lost to me, as if it had been something that had happened when I was drunk. Even now, I remember only enough to describe it and I'm sure I wouldn't even have that much had it not been my lot to fall in love with a woman who believed in family life and who forced me to think and talk about mine.

Her name, when I met her, was Tracy Keating, but she took my name when we married. I wonder why: if she believed so in family connections, why would she abandon her last name? I suggested a number of times that I take *her* name but each time my suggestion got a laugh and I didn't quite dare force her to understand how dearly I would have loved to complete my separation from Earl by changing my name. I loathed my name.

Less than a month after Tracy and I met, we took an impetuous weekend trip to the Bahamas and it was somewhere during the sunny, alcoholic romp that I stumbled on the memory of that night in a motel with Earl. Tracy had asked me a few vague questions about my recent past and I mentioned seeing Earl six months before. I hadn't known it, but until then she'd thought I was an orphan. Then she ascertained that not only was Earl alive and well but that he lived in New York, about fifteen minutes by subway from where she and I had been making love and laughing like lunatics for the past three weeks.

And so, between trips to the beach and trips to the casino, where I swam with the blind vehemence of an urbanite and gambled with the forced flamboyance of an up-from-under boy, I talked to Tracy about Earl. I didn't know what she was making of my traitorous tales but she kept probing, kept egging me on and it was so wonderful to feel someone cared about my life that I didn't mind revealing the depths of my resentment. But then she said something that should have warned even a fool in love.

"We'll go see him when we get back," she said.

But I was not warned at all. What it meant to me was that she planned to keep on seeing me—I loved anything that smelled of a future between us. And the fact that she wanted to meet Earl only meant that she was serious about wanting to mix her life with mine. So instead of telling her to keep her finely tuned sensibilities out of my discordant life, I put my arms carefully around her—she was so thin, so beautiful, and I loved her so much.

During our last day in the hotel, I lost a couple hundred dollars playing blackjack and Tracy took me out for a few drinks, to cheer me up. We had those fruit-chopped-ice-and-rum drinks we wouldn't have touched in New York but which seem somehow ideal in the islands. When I had my second, she casually asked me what I remembered as the best time between Earl and me and it was then that I remembered that one quiet night in a motel as we traveled toward New York. I described it to her and she nodded with slightly irritating, though altogether well-meaning encouragement, as if to say that if I looked I would discover this was only one sweet memory in a galaxy of them.

It struck me as curious that the memory of that night should have eluded me for so many years, for though I rarely spoke of Earl I thought of him all the time and had practically memorized my life with him, as if our past was an extinct language that only I could keep alive. But as I thought about it and sipped noisily on my third rum glacier, I realized that that night was for me one of the true and dizzy peaks of filial treachery. I had looked forward to moving to New York because I thought I could disassociate myself from my father and that was exactly what I did. All of the touching moments along the way, all the games of twenty questions, all of the Cokes with two straws, engaged only an infinitesimal part of me because I'd long ago made up my mind about him and waited only for the chance to separate our lives.

I had five more years of living with him and we kept out of each other's way. Whatever dim impulses he might have felt to fuse our lives were either forgotten in the confusion of his own life or tabled in the face of my apparent indifference. I got a scholarship to Cornell and left shortly before my eighteenth birthday and never slept in the same house with him after that. I was not comfortable in his presence. Even that night in the motel, when Earl's whispering stopped and I knew he'd dropped off to sleep, went sour for me because I simply did not feel safe around him. It was not only that I didn't think he could protect me but I suspected that he drew calamity into his orbit. If anything as lofty as philosophy can be ascribed to a twelve-year-old, mine was that the man who stands next to the man who is struck by lightning also gets burned. I wanted a life of my own.

I was never eager for what we generally call success, though I wanted to live comfortably. But with Earl as a negative example, I rejected most of ambition's temptations. I coasted as quietly as a shadow through the semi-fancy private school for which my father had sacrificed so much and then I crept off to Cornell, where I first studied physics, then history, and finally scraped together enough credits to graduate with a major in English. I had the usual quota of friends and lovers, maybe a bit less. But as long as there was someone to invite me to their parents' summer home and keep me out of New York and away from Earl, my need for friendship was satisfied. As for my plans, these were persistently vague: I would graduate, get some sort of job, and go to Europe.

I did just that. I looked at some of the great paintings, learned how to play billiards, took drugs, almost married a Dutch girl who turned out to be fourteen years old, lived for ten days in a cave in Greece. I was out of the draft on an adamant lie and all I wanted was to stay alive and enjoy myself.

When I ran out of money I came back to New York, thinking I would work for a few more months and then return to Europe. I stayed with an old classmate and didn't tell Earl I was back until I was working, afraid, I think, to meet him with anything resembling a vacuum in my life. Through a friend of a friend, I was introduced to a man named Bob Halpin, a cheerful, fortyish businessman who liked something in me and hired me to work for his management consulting company. I never dreamed the job would last more than six months, but I had that knack some people have for fitting in. Halpin had a belief in me, not so much in my talent as in my luck. He said that things had a way of working out well when I was around.

From the very start, I didn't care about that job, but it gave me money and determined to a large (and telling) extent the circles I moved in. I suddenly knew far too many people who were twenty years my senior, who'd been born into wealthy families or who had pursued wealth all of their lives, who were on their second marriage, and who were content to touch the most distant, public edge of my life and leave it at that. I moved into a beautiful apartment on Central Park West and while I knew enough to realize that it's unsympathetic for someone who's suddenly hit the bucks to complain about what it's done to his so-called soul, there were, nevertheless, times when my life seemed so strange that it was nightmarish. I feared I had cut myself off from ever feeling young again and worried that I was living utterly out of my depth. I had no distinct ideas about what to spend my money on after I paid the rent and so I saved it for some future trip. I thought I might buy a piece of land in the country but I felt so alone in the world that I didn't dare isolate my-

self further. I had what people in their middle age call
empty affairs. I bought a wooden valet for my custom-
made suits. I made fun of vegetarians. I was twenty-
five years old.

There was no one I felt comfortable with and no
one to whom I dared give my heart. The exile from my
contemporaries was no accident: the lives of people
my age seemed suddenly perilous. They were beaten
by the police on Fifth Avenue during antiwar parades.
They lost their minds on drug trips. They didn't fit in
anywhere and begged on the street. They took jobs as
messengers and lived in neighborhoods where everyone was unsafe. Their lives were disorderly, given to
sudden eruptions. And those whose lives weren't like
that seemed to have no time for or interest in me. I
was not the only one to impose clockwork order on my
life but those of us who did avoided each other, or
drove each other mad with small, muted gestures of
rancor and envy. Maybe it was just my bad luck, or
maybe I was being saved for something else, but I
didn't meet anyone my age who had taken a place in
the business world whom I could stand to be in the
same room with, or who appeared to be able to stand
me. I had an easier time with women since there were
still a number of them who lived on the outskirts of the
economic world, who lived orderly but wholly marginal lives, but these friendships never lasted very long
because they seemed to be looking for someone who
was an enormous amount of fun and I really wasn't
fun. I was never a "Let's have breakfast in Coney Is-
land and then fly to Paris to buy shoes" type.

What I needed was an outsider on the inside and
that was what I found in Tracy. I met her at a party
that Paramount Pictures threw after a world premiere.
I was in attendance because Halpin and I had helped a
Paramount executive set up a dude ranch in Arizona
and Tracy was there because the publishing company
she worked for had brought out the book upon which
the movie was based. There was a band, twenty

waiters, and five hundred pounds of shrimp. I escorted a young woman who worked in my office and Tracy was with her friend Gary Fish, who, many months later, I was to punch in the nose. It was a miracle that we met at all. The party was held in a hotel ballroom and it was swarming with movie industry people pressing each other's flesh, hippies with Nikons dangling from their necks, paid escorts, out-of-towners, relatives. As I had come to expect, there was no one for me to speak to, so I had the bartender make me two drinks and, with my date happily circulating the room in search of celebrities, I found a pillar near the bandstand, where I could lean, drink, and be near enough to the source of some of the party's noise to feel camouflaged.

It turned out to be Tracy's strategy as well and from there it was basically like anyone else falling in love, only this time it was me, it was us. We talked for a while, her friend Gary Fish sensed what was happening and excused himself, and Tracy and I were lovers that same night—I'm bragging, of course. It's a miracle I didn't frighten her away with my mangled ardor, but I knew immediately that I loved her and my strongest impulse was to throw my adoration over her like a net. After a week of my *hinting* how much I cared for her, and how often I would like to see her, Tracy told me flat out that she was in love with me and I burst into tears. From then on, we made each other dizzy with declarations. We woke daily with vows of love and we'd say it on the phone when we were at work. When we finally moved in together, she wrote she loved me on the bathroom mirror with her one tube of lipstick and once she sent me a telegram: "Dear Fatboy, I love you forever."

Tracy's physical beauty may have struck some as merely fawn-like but to me it was awesome. She was small but high-waisted and her legs had little streams of down, flowing up the thigh and down the shin. Her teeth were bright and straight, her hair the color of obsidian, and her hot brown eyes burned with an intelligence I felt was rather superior to my own. She had the arms of a strong, though slightly undeveloped boy and she wore her hair cropped so closely it was only through old pictures of her that I learned it was curly —I loved those old pictures and I carried them in my wallet, as if I'd always known her. There were two pictures of her on horseback, one at six with tar-colored pigtails dangling down a striped T-shirt and another at thirteen, in full competitive costume, scowling with the shy hatred of a secret outlaw. Then there was the photo of her in sailor pants, taken when she was fifteen, her hips protruding like boomerangs, standing in a deserted amusement park, a roller-coaster track behind her looking like the skeleton of a mountain. I would look at these pictures at work and sometimes in the middle of the day drop everything, take a cab across town, and charge into her seedy offices like a lunatic, my eyes shining like the icing on a cake.

I courted her out of passion, but I *did* see marrying Tracy as a kind of salvation. I was a boy with a lucrative job but I had no one I dared speak to—I couldn't have sustained myself alone. Tracy's life—the patterns it took, the way she moved through it—seemed like an ideal, and I admired, right up to the borders of envy, her solid, cheerful family. Her mother was a physician and her father taught classics and Tracy, with her brother and her sister, was raised in a large white house in Princeton, drank tea beneath striped awnings, had cultural Christmases and historical Seders and lived a life that I imagined to be a mix between the lives of royalty and the lives of people in a Norman Rockwell. If she was not happy there, if her parents were timid and distracted, then so much the better. Let her grow her heart in that perfect garden and let her harvest it with me.

She knew from the start that I had very little idea of what was at the center of my life but that was only fair, it seemed to me, because she had no better idea of what burned at the center of hers. She was like me in that way, though not so quick to admit it. The general foolishness and cruelty of the times seemed to be passing over us, the way a tornado unexpectedly spares one house after demolishing all of the others. I felt real spiritual luxury around her because she seemed, like me, exempt from true and lasting misfortune. Tracy, though, looked at me as a bona-fide product of tough times and thought that at some point I might help her to know the netherside of the world in which she found herself so eerily blessed. We moved with the same ease, but our fears were fundamentally different. Tracy feared languor and isolation and, like one who was born with grace, she could look at all of her advantages as temporary, while I lived with the sense that doom had missed me by an inch. We touched and talked constantly, but now it's difficult to remember much of what we said. It is a kind of wonder, really, how happy we managed to be: so much of what we had had simply been handed to us and, though we never spoke of it, we both instinctually knew what was on the other side of that dime upon which our lives so effortlessly turned. We were always, I think, at least half scared.

2

W E'D BEEN married several months, it was the end of September, and I was sleeping late. Tracy was up, working on the design for a huge, shiny book about soccer tournaments. She was now in business for herself and kept long hours at her office on Seventy-fourth and Broadway. She also kept a set of tools at home—T-squares, packets of colored pencils, enormous paste pots, razors, a magnifying glass, an electronic calculator, and a sloping drafting table interrogated by a gooseneck lamp, all adding a pleasant, industrious edge to our otherwise indulgent apartment. Tracy loved her work.

Sometime after noon, Tracy came into the bedroom and pulled the covers off of me. "It's my day off," she said. "You can't sleep through my day off."

"It's my day off too."

"Every day's your day off."

Barefoot, she stepped onto the bed and straddled me. Her black hair was cropped extra short and her

17

hips looked particularly fragile beneath her bluejeans.
Looking up at her, with my heart swaying in my chest
like an old dignified drunk, I felt a familiar, ferocious
sense of well-being. Tracy made a gentle leap and her
small, bony feet, which looked like shaved squirrels,
landed within an inch of either side of me. I giggled
like a huge infant.

"Come on," she said. "I'll make tea. It doesn't seem
as if life's begun if you don't get up."

Over breakfast, I went through the mail. First there
was an aerogram from vacationing friends in La Paz.
Next I looked at a booklet from a New England realty
company describing some country properties. Since
being married, I'd resumed my search for a country
home and Tracy and I were registered with real estate
brokers from New Paltz to Bangor. There were a few
bills in the mail, a copy of a magazine called *The Management Consultant*, which my boss had sent to me,
even though he knew I'd never read it. At the bottom
of the stack was a large, rose-colored postcard with my
name scrawled in a familiar hand on the front. I noticed, peripherally, that Tracy was watching me as I
flipped the card over. It was a printed announcement.

Earl Morgan, Pianist

Wednesday, October 7

8:00 P.M.

Grieg, Beethoven, Morgan

Carnegie Recital Hall
West 57th Street

Written on the bottom was, "How about it Virgil? See
you there? Dad."

"Are we going?" asked Tracy, her eyes grabbing at
mine.

"I really wish we could. Unfortunately..." I
grinned.

"I think we should," said Tracy, doing her best to sound casual. "We haven't seen your father in months. It's awful. We've seen my parents five times since we got married. We've seen them in Princeton, in Maine. Your father lives forty blocks away."

I looked at the card again and felt a certain tug of filial duty—not such a tug as to take me through the fear and sadness I felt around my father, but a tug all the same. "Okay," I said. "If you want to go. He'll be delighted."

"Do you want to call him?"

"No. We'll make it a surprise."

"We'll go out for drinks after."

"Fine."

"At the Russian Tea Room. It's just next door."

"I know exactly where it is. Even people who live in distant cities know that. Stop being so eager."

"I'm not."

"You're pushing me to feel something I don't feel. We'll go. We'll have drinks. Let's leave it alone now."

"All right," she said, after a silence. "But you'd better make reservations. That place is packed after concerts."

We stayed in all day and through the evening. Tracy worked on her soccer book and for a while I listened to music on the headphones and stared out the window: twelve stories below, people walked through the park, their collars up against the wind.

Finally, I began to work on a piece for my office. My job wasn't difficult nor was it demanding but what I did had to be good because I was paid so much. I prepared a long memo regarding a Japanese fast food chain that wanted to consolidate its twenty outlets into an impeccably chosen half dozen. When I finished—I worked as slowly as I could—Tracy was still hard at work.

I watched her for a few minutes, feeling restless and ignored, and conscious, I believe, of my father's footsteps, of his moving toward the outskirts of my life.

"I love your tits," I said to Tracy, putting my arms around her. "They are completely wonderful and what's more they're perfect. Perfect! It's as if God, in His infinite wisdom, made a perfect pair so He might show all of His assistants and say: 'Here, this is what tits are supposed to look like.' Okay, now take off your shirt."

"I think tits is a lacking word," Tracy said, considering a three-by-five of a beaming Pelé.

"You do?"

She showed me a photo and then placed it in the stack of discards. "Yes," she said. "You're too old to say tits."

"Well, apparently I'm not."

"Women have much better names for the male organ."

"For instance?" I said, putting my hands on her shoulders. She smelled of musk oil, coffee, and glue.

"Nightlight."

"Nightlight? Go on."

"Lie detector. Bugle."

"Women don't say that. You say that. Wouldn't you like to go to bed for a while?"

"I'm getting to the crux of this, Virgil. In an hour."

I smiled at her. I had no reason to be annoyed that Tracy didn't want to go directly to bed with me. I had asked her, in fact, without wholly feeling it. She returned to her book design and the room became so quiet that I heard a Nat King Cole record being played by a nostalgic neighbor, a fresh supply of heat being blown through the grille on the other side of our living room, and I heard, really, the soft machinery of our essentially untroubled life. I had a sudden impulse to throw a fit. I wanted to grab Tracy's wrist, drag her off, force myself on her. I wanted to beg, to bark. I loathed being asked to wait for an hour. "Okay," I said, "I'm going to time you." It was ten o'clock.

To help pass the time, I went to visit our neighbor Mario Nicolosi on the seventh floor. His twelve-year-old daughter was staying with him for the weekend and she sat on Mario's old velvet couch, a blanket wrapped around her, staring furiously at the television set.

"Virgil," Mario said, "you look restless and dangerous." He showed me in. There were thick gray electrical wires on the rug and two portable videotape machines in a big flowered armchair near the windows. "You have not met my daughter," said Mario. "Tyranny, I want you to meet Virgil Morgan." The child looked at me briefly.

"I thought your name was Irene," I said to her.

"No longer. Today her name is Tyranny. She is watching videotapes made of me over the last days. She is in one or two of them. You can tell when she appears. Her entire face changes. It is all she cares about."

Mario and I went into the kitchen. It was painted dark blue and there were candles burning on the table. It was difficult to imagine food being prepared there. We sat and Mario poured apricot juice into heavy crystal tumblers.

"Where is Tracy?"

"Upstairs. Working. Why are you having videotapes made of you?"

"Someone with a grant wants to do a tape biography of me, because of my insignificance. I consented because I am curious to see what I look like as I live the day. Vanity. Why doesn't Tracy come down to see me?"

"She does. She's just busy tonight. I asked her to go to bed and she mumbled at me. So I hope to God she's too busy to visit some Italian decadent."

"I just want to say one thing, Virgil. I have lived forty-two years in every continent except Australia, which is not really a continent. One fact: your wife must sleep with someone other than you. It is a law of nature. She is a skinny woman and you are not a skinny man. Skinny must fuck skinny. Not all the time, mind. But sometime." He tilted back in his chair and ran his ropy brown hand over his flat stomach and beamed at me, as if together we'd uncovered a lost chapter of the Kabala.

"Look at your face," said Mario. "So watchful, so composed. You stare at me like a Rembrandt looking at a thief, warning me not to take you from your rightful place on the wall. Someday your entire world will fall into pieces and you will be very relieved. Until then, you will drive yourself crazy wondering when it will happen. You are such an American. They should put your face on the flag. They should have fifty of you, instead of those little stars."

We went into the living room to watch the tapes with Irene. I sat in a rocking chair and Mario lifted Irene's pale downy legs and placed them in his lap. Her watery blue eyes were fixed on the screen because her own image was on now, dressed in a T-shirt and corduroy pants, swaying back and forth to the beat of rock and roll. "You are a beautiful dancer," said the real-life Mario just as his image joined Irene's on the screen. On the screen, he was dressed in a bulky bathrobe, his skinny, hairy legs wet from the shower he'd presumably just taken. They danced together, Irene making flowing, mystic gestures, Mario slicing up the space around him with his hands, his pointed elbows, his flat, sharp feet. This scene lasted until the song ended. Then we saw Mario sitting on the edge of his unmade bed, working fanatically on his toenails with a cuticle scissors. Here, the camera indulged in a series of zoom shots, zeroing in on the toe in question, Mario's wrinkled, phallic thumb hooked through the fragile scissors, his pursed lips, his penetrating light eyes.

What little work Mario Nicolosi had done in his life involved a biography of Boccherini, which was published when he was twenty-four, and a history of Italian chamber music, which he still sporadically worked on. He wasn't the sort one associated with any particular métier but his love of music did occur to me as he saw me to the door. "My father's giving a recital at Carnegie Recital Hall next week," I said. This seemed to make no particular impression on Mario, which confirmed my fear that such events were essentially meaningless, like publishing a book of your opinions with a vanity press. "Would you like to hear him?" I asked.

"Spare your poor degenerate friends," said Mario. "What will he play?"

"I don't know. Beethoven. Something of his own, too."

"Ah. A composer. One continues to learn about you, my opaque friend. A composer."

"You judge for yourself," I said.

"Good. I will discover him and become more famous for having done so."

"This Wednesday."

"Okay. But I must be reminded."

An hour after arriving I left Mario and walked the five flights up to my apartment. I entered flushed and panting. Tracy was still bent over her work. When I came to her side she smiled apologetically and shrugged.

"Christ, you said an hour."

"Misestimation. Go to bed if you want to. I'll wake you up when I get through this. I'll sit on your head."

I stalked into the bedroom, took off my clothes, and lay down. The bed had been my purchase: a specially made triple, as hard as a raw potato. Lately, it had begun to irritate me. It was so large that we could sleep comfortably without any part of our bodies ever touching and it was so firm that we could sleep impervious to each other's entrances and exits. There was a small green lamp on the marble end table and the light it cast against the smooth white walls seemed a little bleak. Reaching over for a book, I saw that the notice of my father's recital had somehow found its way into the bedroom. I picked it up and looked at it again. *Grieg, Beethoven, Morgan.* Good Lord.

Suddenly, I dreaded going to that recital and felt criminally dumb for having invited Mario. I had done so with the misassumption that I was finally inoculated against my father's vanity and humiliation, and I could stand calmly apart from it like everyone else and feel only interest and compassion. But the thought of that man, all hunched and huge before the piano, humming, tapping his feet, dressed like a genius, the anticipation of it made me want to moan with self-pity. I didn't ever want to witness his life again. The piano would be out of tune. Only ten people would show up. The curtain would accidentally be rung down in the middle of a piece.

There was a dream I sometimes had and I had it that night. I am sitting on a plane, my seat belt fastened. I am reading a magazine, waiting for takeoff. My eyes scan the plane and then I see Earl bounding onto the plane, dressed in a pilot's uniform. He heads for the cockpit. I am utterly panic-stricken. The plane is no longer safe. We're in for rough skies, we are going to crash, the plane will drop into the sea. I call for the stewardess. She looks at me curiously from a distant end of the plane. The engines have started. The plane quivers and then moves down the runway. I try to get up. My seat belt is jammed.

3

THE NIGHT of Earl's recital it rained and the wind blew twenty miles per hour. I'd been out of town Monday and Tuesday, looking at some undeveloped land in South Carolina a client of ours was considering for purchase. He wanted me along for cheerful companionship and marginal advice and since he was a valuable client I was sent along as a courtesy. I'd had two days of sun and Rebel Yell bourbon, cruising fifty feet over marshlands in a Piper Comanche piloted by a young woman named Margaret Jean Blassingame, who seemed interested in going to bed with me but whose steamy, confident advances I ignored. I'd been married less than a year and there was a deep erotic pull to honoring the vows. Besides Margaret was built like a showgirl and Tracy had given me a taste for women shaped like swords.

It was storming when I got back to New York. It was one of those violent afternoon downpours that can make you think the world is ending. The sky turned green and then black; the wind screamed like a huge, injured thing. Tracy had taken the afternoon off to be with me and I don't think sleeping with her had ever been better. Not only did I unleash all of my passion for her but I added the untapped ardor I felt for the Southern pilotess. I mean I played her like a harp. I hit notes I hadn't even known she had. And her surprise and fervor fed my own thunderstruck passion. I handled her with all the delicacy I could manage but what I really wanted to do was snap her frail body into parts and drag them into a corner to gnaw upon. When we had been in the Bahamas, there were so many thumb- and fingertip-shaped bruises on Tracy's body that she hesitated to appear in public in a bathing suit. I was better insulated against the excesses of her passion. Now and again a prickly red crescent appeared above my shoulderblade or a crimson highway of mutilated skin coursed down either side of my spine, but, on the whole, our lovemaking left me intact. It at first frightened me to realize that Tracy would permit herself to be dismantled in the act of love for I realized that permission was also request. It was not within my power. Not only did I love her exactly as she was but I had no confidence in myself as an architect of the soul. Tracy's willingness to be utterly changed was always the most terrifying part of her character.

We dozed through the late afternoon and woke to the alarm at six thirty. Tracy trod across our honey-colored floors and switched on the lights in the bathroom. She leaned over the sink and looked briefly at her reflection in the mirror. Her small ass pushed outward as she turned on the faucets. In the center of her thigh I saw a pale olive bruise that would be violet by morning.

I called Mario to remind him of the recital. I'd put Earl's impending performance out of mind while in South Carolina and I'd also forgotten my regret at inviting Mario. But had I not phoned, it wouldn't have made any difference: Mario remembered and was just about to call me.

Our doorman had a cab waiting for us. It was still storming and the driver moved slowly down Central Park West, slamming on the brakes at what seemed mirage dangers. Tracy wore a brown velvet dress and Mario and I wore unassuming gray business suits. It was a style I enjoyed but I was surprised to see Mario dressed that way. It made him look serious and noble and the transformation of his demeanor made me further regret inviting him. It no longer seemed a lark. I felt as if I'd invited someone capable of devastating my father.

"How much does it cost to use the Recital Hall?" I asked Mario.

He shook his head slowly. A lengthy flash of lightning illuminated the soaking street. "I am not sure. It's an investment. The world of music is somewhat closed and this gives entrance."

"He's really very good," I said.

"Wonderful," said Mario.

There was another streak of lightning and I noticed the heel of Mario's hand rested on the edge of Tracy's dress. She didn't appear to notice. I momentarily felt like saying something about it but I knew his attraction to her was either casual or futile.

"His real ambition is to be known as a composer," I continued, still, in some dim way, buttering Mario up.

"Good," said Mario. "That is more interesting. The source."

"He should play more than just one of his pieces," said Tracy.

"The last time we spoke about it," I said, "he told me he was getting into pure sound, understanding the note in a different, amusical sense." I hadn't meant to but I smiled as I said this, for it sounded a little insane.

In the cream and crimson lobby of the Carnegie Recital Hall was a wall directory with movable white letters. We scanned it and saw Earl was in the recital hall. Though just next door was the *real* Carnegie Hall, where artists were paid to perform for people who paid to hear them, and though my father was playing in a hall rented at his own expense to an audience of invited guests, I couldn't help feeling a blush of pride in him. I could feel exactly how excited he must have been when he came into that lobby and saw his name.

It was a narrow gray room with maroon seats and a small planked stage. As soon as we walked in we were struck by the scent of umbrellas and wet fur. Full, the chamber would have seated three hundred and now it held perhaps seventy—not bad, considering the typhoon. We were each given a mimeographed sheet of program notes and shown halfway down the aisle by an old woman who dismissed us with a wave. We found seats in the tenth row.

As I'd predicted, Earl was dressed like a genius. Rather than concert tails or recital suit, he wore dark green pants with two-inch cuffs and a checked cotton shirt with the sleeves neatly rolled to the elbow. Beretless, his bullet-gray hair was combed straight back and curled over his shirt collar. He didn't see us enter; his eyes were closed. He sat at the piano, tilting right and then left, his tusk-like goatee pointing heavenward, now to his heart, now to his ivory-colored hands that marched up and down the keys. His hands were the exact color of the piano keys and when he played rapidly you could barely distinguish them.

"Oh, save me," said Mario. "Grieg."

"Shut up, Mario," said Tracy.

"I don't enjoy this," Mario mumbled, slinking down into his seat.

Sharing the tenth row with us were the Albas, Jerome and Lena. They'd lived in the same building Earl and I moved into when we came to New York. They were both in their seventies and sitting unnaturally straight. Mr. Alba tapped his wife's knee when he noticed me. I made a little bow in their direction and they smiled at me with spectral fondness.

As I looked around the hall I recognized a number of people and realized I'd been noticed, for whenever my eyes would light upon a familiar face I would be nodded or grinned at. Here we are, Earl's friends seemed to say, here we are at last. Only a few names came to mind. Ezra Medoff, an antique dealer who sold Earl some sheet music inscribed by Weber, though Earl after purchasing it often doubted its authenticity. Wearing a brown suit and with gray hair down to his shoulders was John Towland, looking like an old Indian chief. Towland had once advised Earl on some mutual fund in the fifties, an investment on which, through some incredible miracle, my father broke even. Towland and my father had a close, sporadic friendship: movies on the Upper West Side, dinners at each other's houses, seven years ago they'd driven through New England with Towland's widowed daughter. Also there were Barbara Falkenstein, Alan Zuger, Clarence Decker, and Mai Yu, all former piano students of Earl's from the days he worked nights and weekends to put me through private high school. Barbara Falkenstein, now about thirty, sat with an aging black man, who was probably her husband, and a bespectacled, gag-toothed, coffee-colored boy who was probably her son. She was Earl's Saturday student and the first woman I'd ever fucked.

The Grieg ended and every one of us gave Earl a good ovation. Tracy caught my eye as we clapped, and smiled at me. It was more than a smile really. She raised her eyebrows and moved her face a little closer to mine: You see, she seemed to say, he's good. I looked into her eyes, the most intense eyes I'd ever seen. When she shut them at the end of the day it was like the end of an era. But what did she know of Earl? And what did she know of his heart-frozen son?

Earl turned to the audience and smiled just as the applause was ending. Rather than seeming gracious, as he'd probably intended, his smile seemed ironic and faintly condemning, as if he were accusing us for not sustaining our appreciation for a decent length of time. "Thank you," he said, in his barking, metallic voice. It was the voice of tunnel vision, the voice of the last-ditch attempt. "I'm going to alter tonight's program," he said "and instead of the Bagatelle I will next play my own composition, 'The Absurdium Continuum.'" He gazed into the audience and his eyes seemed to rest on my face for a moment, but he gave no sign of recognition. He made a move toward the keyboard but stopped. "This is," he addressed the audience, "a somewhat difficult piece and for those of you raised on traditional music—as most of us were—I can only recommend that you keep your mind open. Thank you." He turned toward the keyboard again and drew a deep breath. He raised his hands and curved his fingers: they looked like eagle's talons about to sink into the lamb of peace.

There are a dozen ways I could describe Earl's music but it is a self-indulgence I now avoid. I have tried to entertain friends by giving them a sense of his lurching, pouncing, halting, racing experiments in pure sound but these descriptions invariably sound mean. There is something inherently noble about the desire to compose music even if the result is the tonal equivalent of smudge. But how much better it would have been had he composed clear, melodic, or even mournful pieces that sought to please the ear and touch the heart. There was something grand and assertive about Earl's compositions and you felt at once lonely and besieged when you heard them. They were pieces to take the color out of stained glass, something to remind you that there is no afterlife.

That first explosion of notes had the effect of Tracy's first interrogations and I traveled breathlessly through time. I was listening to his churnings in our little house on Chicago's North Side, sitting, swallowing my hysterical little smiles and sometimes my tears as he explained to me that life itself seemed to be passing him by. I remembered dinners with his occasional

bohemianesque girlfriends, many of whom thought he
was a genius, or said they did, and all of whom seemed
to have cigarets plugged into the corners of their tight
red mouths. He never had a woman friend for very
long. His most regular visitor in those days was a
woman named Eleanor Simmons who would sometimes have breakfast with us dressed only in a trench-
coat. Once, in an attempt to show Earl's silent, staring
son a little affection, she said, "I could never tell my
psychiatrist what I think about *you*, Virgil," and
though I didn't even blink when she said it, the gesture
hit its mark for I had wondered about it a hundred
times since. I remembered the care with which Earl
packed his sheet music in the back of our Pontiac as
we prepared to go to New York and I remembered the
first day he came home from his new teaching job and
the look in his eyes that told me that his heart, which
had been so buoyant for a few weeks, now was sick
with the suspicion that indeed nothing had changed in
his life. I recalled our monthly treks to Carnegie Hall.
He'd often bring the score to what was played that
night and suddenly, watching him perform before me,
I felt his hard thumb in my ribs, jabbing for my attention. "Here. Look. This is where Mr. Bartók makes his
biggest mistake."

"The Absurdium" was in a quiet stage now, though
you never knew what it was going to do next. The
notes were played softly, with long twittering silences
between them. There were ramblings from the lowest
register. I had never discovered what you were supposed to think about when you listened to such music.
Those bass notes sounded something like lions, whose
splashes of chords sounded a little like forging of steel.
Was that it? A piece about the violation of the wilderness? The music grew louder. He slapped at the top
and bottom registers with open palms, in a seemingly
random fashion but I'd heard it before and it always
sounded exactly the same. The bench was quivering
beneath him now. I looked around at the audience

with reflexive pleading and accusation in my heart but everyone seemed to be paying proper attention. Mario sat deep in his seat, his thin legs tightly crossed, his eyes utterly blank. Tracy was leaned forward a little, her chin resting in her hand. I watched her concentrate on Earl's piece and felt the bite of betrayal. Why didn't she lean over and say something funny to me? I didn't want just *anyone* to ridicule Earl but it would have been real deliverance to hear something light from Tracy. The music was building but I don't think it sounded nearly as thunderous and discordant anywhere else as it did in my ears. Drops of sweat fell from his face and onto the keys. Churning. Churning. Halting. A little carnival lilt. Then an explosion. Finally, abruptly, a silence and he pushed his stool back and dropped his hands. There was an uncertain silence in the audience and then applause. Mario clapped with what seemed to be enthusiasm. Tracy leaned over and said, "It's not what I'm used to but it was exciting, wasn't it?" Was it? I had no way of knowing. It could have been the work of a god or it could have been sick and second-rate. The whole performance was coming to me through a net of family trauma and disappointment. I didn't need Tracy's polite judgment of the piece. I needed something tough, something loyal. I wish she could have said something to let me know I wasn't going out of my mind.

4

MY FATHER was due in Brooklyn for a reception in his honor and I was forced to practically beg him to come to the Russian Tea Room for vodka and soup. The Russian Tea Room is a large, elegant, pink and green chamber with samovars fixed into various corners, prehistoric tinsel dangling from the overhead lights, enormous murky paintings of ballerinas, and a five-inch mirror bonding the room exactly at eye level, so those with their backs to the other patrons can still spy upon them.

"I haven't been here in years," said Earl, digging his fingers into my elbow as a waiter showed us to a long table. My father wore a shapeless blue blazer supplied by the restaurant, not having worn a jacket of his own. The mandatory garment hung shapelessly around his tight, muscular frame but he wore it casually, as if it were a trifle. It was, in fact, the perfect attire for a genius in some self-important restaurant, and watching him stride past those tables of prim Manhattanites was a lesson in just that sort of half-assed yet somehow monumental stature you can only get by surviving on your own terms for five or six decades.

We were six: Tracy and her drink-starved husband, Earl, Mario, a woman named Lillian Douglas and her twenty-four-year-old son Tommy Douglas. Lillian walked with her hand resting comfortably on Earl's arm; after the recital she'd tattooed him with kisses; and now at the table I suspected they sat with knees touching.

Most of Lillian's manner and gestures belonged to no specific era, or belonged to a compendium of them all. She had the slightly wrecked, cough-stunned eyes of a pre-war libertine. She had the fuck-it-all hair-do of an aging flapper nihilist, an explosion of mahogany gauze through which the light crawled. She had the ardent red mouth and plaintively gesturing hands of the Free the Scottsboro thirties and the bat-like attire of the be-bop forties. She was a thin, drawn woman, given to staring and pursing her lips. She looked terrified, furtive, and yet somehow proud, a woman with a tin of expensive candies at the bottom of her purse. Her voice was high and wavered so that you might think she was teasing you. But she never said anything funny and there was nothing idle in her. She was solicitous to Earl and looked at him with a kind of guarded softness that made me hope she loved him.

Her son Tommy looked like a cross between an astronaut and a cat burglar: he combined Lillian's furtive delicacy with the solid capability of some unknown father. His hands were massive, hair-less, tapered: they were what people once called "sensitive hands." His hair was long, black, and shiny, his nose was straight, and his cheeks were brown and scrupulously shaved. He wore small rimless glasses and his eyes waited behind them. They were the sort of eyes men came back with from wars or funerals, the kind of eyes that are granted you when you touch bottom and then begin the long float up to the surface again. They were not lifeless eyes but they expressed a life beyond the life you yourself knew, a life whose existence you granted but had only a faltering desire to know. He wore a simple, inexpensive blue suit and I knew if I were ever to see him in a suit again it would be that one. When he reached for his water his bony white wrists shot out and when he turned in his seat his body moved while his jacket remained immobile. The only thing that made the suit his was a button on the lapel, a green dime-sized button that bore the number 1,200,000.

"What's that?" I said, pointing at the button.

"Please, Tommy," said Lillian. "Not now." She gave him a look of genuine pleading, and then gestured subtly toward Earl. Tommy blinked and then shrugged at me.

When our drinks came Tracy touched my hip and I proposed a toast. "To Earl," I said, "and his magnificent recital."

"Wonderful recital," said Lillian, snuffing out her cigaret.

We all clicked glasses and then drank.

"I want someone to level with me," said Earl. "Old King Lear wants an honest answer. Do you think it truly went well? It's so goddamned hard to tell when you're up on the stage."

"I think it went super well," said Tracy.

"It felt good," said Earl. He took another swallow. "I know I don't play easy music. I figure if I can keep them in the hall I'm doing pretty well."

"We all loved it," said Lillian. "It was wonderful."

Earl looked at Tommy. "You think so too?"

"I'm no expert," said Tommy.

"You don't have to be an *expert*," said Lillian, taking Tommy's hand. She looked at it with such interest that I thought she was going to pass it around. "An artist plays for people, not experts," she said.

"I liked the Grieg," said Tommy. His voice was quiet, withdrawn, as impersonal as the weather.

Earl shrugged, a nervous, excessive leap of the

shoulders. "Maybe I *should* just play for experts," he said, attempting a smile.

Earl was fitful and agitated but the overall mood of the table was lethargy. We were not six starving friends drinking our blessings to a budding career nor were we aficionados sighing in the company of a master. We were six private city-dwellers sitting in an expensive restaurant with an aging, struggling eccentric whose career had not, in fact, been launched that evening but whose appearance in the Recital Hall was tantamount to a confession that no one had ever asked him to play anywhere else. We were there to make an accommodation—or perhaps we were there to mask it, to whoop it up and turn it into an unexpected, quirky triumph.

I would have liked to clap my hands and make us all disappear, to have Earl and Lillian at the reception in Brooklyn, to have Mario in his apartment watching his videotapes, and to have Tracy and me in our apartment, she reading *Bleak House* and me watching *The Thin Man* on TV. There seemed to me no reason to go on. We'd seen the recital, we'd ordered our drinks, made the toast—enough. It was not going to miraculously turn into a celebration. Even if there were miracles loose in the world they did not come to my father. He was nearly sixty years old and his life's path was smooth and deep for his having paced it so many years; to climb out now would be like scaling a glass canyon.

"So how did it feel up there?" I boomed, lurching into conversation.

Earl looked across the table at me. We hadn't said much that evening and evidently he was annoyed with me—God knew his grievances were real and numerous. But he wasn't going to permit his evening to be spoiled by leaning into one of the routines that had characterized most of our encounters over the past couple years—subtle harangues that didn't include any balled fists or raised voices but were, rather, an accumulation of questions, little jabs, passing complaints that somehow organically bonded into a mass of disapproval. No, he wasn't about to worry his sense of accomplishment that evening by picking a fight with his sell-out son. There'd be no crack about the size of my apartment, nor the frankly pretentious stores where I bought my clothes (I'd like to take the day I told him I had my shirts custom made and shoot it in the head). He had no intention of hinting I avoided him for any of the motives he had at one time or another assigned to me—fear of his asking for a loan, my own alleged social-climbing instincts, all kinds of cracked notions that should have been disgusting but which nevertheless pained me. Still, though he had every intention of keeping the evening upbeat, he could not allow himself to respond altogether to my question, so he looked at me with deceptive neutrality and said, "What do you mean?"

"Oh, I don't know," I said with a wild shrug, determined to keep it light. "I've never been on the stage. It must be very, very—you know."

"You get used to it," he said, rather cagily I thought.

"Well, you were fine tonight." I was running out of fuel. What I would have liked to do was flatter him, make him laugh, make everybody laugh, order more drinks. There are people who can lift situations by the scuff and I had been able to do that very thing more than once.

The past is a laboratory and we often emerge from it monstrous in one way or another. Those hasty stitches that bound my lips to near silence were not sewn by my own hand. I was, for the evening at least, and maybe for all my life, a creature of Earl's fucking funiculi, funicula in front of my smirking, face-pulling pals some twenty years past. *I* knew that, but no one else could possibly care, nor could they be expected to. I was older, now. And, not to put too fine a point on it, sufficiently on my own to be able to buy and sell the old man several times over. I sighed and leaned forward. Looking in the mirror, I saw behind me the tiers of animated heads, bobbing, eating, smiling, laughing.

"Mr. Morgan," said Mario, as he finished his drink, "I have been trying to express my thoughts at your recital this evening."

Tracy glanced at me and my hand clutched at the edge of the stiff white tablecloth. As Mario prepared to share his thoughts I felt a surge of disloyalty so overpowering I almost moaned.

"I am a lover of music, a great lover of music, yet I do not go to recitals," Mario said, speaking with agonizing slowness. "I have no will to listen to yet another exploration of compositions that have had their final, definitive playings long ago." Mario paused and Earl stared at him with what looked like impassivity but which I well recognized as real terror and yearning. "Yes," said Mario, spreading his hands before him on the table, "I have become somewhat a stranger to the concert hall. I came tonight only because Virgil asked me to. And it fascinated me that he had a father who —plays."

"I don't expect he talks much about it," said Earl.

"Oh come on, Earl," said Lillian, urging with a gesture of her eyes that Mario continue.

I glanced across the table at Tommy Douglas. He regarded his mother with a delicate, superior, hateful little smile.

"But if recitals were like this one," said Mario, "then I would fill my life with them again, as I did in Rome as a youth. Then, back there—well it does not matter. What I want to say is your piece, the, the, the . . ." He closed his eyes and pursed his lips.

"'The Absurdium Continuum,'" said Lillian.

"Yes," said Mario, opening his eyes and smiling. The sudden display of his eyes was like headlights unexpectedly appearing on a country road. "'The Absurdium.' I am not an active lover of twelve-tone music, though I was one of the first in my circle to admit its legitimacy. But you, Mr. Morgan, are a master of the form."

"I love your friend," Earl said to me, with a great, explosive smile.

"You manage," continued Mario the Magnificent, "to express feeling in a form that too often, far too often, has been a hiding place for formal minds. Bravo, Mr. Morgan. I was uplifted."

"I could not possibly agree more," said Lillian, to Mario.

Tracy reached under the table and squeezed my leg; I'd been given credit for Mario's unexpected appraisal. I turned in my seat and gestured for the waiter to bring another round of drinks.

Tommy pushed his chair away from the table. "I've got to get going."

"Tommy," said Lillian, lighting a cigaret and shaking the match out as if lowering the temperature of a thermometer, "can't you manage to stay?"

"I'm already late," he said. Then, to me, "I suppose the drinks are on you."

"Absolutely," I said with the Morgan grin. I half stood and offered my hand, successfully anticipating his Revolution Thumb Lock Grip. "You see," I said, shaking his hand up and down, "I guessed."

The waiter arrived with our drinks and placed them all correctly. Tommy's Bloody Mary stood before his empty chair and he reached across the table for it. "A little fortification," he said, and drained it with stylish bravado. When he slapped the empty glass onto the table, there was a shadowy red line above his lip. "Not too generous with the vodka, are they," he said in a way of a farewell. "For two dollars a drink I should be on the floor. Well, so long, Earl. Everybody." He nodded at each of us and backed away. When he finally turned around, he ran directly into a busboy, who, at least, was empty-handed. The collision stunned them both and they regarded each other with embarrassment and animosity.

"I have no idea where he's going," said Lillian, dipping her fingertip in her drink.

"That's just fine," said Earl. "Now can we please table that topic for tonight? Can I have one night we don't discuss what I don't want to discuss?"

"I wasn't planning to discuss it," said Lillian.

"All right," he said, "I'm sorry. I guess I'm exhausted from the recital." He reached over; their fingers laced.

I signed for the check about twenty minutes later. We'd been there longer than any of us had planned for or desired. Mario was urged to report to my father what Rome was like in the fifties, but what he was really being asked for and what he was kind enough to deliver was a reprise of his praise for "The Absurdium." I detected a faltering of enthusiasm in his voice the second time through and realized that all along he'd been acting out of generosity. Mario! Thank you.

The waiter came, detached my receipt, and said, "Thank you very much, Mr. Morgan." He didn't know me; he merely looked at my signature, but hearing me addressed as if I were a Russian Tea Room regular seemed to annoy Earl. One eyebrow rose demonically and he put a drunken elbow onto the table. "A real man about town," he said.

"Yeah," I said, pretending it was all part of a good-natured joke.

"You were smart to become a businessman," he said, nodding.

"I'm not a businessman, Dad. I'm just a man." I could not stop smiling. I offered my father my smile as if feeding a little treat to a violent child. And yet, as with most half-formed men in the presence of their fathers, there was always within me the shadow of temptation to burst into tears, to beg him to change his mind, to change his heart, to change utterly in every way.

"You know what comes to mind here?" Earl said, leaning back. "When we first moved to New York.

Remember? I always liked to take you to Carnegie Hall. The *real* Carnegie Hall, not that little outhouse next door. We'd take the subway to Manhattan and"—he turned to Lillian, and the effect of that shift was, for me, like being moved from a ringside table to a table near the kitchen—"Virgil would be sitting next to me, his legs folded, his hands folded. A very reserved kid. People worried about him. But he was mine, you understand. You know that pride. And maybe I was wrong, but I couldn't help thinking I was doing something pretty damn nice for him, taking him along, turning him on to good music. But then you know what happened? Why we stopped going to Carnegie Hall together? You know what tickets cost and you know my financial situation. It was no better then. Well, my young son didn't want to go anymore. He said it made him feel odd because we always sat in the lousiest seats. He said he felt the orchestra was playing for the people in the good seats and we, way up there in the balcony, were just eavesdropping. Eavesdropping! A real kick in the teeth, huh?"

Lillian shook her head sadly and looked at me, apparently expecting an explanation of my hateful behavior. Tracy and Mario seemed to be looking at me, too. I wouldn't have been surprised to have noticed the cook peeking through the swinging doors to the kitchen, ladle in hand, looking at me, as well. Finally, after a silence, I set the record straight: "That was in Town Hall."

By midnight, I was slumped on the couch wearing a pair of pajamas feeling giddy and mournful. Our cat Joshua was perched on my hip, licking his shaggy silver paws, blinking his golden eyes with awesome, enviable self-satisfaction.

"Drink, please," I called to Tracy. "Don't go to any trouble. Just a bottle and a straw."

At her extrasensory best, Tracy that instant came in holding two glasses of Scotch.

"You're wonderful," I said. We clicked glasses; Tracy tapped my ankles and I made room for her on the couch.

"That was a difficult evening for you, wasn't it?" she said.

"What makes you think so? The weeping in the cab?"

"That was my first clue."

"He hates me, doesn't he?" I said.

"Who? Earl?"

"No. God."

"Cool out, Virgil."

"Sorry."

"You two have some reckoning to do."

"I'll be doing a lot of that," I said.

Tracy shook her head. "I worry about you, Virgil."

Like most motherless children, I liked being worried about and I had once hoped that the regularity of Tracy's family life would break her heart upon considering her husband's dicey origins, but it didn't seem to work that way. My long-consummated divorce from Earl was something she still hoped ultimately to correct.

"You don't have to worry about me," I said.

"Yes, I do. I worry about you because I love you."

"That's plenty, then. That's more than a lot of people ever have."

"I want our lives to make sense," said Tracy.

"Why?"

"I can't answer that. I just do. I want to be connected to something."

"You're connected to me."

"I suppose. But *you're* not connected to anything. Nothing. Not even your own family."

"Okay. I'll try to see more of him. You shouldn't insist, though. You should really be ashamed of yourself."

"I'm not. I'm pleased."

I finished my drink and shook the ice cubes in the

glass. "He has terrible luck," I said. "It drives me mad to see it."

"That's another thing, Virgil. Out luck seems so good. Too much seems to be based on it. It's so arbitrary."

"Don't complain. We're very lucky."

"I know. But everything ends."

"All the more reason not to complain."

"We don't even save our money."

"Fuck it. Let's keep it circulating."

"When you were in South Carolina I couldn't sleep. Gary came over to give me Seconals."

"Gray Fish came here in the middle of the night? Jesus, Tracy. You should have called me. Maybe you were lonely."

"It wasn't loneliness," Tracy said. "I don't know what it was."

"Angst?" I said with an idiotic grin.

"No. More like fear and trembling," she said, sinking into my mood.

"You're sure it wasn't a confrontation between being and nothingness?"

"Could have been. Or perhaps it was that basic ontological puzzle of essence and idea."

"Let's take off work tomorrow," I said. "We can go to the movies."

"I don't make money if I don't work."

"You don't even know what's playing."

"What's playing?"

"*The Big Broadcast of 1938* is at the New Yorker."

"How irresistible."

"You don't know what you're saying. That's the one Bob Hope sings 'Thanks for the Memory' in."

"Bob Hope?" said Tracy.

"That's right. Bob Hope. Who spent his life making people laugh." I clutched my breast.

"He did? How come he skipped me?" said Tracy.

"'Thanks for the memories,'" I sang. "'Of tinkling

chapel bells, alma mater yells, Cuban rum and towels from the very best hotels . . .'"

"You have a pretty voice," Tracy said, in a soft abstract way.

"I do?"

The house phone rang, a double flattish ring that couldn't be mistaken for an outside call. The phone was on a glass table directly in front of the couch and I lifted it from its cradle without thinking.

"'Thanks for the memories,'" I sang.

"Hello? Mr. Morgan?" It was the building's night doorman. "May I send up Tom Douglas?"

Working in business in New York had taught me at least one thing and that was how to make snap decisions. "Tell him we're asleep," I said. My nerves registered the intrusion and my lie.

"Who was that?" Tracy asked.

"Lillian's son. Tommy."

"You should have let him up."

"Whatever for?"

"First of all, because he came here. Second, because he's handsome and I like looking at him. And third, because I wouldn't be surprised if he'll be your stepbrother before long."

"Very cogent. Now I'll give you the reasons I didn't let him up. One, I didn't want to. Two, I didn't feel like it. And three, I saw no reason to."

We finished our drinks and prepared for bed. I took a stinging hot shower and entertained myself singing in the flattering echo chamber of the glassed-in tub. I thought briefly of Tommy, of that green dime-sized button his mother had asked him not to explain, and of his aborted visit. I had no idea what he wanted and the absence of an explanation left me unfazed.

I emerged from the bathroom enshrouded in steam, my legs and hands red, a pearl-gray towel around my midsection. I left perfectly formed footprints on our bedroom rug. Tracy lay on the comforter, naked, reading *Bleak House*. Next to the bed, on a little mahogany table that the harpy who sold it to us said was made in Vienna around 1800 and which stood on four gorgeous, mincing paws, was a crumpled Hostess Cupcakes package. Tracy turned to smile at me and her teeth were brown.

"Blood sugar was a little low," she said.

"Well, now you better fuck like a teen vixen," I said, with an odd twinge of jealousy. Tracy was immune to the things that would have put halos of fat around me.

"That's partly up to you," she said, tossing her book onto the floor.

The phone rang again. This time it was an outside call. I made a move to pick it up but Tracy beat me to it, midway into the second ring.

"Hello?" She paused. "No, he isn't. I'm sorry. Who is this?" Her eyes narrowed and she waited for a moment. Then, looking up at me, "They hung up."

"Who was it?"

"I don't know. They asked to speak to Tommy."

Was it then, or was it much before, that my life began its reckless turn for the worse?

TWO

5

THROUGH the autumn, through the rain and the beginnings of the snow, Tracy and I took long weekend trips through New England in search of a country home.

Our hunt for property—the need for which had begun as an idle assertion on my part and then naturally bloomed into a naked obsession—moved north as our desire for land increased, along with our rather ga-ga ideas of isolation, self-reliance, and other stream-lined pioneer ideals. We'd begun our hunt that summer in Putnam and Dutchess counties since they were an hour or two away but every real estate salesman seemed intent on showing us only mediocre properties or thought that because my name was Morgan I was the product of heirlooms and safe-deposit boxes. It was easy to decide against buying so close to New York. We didn't want an account executive next door to us and we didn't want to be too close to the poison we lived in most of the year.

We shopped in Massachusetts. We had one good prospect in the Berkshires—perilously close to Tanglewood—but the property had a pasture in the east leg that the owner refused to part with and Tracy suspected he was going to sell it to a moccasin factory or a hamburger chain. Once we drifted into Vermont it no longer mattered how far from Manhattan we shopped and with our sense of choice thus widened we began looking at parcels of fifty acres and up.

We stayed at inns and drank obscure brands of beer. It was one thing to travel through New England and quite another to cruise through all that grandeur wondering which little chunk of it you're going to own. We spun blissfully up and down two-lane blacktops, over singing bridges, around hairpin turns, sometimes with a real estate agent in the back seat and once with a stuttering, half-blind young man who had overheard us talking real estate in a diner and offered to show us his cousin's place near South Londonderry, Vermont. The house was nice but it was only on six acres of land and it would have been a wasted detour had the owner of the house not invited us to dinner, which was a home-cured ham so good that Tracy and I ate it with our hands and made every vulgar eating noise short of oinking. On these trips, we drove our maroon 1968 Mercedes and as the weather turned harsh Tracy sometimes worried that if something went wrong with the car we'd be stuck, for no one up in the country would have parts. But I never worried. I knew nothing could go wrong with our car. We never even had a flat tire.

Though the idea to buy house and soil was originally mine, it appealed to Tracy and in some way comforted her. It struck her, I think, as a form of saving money, for like most Americans we naturally believed that the land would increase in value as the years went on. At the time, the economy of our country (as opposed to our flourishing personal economy) was showing the beginning symptoms of serious troubles, so for those with money to spend it was a good time to buy. Tracy was glad that at last we would know what became of our salaries. We made over forty-five thousand dollars between us and it all seemed to go for rent, taxi cabs, restaurant tabs, haircuts, and leather jackets. We had no idea *where* it went. We had few unexpected expenses—none since Tracy's abortion the first month we were married. Tracy had wanted it done cheaply in a clinic and we fought for days until she agreed to check into Mount Sinai and have a private room, anesthesia, and an expensive doctor.

The state we could get the most property in for the money we were willing to spend was Maine. Tracy had a particular affection for Maine: her parents owned a summer cottage in Tenants Harbor. We went to Portland to see someone named Francis Gatchell, who'd sold Tracy's parents their place many years ago. We told him what we wanted and he drove with us to Kennebunk and showed us what had been an ice farm. I was almost ready to buy it for its past alone but the property itself wasn't right. First of all, only nineteen acres were left unsold—Gatchell couldn't understand why we wanted more and we couldn't easily explain it, but we wanted more—and, secondly, the house that came with the land was built in 1956 and seemed to embody the spirit of those half-assed times: there was linoleum on the floors, fake paneling in one of the bedrooms, and ceilings for walking around with your head bowed in shame. I explained to Gatchell what the problem was. "I've got someone for you," he said. "Evan Tarwater. You see him. Go north, just a little bit. Yes, north. Just a little bit north." He urged us on as if on a dare.

The next day was Sunday and we drove north on Route 1, through an early snow, until we got about one-third up the state and then we turned inland. The name of the town we were going to was Gardner Point but beyond that all we had in the way of directions was

Tarwater's name written on the back of Gatchell's calling card.

We asked the first person we saw in Gardner Point for directions and he sent us about a mile and a half out of town to Tarwater's house. It was a T-shaped house painted dark green. Inside, it was jammed with furniture, as if he'd inherited the belongings of several families. There were a dozen varieties of chairs, several couches, stools, and pictures of rural settings everywhere, some of them hung so closely that their frames touched. Tarwater himself had a face as white and almost as smooth as a bar of soap. He had small hands, a little pot belly, and pursed lips. When we told him who'd sent us and what we wanted to buy, he said, "I love this land. This land is a good place," and looked at us apocalyptically.

He said he had something for us and we followed him over a small winding road, over a few snowy hills, and then onto a very narrow road. The road was so small that Tarwater's pick-up truck rose on the right and left shoulders simultaneously, bounding in front of us like a big dog, a tail of exhaust flapping in the wind.

We passed birch and spruce and acres of tightly packed pines. There was a hard shell of snow on the ground and the sun shone down like a high-intensity light. Beyond some trees, a hundred feet from the road, was a hot bright glare which Tracy correctly identified as a frozen pond.

"I wonder if this is the land that comes with the house," I said.

"I think it is. God, Virgil. It's really gorgeous."

"Well, this could be it," I said.

"You're hot to buy, aren't you?"

"Not to buy. To own. TO OWN!" I almost lost control of the car.

The road was unpaved and when we rolled over a ditch that was camouflaged by snow, my jaw snapped shut so emphatically that I almost bit off the tip of my tongue. Finally, we turned a bend and saw a small stone house on the crown of a hill that had been cleared of trees. The house seemed to sit there on its haunches, its high red-brick smokestack erect, its small glass windows ablaze with reflected sun. That first glimpse of it made me want to buy the house and when I glanced at Tracy I knew she felt the same. The smell of the bright blue air, the towering trees, the unexpected hills, the serpentine road all conspired to awaken fantasies of an utterly different sort of life: I wanted to own snowshoes and a couple of good dogs, it made me want to be a photographer or a painter, a handyman, a cracker-barrel philosopher, a naturalist, an amateur astronomer, a mystic, a Taoist. I had no intentions of abandoning my metropolitan ways but that brief cruise behind Tarwater's truck made me want another way of life and made me think that that existence was ours for the asking, or the buying. As we made our way up the little hill and pulled in next to the clearing around the house, I felt an unexpected pang over Tracy's abortion: it was a perfect house, a perfect kingdom in which to raise heirs.

The house smelled wet and unused. The lights weren't on, but, in the soft light that came through the small windows, it was so beautiful that Tracy and I practically gasped. The furniture—a legacy of mahogany and oak left by the house's deceased owner—could have been sold at astronomic prices in any New York antique store. The floors were bright and even, the kitchen was huge with a good-looking refrigerator and a six-burner stove. Off the kitchen was a small closet with an elaborately carved door; when I saw it was only big enough to hold two brooms, I used the word "cute" for the first time in my life. Off the main room (fireplace, heavy brass pokers, art deco firescreen, Victorian green-velvet couch) was a stairway. There were two bedrooms, a small room for which some eccentric pastime would have to be invented, and a big country bathroom, perfectly ordinary in every way except that the top of its one window was

stained glass and depicted a brown bear staring peace-
fully into a pond from which leaped a red salmon.

The rest was just business. We made inquiries about
the previous occupants, and found out that the house
came with one hundred twenty acres. Then we drove
to Tarwater's to talk money. I carried with me on these
trips a cashier's check big enough for a down payment
on any property within our range but the check paid
for nearly half of Tarwater's first price so we didn't
haggle, though we'd been repeatedly warned that out-
landers must fight for a fair deal. We acted impulsively.
We should have had the place surveyed; for all we
knew, under that bright diamond glare of snow was an
ash pit. We had no guarantee it was really a hundred
and twenty acres. We should have mentioned something about zoning, or taxes, just the way I had remembered to kick the tires when I bought the used
Mercedes. But we'd taken that access road and seen
the stained-glass bear and before late afternoon we
were drinking beer at Tarwater's house, listening to
him bless the soil and the state of Maine, and listening
to him praise our quick, correct decision to buy.

We left Gardner Point that evening manic with as-
tonishment that we'd finally achieved our goal. We
made it as far as Bath, where we checked into a hotel
and lay around and fantasized about our new property;
of the friends we would invite; of ecological experiments. Sometime during that evening we began referring to the house as Preservation Hall, partly after the
New Orleans jazz band and partly in honor of what we
predicted the house would mean to us: a kingdom, a
refuge, a place to be if the world should ever seriously
unravel.

6

As Tracy and I were driving deeper and deeper into New England, finding Preservation Hall, buying it, consulting with lawyers, signing and countersigning documents, turning on the electricity, getting fuel for the stove, buying oil for the furnace, and having the place thoroughly cleaned, Earl was preparing to marry Lillian Douglas.

They were to marry on December 22. In truth, I was open to some genteel version of unforeseen circumstances up in Maine that would force us to miss the affair but the momentum of our lives, which had always been trusty and regular, got us back to Manhattan in plenty of time, with the same awful efficiency of the elevator that appears instantly at your touch to bring you to your dentist.

We'd had a month's notice. The invitation had been addressed to us in a hand definitely not Earl's and since we never heard from him I often wondered if he would have preferred it had we not come at all. But there is no way that you can decently miss your father's wedding and I think I would have gone even if I was a bachelor and there had been no Tracy urging me on to some mythical unity that could be mine if I would only embrace my father, my past, and some opalescent and dangerous version of myself. So, piercing the joy of finding and finalizing a northern kingdom was the problem of what to get Earl and Lillian as a wedding present. I lurched mindlessly between the grandiose (a trip to Morocco, a set of Mark Cross luggage, an eighteenth-century French armoire made of rosewood, with cherubs for handles and glass that looked like frozen tears) and the sarcastically parsimonious (a record of Bartók playing his own compositions, a tie for Earl and a little hat for Lillian, a pound of Barton's chocolates, a can of peas...). In a way, I wanted to bring nothing at all, but of course I wanted to bring the perfect thing, the gift that would unfold meanings in their minds for years to come, a gift-wrapped enigma, a box of philosophy. What we finally settled on was a set of solid-silver antique Russian soup-spoons, with elaborate floral designs on the handles. When we wrapped them, Tracy enclosed a little card inviting them to dinner a few days after the wedding.

For all I knew, Earl was committing a faint version of bigamy. There may have been such a thing as common-law divorce and certainly enough time had passed since Evelynn Morgan left him for that mechanism of law to have been tripped, but I don't think Earl ever gratified any legal forms about the matter. I never really knew *what* Earl's situation was with my mother and I was too shy to ask: I invariably imagined his response would be bitter, hateful, as long as an opera. What I wanted was a ribbon of paternal wisdom with which I could complete the miniature memorial I kept in my mind—a memory of her pale green, sloping eyes, her high Slavic cheekbones, her fine perfumy hair—but Earl could not deliver such a thing. It wasn't his nature to tell you what you needed to know; he said what he needed to say.

I was seven years old when my mother beat out and I make no retrospective demands that Earl should have then and there cut me in on everything that was happening. But the fact is that he talked more about it those first six months—when what I wanted to do was pretend she was due back any day—than he would later in my life, when I'd finally covered that pit of mortification and loss and was ready to make some sense of it. "It was just one of those things," he'd say. "She did not understand your father, Virgil." Then, waiting until I'd crossed the pubic Rubicon, he said, "The trouble with your mother was she didn't care *who* she, well, made love with." Oh, so *that* was it. Well thanks a lot, you faggot. There were no pictures of her in the house and no mementos, except for the postcards I kept squirreled in my closet. I didn't spend much time fantasizing about her because I had developed a deeply realistic nature and I had no hopes about her one day coming back. There was every temptation to dream up a superwoman: she had the good sense to head west, she was out on her own. But why did she marry my father in the first place? And why hadn't she recognized that I couldn't fit into his household any better than she had? Why hadn't she taken me along?

A week before we made our move to New York, Earl came home pale, as if he were about to vomit. I asked him what was wrong. "Life catches up on you, Virgil. It grabs you when you don't expect. I was walking in Walgreen's to get some spot remover and I thought I saw Evelynn. Your mother, Virgil. It looked so incredibly like her." Well was it? I asked. "I have no idea. I simply turned around and walked out. Why did I do that?" I had no answer; I just looked at my hands and wondered if they were large enough to fit around his throat.

Earl did not live in what is commonly known as the

"real world," or so the two of us chose to believe. He lived in the fever dream of undiscovered genius. I believed more in his strangeness than in his genius but I had no heart to challenge him so our time together was at least half silence. We talked about meals, we divided the chores, we kept each other posted about our comings and goings, we dutifully introduced one another to the guests we brought into the house—he presenting me with a tall, gaunt clarinetist who smelled like a lawn, or a silver-haired woman in a black waitress uniform who shook my hand in a way that dug her rings into my fingers and nearly caused me to burst into tears. And I presented him with such luminaries as Micky Miller, who at the age of ten had somehow gotten detailed information about the function of the clitoris, or Marshall Roberts, a swarthy, athletic boy Earl had thrown out of music class the year before because of a noise Marsh made with his hand and his moist, bald armpit. Earl and I lived like poorly matched roommates in a college dorm. It was a house in which polite interest passed for concern and fits of piteous rage stood in for love. I always felt I was in his way, or, more exactly, felt that among his delusions was one that made him think if he were free of all responsibilities he would be better able to pursue his ambitions. But even this furious inkling was only surmised. In a thousand ways, I never knew him. I only knew what he wanted; I had no idea who he was.

The wedding and the reception afterward were held on a Sunday afternoon at my father's apartment on West Nineteenth Street, where Earl had lived since moving from Brooklyn—slowly, slowly he crept up upon the heart of Manhattan, his talent poised like a knife. It was an old building that was, architecturally, a hybrid of brownstone and tenement. A quartet of suspicious Irish children usually brooded about the steps, drinking grape soda and eating Fifth Avenue candy bars.

Earl's apartment was on the second floor, a railroad

apartment that began in the center of the old building and pressed itself against the barred windows on the street. It was carpeted in dark brown and the rug seemed always to have a wet spot somewhere. There were Venetian blinds on one of the windows that looked onto an airshaft and a number of armchairs that looked as if they'd been snatched from a retirement home. He put his old scarred piano in the front room, the only room that got any natural light, the one room in which you might have sat without feeling as if you'd been condemned. The instrument filled the space, forcing us from the one room in which we might sit in comfort, its yellow keys grinning in profile. Earl lived with true bohemian nonchalance and even if that ruin of an apartment was a sign that somewhere he had failed to grasp the form of his own life, the fact was that even in that depressing turmoil he managed to keep a job and work as a composer. Unfortunately, this is not what I felt the few times I'd visited him. The piano was a demon; it swallowed all the available light. And what was it for? It was for the manufacture of obscurity. Earl played music theory not music; geometry not rhapsody. Robot tunes. There were times when I felt pulled out of a good day, with the sudden knowledge that I was skimming across the smooth ice of my own life, Earl was jammed into that room, doggedly pursuing the same nutcase theories of music he had when he was in college, Temple University, class of 1935.

On the day of the wedding, however, the piano was gone, as were the armchairs and his metal-framed single bed. The kitchen had been turned into a bar. Replacing the apartment's characteristic odor of espresso and dust was the smell of perfume, flowers, cold cuts, and pipe tobacco. The blinds had been pulled all the way up and the blackened window was covered by a painting of a Picassoesque bride and groom. "To Earl and Lil," it said, "Once more into the breach."

The twenty-five guests were distributed along the

length of the apartment. Some of Earl's oldest pals, a few were friends of Lillian's, and there were a couple of aged representatives of Lillian's first husband's family—a pale, stooped, eighty-year-old man with spotted, trembling hands and his wife, who looked as old as he did but far more vigorous, wearing a large sparkling Jewish star around her neck. There was a leathery fiftyish woman in gardening clothes, and a chubby man in a wool suit sat on the floor in a half lotus, with a little black pipe stuck into his smiling face. From my father's contingent, there were people I'd seen at the recital, the Albas, Alan Zuger, John Towland. Every guest seemed to be animated by public convictions: they dressed either inexpensively or idiosyncratically, they were gray, brave, and a little sad, and most looked as if they would have been happier had they lived in another country—in France, Romania, some place where competition wasn't the dominant rhythm of life. Unlike Tracy's and my friends, who took the accident of having been born in America as a kind of weird, dangerous joke, whose sense of culpability was most often translated into a sense of humor, and who, in the meanwhile, managed to make handsome livings, Earl's friends did not so much live in their time and country as linger there, waiting for either monumental changes or extinction.

Tracy and I moved into the front of the house. She was wearing an expensive blue dress and hundred-dollar shoes; I was wearing a chic English suit. We looked as if we might have wandered into the wrong party. A small stereo played Indian sitar music in which my father had been interested long before it was a fad. The front window was open a few inches to keep the air circulating and the wind formed an icy ledge across the room.

I heard a voice raised in annoyance and saw a white-haired woman with large hands and red-framed glasses, wearing a pair of dark gray trousers with creases sharp enough to slice cheese. She made gestures of frustration and dismissal at a young man whose back was to us but whom Tracy and I recognized immediately. "That's Tom Douglas," said Tracy. "We should tell him someone telephoned him at our house."

"You don't forget anything, do you?" I hadn't forgotten either.

The wind must have blown some clouds over the pale distant sun for a shadow moved over and darkened the room, like the first layer of evening.

Suddenly, John Towland appeared. His long gray hair was tied back for the occasion and his hard blue eyes were encircled by an alcoholic pink. "Welcome, Virgil," he said, in a voice that tried to lilt. "I'm official bartender. What's your poison?"

"Tracy?" I asked.

"Sherry, if you have it."

"I'll have the same," I said. "I don't know if you've met my wife, John." It was the first time in my life I'd called him by his first name. "This is Tracy Morgan. Tracy, John Towland is my father's best friend."

"I am?" said Towland, completely astonished. He disappeared into the back of the apartment and we were joined by Tommy Douglas, who wore the blue suit we had met him in. With him was a tall blonde, a large-boned, open-faced girl who wore a floor-length flowered dress.

"Hello, Virgil. Howdy, Tracy," said Tommy. "I'm supposed to be best man."

"Isn't that against the law?" I said.

"Here we go again," said the girl with Tommy. She put her fists on her rounded hips and let out a massive sigh.

"Let me introduce you to my wife," said Tommy.

"Oh stop, Tommy, please," she said.

"All right. Let me introduce you to my chippy. Melissa Cavanaugh, this is Virgil and Tracy Morgan. Virgil's my new brother and . . . I'll have to consult one of my lawyers to find out what our relation is, Tracy." He smiled with terrific charm; it was the smile that opened doors, that changed wills, a smile that pulled you from one state of mind into another.

Tracy and I shook hands with Melissa Cavanaugh. Her palms were dewy. Noticing this, I glanced into her eyes: they were glassy and huge.

"Is this the most horrible place in the world or did I forget to take my mood elevators?" Melissa's voice was a marvel; smoky, wasted, ambisexual, a small-time nightclub voice, the voice that women have in the dreams of saxophone players.

"We'll be out of here soon enough," said Tommy.

"You got a phone call at our house the night of Earl's recital," Tracy said. After Melissa's voice, hers sounded like the ringing of a small, silver bell.

"Yes. I gave a friend that number." Turning to me, he added, "I expected to be let in."

John Towland appeared with our sherries. "The minister's here," he said. "He doesn't feel very well. I suppose the cold got to him. You know how these men of the cloth are. Living off the fat of the land." He handed us hot glasses, fresh from the sink.

"So where's my father and your mother?" I asked Tommy, after Towland moved on. "I'd think they'd want to be here."

"They went uptown to borrow a car from Mom's cousin."

I nodded, somehow stunned by the information. Borrowing a car? What for? Their honeymoon? Up to Niagara to look at the frozen falls? They could have asked me for a car. I didn't use mine during the week, it just took up space in an underground garage—seventy-five dollars a month. Christ, I wouldn't have minded.

"What are you two doing after the reception?" Tracy asked. "We can go for a drink, if you like."

"I'm not supposed to drink," said Melissa.

"Melissa's on the down slope of a manic-depressive thing," explained Tommy. "It can get pretty grim." He glanced at Melissa. "I don't see anything wrong in talking about it," he said. "It's our source of income. Melissa's a part of a state rehab program, this bureaucratic outpatient experiment. They give her a monthly check for going to school. That's what we live on." Again, that smile, that astonishing trick he had taught his mouth.

"Now to be fair, you have to tell us something about you," said Melissa. "Something personal. It won't be fair otherwise."

"A fair trade for that information would be for us to tell you how we make a living," I said.

"I already know that," said Tommy. "It's one of your father's recurring topics."

"Good. Then we're even."

"What does he do?" Melissa asked Tommy, about me.

"He makes money," said Tommy.

"Thank God," said Tracy, protectively.

"And what about you?" I asked Tommy.

"Me? I make trouble."

"How?" asked Tracy.

He pointed to the same small green button he wore on his lapel the first time we'd met, the one that bore the number 1,200,000. "Prisoners' rights," he said.

"Good cause," I said, much too quickly.

"You think so?" He seemed surprised.

"Sure," I said. "You've got to be insane not to be for prisoners' rights."

"I *am* insane and I'm for them," said Melissa, apparently lifting a bit out of her depression. She and Tommy had a nice, comfortable laugh. They were the sort of couple one immediately thinks of in sexual terms; their bodies seemed molded for each other and they brushed against one another when they stood.

"We're all prisoners anyhow," said Tracy over their laughter. I felt a pang of husbandly sympathy: she'd said it too late and it annoyed her to miss a beat.

* * *

Earl and Lillian blew in about half past two, thirty minutes late. Lillian was dressed in a nice green and silver dress, with long tight sleeves and pale green gloves. I was glad she hadn't tried to do much with her hair for that anarchist hair only looks ashamed of itself when it gets plastered down. Earl—and for some reason I didn't guess this, for some sick, childish reason I expected him to appear in a blue suit and boutonniere—Earl dressed in genius togs. He wore a red smoking jacket with cranberry silk lapels and a cranberry belt. Beneath that he wore a black shirt and a lemon-yellow ascot. His wool pants were a color that can only be described as bronze and instead of shoes he wore black ankle-high boots with functionless silver buckles on their sides. His friends appreciated his outfit and he turned around for them, in a rather funny burlesque of a model.

I drifted over toward them as soon as they entered but Earl gave no formal recognition of my presence. He and Lillian drank vodka and pineapple juice while Earl entertained the Albas and the old woman with the Jewish star with a story of the difficulties they had encountered in collecting Lillian's stingy cousin's Oldsmobile, which they planned to drive to Pennsylvania to visit Lillian's ailing mother. I stood next to him in silence and after a while, after what seemed, in fact, to be an initiation, his hand began to stalk my arm, like a big cat preparing to settle down to sleep. I took a deep breath. I needed to fully realize that the man in bronze pants who was about to venture into the mysteries of matrimony, who was about to plunge into an ancient ceremony with a woman to whom he had undoubtedly whispered all manner of endearments, that this man was my father, and twenty-seven years before he had exploded a spray of his essence into a long-vanished woman and out of that moment had come me.

"I want to talk to you for a moment," he said to me. "Let's go to the kitchen." He looked at Tracy, who'd come to my side. "Do you mind if I steal him for a minute?"

"Be my guest," said Tracy.

He did a not terribly subdued double-take just as he was linking his arm into mine. "You look marvelous today, Tracy," he said. "A princess."

The minister, an old friend of Lillian's late husband, Ivan Douglas, a jittery, obese, phlegmatic cleric named Gerald Healey, the Reverend Gerald Healey of the Congregationalist Church, was at that point in the bathroom, apparently much sicker than he'd first let on. He'd had a terrifying attack of coughing and shivering and then insisted what he needed was a place to be alone and compose himself. He'd been locked in the bathroom for about twenty minutes and once in a while John Towland knocked on the door and asked after him.

There was no rush, at least as far as my father was concerned. A few of the guests seemed to be hungry so Mrs. Alba served the cold cuts. Earl and I went into the now empty kitchen. The light was strong and watery. There was a brown bag of cloudy ice cubes in the old-fashioned sink. Someone had spilled a drink on the linoleum and on the wet spot there were a few yellow paper towels. Earl and I stood in the middle of this and were both physically uncomfortable and confused. There was no place to sit and nothing we dared lean against. "I'll be glad to leave this place behind," he said. He waited for an answer but what could I say? I was glad, too. "There's just one thing I need to tell you," he said.

"What's that?"

He looked at me as if deciding if I could take it. "We've decided to let Tommy be the best man."

"I know. He told me."

"He told you?"

"Sure. As soon as Tracy and I came in."

"Look, Virgil, I hope you're not upset. I honestly did suggest to Lil that we have you as best man but this business between her and that kid is very delicate at this point. Between his jealousy and his prison and his prisoners' rights, he's made what should have been a beautiful romance—a simple, beautiful romance—into something tense and difficult. I don't mind saying that to you. But you're not to repeat it."

"Look, if making him the best man makes things better between you and Lillian than I think you were right to do it."

"You know, he doesn't even care. What he cares about is that we asked him. That was his victory."

"What is it with him and prison?"

"A cause. You know. The Jewish disease. Or, in his case, the half-Jewish disease."

"Has he been in prison?"

Earl faltered for a moment. "Yes. Two years. The draft. During the war." He paused and smiled. "He wasn't shrewd like you."

"Shrewd's a lousy word, isn't it?" I said.

"Not when it keeps you out of jail and out of the army. Not when it keeps your life moving along while other boys your age were fleeing the country or getting crippled and killed."

John Towland appeared, slapping an empty tray against his side. "Reverend Healey is functioning again," he said. "Just a false alarm. He's ready whenever you are."

"Is Lillian out there?"

"You bet."

"Okay. Tell them I'm coming."

Towland rested the tray against the sink and started out toward the front of the apartment.

"Hey John," my father called. "You don't think I'm crazy for going through with this, do you?"

Towland turned, apparently quite startled. "Of course not," he said, squinting and shifting his weight, as people will when they've been asked what seems an unfair question.

* * *

When Tracy and I were married at her parents' home in Princeton we had our closest friends from New York, some old friends of Tracy's from school, a few friends of mine from school, about two dozen members of Tracy's relaxed yet firmly extended family, friends of the Keatings, and finally Earl, who did not know a soul there. Nevertheless, among all those strangers, with his suit limp and his stomach soured by the heat, Earl managed to generate enough of his own *loco* power to be one of the focal points of the affair. When Tracy's brother went to pick him up at the station I paced the Keating house in pre-ceremony anticipation and I stopped to admire a floral display. The flowers were standing on top of a big black piano and at that moment of prescience I realized that before long my father would be sitting at the keys. He didn't wait to be asked. He did, however, begin in the quietest possible way, a few arpeggios, bits and snatches of upper-register pastiche. Then some polite fool asked him if he'd like to play and within moments he was in the midst of a piece so torrential that everyone was paralyzed into strict attention, as if the discordant explosions had been diabolically conceived to befuddle the motor senses. There seemed to be at least fifteen minutes during which I was in a room of wide-eyed mannequins, dressed in summer finery, drinks in their hands, some with their mouths open, a few with knit brows. Only I, who was used to it, escaped the spell and I just swayed there, my heart thumping, wishing there was a way I could end it, a switch I might throw.

After an extended bout at the keys, Earl drifted vaguely through the house, randomly entering and quitting conversations, confusing the bartender with his requests for complicated mixed drinks, and, or so it appeared from a distance, flirting with a friend of Deborah Keating's, a white-haired lady whose face went electric pink as she stuffed a lace handkerchief into her wicker purse and high-tailed it out of there. Now and again, I'd notice a guest giving me a noblesse oblige blink of vague, theoretical pity.

Earl left around six but before he did he asked me to go into the dining room, where the long table was covered with gifts and envelopes.

"I want you to see what I brought you," he said.

I looked at the table and shrugged. I wore a white summer suit but beneath it my sweat touched me at all points, like a second person.

"It's right on the top," he said. "I keep putting it on top so it won't be broken. The blue package. There."

I picked up a flat, hard package. I could feel the frame and the backing through the wrapping and knew it was a picture. I tore it open and saw a photograph of my mother. It was a shy, smiling Evelynn, age twenty-one, her full, hard lips touched by primitive photographic pink, her eyes as bright as dance floors, her brown hair pushed back from her high downy brow in tight little curls. I stared silently at the picture.

"I thought you'd like to have it. And I think she'd like you to have it, wherever she is."

"It's a good present." My voice slipped away from me. I put the photo down and extended my hand.

"I'm counting on you to be very happy," he said, pulling me toward him in a sharp, convulsive, and utterly unfamiliar embrace. "Please. That's my only wish for you. Just beat this lousy world at its own lousy game. Be happy."

The Reverend Gerald Healey closed the window, blew on his small red hands, and stood before us holding a large sheet of paper. He looked like an innkeeper. He wore bifocals and unruly tufts of white hair peered from either side of his apple-shaped head. He had short legs and his feet looked more like hooves. I'd been told that Healey had met Ivan Douglas in the army but it was difficult to imagine those pudgy hands holding a gun, or saluting. It was hard to imagine them doing much of anything, except serving pints of stout or waving at the postman.

Earl, Lillian, and Tommy stood before him. Tracy, Melissa, Towland, the Albas, and I stood in the front row. Someone turned on the record player again which played a stirring rendition of the Wedding March from *Lohengrin*, which lasted a good five minutes.

When the music stopped, Healey took a deep breath. "We are gathered here together," he read "to join in marriage Lillian Belsito Douglas and Earl Morgan. Lillian is one of my dearest friends, a woman in whose strength I have more than once taken solace. Earl is a man whose life I hope will be intertwined with my own. They are adults in every sense of the word: responsible, committed, and each coming to the other from baptisms of sorrow and knowledge.

"I served in the United States Army with Lillian's first love, the father of Lillian's only son, Tom, and the man of her life for the first twenty-five years of womanhood. Though I was destined to be a minister and Ivan, my friend, was a Jew, there were no petty differences to keep us apart. He kidded me about my desire to serve my church and I kidded him about his Christianized surname and about his agnosticism. Ivan Douglas has gone to the other side. But he was the sort of man whose encounters with others changed them. I know he changed my life and though my dedication is more to God than to any one man, sometimes my dedication to the memory of Ivan Douglas is my primary avenue toward my God. I realize that a wedding is no occasion to speak of the departed, but it is this presence of past lives, or hard-won knowledge, that makes this wedding so important to me.

"Earl Morgan himself is no stranger to the sudden vicissitudes of wedlock and while I did not know his first wife, Evelynn Morgan, I do know that death took her away from Earl during the tenth year of matrimony, leaving Earl with the care of their only child, his son Vernon."

I supposed that in the excitement of murdering my mother for Healey's notes, my father must have mumbled my name. I glanced at Tracy but she didn't fucking *dare* look at me.

"We are joining two people," Healey continued, "who have had love snatched from them by the cold, uncompromising hand of Death. People who've weathered storms that have crippled others but who have come through them, not shrinking from life, not fearful of its manifold challenges, but open of heart, optimistic of spirit, full of faith, if you will." He made a little smile at my father, who'd probably asked him to keep religion out of it.

"Lillian, you came to this city from Scranton, Pennsylvania, where you were, as you yourself described it, an obedient rebel. You married your first husband without your parents' approval. To them a Jew was a fearful, unusual thing and the light of love in your eyes could not melt their fear. You and Ivan lived in New York until your marriage was interrupted by the war. When Ivan returned you were both determined to seize your lives. You began to fulfill your lifelong dream of dancing by studying with a series of teachers —studies that eventually led to your opening your own dance instruction school in the 1950s, and Ivan began the pursuit of his desire to be a journalist and secured a position on a newspaper many of us will remember, *P.M.*, a fine, forward-thinking paper whose own life was tragically short.

"By this time, you were a family of three. I remember when I asked you if there was a guiding light you followed when you raised your son. And you said, 'I want him to have a soft heart in a hard world.'

"No words could I find to better describe Lillian Douglas who today becomes Lillian Morgan. She is a woman who has made adversity the plow with which she has tilled the fields of human love. Through the isolation of childhood, the challenges of marriage and the initial rejection of her family, through the pain of arthritis, the sorrow of widowhood, the pinch of material want, and now onto the challenge of second love, Lillian Douglas has been a model to me and it is with the utmost pride and joy that I have journeyed to New York to preside over this special day.

"I cannot pretend to know the groom, Earl Morgan, nearly so well. We had dinner last night to discuss this ceremony and various other topics and I was impressed by his fervency, his enormous dedication to his craft—Mr. Morgan is a musician—and, most importantly, by his dedication to Lillian and her son Tom. He is an open-minded man and there is no question but that he, like so many of us, marches to the beat of a different drummer. When I asked the bride and groom last night where they planned to live, Earl said, 'Her place.' I asked how they reached that decision and again it was Earl who answered. 'It's bigger and it's a lot cleaner.' I was, in all honesty, taken aback, but then I realized that was only because I'd unconsciously assumed it was the man's home in which a new marriage would sink its permanent roots. When I considered Earl Morgan's candid answer I believe I was given a measure of the man. He is not bound to outmoded traditions nor is he bound to any base pride.

"And so, we bring two broken families together and make them one. Lillian and Thomas Douglas, Earl and Vernon Morgan. Earl and Lillian, will you repeat after me?"

7

I DRANK MORE champagne than I ought to have. Earl and Lillian were occupied with my father's new extended family and I informed Healey my name was Virgil. Or did I? I meant to, but I can't remember any response on his part so perhaps I never got around to it. Finally, I made my way to the corner in which Lillian and Earl were holding court and, holding my champagne glass aloft, I proposed a toast. "To their joy," I said, but only Lillian's cousin Arthur Tagg was holding a glass so it wasn't a very successful gesture. To make up for this, I began bragging about my new property.

Certainly it seemed strange that the son of the man who'd just borrowed a car on his wedding day was himself a baron of the northern woods and I don't think this irony escaped anyone. As soon as it was out—"One hundred twenty acres of heaven" is how I phrased it—I looked to see where Tracy was and when I saw her across the room talking with Tommy and

Melissa I was relieved, which proved, I'm afraid, that I knew exactly what I was doing.

"That's a lot of land, Virgil," my father said.

"It's mostly just wild," I said, backpedaling.

"You saved some of it for us," said Lillian, with a thin, just-kidding smile. "We'll retire to it."

"Where is it?" asked Earl.

"Up in Maine."

"Where?"

"Way up."

He turned to Lillian. "You see? He doesn't want to tell me."

I wanted to protest, but he was right. "I'll tell you all about it later," I said, thinking it was just not the place to discuss it but unable to admit, then, that had I my free and open choice I would have seen to it that he never knew where it was.

"Sure," he said. "Later. Next year." Then, before I could say anything more, he turned to John Towland, who was standing near the record player. "What is that, John? 'Transfigured Night'? That still sounds awfully good."

Tracy and I left in the late afternoon, accompanied by Tommy and Melissa. We went to a nearby bar, a dark purple chamber with relaxing pictures of Puerto Rico on the walls. Tommy knew the bartender and he gave us complimentary brandies when Tommy told him we'd just come from a wedding.

"Is anything happening in back this afternoon?" Tommy asked.

"No, not today. Maybe later," the bartender said, a soft-looking Latin named Hector who wore a black silk shirt with golden lightning bolts over his chest.

"What goes on in back?" I asked, after Hector was gone.

"Cockfights," said Tommy.

"Great," said Melissa, "that's all I need." She slid her Don Pedro over to Tommy.

"I know it's awful, but I'd love to see one," said Tracy.

"Sunday's usually a good day here," said Tommy, leaning toward Tracy. "Sometimes Thursday nights. Weekdays are better in the Bronx. But the betting's better here. You want to go to the South Bronx? Maybe there'll be something happening. I can call."

"If you think you're going to bring me to some little shithouse packed to the rafters with macho pigs and have me watch two chickens claw each other to death," said Melissa.

It was somewhere between the third and fourth drink that we began talking about the wedding. "I suppose Reverend Healey's had more experience with funerals than with weddings," Tracy said.

"Is he a close friend of yours?" I asked Tommy.

"That's okay," said Tommy, "you can denounce him for getting your name wrong."

"And that bit about my mother being dead," I said, shaking my head.

"What do you mean?"

"What do I mean? She's not dead. Or if she is, we don't know it."

"Your father said she died of polio. He said she was paralyzed and he had to put her in the hospital. Before the vaccine."

"What a goddamned lie. He actually said that?" I was fairly angry but I was laughing.

"That's right," said Tommy.

"You mean your mum's not dead," said Melissa.

"I hope not," I said.

"Virgil's mother left Earl when Virgil was about seven," said Tracy.

"Frightening," said Melissa.

"Why's that frightening?" said Tommy, annoyed.

"I don't know," she said. "It's like someone coming back to life. It pulls the rug out. I like the dead to stay dead."

"Well, I don't mind a little traffic between dimensions," I said. "Come on, let's drink to my mother's health. God, what a wedding."

"I never saw people their age get married," said Tracy. "It brings out the sentimental in me. It seems incredibly brave and romantic. I've always thought that older people experience a kind of passion completely unique." She paused for a moment. I felt an unaccountable reluctance to hear what was on her mind. "Look, Virgil," she said, "I know you're not that fond of your father but there were moments when I wanted so badly for them to be happy that I thought I was going to pass out. They were holding hands, borrowing a car to ride out and see her mother. Both of them have been alive for so long. They've had so much happen to them. And we're so young. So much of our life is being young together."

There was a silence. Listening to Tracy had filled my throat with hot tears, the sort of tears not for shedding but for swallowing. I was glad she'd been moved by Earl's wedding, glad she hadn't recoiled from it, as a large, untamable part of me had. I was glad to be with her in a dark Latin bar, getting drunk with my new stepbrother and his unraveled mistress. I was a little wounded that Tracy thought our love depended on being young together but, at the same time, I was grateful for all the years I assumed were mine to prove her wrong.

The silence was broken by Tommy slapping his glass onto the bartop. "I'm trying to make a decision," he said. He drummed his fingers and looked at Tracy and me. "We need one more thing to consecrate this day, to make us all a family. I want you two to come up to our apartment. I want to show you something."

"I'm game," said Tracy. "We should get out of here while we can still walk."

"Tommy," said Melissa, "what are you going to show them?"

"Just shut yourself up. I know what I'm doing."

Their apartment was on Fourteenth Street, near

First Avenue. Just a little east, the generators and smokestacks of the Con Ed plant heaved in the twilight, like monsters in an H. G. Wells nightmare. The streets were strewn with papers, burned-out couches. Most of the stores were closed, the windows protected by bars or gates. No one was outside except two young men who stood in a littered doorway with their hands jammed into their pockets, their collars up, staring into the globes of steam that rose with their breath: citizens of a world that didn't work very well.

The building Tommy and Melissa lived in was a narrow five-story tenement, next door to a bingo parlor. "The bingo makes this place safe," said Melissa, as we got out of the cab. "There's always crowds. Even at two in the morning." They lived on the third floor, in the front. The halls were lit by weak, jittery fluorescence, and lurching up those steep stairs was like climbing through a submarine. The door to their apartment looked newly constructed: thick wood, reinforced with lumber and steel around the frame. The name on the door was neither Douglas nor Cavanaugh. It said DePasquale.

Inside, it was cave-like. The apartment consisted of two large rooms, both painted the blackish green of leaves after an early morning storm. There was a tiny gas stove and an old refrigerator, but no signs of domestic activity. Lined against the lumpy walls were piles of newspapers and magazines and a few stacks of carefully folded clothes, as if everything were about to be donated. Beneath the windows—which were kept deliberately dirty in lieu of curtains—was their bed, neatly made. Although I'd expected an anthology of them, there was only one poster on the wall. It showed a black man in prison clothes thrusting his fist into the air. Beneath the picture was the now familiar number, 1,200,000, and the name of the organization to which Tommy apparently belonged: National Association for the Rights of Prisoners.

Tommy had a very small bit of cocaine which we all

shared. Tracy and I were never very involved with drugs but we had a taste for what's good and Tommy's coke was deeply inferior. It burned the nose, strafed the throat, and turned the mind over only once. Melissa turned on a dim light next to the bed and to further mute it she draped a red and blue neckerchief over the shade. Their apartment was now exactly the light of the bar we had just left, but there was no jukebox, no drinks, no easy proximity to the life of the street. There was only the smell of joss sticks, the guttural hum of the Con Ed plant.

"What did you want to show us?" I sat down on the edge of the bed.

"Okay," he said. "The time is now. It's in the closet. You sit tight. This is going to turn your mind around."

He disappeared into a long closet across the room and a few moments later we heard something heavy being dragged—a body? a howitzer? I leaned over and put my hand on Tracy's shoulder. Just a few minutes before she'd been drunk, loose, loquacious, but the lousy coke and the mystery had silenced her and she started a little when I touched her.

"What do you think it is?" I whispered to her.

"A trampoline?"

"Maybe. Perhaps an enormous metal goose."

"Oh shit," said Melissa, pacing, "this is wrong."

As Melissa went into the other room, Tommy emerged from the closet carrying two bright silver cases, each circumscribed by a black canvas belt. He banged one of them into the frame of the closet and cringed.

"Do you need any help?" I asked, relieved by the innocuousness of the objects.

Melissa came in holding a carton of milk and placed a dark red pill deep in her mouth and then washed it down with a great, excessive toss of her head. "You shouldn't be doing this," she said.

"Now's the time for you to take a pill that makes you shut up," said Tommy.

Tommy opened the larger of the two metal cases. It was lined in plush and contained a radio transmitter about the size of a tool box. It had twenty silver switches and a number of dials. He turned the case around so we could get a better look at it. He was on his haunches now, moving his hands excitedly over the instrument, but not touching it, like primitive man before a fire. He hurriedly opened the second, smaller case. From it he extracted an old-fashioned broadcasting microphone and an antenna that looked like a small abstract rendition of a Christmas tree. "I don't think I'll connect it now." His voice wobbled at the edges; for the moment he was a manic matinee doctor reveling in quackery's most romantic notion—the cursed thing.

"Well, what do you think?" he said.

I didn't know what to think. It was a radio.

"You don't know what to make of this, right?" he said, pulling that smile out of the hat again. You knew it was invented but still it moved you—you wondered what sort of person would make up a smile like that.

"I love this machine," he said. "You're never going to see anything like this again."

"What does it do?" asked Tracy.

"It does a great deal, let me tell you. And no one knows about it. That's very important. No one must know a thing about this."

"Are you in contact with outer space?" I asked.

He said, "Do you have a television?"

"Sure."

"Then watch it. Tonight. Channel 5, around nine, ten o'clock." He went to his knees and closed the cases. "This has been my present to the two of you. Now we're all a part of the same family. The ceremony wasn't enough. I wanted to do something to really draw us together. I went first. I opened a door so you could look at my life."

* * *

Tommy had urged some pamphlets on us and Tracy flipped through them while I made a light supper.

If Tracy had not been the kind of woman capable of opening her heart to the horror stories of prisoners then my love for her would perhaps have been different, less ardent. She read *Prisoners and Sex*, *Prisoners as Guinea Pigs*, and *Crimes of Consciousness* and I thought of that part of my wife capable of caring about the world. It was no surprise that she clutched at those pamphlets, reading them in the cab, in the dim fleeting light of the streetlamps, reading them at the table as we ate our cheese and pears. Silently, I made what retrospect reveals as an extravagantly optimistic prediction: I thought that before long we'd be writing a check, a donation to the National Association for the Rights of Prisoners.

"I'm going to make coffee," I said.

She looked up from the booklet. "Your stepbrother is remarkable, isn't he?"

"I don't know what to think of him, or her," I said.

"We're not used to people like them. But you can certainly feel something torrid and astonishing between them. I suppose it comes from living so close to the edge."

"I think you might be confusing the edge with the bottom," I said.

"There's not much difference, is there?" she said. "I admire them."

"I know you do."

"They've been tested," Tracy said.

At nine we went into the living room and turned on the TV. As luck would have it the channel Tommy asked us to watch was showing one of my favorite movies, *The Invasion of the Body Snatchers*. The frequent commercials reminded us that it was three days to Christmas. We'd promised each other not to get gifts this year—Preservation Hall was to be a gift to and from each of us—but I thought I might break my word. Even if I didn't, there were presents we had to see to. Last year we'd exchanged presents with ten people and we would be seeing those same friends on Christmas Day, at a party on Riverside Drive. Tracy and I made lists of people and what to get them while we watched. I tried to make her shut up when the movie went back on but she deliberately made light of it.

"Yes, yes, I know. The pods take over their souls and make replicas of them as soon as they fall asleep."

Her refusal to take the movie seriously touched me; I knew Tracy had a capacity for being frightened out of her wits by horror films and the vulnerability of her unconscious made me ache with love. There had been times when she'd awaken from a nightmare whimpering and I'd take her in my arms and kiss her until she fell back to sleep. The next morning she had no recollection of waking at all. Maybe I was wrong to, but I loved it when she'd come crashing out of sleep and into my arms. Afterward, I would lie beside her and watch her sleep, fighting my own onrushing sleep with the hope that a good dream might be delivered to her and she might murmur my name.

But I could not involve her in the movie. There was that list of friends, starts of conversation about Tommy and Melissa, a trip to the kitchen which somehow took five minutes, and then, just as an eerie replica of a significant minor character materialized on a billiard table, my efforts to make her concentrate were sunk for good: we knew why Tommy had asked us to watch.

The first sign of interference affected the picture reception. A few lines danced through the picture tube and the image shook for a moment. Then there was a crackling noise, followed by a loud pop. The four characters in the film continued their gestures, as the alien being came into existence on that billiard table, but we no longer heard their voices. We heard another voice, one that was unmistakably Tommy's.

"I've spent two Christmases in jail. For one, I got a loaf of whole wheat bread and a magnetic chess set. For the other, I got kicked in the testicles and had two fingers broken. Who I am is of absolutely no importance. What is important is that there are over a million of us behind bars on this day, being used as guinea pigs in experiments you would not believe—given drugs, locked into black holes, getting shot up with viruses. The others are being driven crazy and the others are just waiting. But one day the doors will fly open and we're going to be loose in your cities, I can guarantee that.

"I'm almost out of time. And so are you. You cannot ignore the prisoners in your jails. They are *your* jails. You paid for them, you built them, your taxes pay the salary of every faggot maniac that works in them.

"You can roll over and play dead or you can start doing something. Anything. Put carpets in the jails, radios. It's not crazy. In Sweden—oh, fuck Sweden. No bails over a grand—you can't make us pay for the right to trial. Mandatory life sentences for any prison official who commits any offense against a prisoner. And an end to all physical, psychological, and sociological experiments performed on us. You can't—"

Suddenly, his voice was gone and the dialogue of the film came out of the actors' mouths once again. They were in the moonstruck garden now, discovering a coven of pods. I was sitting on the edge of the couch and when I looked over at Tracy she was too.

She let out her breath. "Oh, my God," she said. "He'll get busted for certain." She said it in a voice more frightened than any I'd heard from her. I moved closer to her. She practically leaped to her feet, stretched her arms far from her body. "God," she said, with a crooked, lunatic grin, "what a fucking incredible thing to do. It really made my heart stop." She paced to the center of the room and stopped there, folding her arms over her breasts. She was still for a moment. Then she said, "Do you think he'll do it again?"

8

H E DID DO it again. He broke into a broadcast the next afternoon and he jammed in twice on Christmas Day. For a while he was the talk of New York: the talk, that is, of a city perpetually in the throes of some metropolitan amazement. One week it's a Hungarian refugee blasting the United Nations with a shotgun. The next week a woman with an enormous bosom causes a furor each time she emerges from her subway stop in Wall Street, and before long photographers and TV cameramen are standing around with the throngs of clerks and brokers who daily await her. It doesn't have to be tragic or violent to capture the collective imagination. It's all a part of the city's sense of life: half antic, half peril.

Tommy became a part of that. Whatever laws he broke, however many policemen might have been on his trail, the fact is that the *Daily News* called him the "Phantom Broadcaster," and by so doing made him community property. Somewhere he may have been forcing people to think and talk about prison reform but for the most part he was a fad. If you hadn't heard him you felt left out. Christmas, even in New York, is a festive time of year and Tommy became a part of that mood. Phantom Broadcaster. Nobody seemed to pay much attention to why he was doing what he did, or what he had to say, but the fact that he was doing it at all—that he was getting away with it—was everything.

Tracy rooted for him with total, uncritical ardency and I paced around my knowledge of him with growing suspicion. Why, I wondered, had he wanted to reveal himself to us? When the Broadcaster was mentioned in the office I worried that my face might color. When I saw someone reading about him on the subway I lowered my eyes, shifted away. I tightened inside, as if they might be reading about a crime *I'd* committed. But mostly I waited for Tommy to make contact with us again. I couldn't help but believe there was more he wanted from us. Yet what could I give him? All I could think of was money and I didn't quite see what good that would do. I felt probably exactly what he wanted me to feel when he had pulled his transmitter out of the closet: I felt mystified, badgered, and somehow exposed.

Tracy brought home a copy of *Newsweek* with a small story about the Broadcaster. He had become national news. Soon there would be imitation Phantoms. I just glanced at the story, unable to read it.

"What's wrong?" Tracy asked.

"I find this so annoying."

"Jesus, Virgil. Annoying?" said Tracy. I think she was so disappointed in my response that she was unable to say anything more. Somehow, Tommy's struggle reminded her of her own, the struggle she had promised herself to make one day, while it reminded me of all the things I had secretly promised myself never to do.

* * *

The day after Christmas, Bob Halpin told me he
needed me to go to Arizona and California at the end
of January, for five or six weeks. He had just secured
an account with a chain of resort hotels and he wanted
me to be there. It was some kind of honor and there
was no decent way out of it. Besides, that mild, fortyish man with his orthopedic shoes and rumpled suits,
and that steel glint of pure, functional intelligence in
his narrow eyes, knew how to spring such things. Just a
half hour before, a memo had appeared on my desk
informing me that my annual salary review had af-
forded me a $4,500 raise. Annual salary review? I
hadn't even known there was such a thing.

I could have arranged to bring Tracy out West but
she wasn't interested. Her business with Gary Fish
didn't take enormous energy but it demanded steady
attention. The Fish never allowed her to imagine that
he might carry on in her absence. The son of a steel
executive from New Jersey, he was a skinny, pale,
coughing egoist who'd inherited from his overbearing
old man the moronic theory that people wanted someone to tell them exactly what to do, and that the way
to get ahead in the world was to be a power in the
will-less void of other people's lives. That Tracy tolerated Fish was, from the start, a faintly unpleasant mystery to me. They'd met as co-workers at a publishing
company and their partnership had been his idea. Fish
had originally bankrolled it, as well.

The impending five-week separation weighed upon
what was already a difficult holiday—not difficult in
the usual sense, but ambiguous, puzzling, like one of
those arithmetic problems about how many apples are
yielded by a particular orchard, a problem in which
one vital clue has been omitted, a printer's error. My
father's wedding took some underground toll in me, as
did Tommy's broadcasts; these were not events that
beat me with a stick but they did barge into my life and
one of the things I knew and accepted about myself

was that I was at my best when my life contained only those things I admitted to it. Though business had taught me all I needed to know about spot decisions, the general tone of my growing up had taught me stricter lessons about what happens to life when events begin tumbling about. I had a general's scorn for chaos and I felt disorder snapping at the edges of my life, moving up on a flank, taking a distant hill.

I don't mean to say that my decision to spend New Year's at Preservation Hall was a form of preventative warfare, nor was it purely an adventure to mobilize the benign spirits that had watched so conscientiously over my life alone and my life with Tracy. There was a measure of all that but mostly it seemed like a perfect place to be at the moment. Neither of us had much appetite for the parties we were invited to and the idea of a week in our new house, identifying our trees, watching the sun rise and set, naming the constellations, fucking in absolute peace—the prospect was ravishing. We had planned to spend a little time up there that winter but now with a piece of January and most of February being donated to my boss it seemed right to go immediately.

Like characters in a film running at twice the normal speed, we shopped the next day for a few of the things we wanted to bring to Maine. We bought an Amish quilt from the author of a quilt book Tracy had designed. We bought light bulbs and pot holders, a rug for the bathroom, and a reading lamp for the upstairs front bedroom, which we would soon make our own. We bought what was necessary for a New Year's toast —a bottle of Dom Perignon 1962—and a couple of bottles of claret for special meals. We got a bottle of Russian vodka and a bottle of unblended Scotch. We bought a cassette tape recorder and twenty cassettes. Tracy got a sketch pad and charcoal pencils. I bought some Marquez in Spanish, hoping to resuscitate my one foreign language, and Tracy, perhaps inspired by

me, bought some Gogol in Russian, which was the language she had studied in school. Other than that, we
weren't worried about what to read. One of the unexpected treasures of the house was that the deceased
owner had left behind a nice collection of old books—
first editions of *Seventeen, Flappers and Philosophers*,
and *The Sound and the Fury*, aside from a collection of
old paperbacks with baroque, melodramatic illustra-
tions on their covers: a woman being choked on a
staircase, a young boy grinding an old watch beneath
his heel, a bearded sailor shaking his fist at heaven.
You had to be careful when you turned the pages because the paperbound books were not made to last;
they had cost ten cents, fifteen cents, a quarter. But
their smell went straight to the heart and when you
read them you felt you were reading in the archives of
lost time.

As we were leaving the appliance store with our
cassettes, I saw ten or so people in the showroom,
looking at the bank of TVs, comparing the reception,
the color. A quiz show was in progress and the contes-
tant, a smiling nun in dark glasses, had just been asked
what color was the face of someone who was "livid
with rage." I thought the answer was light purple but
she won when she said white. I was about to confess
my error to Tracy when that now familiar sequence of
dancing lines made its way across every set before us.
Everyone knew exactly what was going on. It was the
Phantom's fourth day in New York. There was, or so it
seemed, a small collective gasp. Someone said, "Here
comes the guy who talks about jail." The guy who
talks about jail? Somehow, that didn't seem sufficient.
Involuntarily, I stepped back. If I'd been alone, I think
I would have turned on my heel, disappeared.

After a moment's static, Tommy's voice came on.
"Well, we're back," he said, but that was all. The
video portion of the transmission went suddenly dead
and, after that, silent electric snow filled the screens.

Someone at the studio had stopped the entire broadcast. They must have been waiting for him.

I explained to Bob Halpin I wanted a week off. Gary Fish was no problem because he was on his way to Aspen, Colorado, to commiserate with his sister after her divorce, so Tracy's office would simply be closed. We got Mario to look after our plants and our cat. His daughter was with him again and they weren't getting along so Mario asked if she might stay up at our place, which was fine with us.

The only thing that existed outside the corral was the invitation to dinner we had extended to Earl and Lillian on the day of their wedding. It was an evening I would have liked to sidestep, even before I knew it would turn out so poorly. Part of my desire to scoot north was to remove myself from the orbit of my father's life—a life that seemed to be brushing closer to mine than it had in years, circling my cool moon like a mad comet. On the card we'd inserted in their wedding gift, we'd invited them for the twenty-ninth of December, one week after their wedding and one day before our departure. By the twenty-eighth, however, they hadn't called to acknowledge the date and I felt certain hope.

When we woke up Sunday morning, Tracy asked me, "Do you have your father and Lillian's number?"

"What for?" I said, playing it dumb.

"Dinner's tonight. Maybe they forgot or maybe they need a personal reminder."

"They didn't let us know about dinner? Then fuck it. It's not a good time now, anyhow."

"But we invited them."

"You invited them."

"No. *We* did. Do you have the number?"

"No. It's probably in the phone book. She lives on East Twenty-third. But I still . . ."

It was a wasted argument. As we had our breakfast, the phone rang, and, heavy with that sense of failed

luck that can come over you when things are starting
to slip out of your grip, I knew it was Earl, and it was.

"Hello. It's Dad," he said. He paused.

"Hi," I said.

Satisfied, he went on. "There's trouble about dinner."

I knew my luck in the matter wasn't good. It
wouldn't be a cancellation, just a complication. What?
His gums had gone bad and we'd have to process his
food. "What's wrong?"

"What's wrong. Umm, Lil's not feeling great. I'm
going to have to come over solo."

"Look, if she's not well why don't we make it some
other time?"

"No. She's just going to sleep. And I'll just be sitting around. She's very sorry. You want me to put her
on?"

"There's no need for that."

"She is very sorry. We're going to have you and
your wife over as soon as things settle down."

"Good. There's no hurry."

"No hurry, huh. That's nice."

"I didn't mean anything. I just wanted you to—"

"Forget it. What time is good for this afternoon?
Three? Four? How about three thirty? Okay?"

He arrived close to five. No surprise. It was an
arithmetic I'd worked out long ago. Earl felt that
showing up on time betrayed anxiousness, neediness, a
desire to please and it was the concealment of just
those things that made him at once intolerable and
brave; intolerable because it was a lie, a rude, silly
fabrication, and brave because as he aged it would
have been easy to rip loose and abandon pretense, to
drop his guard and reveal the great hole in his chest.
But if he'd made his pain public I don't think a person
alive could have stood being in the same room with
him. So he sauntered in at five, dressed in a ski jacket
and bearing a jar of brandied peaches. His arrogant,
watchful face still looked cold from the walk from the

subway—it was a harsh day and the wind blew hard off the park.

"I'll make you a drink," I said, leading him into the living room.

"No. Just a cup of coffee. Okay?"

"Okay. It'll take a while."

"No instant?"

"No, but it's all right." It wouldn't be more bother than mixing the drinks he liked to ask for: rum, tonic, grenadine, cream, a chunk of fruit. Sublime nitwit drinks.

Tracy came in from the kitchen. As she and Earl embraced I could see her face and sense that when he touched her with his large waxy hands the cold went right through her.

"You're too beautiful for my son," he said. "No wonder he tries to keep us apart. And this place," he said, making a quick transition, taking in the room with a dramatic sweep of the eyes. "I keep on forgetting how fabulous this place is. You should have chamber music recitals right here. Windows. Furniture. Wood."

Windows, furniture, wood? Where was he living?

"Is Lillian all right?" Tracy asked.

Earl sat heavily on the couch. I was half out of the room on my way to the kitchen, but I lingered.

"She's not particularly well, no," he said.

"What's the matter?" asked Tracy. She sat near him.

"What's the matter?" He took a deep breath. "Okay. No sense in secrets. It's her son. Tommy. He's in trouble. Pretty serious. And Lil blames herself. She takes everything on. To her, everything's her fault. That boy has broken everything youthful in her right over his knee."

"We know," I said.

"You know what?"

"The day of your wedding he showed us his transmitter."

"He did. Well." Earl thought about it for a moment, a purely animal calculation: Is this good for me/bad for me? "Okay. I'm glad. It's a relief for someone else to know. What do *you* think about it?"

"Don't ask me," said Tracy. "I've got a weakness for it."

"Tracy has a sense of the fabulous," I said.

"You must think it's pretty crazy," Earl said to me.

"I don't know. It doesn't seem to do much good. He'll probably get caught, too."

"You understand, even the wastrels and ex-cons he knows in that organization are against what he's doing. Even them. But Lil won't see it. She likes that girl of his, too. That sick, rich, spoiled girl. Poor Lillian has much too much sympathy. You'd think loving me would be enough of a cause for her." He made a sharp, barking laugh. "That little no-talent Rimbaud is wrecking my marriage. Lil's too exhausted to come here today. It's a real pain in the ass."

"Are the cops after him?" I asked.

"They're after whoever's making those broadcasts," said Earl.

"They don't know who, do they?" said Tracy.

"Who knows what they know," said Earl. "I'll be honest with you." He paused for a moment and then warned us: "This is extremely honest and I don't expect it to get around. If it wasn't for what it would do to Lil, I wish they'd arrest him and put him away again."

I went into the kitchen to grind coffee and boil water. While the kettle heated, I sat at the kitchen table and leafed through Tracy's copy of *Persuasion*, which was open on the table. I heard my father's voice in the next room—he was telling a story about Berlioz insulting the owner of a cafe. I stalled. The kitchen had a symmetry that pleased me. I liked the light blue and yellow tiles on the floor, loved the old wooden table with its dark varnished knots. On one wall there hung copper pots and German knives; on another was a plexiglass spice rack and a genial poster illustrating weight and volume equivalents. Sitting there, with my thumb marking Tracy's place in her book, gazing around that kitchen, I had a sense of utilitarian privacy, of safe harbor. The roast was already seasoned and in the oven but I prolonged my stay by breaking the tips off of the string beans and dropping them into a ceramic bowl—each one looked lovelier than the last.

A few minutes later, I brought in the coffee. Earl was turned toward Tracy on the couch, one leg folded beneath him, his finger wagging at her, a great, manic smile on his face.

"You haven't even seen your land?" he said. "How do you know it's really there, or all there? You know, these backwoods types are a lot shrewder than you think."

"We trusted him," said Tracy. "Besides, Virgil was hot to buy."

"And what might we be talking about?" I said, setting down the tray.

"Tracy's telling me about your land," said Earl, fixing his coffee. "So what have you got there, Tracy? The house, a hundred acres or so. What else? A lake?"

"No," said Tracy. "A pond."

"It sounds really wonderful. Wood nymphs. You'll probably spot a flying saucer. It sounds very much like Benjamin Britten's place. I read about it."

"You know," I said, trying to step good and hard on the conversation, "I don't think I've ever heard anything Britten's composed. Or have I? Did you ever play me any of his things?"

"Well," said Earl, "when are you going to invite us up? I'd like to see springtime in a place like that. The only way I can tell the seasons have changed here is when the Puerto Rican girls in my school change the color of their nail polish."

"I love those bizarre nail polishes," I said. "I like

those two-tone jobs, the three-tone ones, as well. I like the whole Latin feeling this city has."

"Sure you do," said Earl. "That's why you have a house five hundred miles away. Where is it anyhow?" He looked at me for a moment and then shifted his hard, watchful eyes toward Tracy.

"It's not really much of any place specific," Tracy said, her voice faltering.

"What was that type's name, the one who sold it to you? You just said it to me. The one who loved the land so much? Rainwater?"

"Tarwater," said Tracy.

"He wouldn't ride in our car," I said, "because it's German. His brother was killed in the war." The chance that the conversation would trail off into memories of World War II was pretty fucking slim but I had little to lose.

"That's right," said Earl. "Tarwater."

There was a silence. I looked at Tracy, hoping to telegraph my ardent desire that we not speak to Earl about the land, and that we, above everything else, not tell him where it was.

"You two are putting me in a very undignified position," said Earl. "You know very well that I'd like to know where your house is and you're deliberately not telling me. I don't understand that. You're turning good news into a very insulting mystery."

"Oh come on, Earl," Tracy said. "You're misinterpreting us."

"Am I?"

"Yes, of course. And you're not behaving well at all."

"I'm sorry if I'm misinterpreting you," he said.

"Well, you're not, exactly," I said, aware that in a moment the lever would be tripped and he would know everything. "I *do* want where the house is to be a secret."

"From me?" said Earl

"From everyone."

"I don't want to be in this kind of argument," Tracy said. "I'm getting drawn into something I really don't approve of. I'm not keeping it a secret, Virgil." She looked at Earl. "And I'm not playing cat and mouse." She took a deep breath and slumped back on the couch. "You two. You meet like enemy generals, knocking your sabers against the table, bluffing each other. Really."

"We are mistrustful of each other," he said to me. "I feel that too."

"We are," I said.

"But it's not because we don't love each other," he said to Tracy. "In England, the Morgan family was a soldiering one. Fighters. It's how our energy works. I don't want you to think we fight because we don't love each other." He patted her knee and smiled at me. "The women who enter our little clan have a hard initiation, isn't that right, Virgil?"

"I never thought of it that way," I said.

He added another sugar cube and some milk to his cup and then broke the sugar with the back of his spoon. "I'm not going to have a good time if you don't tell me where your house is. It sticks in my throat."

I shook my head, perhaps imperceptibly. I wanted to bellow my refusal but Tracy's presence inhibited me, civilized me in a way that was uncomfortable and seemed potentially dangerous. Still, I could not harvest the fury that grew wild within me. Tracy said the house was near Gardner Point and people around there knew it as the Page Place. She told him only the essentials—she too seemed to feel trapped and edgy —but by the time she was through he knew enough to find us, if he wanted to. I was encapsulated in my silence. I looked at my hand: it was navigating a spoon around and around the circumference of my coffee cup.

When Earl left, Tracy and I still had more packing to do and we wanted to go to bed early, so there really wasn't time to fight. I didn't know what to say. Perhaps I should have made more of it but my dread was right at the center of me and I could not explain it, I could barely touch it.

I set the alarm for five but Tracy changed it to a less hysterical seven.

"You shouldn't have told him," I said, once we were in bed.

"I didn't feel I had a choice."

There wasn't more either of us could say. I would never accept her reasons for telling my father where our house was and Tracy had no impulse to defend herself: she had seen the sleeping dogs of my feelings about Earl and rather than let them lie she'd chosen to give them a swift kick in the ribs.

THREE

9

IF YOU BORE down, you could make the ride in about seven hours. We left early in the morning and figured we'd be at Preservation Hall by midafternoon. We drove through Manhattan, through the geysers of white steam that rose through the manholes. We played our cassette recorder and were accompanied by the Brahms Horn Trio as we sped past the Bronx and out onto the Connecticut Turnpike. Thin snow flurries blew past us and when we turned on the radio to listen to the Top 40, the disc jockey, who like most disc jockeys sounded like a large insane man locked in a smoky room, said there were travelers' warnings posted. At the time, Tracy was at the wheel.

"Do we heed them?" she asked.

"Absolutely not."

"Good for you. Onward!"

The sun appeared for a few minutes: a luminescent dime encased in ice. The snow fell steadily and our progress slowed. It would be at least a nine-hour drive.

The blizzard pleased us; it was a greeting to strangers, the North of the country dressing itself in its typical costume. The snow was extreme, forceful, and remote. By the time we were in Massachusetts, cars were parked haphazardly along the highway, some of them still holding their grieving owners, others merely abandoned. We opened a bottle of Scotch and ate sunflower seeds and dried apricots. Gordon Lightfoot was on the cassette recorder. The wind blew with astounding volume: I thought it was a sound you'd hear only at sea. We turned up the music to cover the noise of the wind, because it frightened us.

"We better forge on," Tracy said.

"Definitely, chief. Definitely."

In Maine, the highway looked at first like a back country road and, as we went north, a snowpacked path, but the snow was no longer falling. It was very late in the afternoon and the headlights of oncoming cars detonated rainbows in the heavy gray air. We were both a little drunk. I'd been staring for some time at the small impression Tracy's nipples made against her shirt, wondering if I were to grab her would we crash, die. It seemed as if we'd been in that car for weeks. I unzipped my fly and pulled out my cock. "Umm, Tracy?"

She looked over and her foot pressed the gas too hard. The car wagged from side to side and the wheels made an odd sound on the snowy road, like a lawn mower. She reached over and put her hand around me.

"I think I'll shift down to second gear," she said, moving it forward. "Or maybe third? How about fourth? Oh, good old fourth."

Even with the technical delays of nailing down the deal, we'd bought the house in a flash of desire; when we walked in early that evening we both felt alien. It was like breaking into someone else's house, someone else's life. We stood on the threshold, me staring at the big old-fashioned door key, Tracy looking around with her hand against her throat. "Hello?" I said, as if someone might be there. The sound of my voice seemed to get about three feet before it was absorbed by the silence of the house, a great gray and white silence, the silence of a deserted laboratory, the silence of dreams.

We turned on the heat and unpacked slowly, as if still expecting the rightful owners to appear and chase us off. The floors creaked unfamiliarly, the dark blue night pressing against the small windows was soft and strange. The little pyramid of wood next to the fireplace seemed to be proof that someone else lived there. We brought in our food, our booze, suitcase, and music. We made the big four-poster bed. There was a Chinese vase lamp next to it and in the center of the room a tulip-shaped light bulb hung from a chain.

As soon as the bed was made we fell into it, too tired to make love. Just as I was slipping into sleep, I sat upright in the bed, confused, a little panicked. I remembered where I was and tried to go back to sleep but a memory of the downstairs door being left wide open kept me awake. I dragged myself out of bed and went downstairs. Not only was the door closed, it was locked.

The house was unique to the state, or so we were told. It was a miniaturized stone version of the sea captains' houses on the coast. It had an exterior end-chimney, a steep gabled roof, small casement windows, and the second story overhung the first by a foot or two: all of these things that seemed architectural idiosyncrasies were copied from a basic design used in the state of Maine. The house had been built in 1934 by a man named Cleveland Page, who lived there with his daughter Christine in what seemed unnatural closeness after the death of his wife. Page had taken fierce care with the details: the fireplaces were as smooth and perfectly fitted as Incan walls, the floors so level that if you placed a marble in the center of a room it would stay there until you blew on it. We'd bought in such haste that it would have served us right had we found a cluster of hidden defects, but everything discovered only enhanced the house's value. The doorknobs were all brass. A little shelf between the basement and the ground floor was perfect for wine storage. The upstairs bathtub could easily fit two. We found beneath the snow a flagstone path that led from the house to the pond, a five-minute walk. The lake itself was visited by ducks and Page had raised trout in it, or perhaps Tarwater had, for it was he who, after Cleveland and Christine Page died, picked up the property cheaply for quick sale.

Page had been a carpenter. His workshop was in the basement and his tools were still there, hanging from oak pegs, as sad as dogs who wait at the gate for a dead master. The kitchen chairs and table had been made by him, as had the bookcases, the magazine rack, and the flower boxes.

There was no phone, but we weren't anxious to have one. The only electrical implements left behind were the lamps, an old console radio with a dark green dial, and an ancient phonograph, a Victrola, with bright felt on the turntable and a big metal arm so bright and shiny that it seemed as if it had just been polished. Next to the turntable was a little box that said Somoset Chocolates in which were hundreds of B&H Fibre Needles, little sharp steel pegs to be inserted into the tone arm. Beneath the speaker was a compartment for records and there were about two hundred of them. "In the Valley of Sunshine and Roses" by Henry Burr, "M'Appari" sung by Theodore Kittay, "In the Garden" sung by Mrs. Wm. Asher and Homer Rodeheaver, "Love Nest" by Fritz Kreisler. The records were brittle and gave off a faint odor of photographic fixer. Some were recorded on only one side, some were on labels so obscure that you could only think that making and merchandising them had been some quirky vanished entrepreneur's labor of love. Just handling those shiny black circles spun us back through time, head over heels. We ached for an era we'd never known and unconsciously mourned for the fragility of all time, for the elusiveness of even the moments that passed in our own lives, coming from points unknown and vanishing in a blink.

The first night we arrived at Preservation Hall was taken from us by fatigue. We went straight to bed but woke again around eleven that evening, made supper, drank a bottle of wine, and went back to bed. The next day was New Year's Eve. We walked around our property for a while and tried to identify the names of our various trees; there was pine, fir—oak? ash? maple? —it was difficult without the leaves and under all that snow. We walked to our pond. It was partly frozen but the ice wasn't thick. I found a heavy rock and dropped it through.

"Now the trout can breathe," said Tracy.

"Let's name the little lake," I said.

"It gets ducks, right? And ducks have those big orange bills and matching feet. Very forties."

"Let's call it Veronica Lake, then," I said.

"Why not be subtle: Lake Veronica."

The snow fell in flurries. The wind was so severe it was like being hit in the face. I wore boots and Tracy wore a pair of old snowshoes we'd found in the cellar, stepping around in them as if she were walking on eggs, waving her arms for balance. We were careful never to let the house get out of sight once the snow began. It was too cold to wander far and with snow obscuring the access road the thought of getting lost was terrifying.

Inside, Tracy taught me how to build a proper fire without using an entire newspaper. Then we had lunch and read before the fire. I'd built a raging blaze and Tracy, itchy from the heat, took off her shirt—heaven! We talked about going into town to get more supplies but we weren't in the mood: I think we wanted to pretend for another day or two that we were the last ones on earth. Besides, there was plenty of time: though time in the country, and time in love, does not slow down, it has a kind of transparency to it.

"This is the best place in the world," I declared.

"It's the nicest house I've ever been in," said Tracy. "It's almost scary it's so perfect."

"It's *much* nicer than your parents' house in Tenants Harbor."

"Oh, much," said Tracy, pulling my hair. "Infinitely."

"Good. I've finally raised your standard of living."

"Even though their house is right on the bay, with lobstermen chugging back and forth, and a sailboat, and tennis courts three minutes away. But who cares, right? Ours is so much more *rustic*." She laughed.

We had brought New Year's Eve dinner from New York: eight little rib lamb chops, an elephantine head of broccoli, wild rice, and a bottle of 1964 Petrus, which we had opened at five that afternoon. Though my drinking had increased over the months in frequency and volume, my tolerance remained low and by the third glass of that rich, nearly overpowering wine, with its smell of mud and roses, I was sinking in my chair. After dinner, we brought the dregs of the wine and a bottle of champagne into the living room and tossed a couple more logs onto the fire. The room danced in its own radiance. It seemed that life itself was coming to a quiet, golden epiphany.

We both were on the floor: Tracy's head rested in my lap and her legs were crossed. I ran my thumb along the line of her jaw.

"It's a good way to end the year," I said.

"It is. And a good way to begin the new one." She finished her wine and, with impeccable nonchalance, tossed the glass into the fireplace. "No resolutions for me this year," she said.

"I didn't know you made them," I said.

"I've always made them. For as long as I remember I've wanted to be different in one way or another. First I wanted to be kinder, then I wanted to stop jerking off, then I went through a string of resolutions about keeping up with my music lessons, keeping up with my poetry, all that stuff that never worked out."

"I can't imagine you ever making resolutions," I said.

"That's because you think I'm a sprite."

"I don't."

"You do. Open the champagne, okay? It's almost midnight."

"I want to tell you something," I said. "Do you remember when I came to see you in your room after your abortion?"

"You cried then."

"I know. You thought I was crying because of the abortion, because of the life we'd almost made together. I thought it was that, too. But it wasn't. Or it was only partly that. I did want a child."

"You probably still do."

"I do. But that wasn't why I was crying."

"You wept so beautifully. If I hadn't been so drugged I would have cried with you."

"I cried with relief because you were awake again. That was the worst part, knowing you were under an anesthetic. It was as if your soul was in danger. It wasn't like sleep because you couldn't awaken yourself. You were just lying there suspended. If the world had ended you would never have known it. I couldn't bear your helplessness."

"I'm sorry about that dinner with your father, Virgil."

"It's all right." I twisted the cork out of the champagne bottle.

"I don't want you to think I'm not on your side."

"Let's leave it alone. Anyhow, I never expected you to be on my side." I poured the champagne into my glass and it mixed with the wine sediment and turned red. I handed the bottle to Tracy and she took a long drink from it, for she had no glass.

"I've never had so much fun with anyone I've ever known in all my life," she said.

"I love you."

"I know. And I love you."

"I never thought anything this wonderful would ever happen to me."

"Oh, you did too," she said. "You thought your life was going to be just fine."

"But not *this* wonderful. Never this wonderful."

"I hope we always love each other," said Tracy, "even after we change."

"We won't change."

"We will. We have to. You'll see."

"We won't if we don't want to."

"It won't be our choice. We're walking on thin ice."

"But that's us. We've always been like that," I said.

"I know."

"I'm used to thin ice."

"I should be too but I'm not. I don't know that I'll ever be. I hear it squeaking when I fall asleep."

I shook my head. "Okay. But as long as we're on it, let's not jump up and down."

"I can't promise that. It's going to be a relief for me when it falls through."

"You're nuts."

"No. Then we'll be tested. We'll see what we're made of."

"Enough."

"Okay. What time is it?"

"Eleven fifty."

"Let's go to bed."

"And do something unusual?"

"Okay. Good idea. Something illegal and truly demented."

"Like making love with our socks on?"

"Or making love with our socks," she said.

We finished the champagne and turned off the

lamp. The only light now was from the faltering fire and it was a pale, electric orange. We put our arms around each other—as I remember it now I can feel her small, strong hand on the rise of my hip—and we walked to the window to look at the last minutes of the year. The night was thick, undifferentiated. A light snow fell. I looked up at the sky and a favorable wind must have come up because the dark long clouds broke up for a moment and there in the space, full, brilliant, and unimaginably gold, there directly above us floated the moon, a high flat winter moon, the safe moon.

10

T HE NEXT morning we woke early and rolled into each other's arms. It was cold in our bedroom and whenever we stopped making love, I felt the perspiration hardening along my spine. Tracy called out my name and I called out hers—or a mangled version of it—when the third ejaculation ripped through me like hot knotted rope. As we lay there the sense of solitude, enfoldment, and the invulnerability of living in that house filled and warmed me. I felt that my life had reached the only sort of perfection available to it—is it always so when life is about to explode? Does it swell up like a frog, displaying every muted, astonishing color along the line of its throat?

"Who's going to make breakfast?" I asked Tracy.

"I'll think of a number between one and seven," she said. "If you guess within one digit then I'll go down and make something. If you miss, then you go."

"Are you sure you want to do this?" I asked.

"Just guess."

"Six."

She rolled away and grabbed for the covers. I slid next to her and put my arms around her. She took my hand and put it to her breast and then drew her knees up. She breathed a deep sigh and pulled me closer.

"Don't make me go, Virgil. It's too cold down there. My nipples will implode. This, this implosion is an often ignored danger of country life. We're hundreds of miles from the nearest breast clinic. It's an insane risk."

I slipped my other arm under her and covered her other breast. "Okay. Now get up very slowly. I'll keep my hands on you. There'll be no danger."

We got out of bed like Siamese twins, joined at the palm and the bosom, the pelvis and the rump. I matched her step for step. As we passed our bedroom window I saw that a light snow was falling again. We walked down the stairway, my hands still on her. We stalked into the kitchen, where the heater purred beneath us and sent its scentless breath through a yellow grille in the wall. Tracy put a copper tea kettle beneath the faucet and the water thundered into it. With my hands still affixed to her, she walked across the kitchen and turned on the stove. Through the windows in the back door, I looked out at our land: powdery snow was falling, the trees seemed closer to us than they had the day before. It was a vision of New England winter that soldiers must have wept themselves to sleep over in Vietnam.

Naked, we ate our breakfast at the kitchen table. We were both chilly but our nakedness helped us possess the house. We made a half dozen eggs and instant coffee, and ate half a loaf of rye bread. We talked about going into Gardner Point to buy food, but still there was no hurry. After breakfast I boiled some more water for coffee and unpacked our coffee grinder so we could have a special blend.

"Well, here we are," said Tracy.

"Absolutely."

"Well? What now? It's just the two of us. It's a little imposing, isn't it?"

"Not at all. We'll hang out. We'll both learn how to hang out." Coming from a great distance was a low mechanical hum. It darted at the edge of my attention but I turned away from it. "And we can always make love," I added.

"Paul Valéry said that when people don't know what to do they take off their clothes," Tracy said.

"Well, we'll have to take off our skins," I said.

"Do you hear that?" Tracy said. "Shh. Listen. Hear?"

We walked to the back door and looked out the windows. The winding access road that led to the house from the woods looked like a serpent or a river twisting through the snow and then blending into the distant, mysterious haze. The sun glared off the snow and our eyes fought for vision as we stared before us. The hum grew louder and before long I saw a cream-colored Volkswagen bouncing toward our house. It wagged uncertainly on a slippery spot, righted itself, and continued toward us.

"What's your guess?" asked Tracy.

"I better get our robes," I said, turning quickly. I took the stairs two at a time, feeling as if I were making an escape. I found our robes hanging from an oak clothes post in the bedroom, snatched them, and then sat on the bed. I wanted just one moment to think.

I made it down to the kitchen just as the VW pulled next to our car. It idled for a few moments; its exhaust blackened the snow. The car's windows were so dense with frost we couldn't see who was inside it. Finally, the motor switched off, the car shuddered for a moment, and the door opened. A woman stepped stiffly out. She wore bluejeans, a short fox jacket, and a multicolored stocking cap. A gust of wind lifted a corona of blond hair around her shoulders and she hugged herself for warmth. As she staggered closer to us it appeared that she'd been sobbing: mascara stains as black as tar ran from her eyes to her full downy cheeks. It was Melissa Cavanaugh.

We opened our door to her and she staggered in, shaking and weeping. Her breath caught and broke in her throat and the cold that radiated from her body seemed to strip off our robes. She covered her face with her hands—her hands were salmon and streaked with dead white. She made noises which might very well have been speech. Snow stuck in her hair, and on the side, where her thick hair parted, emerged an ear so red that I was certain it would snap off if touched.

"Sit down, sit down," said Tracy.

Melissa slumped into one of the bentwood chairs in the kitchen and stamped her feet on the floor. She wore suede desert boots. She didn't say a word but petitioned our patience with a few exhausted gestures. Tracy ran some more water into the kettle and put it back on the stove. I went to the front of the house for the Scotch.

We waited for her to do something, to make her purpose clear, but she didn't seem capable of receiving questions. Tracy and I doddered around, waiting with the breathlessness of suitors for her to say something.

She accepted a cup of tea from Tracy and when I poured out two fingers of Scotch she accepted that, too. As she warmed herself and tamed her nerves, she made disjointed exclamations about her ride. "Heater broken . . . They said half hour, more like . . . All that snow. I hate the snow. I've always despised snow. . . ."

After her tea and Scotch I asked, "What brings you here?" trying to sound as neutral as possible.

"Look," she snapped, with suddenly focused energy, "no questions, no hassles. Not now." She turned quickly to Tracy. "I'm waiting for Tommy. He should be here in just a little while. An hour or two. We're not going to hurt anyone. We haven't done anything wrong."

"I still don't understand why you're here," I said. I overheard myself speaking: I *did* sound relaxed. "And how come you didn't come up together?"

"He wanted to travel alone, in case something happened."

I took a deep breath and seriously considered shutting up. "I'm still not following you," I said.

"Listen, Virgil." Melissa stood up. She took a long look at me, as if trying to decide how such a person might be spoken to. "Now you just listen. We have done something incredible. You *know* what I'm talking about. All right? This past week has been like nothing else that's ever happened. We've been followed, threatened, informed on, fucked over, everything. We've stuck our necks out further than anyone. Okay? So I can't be hassled. Not by you. Not by anyone. I made it here. I didn't even know where I was going. I didn't know what was waiting for me. I thought about turning around every minute. But I didn't. And now I'm here. I can't be pushed around." Her voice was so smoky and rich that practically everything she said sounded flirtatious. Her skittery, indigo eyes glared at me, ignited by alternating surges of panic and determination.

All that those eyes inspired in me was my habitual, inherited tenaciousness. "I would still like to know what you're doing here. And I'd like to know how you found we were here." I gestured toward Tracy. "We'd *both* be interested in that."

"Tracy," said Melissa, "where's the john?"

"Upstairs," said Tracy. "You'll see it."

"This is my house, too," Tracy said as soon as we heard Melissa on the staircase.

"So?"

"You're not in charge of immigration. It's not fair that you stand at the door and say who can come in and who can't."

"I want to know what she's doing here."

"Before she even catches her breath?"

"Earl sent them up here."

"We don't know that. And even if we did..."

"Yes?" I leaned forward.

"We don't know anything yet, Virgil."

"Not so. Earl sent them up here because the police are after Tommy and it's getting on Lillian's nerves. It's totally apparent."

"It's a side issue."

"How's that?"

"It simply is. The important thing is that she's here. That's what's happening right now. We're not going to throw her out, are we?"

"And what do you think happens when Tommy gets here?" I said.

Tracy turned away. I followed her gaze out the window. The snow was falling with more force now and it had lost some of its brilliance and whiteness.

"How am I supposed to know?" she said.

"This week was supposed to be ours," I said. I reached across the table and touched her arm.

"It is ours, Virgil."

"These people are in deep trouble," I dropped to a whisper. "She's a goddamn lunatic and he's wanted for that radio bullshit. God only knows what he's capable of."

"Only God knows what anyone's capable of, Virgil."

"You know what I mean."

"You sound frightened."

I thought for a moment. "I am. But only a little. Mostly I feel imposed upon. These two have nothing to do with us."

"He's your stepbrother."

"What's that mean?"

"Whatever you want it to, Virgil."

"Earl sent them. We're being completely exploited. I'm not going to let this happen."

"You're not going to throw them out."

"No. She can wait for Tommy. But I'm not going to

hide them. Nothing can convince me that would b
right."

"I don't like this in you, Virgil."

"Stop using my name all the time, for God's sake.
We just looked at each other for a moment. "It sound
so impersonal," I added, by way of explanation.

When Melissa came down we settled into a mood o
tentative, somewhat strained politeness. She seemec
anxious to charm us, though she seemed to have littl
experience for such a task. She talked about herself—
raised in Vermont, parents converted Catholics, rib
bons for riding, father a minor politician who'd writter
speeches for John Kennedy, nastiness and extendec
social persecution at a girls' school, accused of stealing
something or other, a stormy break with her family, a
tearful good-bye to her horse. I confess I wasn't paying
strict attention.

A thread connecting it all, however, was the perpet-
ual assumption of her madness. It was this bleak reckless air of incurability that made her seem older than
she was. Twenty-three years thinking of herself in the
same feverish terms had streamlined her and focused
her effect. You looked at her and it seemed inconceiv-
able that she would ever change: she was eternal,
archetypal. Those eyes would burn holes in the land-
scape even when she was seventy-five. She was somehow fixed in the scheme of things and while you never
wanted to be like her you could not ignore the strength
she had gotten from the repetition and stasis of her
life. It bound her to herself. She was, in that way, like
someone from the previous century, someone who had
never vitiated her strength by wondering who exactly
she was. Like Earl, she didn't seem to suffer from the
mysteries of self; she knew her character in the way a
boxer knows his opponent after a fifteen rounder,
knew its moves, its treacheries, and loved it.

We sat around the fire and I poked at the logs and
watched out the window. The snow flapped like an

endless white blanket. Sometimes the wind made a curious noise and Melissa would turn quickly toward the door but, then, recognizing the sound, she would sink into a peculiar sort of languor. She rested the way you imagined firemen rested, always ready for the alarm. She lay on her back and when she stretched her arms her shirt popped out of her jeans. Her neck was as smooth as a child's. She wore a delicate gold chain that dipped beneath the second button of her shirt and seemed to nestle in a fan-shaped burst of freckles.

"You want another drink?" I said, pouring myself one.

"I want to be okay when he gets here," she said. She closed her eyes. "I'm obsessed with him. It's obvious. My doctor won't even let me talk about him anymore. Isn't that stupid? Sometimes I think it's the worst thing that ever happened to me. I've cut myself off from every person I ever knew because of him. If I didn't take classes I wouldn't even *see* anyone else. I can't talk to anyone about him because it's too dangerous. If he ever left me, no one would know except me. It's like a nightmare, a beautiful, erotic nightmare."

"How did you meet?" Tracy asked.

"When Tommy quit Yale—"

"Yale?" I said, with far too much surprise in my voice.

"That's right. Yale. Full scholarship. Everyone loved him there. Anyhow, he knew my older brother Royce at Yale and they both dropped out and went west. Royce turned gay and pretty soon they stopped traveling together. Then Tommy came back to New York and looked me up. I was in really bad shape then. I was seeing this filthy psychiatrist who just dumped on me, seeing him four times a week. I wasn't getting any money from home. Just a little from my grandmother but then she died and it all went into trust. Tommy moved in with me and we both started working. We wanted to save enough money to go to

South America. He wanted to do a big deal down there."

"A big deal?" I said.

"Never mind. Anyhow, we had a fight. And he left. Then he got in trouble and had to go to jail. I wrote him every day and tried to visit him, but they wouldn't let me because I wasn't related. When he got out he came back to New York and we moved in together."

"Where was he in jail?" I asked. "And what for?"

"Oh come on, now," said Melissa.

I smacked a spent log with the poker; it turned lurid orange and caved in.

"One thing I've learned," said Melissa. "You never ask about someone else's jail. You just never do that." She rose with some difficulty and walked to the window. She pressed her palms against the pane and then put them on the sides of her face. "I wish he'd get here," she said.

"How long were you really planning to stay?" I asked, in that casual, shambling voice you use when you fear someone's temper.

"Are you going to throw us out?" She turned to me and put her hands on her hips.

"I want a better idea of what's going on."

"We didn't think you two would be here. We thought we'd have the place to ourselves for a couple days."

"Then what?" said Tracy.

"That's what we need to figure out. Tommy said the reason most everyone in trouble ends up getting caught is they never get a chance to plan. You just run and hide, and live by instinct."

"Are things that desperate?" I asked.

"Not really. I don't know. We need some time to live, rather than all this enduring. All we need is some place to sit while things cool off in New York."

"That could be months," I said.

"Don't worry. It won't be. All we need is a day or two."

Melissa asked if she could take a bath and I was sent to her car to get her suitcase. The sun had either set or was utterly obscured by clouds. The snow, thick upon the ground, reflected the slate-colored dome above. The insides of my nostrils petrified as soon as I stepped outside and though I wore lined boots and a leather coat my skin shrank from the precision of the cold. I took the valise out of the trunk and threw myself toward the house, fixing my eyes on the soft yellow light in our windows and letting that vision carry me back. Altogether I'd walked perhaps twenty yards.

"It's really something out there," Tracy said, as she bolted the door behind me. "I could barely see you." She brushed the snow out of my hair and I felt wanted again.

"Check out this suitcase," I said. "Welfare people see this and she gets kicked off the rolls." I held Melissa's valise up for Tracy to inspect.

"It's gorgeous," said Tracy. "Doeskin, I'll bet. And look. A strip of real turquoise right in the grip."

"It's heavy," I said. "Maybe she's carrying a piece."

"Perhaps a harpsichord."

"No, really, feel how heavy it is." I handed the bag to Tracy and she grudgingly took hold of it.

"Seems normal to me."

"You're nuts." I laughed and took the suitcase away from her.

She leaned against the refrigerator door. "You blame me, don't you?"

"For what?"

"You're too transparent for that. You blame me for her being here."

"I should but I don't. You never believe me about Earl. None of this is a surprise to me. You think my family life has something in common with yours. It doesn't. There was a time, you know, when I was *sure*

I'd never see him again, when it was so fucking un-
bearable that I used to wake up in the morning with
my jaw aching and know, without even remembering,
that I'd dreamed of him. There were times when I'd
leave the house in the morning and *know* that I was
going to get a call from him at my office and I was
right every time. The way I feel, I should have listened
to that part of me that's the hardest, the cruelest, and
just cut him dead. But I can't do it. And this is what it
leads to. Inevitably. There is no other way with Earl."

"Why do you think this is necessarily something bad
that's happening?" asked Tracy.

I brought Melissa's suitcase up to the guest room. I
heard her splashing in the tub; the plain pine door to
the bathroom was ajar and steam floated out into the
hall. I sat on the bed; its springs wheezed beneath me.
It was pitch dark in the room. I felt around for the
chain to the overhead light and pulled it on, but the
bulb was small and weak, dropping a faint depressing
light onto the bare striped mattress, the smooth pine
floors, the orange and green hooked rug. I put Melissa's suitcase next to the bed. What I wanted was to
take a walk but that of course was impossible. The
weather and the enclosure it engendered was beginning to get on my nerves. Had it been just Tracy and
me in the house I would have let the night and its
storm wrap around us like fur but with Melissa in the
tub and Tommy on his way, the house seemed small,
fragile, and just a little ridiculous. All those acres lost
their majesty and taking the place of the former grandeur was an air of pure menace. I thought about Lake
Veronica and all of our trout beneath the ice; the
thought of those trapped fish sent a tremor of dread
through me.

"Who's up here?" Melissa called from the
bathroom.

"I am," I said. "I brought your suitcase."

"Go downstairs. I don't have any clothes and I want to go into my room."

As I got up to leave I noticed her clothes on the wicker chair. She must have taken them off in a rush: the blouse was still half buttoned, one leg of her jeans was turned inside out, and her peach-colored underpants rested in the inside of her trousers.

Against my will, or independent of it at least, my eyes slid toward the opening in the door as I passed the bathroom on my way down. I saw a flash of red towel and the door slammed in my wake.

Though it was never specified, we were waiting for Tommy to arrive before having dinner. I sat in an easy chair near the fireplace and read an old paperback copy of *Double Indemnity*. Tracy and Melissa were curled up on opposite ends of the couch, Tracy reading a slim Russian grammar and moving her lips, Melissa flipping through a copy of *Twenty Grand Short Stories*, waiting for one to arrest her attention. She wore pink and gray silk lounging pajamas and her hair was wrapped in a red towel. She looked rather beautiful.

The only sounds were those of turning pages, the fire, and the wind outside. It seemed a little colder than it had been but I wanted to conserve wood so I let the fire dwindle. I noticed I was on page 125 in my book and was surprised that so much time had passed. I looked at my watch: 8:20.

I heard a fluttering noise and looked up. Melissa had dropped her book onto the floor. One of its pages peeled loose from the old binding and floated across the room.

"Oh shit," she said. "Where is he? He should be here by now."

"He's probably waiting for the weather to clear," said Tracy.

"I want to kill myself when things like this happen," said Melissa.

* * *

I went to bed early that evening. There was such a sultry, hopeless tension in the air that I dragged myself upstairs as if it were four in the morning and I'd been smoking opium. I fell onto the quilt and listened to Tracy and Melissa talking downstairs. The wordless hum of their voices laced itself through the net of wind that had dropped over the house, and the curiosity I had about what they discussed in my absence almost lifted me from bed. Before I'd removed myself from their company, Melissa had been in the midst of a seemingly endless moody saga about Tommy—his triumphs at Yale, his attempts to galvanize the National Association for the Rights of Prisoners into bold action—and about the people who gave him money and support because they "believe in his energy." I think it was the phrase "believe in his energy" that had sent me upstairs.

I tried to stay awake and wait for Tracy. I had slipped off my shoes but kept my clothes on. I heard my name mentioned—the sound of one's own name can cut through lead. But I couldn't recognize whose voice had said it or make out what followed. I closed my eyes and remembered one of the postcards my mother had sent me a few months after she left us. "I wanted to call you David," it had said, "but he wanted to name you something artistic. If I were you, I'd change my name as soon as I could." I tried to recall what the picture on that particular card was. Was that the Redwood Forest? Or was that one Boulder Dam?

The next thing I knew, Tracy was beside me, sound asleep. I was still on top of the quilt and my weight pulled it tightly across her chest. I got up to take off my clothes; the chill in the air raised the hair on my arms. I wondered if Melissa was still downstairs and the thought of her ignited a little surge of nastiness that pulled me further from sleep. I stood in the center of the dark room, listening to Tracy's distant breathing, feeling my blood start to move again. I rubbed my eyes and fought for vision. I tried to look out the window but it was opaque with frost. As I stared at it, a crack appeared along the right side. It made a high, twittering noise and then a jagged, thin incision appeared. The wind seeped in through the fault and carried a ribbon of snow that moved like a snake across the floor.

11

TRACY AND I awoke in each other's arms the next morning. We held each other silently and then I rolled over to look at the window. The crack was no longer there. The incision had healed over night and in its place was an icy scar. There were dark streaks on the floor where the snow had melted.

"You took the night train out yesterday," said Tracy.

"I waited up for you."

"Sure. For ten minutes. I came in here and you were dead out. I even made noise. I had my diaphragm in."

"You did?" I took her in my arms again, somehow astonished she'd wanted to make love. "I'm really disappointed."

"You ought to be."

"However, one assumes that that which was inserted remains inserted."

"Yes it does. Suspended like an inner space station."

I gathered her still closer to me and as I kissed her we heard two shots and then a scream. The shots sounded distant and inconsequential but the scream was violent, not really quite human. Only in retrospect do I realize how powerfully shrill it must have been. Melissa was downstairs, our door was closed, but it sounded as if the cry came from beneath our bed.

We grabbed our robes, opened the door and went into the hall. We ran down the stairs expecting to hear another scream but the wind was the only sound. It was like being in a nursery filled with the most miserable children in the world; the cry of that wind made you want to slit your throat. Downstairs, it ripped through the house—ashes eddied in the fireplace, the curtains pressed flat against the iced windows. There was a fine powder of snow on the floor.

We followed the glacial stream into the kitchen. The door was wide open. A two-foot drift stood just beyond the threshold and in the center of the bright white crest Melissa's footprints had stamped out a canyon. The severity of the wind stabbed at our hearts. Tracy hugged herself and turned away; I raced to the door to slam it shut.

We wanted to run to find a warm spot in the house but we stood at the windows staring into the whiteness. Tracy was shaking and I put my arm around her; the touch of her reminded me how close to making love we'd been. The room smelled of dampness and wind, that smell from childhood when you are waiting for a bus in a blizzard and the cold is so intense that your head pounds and to warm yourself you press an ice-pocked mitten against your mouth.

"Look," Tracy said.

I squinted, and through the snow, roughly in the direction of the access road, I saw Melissa, or a pale reverberation of her red fur jacket. I couldn't tell if she was heading toward us or away from us. The snow was so thick by now and fell in such complicated, crossover patterns that linear perception was shaken and upset.

I thought of going upstairs and dressing so I might help Melissa, but staring into that opaque blizzard and listening to that wind—I felt I could never do it. Suddenly, she emerged more clearly. She fell, quickly righted herself, and continued. I knew then that I was essentially unprepared for the kinds of tests and hardships that others might barrel bravely through. I was not brave. What valiance I had was in keeping things away from me. Even in the cold, my eyes felt warm at the thought of this.

Directly behind Melissa—or to her side—was another figure. For a moment they merged into one creature. Were they hanging on to each other? It wasn't until they were near the cars that I saw it was Tommy Douglas, but of course I'd known it all along. His hair was iced. Even Melissa's hair was caked with snow, with only an underglow of its natural color. She was pulling him by the arm toward our house. He stared straight ahead, as if he were blind, or out of his senses. In one hand he held a rifle which he waved for balance as he stumbled toward us.

They exploded into the house, staggering, tripping, the cold pouring off them in waves. Tracy and I backed out of the kitchen. The temperature had fallen at least forty degrees and snow danced over the floor like iron filings in a magnetic field. Tommy and Melissa gasped and spat. Though we were no further than ten feet from them they seemed totally unaware of us.

They hadn't closed the door, so the wind poured in. Tracy and I put our hands over our faces. Melissa groaned and made a motion toward Tommy but he lurched beyond her and crashed into the sink. His rifle slipped from his hand, landed on its butt, and stood for a moment. Then it fell with a sharp crack. Tommy's eyes were flat and dead—a fish's eyes. He let out a long rattling moan, groped at the air, and fell to one knee. Melissa tried to grab him but he was too heavy and he collapsed to the floor with a dull, sickening thud. Melissa cried out and dropped to her knees. She pulled snow out of her hair and pressed it against his gray forehead.

"Close the door," I shouted over the wind.

She looked up at us; the power of her eyes could have bent a key or crippled a horse. "Help me," she said, shaking her hands.

Tracy could not help herself; the cold pushed her deeper into the house.

"Just close the fucking door," I screamed.

Melissa reached over and threw the door shut but the wind pushed it back open. It banged into the wall and two small windows noiselessly shattered. Melissa crawled over to the door and pressed it closed. Barefoot and naked beneath our robes, Tracy and I crept into the kitchen.

We stood over Tommy and for all I knew he was dead. My throat closed. A violent stench rose from him. His face was the color of an old dime; his body was rigid. Steam rose from him. His skin looked as smooth as ice. His eyes were open but they did not look like eyes, not even fish eyes. Stones. Pieces of blue quartz. An icicle hung from one nostril and as Melissa rubbed more snow onto his face—she never doubted he was alive and watching her work relieved me—she accidentally brushed the icicle away with the back of her hand and a quivering globe of blood appeared. The blood trembled there for a moment, wavering with the slow-motion persistence of mercury, until it fell into the pale frozen whiskers of his boyish mustache and another, somehow redder drop of blood appeared in its place.

"He's alive," I said, before I knew I was saying it.

"Let's get him out of this room," said Tracy. "Into the front."

Tommy was a little over six two, with long arms and legs, a narrow collie-like face, and delicate bones. He had the body of a hypersensitive college boy, or a moody delinquent, and he couldn't have weighed more than one hundred sixty pounds. But as we took him by the shoulders and feet to bring him to the front, it seemed as if we carried a small church. He came to as we moved him and moaned in our arms. I had him gripped around the armpits; his jacket was frozen over with a sheen of ice; I had to claw to keep hold of him. His head lolled back into my stomach and his gray face, with the blood-tinged mustache and those wide frozen eyes . . . What did they show? Meanings lined up at the edge of my consciousness but I glanced away.

We placed him before the empty fireplace. The snow and ice from his clothes and hair mixed with the ashes and soot. Melissa leaned over him and yanked at the thumb-sized zipper beneath his chin. It was frozen. She tossed her head back in frustration and yanked again. It opened with a tearing hiss. He was breathing heavily now and I had the nauseating feeling that the whites of his eyes were melting. With every painful breath, a large tear fell from either eye. He opened his mouth to speak and the skin at the corners cracked; he grimaced with pain and it cracked more. Torture. It was like watching someone be worked over by something invisible. I lifted his shoulder and Tracy and Melissa worked off his big soaking jacket.

Since that day, I have tried to recapture even an inkling of the punishing freeze that gripped him. I have pressed my hand for ten minutes on the frost-caked side of an ice box; I have taken walks through Central Park at night in the snow wearing a summer shirt. I have taken every chill my body ever felt and subjected it to a ghostly arithmetic, multiplying its impact on my senses. I know I haven't approached what Tommy felt and I am even further from a sense of what it was for him to make that walk along our access road. The real power and range of a storm is only felt when you have no protection from it whatsoever, when you don't know where you are, when you don't know where your next step will fall, when you are choked with that kind of fear that has nothing to do with the imagination and nothing to do with dread.

Snow and ice formed a dark pool beneath him, as if he'd been punctured. Melissa crouched before him, kissing his chest and hands. He wanted to get up. His body shook with the effort of it but his face remained impassive. He gasped for breath and coughed, bringing up a cylinder of phlegm which he spat weakly onto the floor. After an effort that would have made anyone ache to watch it, he was on his feet but he didn't have the strength to stay upright. Quickly, he sat down on the floor; his head jerked forward, his chin bounced off his chest. He sat for a moment, his legs useless before him. When he lowered himself back onto his elbows he fell flat on his back, banging his head with a vicious crack.

"Let's get his boots off," Tracy said to me. His laces were frozen and we couldn't untie them. Using a kitchen knife, we cut the laces off in pieces, while Melissa smoothed Tommy's hair and whispered his name, as if her voice were a line she dropped into the pit of his suffering. My hands throbbed from the cold of his boots. I glanced at Tracy. Her hands were translucent blue. I pulled at Tommy's left boot. He yelped with pain.

"You bastard," said Melissa.

"Sorry," I said.

"No," said Tommy, in a faint voice, "it's good to feel something."

"Tommy," said Melissa.

"Do it again. That thing with my foot. Give me something to hang on to."

We covered him in blankets and watched him breathe. He drifted in and out of consciousness but when I finally got him the Scotch he was conscious. He said he was numb practically everywhere. He looked at his hand and saw it was white. The fingertips were bright and silvery—frostbite.

I wanted to build a fire but Tracy said that sudden intense heat would be the worst thing.

"That's right," said Tommy. "That's right."

We put a pillow beneath his head. His breathing came easier and he looked disinterestedly at the ceiling as we peeled off his clothes and began massaging his body at Tracy's suggestion. I worked on his feet, somehow exiled to the least erotic part of his body, while Melissa worked on his face and neck and Tracy rubbed his arms and hands.

"That's good," he said, now and again. "Thank you."

"Oh, don't you thank us—you're going to pay for this," Tracy said, in that gruff, reassuring voice I'd thought she had invented for me.

His car was stuck somewhere on our land. He'd been driving slowly but the snow was blinding and the road meager and finally he'd guessed right when the road bent left and he'd ended in a thicket of ice and shrub he couldn't back out of. Panicked and furious, he tried to dislodge his car but it seemed hopeless. He was getting colder, the snow was getting thicker, more forceful, so he gambled on walking the rest of the way. At one point, he had an urge to simply lie down and rest for a while: those drifts of soft snow looked like featherbeds. He'd recognized this desire as the snow's suicidal lure and though he couldn't stop himself from sitting down for a few moments, he kept himself awake by firing his rifle into the air. It was those shots that had sent Melissa out to him.

His feet were dry and hard and the arches were abnormally steep. Each of his toes had three sprouts of wiry black hair. The nails on his big toes were long, cracked, and yellowed. His middle toe extended a half inch beyond the natural curve of the foot. His smallest toe had practically no nail at all and looked like a small grape someone had stepped on. It was only natural to think of the martyrs of legend and prayer as I held his foot in my hands. My nerves were pulled sufficiently tight for the aimless association to make me feel somehow accused.

I looked up at Tracy's face as she massaged his arms. She had the expression of an intelligent child who has found something beautiful on the beach, a look of pure, rapturous attention.

"Are you getting any feeling back?" she asked Tommy. "Are we doing it right?"

"I don't know," he said. He closed his eyes and attempted to concentrate on his body. "I don't hurt at all. I don't think that's a good sign."

"I'll put him in the bath," Melissa said.

"Good," he said.

"Lukewarm," I said.

"Right," said Tracy.

We all fell silent then. I felt an absurd warmth radiating through me, like the way one feels at the end of one of those patriotic old movies, when you realize that finally everyone is going to work together and get the job done. I looked at Tracy and smiled.

We took Tommy by the arms and supported him from behind as he stumbled up and tried to find the center of his balance. Standing before us, in his jockey briefs, with a trail of dark hairs emerging from his underwear up past his belly button and halfway to the slightly sunken center of his chest, his long sinewy arms dangling at his side, his high fine collarbone black and gray from the frost, shifting his weight from one tender foot to the other, he looked weak, exhausted, and helpless, like a man who has been discarded by an enemy who has no further use for him. His eyes were still unfocused, the blood had dried in his mustache and formed a tarlike scab on the ridge of his nostril. He tried to take a step but winced in pain—or in anger—and fell toward me. I caught him easily and tried to right him, but he was content to lean on me for a few moments, breathing heavily, pressing his forehead onto my shoulder. In memory it lives as a variety of embrace, the only kind available to us, and as such I honor it. But it would be a pleasant, silly lie to say that at the time I welcomed it: the cold seeped off his body, his bones were sharp, and as he grasped me I felt there was something willful about it, something mocking, as if he knew how much I didn't want him there, which, of course, he did. He knew full well and it probably gave him a kind of pleasure to know, for those few moments at least, I was cringing beneath him.

While Tommy and Melissa were upstairs, Tracy and I swept up the snow and mud and lay towels on the wettest parts of the floor. I pulled off a door from the kitchen cabinets and, using one of Page's old hammers and his bright silvery nails, fastened it over the broken windows in the back door. We put the magazines in order, straightened the furniture. Still, there was an odor of chaos: a damp, unclean smell, like that of a frightened animal.

"How are we going to get them out of here?" I said to Tracy. We were in the kitchen and she had just put a kettle on the stove for tea.

"Virgil!"

I put my hands up and grinned appeasingly. But what was it that I felt? I want to call it a long, hot jolt of prescience but it probably wasn't anything that clever: I did want them out. I wanted them erased.

"I just think we should do something," I said. I looked out the window. "I suppose they're no more anxious to stay here than we are to have them."

"We'll have our time alone," Tracy said.

"I know. It's not that."

"Then what is it?"

I shrugged. "I've got the creeps, that's all. I suppose it was seeing him come in half dead. And knowing who sent him up."

"Please don't close yourself off, Virgil." She sat at the table and folded her hands before her: she looked like a memory an old schoolmaster might have—his best student. "Try and go with what's happening to us."

"You're so good, Tracy. The only thing wrong is you make me ashamed for what I'm thinking."

"Then change."

"I can't. I don't even want to."

"You will. You'll have to. He really made an incredible walk, didn't he?"

"He did."

"Real endurance. I wish—" She cut herself short. Her attention was taken by a smell coming from the stove. I followed her glance and saw threads of dark gray smoke rising from the kettle. Tracy ran to the stove and picked up the kettle with a towel and threw it into the sink. It rattled noisily against the porcelain and you could tell by the sound it was empty.

"I forgot to put water in it," she said. "I'm so stupid." She turned on the cold water tap and a little rust-colored water trickled out. She turned on the hot water tap and the force of the flow didn't increase. The water turned a darker orange and then the pipes made a violent clatter, shaking with so much force that we felt the vibrations right through the floor. We held our ears and stepped back as the vehement hollow banging grew louder.

Tommy and Melissa went straight to bed. Tracy and I went up a few minutes later. When I went to the bathroom I saw the tub hadn't been drained; there were about six inches of tepid, cloudy water in it. The toilet hadn't been flushed either. I was at first annoyed but then I realized they were trying to save water. On the off chance that things might have improved spontaneously, I turned on the sink but, again, there was a terrible throbbing clatter. The faucet shook in my hand as I turned it off. I stood silently for a moment, listening to the wind. The gray water in the tub and the fouled water in the toilet was the last of our running water.

Tracy was already in bed when I came in. The light shone in her hair and, as I looked at her, I imagined our house was uninvaded, warm, and airtight. I took off my shoes and started to unbutton my shirt.

"Don't get undressed too far," Tracy said, opening her eyes. "The sheets are clammy. It's cold in here." She removed an arm from beneath the quilt to show me that she wore a sweater. "I've got pants and two pairs of socks on, too."

"I don't like sleeping with clothes on," I said.

"You'll freeze your nuts off," she said.

I placed my hand on the wall grille. It was warm, but only faintly. "There's heat," I said.

"Do what you like. My cells are cold."

I stripped down to my underwear. It was cold and wet in the room but I was determined to honor some form of a normal night's sleep. When I rolled next to Tracy and put my arms around her, I felt an unexpected erotic nostalgia being in bed with a clothed woman. It brought back high school, those passionate, demure girls, and all the dry humps that stretched the nerves and filled the heart with deep, provisional joy.

In the next room, Tommy and Melissa made love on our noisy guest bed. It was like the soundtrack from a movie about the beginnings of the Industrial Revolution—the wheezing inefficiency of primitive machines. "He seems to have recovered," I whispered to Tracy. The sounds of love next door further incited my erotic impulses. I put my knee between Tracy's thighs and pulled her close to me.

"If you think I'm going to take one article of clothing off my poor skinny body then you really are crazy."

"What if I begged?"

"Forget it. I want to sleep. The sooner I'm asleep the sooner I can stop shivering. I want to dream about Jamaica."

She rolled over and was soon asleep. I lay in bed with my hands behind my head. It seemed to grow colder in the room. Tommy and Melissa were quiet in the next room but then they started up again, this time at a slower pace, with the bedsprings heaving long high-pitched sighs beneath them. They made love in a graceful loping rhythm and for all I knew they kept it up for hours. I rolled over, wrapped the pillow around my head, and forced myself to sleep.

12

I WOKE THE next morning and in the sweet afterburn
of a night's dreaming I was certain that everything
had changed. My mind had created the world in its
own image and rather than snow I expected to see
the first pale shoots of spring. Instead of Tommy I
expected Mario. In place of my receding wife I expected to see Melissa. These illusions had an eternity
of their own but in the clock time of full consciousness they lasted only a moment. When it struck me
that indeed nothing had happened to unhook my fate
with Tommy, Melissa, and the endless whiteness that
surrounded us, my life felt haunted. There are cala-
mities that ricochet from out of nowhere but the
ones that inspire true helpless terror are those that
unfold from the distant, unexplored center of your
life: escaping them is like outrunning your shadow or
touching your voice.

Careful not to awaken Tracy, I slipped out of bed.

Of course it was my imagination, but that screech owl wind seemed to lift and shake the house.

In the kitchen, I found Tommy and Melissa at the table, with steaming bowls of brown rice in front of them. There were still black and gray discolorations on Tommy's face but his hair was combed, he wore a fresh shirt, and he was smiling. Melissa looked unkempt, unslept, and private.

"How you doing, Virgil?" Tommy said. "Want some rice?"

I sat at the table. "Is there anything else?"

"Not much," he said. He tapped Melissa's hip. "Another bowl." As she got up, Tommy leaned back and placed his hand on his flat belly. "Thanks for helping me out yesterday. I was really wrecked." He shrugged and shook his head, as if we were talking about flamboyant behavior at a party.

"How's the snow doing?" I asked.

"Snow's having the best time of its life. Don't never want to quit," he said, in a black cadence subtle enough to seem almost natural.

Melissa slid a bowl over to me and I spooned some rice from the pot in the center of the table. When I lifted it up there was a dark circular burn on the oak surface. "As soon as it lets up—"

"As soon as it lets up, we're gone. Never know we were here."

"I'll drive you out to your car," I said. "With all of us working we can dig it out."

"Okay," he said. "I'm going to hold you to it."

"Fine."

"There's no phone here, is there?" asked Melissa, directing the question to me but not looking my way.

"No," I said. "We were going to—" I stopped myself. It seemed that Tommy and Melissa had traded quick furtive smiles. I felt a tug of uncertainty and an accompanying sense of embarrassment: secret gestures. "How come you were so late getting here?" I asked Tommy, sticking my thumb back into the conversation.

"I took the high road and she took the low road. I took a stopover at the state prison. I want to see every state prison." He held a spoonful of rice. He looked at it for a moment and then tossed the spoon into the bowl, chipping a side. "Town was pretty closed up but I got to see the prisoners' craft shop. You know, where they sell all the super groovy things the fellas make. I asked the guard who worked the cash register what they did with the money they took in and he gave me that special look: they know when you've been inside and when you've been in, you can recognize one of them if he gets washed up naked on the shore.

"This craft shop is full of things, but everything is the same. They sell footstools, right? Not one, not a dozen, but four hundred of them. Not one cedar lamp but a thousand of them. Not one pine dresser but two hundred and fifty. This is all supposed to show rehabilitation. The men have projects, a chance to be creative. But you look at it and you've got to be stupid or crazy not to understand that everything's been *assigned*. The men don't choose to make anything. They're told what to make and they make it and then it's sold in the gift shop about two hundred yards away. To people like me. People passing through." He turned to Melissa. "I can't tell you how sick those things looked, all lined up next to each other, each one the same. It was like those pictures of all the prisoners' belongings, after they'd been gassed in the concentration camps. These little meaningless objects, repeated and repeated until it drives you mad. I really felt like trashing that place."

"Where were you in jail?" I asked.

"A nice little place called Rhodesfield. In the state of Pennsylvania."

I nodded.

"Anything else?" he asked.

"Earl said you were in for a draft violation of some sort."

"He did?" Tommy laughed. "I thought only my mother said that anymore. Heaven protect us from middle-class dreamers. Draft-dodging. How they love that."

"So what was it?"

"Just breaking the law, that's all. Like any other nigger. Nothing noble."

"Stealing?"

"Why are you so curious?"

"I just want to know how people start in one place and end up in another. I have trouble understanding how people's lives add up."

"You don't know where my life started or what it's adding up to."

"You're in all the newspapers."

"True."

"You went to Yale."

"Where'd you learn that? My mother still bragging about it?"

"Melissa mentioned it."

He turned toward her. "Smart," he said.

"Thanks a lot," she said to me.

I heard a noise behind me and turned around. Tracy came in wearing a sweater, scarf, and a hat. She looked bleary and a little feverish.

"Good morning," she said. She leaned over and kissed me on top of the head. "I'm starved," she said, sitting down and taking over my bowl of rice.

"Well, I did go to Yale," Tommy said, leaning back in his chair. You could see him organizing his biography: it was like arranging a tray of leftovers, something to present to people you didn't care about. "A full scholarship. I could have been trained to be a gentleman. I could have gotten a Rhodes scholarship eventually. I was second-string all-city basketball team in high school. I could have done half a dozen fucked up things. Sometime when you've got a few hours go visit your old man and get my mother to talk about all of my potential. It's one of the subjects she's a real orator about. She's like Lenin at the Finland Station when it comes to all the things I could have been."

"My parents were exactly like that," Tracy said. "It made them so frustrated that I could never do any one thing. I went through three different kinds of music lessons, dancing classes. I was even into mapmaking. But nothing took."

"It sounds as if your family problems were a little different than mine," said Tommy. "It sounds as if you were supposed to be the ornament of your family; I was supposed to be the savior of mine."

"And from there to phantom broadcasting?" I tapped my thumbnail against the back of a spoon.

"I had a little bit of my skin removed," he said. "That's all it took. A couple of layers peeled off."

"In jail?"

"Mostly in jail."

"But I still don't see how you ended up there."

"You don't see because I don't want you to see," he said with that tender ravishing smile.

I knew he was condescending to me but I didn't really care. I glanced at Tracy; she seemed to be looking at him through a mist of sheepishness. I realized then that he'd insulted her with his remark about her family wanting her to be their ornament. I was annoyed with myself for not having sensed that immediately and annoyed with Tracy for being vulnerable to that kind of shit.

He had a strange kind of radar. As soon as I felt that twin surge of annoyance, Tommy's manner suddenly changed: you could feel him reaching out, making certain that no one moved too far away from him. "What I'm trying to say is if I hadn't gone to jail . . ." He stopped, shook his head, pretending to remember in front of us, pretending to grope for words. "I don't know," he said, with a wistfulness

that was clearly manufactured. He knew exactly what
he was going to say, there was no question about
that, yet he needed the pretense that he was trying
to talk to us, needed the pretense that we occupied
in that house the same space and time, and he
needed somehow to obscure what I felt was the central fact of his case: he had come there with something to sell and something to hide. He had no real
impulse to be honest with us; we were merely useful
and, in his eyes, Tracy and I had done nothing to
warrant trust. Perhaps I should have been more
skillful in coaxing him out, but, in fact, I wanted him
to remain encapsulated in his attitudes, the poses he
struck: I wasn't anxious for him to become still more
real. My curiosity vied with my aversion and my
aversion got the upper hand.

Yet as he felt me back away from him, he leaned
toward me. "I did go in for robbery," he said. "I
robbed a rent-a-car office. A friend of mine was working there. We figured it would be a snap." Smile. "We
were wrong. About eighteen months' wrong."

"That was an unbelievably unfair sentence," said
Melissa.

"Could be," he said with a shrug. "But it was the
best thing that ever happened to me. It's so hard to
know what this country is about. I really do think you
have to go to jail to understand. And it's good to find
out just how scared you are, and how scared you're
not." He nodded, again affecting that look of fake reflection.

I'd always been able to imagine even casual confron-
tations coming to a violent end: the fathead in the
sports car I honked at on Third Avenue came to
blows with me in my imagination, he pulled a knife,
but, in the end, begged for mercy; the noisy transvestites on the thirteenth floor responded to my demand that they turn down their stereo with a wild
amphetamine-crazed attempt to burn down our

building. It was a habit of thought, a reflex, a way of staying in shape. It kept your nerves in fighting condition. Your stubbornness was a moral gymnasium in which you practiced your moves. In normal life, of course, the cruising roadhog in the emerald Sunbeam merely cringed when you honked and turned east after a couple of blocks; the transvestites above you turned off their stereo just as you were dialing their number. But the years of rope skipping and shadow-boxing developed you. It set a standard for behavior and you came to take it for granted that if push came to shove you would do the shoving. It was a romantic notion, a naïve one, willfully naïve. There were a million people in your borough alone who could beat the shit out of you, but in a battlefield that was primarily mental your *willingness* to fight seemed sufficient.

The knowledge that, finally, I would be willing to go to some lengths to unfasten Tommy and Melissa from my life was my hidden weapon and I turned it over in my mind the way one turns a little pistol over in one's hand: those deadly contours that comfort and beguile. As their first full day at Preservation Hall passed, I realized it wasn't necessary for me to protest their intrusion into Tracy's and my life, nor was it necessary for me to hint darkly that their hours with us were numbered. By the late afternoon, with the impending darkness triggering little bursts of alarm within me, I calmed myself by settling on the only strategy available: I would bide my time.

But why was I so anxious to get them out? A manic-depressive and a messianic ex-con may not be the perfect guests for one's newly christened cottage but there was enough remarkable about them to justify a certain hospitality. And certainly only a moral mutant would expel anyone into the storm that wrapped itself tighter and tighter around us. They had no real affection for Tracy, and I suspected they truly disliked me, but with conditions so difficult we needed them, in a way. Tommy spent time in the cellar, banging at the pipes, fiddling with the hot water heater, and turning off the furnace, which annoyed me at first because he hadn't asked but which finally made sense because we were low on fuel.

My desire to be rid of them was not reasonable, it was scarcely civilized. It was vague, superstitious. In their presence, I staggered through a waking dream of imminent calamity. They carried something foreign on their skins and they threw a sense of disaster in my path as if it were a bouquet. Tracy and I were fixed to life, rooted to it and protected by it; Tommy and Melissa seemed borderline, desperate, and darkly reckless, like people with a lot less to lose. It's important to be among those whose stake in this world approximates your own—it's important wherever life might attempt to shake you loose: you wanted everyone comfortably seated and holding on tight.

I had carried my heart and mind through a world of malice and trouble and had thus far made it safely through. I'd lived most of my life in a city full of robbers and beggars. Daily, there seemed a thousand spears unleashed at the moving target of my life and there was a mood in the air that sometimes made one a little bit ashamed for surviving. Your government destroyed a country, dropping flaming jelly on children as they slept, and still your life ran smoothly. You walked into your friend's apartment to discover, along with him, that it had been burglarized and as he sat trembling on the couch, too shaken even to call the police, you looked out the broken window into the cool night, sick and delirious with the knowledge that such things did not happen to you. When you went to work, you passed an old swaying blind man, with his melancholy dog and a cup of broken pencils. You dropped in a half a buck and took a pencil, and twiddled it in your fingers as you rode the elevator to your office. You'd make more that day than the old supplicant would see in a week, or a month, or a year. You didn't quite know anymore, you were losing touch. There had been a time when I could imagine other people's lives but now I had gripped so firmly onto my own that I had lost the talent: they came to me through a blur of menace. I had trained myself to stop paying certain kinds of attention.

There was no lack of emotion in my life, or so I told myself. I had a torrid, worshipful love for my wife, engulfing, consuming, and comforting. I sighed with pleasure when I saw lovers embrace in the park. Popular tunes could raise bumps on my arms. The past moved me. The tastes of old wines. Country skies. If anything, I was a patsy for sensation, which seemed to me proof of living at full throttle, open-armed and prancing. For all my superstition, for all my dread of wandering menace, I loved my own life. I generally woke up smiling. There was little I wouldn't do to give a friend a hand. In a decent world, it would have been enough, it would have been plenty.

That night, we melted snow in a cast-iron pot so we would have water to boil the last of the rice. I stood over the stove and watched a heap of snow reduce to two inches of hot water while Tracy, Tommy, and Melissa sat at the table. Melissa was telling Tracy about how miserably everyone had treated her when she went home to Vermont and Tracy nodded receptively, expressing an interest in the story I didn't care to admit was genuine. At the time, it merely seemed elaborately gracious.

"Say," I said to Tommy, "you never did tell me how Earl put it to you about coming here."

He looked up and smiled. I'd apparently struck on a topic that interested him more than his sidekick's biography. "He was glad to get me out of town."

"He was glad to get us both out," said Melissa.

"The police were looking for *me*, not you. My mother was getting nightly calls from my parole officer. And Earl was freaking out completely. He accused me of trying to ruin his marriage. I can see why you hate him. What an asshole."

I briefly imagined defending my father—an asshole, eh?—and flinging the pot of boiling water in Tommy's face.

"But what did he say? How did he put it to you that you should come here?"

"He asked if I needed a place to stay while things blew over in New York. I said yes. He said you had a house in Maine, that I could come here."

"Just like that?"

"I didn't pursue it. It was a good idea, being so far north. I could stay here and figure out what to do next. And if I decided New York was too risky I could stay up here, or head west, or go to Canada. I've already violated parole. It doesn't matter. When you're in enough trouble your choices become very, very open."

"Old Earl really sent you up here because you were ruining his marriage," Melissa said. "That was really where he was at."

"He had to do something for me. Mom's a lioness when it comes to my welfare. If he didn't do something I think she would have given up on him. And after all that sniffing around and begging he did to get her to marry him I don't think he wanted to press his luck. So he offered me a place to hide. Probably the first time he got laid that week. He had to offer something and he didn't have a whole lot to choose from."

"And what's that supposed to mean?" I said, with what I hoped was a murderous edge on my voice. Suddenly, after so many years of doing the soft shoe around his reputation, I was ready to defend my father.

But Tommy retreated immediately, sensing that I'd welcome an issue to go the limit over. "I don't mean anything by it. I'm mother-crazed. It's a well-known fact about me. Think nothing of it, bro'. I'm just talking to pass the time. I don't even know your father."

"That's right," I said. "You don't know him. So why don't you talk about something you know about. Talk about jail or something." I moved toward him and my voice, rather than evening out, took on a thick hateful tone. Even I was a little disquieted to hear it.

"He said he was sorry," said Tracy.

"Virgil wants to make everything as unpleasant as possible," said Melissa.

I turned to Tracy. "You're on his side?"

"Give me a break, Virgil."

"I'm giving you a break. I'm asking you."

"Look," said Tommy. "I'm sorry. I shouldn't have said it. Come on. The water's boiling like a mother-fucker. Let's throw in the rice."

"Here," said Tracy, pushing the cup toward him. "It's the last of it. Let's just throw it in. Tonight we feast!"

We went to bed as soon as we'd eaten, all of us hoping that the rice would sit in our stomachs like a soft brown coal, radiating warmth. This time I didn't undress either and Tracy and I sprawled next to each other like two derelicts on a bench, needing each other for heat, sharing a destiny, but too confused to grab hold of each other. I suspected Tracy didn't want to be touched and I didn't feel like making gestures. "Are you angry at me?" I whispered. As I said this, Tommy and Melissa started up in the next room.

"No," Tracy said. "I'm not angry. I'm worried."

"About what?"

"You. You frightened me downstairs."

"Because I was angry?"

"You really felt like slugging him."

"Look, Tracy, I'm not going to throw them out. But at least I can resent them being here. They hate me, anyhow."

"They hate you because you don't care what happens to them. You're very transparent."

"Good. I don't like them here. They hate normal life. That's what they're really against."

"I'm sick of normal life."

"You are not and you know it."

"Aren't you interested to find out how we behave when things aren't safe and made to order?"

"My life has never been safe or made to order. It's you, Tracy. When are you going to stop waiting for some miracle, some cataclysm?"

"Spare me."

"You spare me. You like experiences." I waited for her to answer but I felt her lowering her center of gravity, sinking into the mattress and away from me. Whatever it was that was going awry between us, Tracy didn't want to fuss with it now. As soon as there was silence the metal rasping of Tommy and Melissa's bed asserted itself. I didn't want to end on such a poor note but I could think of nothing to apologize for. Tracy, however, had taken aim on sleep and I felt I must distract her. "It's your fault they're here in the first place. It's because of you that Earl found out where we were. I told you this would happen. Why didn't you believe me? I know my father. I know what happens when you mix your life up with his. I may not know much about a lot of things, but I'm a fucking expert on that subject."

It was a stupid, useless thing to say but it gave me some dim satisfaction to accuse her and, sensing the measly pleasure, I began to wonder if I might have become unmoored from my right mind: truly, my touch for the situation was receding from me the way a frozen lake will recede from its own shore. I had no analysis, not even a strategy. All that was mine was a brutal, animal suspicion that taking steps to protect ourselves from Tommy and Melissa was not only forgivable but something that I was obliged to do. A couple days before, when I realized the lengths I would go to keep Earl away from my house, I had a terrible sense of my own violence, but now in bed, with Tracy drifting away from me, and Tommy and Melissa tearing at each other in the next room, I swallowed another dose of my own confusion. I didn't know what to make of it but I felt myself being pulled toward something—something in the world or something in myself—that seemed to hold within it my ruin. There is a sense of danger that even the heedless can taste: you know without thinking that something waits for you, something patient, overwhelming, and it can change you. You back away from it, but there's no place to go: the only possible route is inward and for all you know your very heart is the source of all the chaos, all the danger, all the fierce, unpredictable malice you fear.

The house had been built to withstand the winter but we'd barged into it without preparation and now we were paying for it. We were short of fuel. Soon the bottled gas for the stove would be gone. The water pump was frozen. We had just a few scraps of firewood left, and in the way of food we had a bag of onions, an enormous purple and beige garlic bulb, and a bottle of vintage claret. In most parts of the house we were safe from the wind, but the cabinet door that covered the broken windows in the kitchen was only temporary and once again our bedroom window was making that high twittering noise. Then the glass let go with a sharp crack and parted again: the wind and snow rushed in as if it had been waiting, longing for an opening.

I didn't raise my head to watch the snow twist across the floor but I knew it was there. I closed my eyes and then opened them again: the room came into focus, materialized like an image on photosensitive paper, but only so far. It was a picture taken through a black bandanna. I breathed deeply and smelled the snow, that clean, cold, vagabond odor.

I thought Tracy was asleep but I felt her body shaking. I rose on my elbow and peered over at her. In the dark, I saw her eyes were wide open and she was crying. It was the most proprietous weep I'd ever seen. Her features were a shade shy of absolute calm, her mouth was a pale straight line, her eyes opened to their widest, as if to insure that each tear rolled out perfectly formed. It was not the kind of crying to melt the heart but she so rarely wept that I was in no way inured to it. It made me want to carry her down to our car and drive her away.

"Tracy," I whispered, putting my hand on her shoulder.

At first she didn't acknowledge my touch but I kept my hand on her and she rolled onto her back, stared at the ceiling, and continued to cry.

"What's wrong?" I asked.

"I'm terrified."

"The storm?"

"Everything. The storm. Everything breaking. Prison. You."

"Me?"

She nodded. "I keep thinking you're going to do something terrible."

"I'm not. You don't have to worry about that. Okay?"

"I despise everything. I feel filthy. The fucking toilet won't even flush."

"I hate it too."

"Our window's broken again. I can't get warm. I'm going to come down with something and then what'll we do?"

"I'll go downstairs and turn the heat on," I said.

"We better not," said Tracy. "We've got to conserve fuel."

"Fuck that. Maybe we'll be out of here tomorrow. This might be our last night here. Let's get comfortable."

"We may be here for days."

"No. People up here are used to storms. They have search parties to come after people."

"No one will come here, Virgil. Who even knows we're here?"

"Those two asked people in town how to get out here. It'll work out." I put my hand under her sweater and felt her belly; it was like a patch of half-frozen moss.

Early that afternoon, Tommy had been talking about how parole boards substituted for court and jury. He then told us that because there were Catholics on his parole board he used to attend Catholic services in jail. During his recitation, I had stolen out of the living room and found our bottle of Scotch. There were about five fingers of it left and I took the bottle upstairs and hid it in the bedroom closet, an act of penny-ante anger but an act of premonition as well, for lying next to Tracy I realized it was just what she needed.

"I've got just the thing for you," I said, sliding out of bed. There was snow pulsating on the floor as I made my way to the closet.

I presented Tracy with the bottle, making a quick, courtly bow, certain, in my foolishness, that I was making myself a hero of providence in her eyes.

She took the bottle, unscrewed the cap, and brought it to her lips. Just before drinking, she said. "Where'd this come from?"

"Just drink. It'll warm you. Go on."

She took a good swig and let out a sigh that could have been ignited. "It cauterizes you," she said. "Here, take a little."

"Don't mind if I do," I said. I belted down a mouthful and coughed. The bedsprings next door had stopped their wailing and I had a momentary tremor, thinking that Tommy and Melissa might hear us and know what we were doing. I handed the bottle back to Tracy and she took another long drink. She tilted the bottle to the side to see how much was left.

"It's almost gone. God, my head." She handed the bottle to me and collapsed flat on the mattress, with one of those goofy smiles people get in cartoons after they've been clobbered: I expected to see shooting stars and hear cuckoo clocks.

I finished off the bottle. With very little food in us, we were both drunk. It felt wonderful to be drunk.

I woke with a start from my blazing, drunken stance. Tracy was reeling across the bedroom and down the hall. In the bathroom, she vomited with such shuddering violence that it seemed as if she were being turned inside out.

13

THE NEXT morning Tracy was vague and mercurial and I was hung over. The snow was still pouring out of the sky but every now and then it seemed to fall with less force.

Tracy and Tommy tried to open the back door to gather snow for melting but the door was too tightly packed by the drifted snow to budge. Finally, after they kicked at it, the door opened an inch or so. Tommy got on his knees and put a long teaspoon through the opening and gathered hard, brilliant helpings of snow. I wanted to go into the basement to turn on the furnace but Tommy said Melissa was still asleep and, to be fair, we should wait for all of us to be awake before we heated the house. I was outvoted in this matter, two to one.

That afternoon, the storm grew wilder and by three it was dark. We boiled up a few onions and the four of us ate them with our last bottle of wine. I got up to turn on the living room light but the bulb remained flat gray. I clicked the switch a couple of times.

"Electricity's out," Tommy said, as if he'd known about it before or had long expected it. "And that solves arguing about the heat," he added, with apparent satisfaction. "Without electricity, the furnace is just a piece of tin."

Unconvinced, I went to the kitchen to check the lights and then ran upstairs, trying every light, slapping at switches, yanking crazily on chains.

I went to Tommy and Melissa's room. In the weak gray light I saw their tumultuous bed, with the sheets and blankets entwined, looking like a string of foothills in the desert. Melissa's suitcase was open at the side of the bed. A dirty shirt, underwear, socks, a pale pair of frayed pantyhose, and a great, faintly sexual scatter of balled-up tissue paper lay on the floor. At the front of the room, opposite the bed and right next to the small plain chest of drawers, was Tommy's rifle. Unthinkingly, I picked it up and felt its heft. I curled my finger around the freezing trigger. I thought wildly about going downstairs and pointing the gun at everyone. But I had no demands. I still wasn't ready to send Tommy and Melissa away, though I'd played the scenario in my mind: the shove into our car, the quick, grim ride to the edge of our land, the rapid U-turn, the sight of them getting smaller and smaller in my rearview mirror.

I'd never fired a gun. I'd been called to serve in the army but I told my draft board that I was a homosexual. Summer camp was never on my agenda. In college, I once considered joining the rifle club but the boys in it were aliens to me, small-town right-wingers who had to leap through hoops of contrition to get laid.

I squinted through the rifle's sigts. I turned toward the wall and took aim at the useless light switch. I had a fleeting, persuasive desire to squeeze the trigger.

There would be a violent crunch of noise. Shouts from downstairs. Tommy would run in and try to disarm me. I would put the barrel's tip flush against his prominent adam's apple and warn him not to make a move.

With a sharp intake of breath, I pulled the trigger. Locked. I found the latch, unlocked it, and pulled the trigger again. There was nothing, not even a click. I looked at the gun for a moment and realized that the ammunition clip wasn't in.

I looked for it in the dresser and then under the bed. I felt certain it must be in the room and I wanted to find it before the house went utterly dark. Looking for it gave me something to do and having it would give me something to have. It was no clearer than that. I wanted that clip, not so much to insert into the rifle and so turn it from a piece of prosaic metal into a soaring epic of potential death but so that only Virgil Morgan would know where it was. That was my only plan: I wanted to re-hide it.

I pawed through Melissa's suitcase, doubly cautious so I wouldn't be heard from downstairs and so I could hear anyone who might approach. A pair of faded jeans with a clenched fist sewn to the back pocket, a striped silk tie, expensive to the touch, an unpressed white shirt carefully folded—that one looked a little suspicious. I opened it up. Nothing. A pair of tennis shoes. Empty. Some flimsy, rather thrilling women's underwear. A pornographic magazine with Oriental models. No time for that. A black leather wallet. I opened it. At least two hundred dollars in it. The sight of the money made my heart pound: it was like a letter from home. I'd forgotten there was a world where orderly, symbolic exchanges took place, where people ordered ham and cheese and bet which horse could run fastest. I stuffed my eager hand into the side slots of the valise. A bottle of dark red capsules with Melissa's name on the prescription, another bottle of small cobalt-colored tablets, also bearing her name. There was a plastic container for a lady's razor which she used as a jewelry box for some Indian beads and a small silver buckle. Something was happening to me. I felt an involuntary twinge of affection and shame: an ambivalent voyeur who drops his spyglasses, overcome with the innocence and frailty of his victims, of all victims. There was a deck of cards and a case which couldn't possibly have held the clip but which I opened anyway. Inside was a photo of someone, perhaps Melissa's father, but by that time the room had gotten practically black and I was only guessing.

"Virgil!" It was Tracy's voice and I spun around, under the guilty dumb delusion she had sneaked into the room. She called me again and I realized the signal came from Level Two of the house, calling the cellar Level One, and that I was on Level Three. In a way, I was losing my mind.

"Yes?" I trilled, mashing Tommy and Melissa's belongings back into the suitcase.

"We've got a decision to make. Can you come down?"

"I'll be right there." I gave a few last pokes around. The clip wasn't there.

I was wanted to help Tracy choose which of our books would be burned in the fireplace. We had two fairly good logs left, but no kindling. Tracy and I solemnly chose the books we'd brought up, electing to spare the ancient paperbacks that had been left by the house's former master. Tommy and Melissa looked bored and slightly contemptuous as Tracy and I deliberated over this matter. When we finally made our decision, Tommy said, "You may as well get used to the fact that tomorrow we're going to burn a little furniture."

Tracy and I had brought two small pewter candleholders and two white candles, now our only light. They flickered in the steady breeze and watching those pale yellow points of flame shudder to the edge of ex-

tinction reminded us of the house's little leaks and the
broken windows in the kitchen.

I took one of the candles and went to the basement
in the hope that among all the tools there was a flashlight. The basement was about ten degrees colder than
the upstairs. It had that dull messy smell of wet newspapers, of mud and dust. I kept my hand cupped before the flame and crept carefully, afraid of tripping. I
could see very little but when I dropped my hand the
flame did its St. Vitus's Dance and I had to protect it
again. After a long slow look around the cellar—during which I felt the need to empty my bladder with
such sudden urgency that it seemed to be the advance
guard of lunacy—I found the pegboard hung with
tools. Hammer, handsaw, screwdrivers, level, plane,
pliers. No flashlight. I looked on the worktable. A
vise, a pastic tray with dividers for nails, tacks, screws.
A glasscutter. Putty. A drill.

Everything seemed a potential weapon.

As this occurred to me I had a panicky thought that
Tommy and Melissa were at that very instant convincing Tracy to join them against me. The cellar door
would close. Did it lock from the kitchen? It did. I
took a hurried last glance. Fuck the flashlight. I took
the stairs two at a time, allowing the candlewick to
swallow the flame.

"You let the candle go out," said Melissa. "We don't
have many matches, you know. You could have been
more careful."

Without bothering to answer her, I relit the extin-
guished candle with the flame of the other one, and
then glanced at her briefly.

"How many candles are there?" Tommy asked. He
sat on the couch and rubbed his hands together. Although his body was hunched a bit from the cold, there
was something in his eyes—a steadiness, a dryness—
that contrasted with the flickers of panic that reverberated in the rest of our gazes, and I knew that Tommy
was in his element. Just as my character had been

formed by and for order, his was shaped for emergency. I remembered his tentativeness and uneasiness when I first met him at the Russian Tea Room and, with a deep inward shiver, I felt that here, in this growing torment, he was in his element. He felt closer to the part of himself he valued most, and he looked it.

"I think we've got about six left," said Tracy. There was scarcely a flame in the fireplace, but she moved close to it, holding up the palms of her hands.

"I think we'd better put these candles out then," Tommy said. "We don't know how long we're going to be here."

"It'll be so dark," said Melissa, softly. I looked at her and she glanced away, a little panicked that she'd contradicted Tommy. Her willed and convulsive subservience to him wasn't typically female: the command between them wasn't decided by an aristocracy of gender. It was wholly a question of who understood suffering and disorder most deeply and, granting Tommy his advantage in that realm, she had no choice but to obey him. Tommy had the last word between them because he had been to prison, because he made broadcasts. Melissa's struggles had been merely personal but Tommy had the glory of jousting with the state. The end of Melissa's struggle could only be peace, but Tommy's amorphous, faltering fight—with all of its false starts and stops, its secrecy, its obscurity —promised some grand and general liberation, and something had convinced Melissa that the breadth of his struggle gave it special importance.

"What are you looking at?" Melissa asked me, tossing her head in indignation.

I shrugged and looked away.

Tommy picked up one of the candles and blew it out. Darkness rushed in like wind. It was like being at the bottom of a very cold ocean. I knew there was nothing to it, but the darkness emphasized the cold.

"I say we leave the candles burning," I said. I

placed myself before the candle that burned on the mantelpiece.

Tommy shook his head. "You don't have any idea how long we're going to be here."

"These candles burn very slowly," Tracy said.

"Look," said Tommy, a commander addressing his nervous troops, "we're going to have to spend some time in the dark. That's all there is to it. We have to save the candles for when we really need them."

"We need them right now," I said.

"You want to pretend that we're going to be here for another fifteen minutes," said Tommy, "and I'm telling you that just isn't true. We may be here for a very long while and we've got to conserve what we have."

"Look," I said, "I'm sorry I didn't take a bath while the water was running and I'm sorry I didn't put the fucking thermostat up to one hundred when the furnace was still on. I think we should use what we have, while we have it." I wanted to accuse him of wanting to make everything as uncomfortable as possible, but at that point I still believed I might contain my malice toward him. I wanted to minimize our points of conflict, understanding, in my way, the intimacy of battle.

"Why don't we vote on it?" said Tommy, confident of Tracy's vote. He smiled at me, as if parliamentary democracy was an invention of my class and now it was to be used against me.

Tracy, however, voted with me and, with the vote tied, we flipped a coin to decide. Once it was left to chance, I knew the outcome: I won three straight tosses in a best-of-five match. Melissa groaned loyally each time I correctly predicted which side of the quarter would come up, but she looked relieved when I finally won.

It was still early in the evening and though we were tired from the cold and hunger no one wanted to go to bed. Melissa announced she was going upstairs to get a deck of playing cards. When she was gone, I wondered if she would detect that I'd been through her valise. She came down, apparently unsuspecting, and asked if we wanted to play a game called Swiss Chairs.

"You better watch out for Virgil," Tracy announced in a fairly good-humored voice. "He's pathologically lucky."

"So the story goes," said Tommy.

"Oh, yes?" I said.

"Your old man says you lead a charmed life."

"He means that in the most condemning possible way."

Tommy shrugged his shoulders. "I suppose so."

"Do you want to learn how to play Swiss Chairs or not," said Melissa.

The four of us sat before the fireplace, on the hooked rug, with cushions beneath our asses. Melissa dealt out eight cards each and then put four cards in the middle. Then she added a fifth center card, thought about it for a moment, and then re-collected all the cards. This time she dealt out six cards each and put eight cards in the middle. "My brother taught me this," she said. "It's the only card game I like, except solitaire. The idea is to go out before anyone else."

"Go out?" said Tracy.

"Get rid of all your cards."

I threw my cards into the middle. "I win," I said.

"Do you mind?" said Melissa.

Obligingly, I picked up my cards again.

"Okay," said Melissa, "everyone look at your cards. Everything under five is a potential chair. Tens are carpenters. Sevens and kings automatically break a chair. The cards in the middle are the warehouse."

"Last time you said the deck was the warehouse," said Tommy.

"No, I didn't."

"Yes, you did. And you said that sevens and *queens* automatically break a chair."

"What the fuck is a chair?" I said, glancing at Tracy

and sending her a grin of patrician malice she could not resist.

"I'm getting to that. It's a combination of low cards. The sturdier the chair the more cards it can support. Like an ace-two chair can support a six and an eight. An ace-two-three chair can support a six, eight, and a nine. But if you put down a chair and I have a seven or a king—"

"A queen," said Tommy.

"—then the chair is broken and you don't get credit for it. We need a pencil and paper, by the way."

The game developed complexities as she continued to explain it. Red chairs were more valuable than black chairs. There were chairs of bonded suits, temporary chairs, and something called a shifting chair which she could not make clear to us. The cards remaining in the deck were to be drawn if you couldn't make a chair, but the person who drew the card had to offer it to the other players first and had the last option whether or not to take it. But, and this really *was* important, in order to take any card ... And so forth. She corrected herself a number of times, hesitated, and argued with Tommy, who was either doing an imitation of caring about the game or was merely subverting her attempt to explain it. Finally, after about twenty minutes of listening to those nitwit directions, I tossed my cards down.

"Why don't we play something simpler. How about casino?"

"You're not even trying to learn my game," said Melissa, her face darkening.

"It's impossible. You don't even know how to play it."

"I'm *telling* you how it goes. Christ, do you have to have everything your own way?"

"All right," said Tommy. "Easy."

"Don't *you* stand up for him," said Melissa.

"Lighten up," Tommy said.

"You don't like him any more than I do." She was starting to cry.

"Shut the fuck up." It would take a lot of ravishing grins to take away the memory of the violence and cruelty in that voice. He grabbed her arm and squeezed it, fixing her with his stare.

"You're hurting me," she said.

"Let her alone," said Tracy.

"Let her alone?" said Tommy, dropping Melissa's arm and facing Tracy.

"That's right, let her alone." Tracy's hands were clenched but I don't think anyone but me noticed her fear.

Tommy made a move toward Tracy. I felt a jolt of adrenalin and a burst of fearful joy. I felt in an even fight Tommy would be superior to me but if we fought over Tracy I would be possessed: I would dismantle him.

Tommy looked at his hand as if he were consulting with it: Who do you want to grab? this one? that one? But then his features went soft and he shook his head. "I don't know what's the matter with me," he said. "Stir crazy. Being cooped up reminds me of jail." He put his arm around Melissa. "I'm sorry. Did I hurt you?"

She rubbed her arm. "Not really."

"I did. I know I did. Take the weight off me. Hit me. Okay? Give me a break. Hit me anywhere you like."

Without any hesitation, Melissa leaned over and slapped him hard across the face.

"He terrified you, didn't he," I said to Tracy as we got into bed.

She nodded. "I want them out of here," she said in a very quiet way, as if neither of us were meant to hear it: for the record.

"If the snow stops and we can find the road, there's a chance," I said, taking her in my arms.

Making love in the freezing bed was a delicate, nervous event, yet the opposition of the elements added to our pent-up ardor. We would have liked to cut patches in our clothes at the strategic points but we settled for the sordid, delightful alternative of coupling with our drawers pulled down to a level that maximized movement and minimized exposure, somewhere between our thighs and our knees.

I woke in the middle of the night. Tracy had rolled away from me and her body was tight and folded into itself, as if she wanted to make herself smaller on the chance the cold might overlook her. I felt miserable and unclean and though making love had calmed me, the moisture we had created now felt slimy and half frozen on me. I tried to drift back to sleep but the cold in the room tormented me. As I became more awake, I felt more miserable, as if consciousness had been reduced to a species of terror and the more conscious I was, the more terrified. The thought that I was a prisoner in that house clanged like pipes in my mind. I felt that the storm wouldn't have seemed so devastating if only Tommy wasn't in the house. The natural disaster had bestowed authority upon him and with life suddenly dangerous and unpredictable, I was his underling. I felt deep, prideful panic and longed for a way to put *him* beneath *me*, to make this my house again. The prospect appealed to my superstitious nature: if I were in command everything would be different. The snow would stop, heat would come pouring out of the icy grilles.

I promised myself to be more assertive, to insist on the validity of my perceptions, which seemed rosier and more conservative than Tommy's reflexively desperate vision. Yet my point of view, because it was, I thought, more *reasonable*, lacked the force of Tommy's. Like a gentleman at the Apocalypse, my presence was a little frivolous: we were now in the realm of emergency.

I slipped out of bed and stuffed my feet into my shoes. I didn't know what I was doing until I began to creep out of the bedroom. Then I realized that I was going to continue to look for the ammunition clip to Tommy's rifle. I still didn't know what I was going to do with it, or why exactly it was crucial that I know where it was, but finding it, I thought, would somehow equalize the balance of power in the house. I moved toward the staircase, certain everyone was sleeping. It would be one of my only chances to look downstairs for the clip. The house was dark but I could make out shapes; it felt good to glide like a creature of night through my house. I stepped off the last stair and into the living room. The windows were frosted over and almost black but I could sense the snow falling beyond them as the sky emptied itself upon the house and everything around it.

"Can't sleep?" a voice said.

I turned and saw Tommy sitting on the couch, his legs crossed and a glass of snow in his hands.

"Restless," I said, my heart shaking.

"Me too," he said. He made a small laugh.

"What's funny?"

"Oh nothing. I heard you and Tracy making it up-stairs. I figured you'd be out for the night. I certainly would be sleeping if Melissa had wanted to make love. But . . ." He ended with a shrug.

I felt like kicking him in the teeth; my bones ached with the wanting. But there was nothing I could even say since I'd been listening to him and Melissa for the past few nights.

"It's colder down here," I said.

"It doesn't make any difference." He dipped his fingers into the glass of snow and dabbed some on his hand.

"What are you doing that for?" I asked.

"Sores on my hand."

I nodded.

"Why don't you sit down?" he said.

"No, I'm going upstairs."

"Please. Sit down. Just for a few minutes."

I sat down. I felt a wave of disappointment, knowing I would not be able to look for the clip. I sat a few feet away from him on the couch, with my hands on my knees.

"I know you hate having me here," he said. "You don't even know me and I know you don't understand what I'm doing. And I *was* sent up here by your old man. Look, I know how complicated this is. I can't even get into it, it's so complicated. Sometime soon when I've got the chance to think about everything that's happened to me these past couple years I'll think about that, how your old man sent me up here and what that felt like to you. I'm not a total fucking idiot, you know. I'm not here thinking everything's fine."

"I assume that," I said in a small, fussy voice, and shrinking a little at the sound of it. "I don't know what to think about you. You don't let yourself be known. I forget everything you say right after you say it."

"It's not important what you think of me," he said. He looked away. I sensed I'd wounded his vanity.

We sat in silence. I almost told him that, in fact, I would *like* to know him, but when I said it to myself it sounded merely inquisitive. Finally, the silence made me nervous enough to break it. "How long were you at Yale?" I asked.

"It's not important," he said with a wave, but then, quickly, he continued. "I always wanted to go to a place like that. Harvard or Yale. I wanted it without even knowing why. But once I had it I learned what it was for. It was for spitting on. It was for holding it in your hand for two seconds and then tossing it away. Those places really do want to groom gentlemen. I hate privilege."

"It's a privilege to throw it away."

"Paradox," he said, conclusively. "Anyhow, I learned more in jail than I could ever have learned in school. And not all of it was pleasant."

"It was very hard, wasn't it," I said. I'd had one of those unexpected flashes when suddenly you can tell something about someone: it was not a startling insight but I knew then that prison had broken something in him, had forced him to touch the center of his own fear.

"You're goddamned right it was hard," he said with unexpected feeling. "You'll never know how hard it was. You don't know how *embarrassing* it is to be in jail, to have no freedom, no privacy. Anyone can come by and look at you. Anyone can tell you what to do. You're everyone's inferior. I'm talking about stupid men with triple chins, who fart and belch all night and day, and *they* have the right to boss you around."

"You were in for a year?"

"That's right." He paused. He could tell the conversation had drifted out of his complete control, but he knew well how to regain it. There were a dozen compelling half-truths he could tell about himself and he knew how to pull them out like a magician extracting colored silks from his sleeve. "You know, some of the members of my parole board were Catholics and I went to mass in prison just to make an impression on them."

"I know."

"You know?"

"You mentioned that already. Yesterday, I think."

"I did?" He seemed rattled, but then he smiled. "I thought you said you couldn't remember anything I said." He raised a finger, scoring the point. Suddenly he was completely relaxed again.

"Listen," he said, "I don't fool myself. I had it easy. I was only in for a year. I didn't get fucked over too badly. It was like a walk in the park compared to some. The guys who had records, or who didn't have mamas to hire them decent lawyers, or who weren't white, or who wouldn't"—he broke off for a moment —"cooperate. The way I did. I *owe* all of them."

"You can do a lot more out of jail than you can inside," I said.

"I don't really know what to do. I just know I've got to do something."

"Do you think they do any good?" I asked. "The broadcasts."

"Sure. People at least have to know. How else can anything happen? You tell me."

"I don't know," I said. "Doing good isn't one of my talents." I got up and looked out the window. "It seems to be letting up," I said.

"I'd like to get back to my transmitter. I hate this waiting around."

"There's a lot of snow out there."

"I have to get back to New York. My mother's holding twenty-five hundred dollars for me. Everything's there. I got to get that radio going again. I wish I could count on you, Virgil."

"For what?"

"To try and get me out to my car."

I didn't dare look at him. "Sure. We'll all try and get into town. With the four of us, we might make it."

"I don't want to force anything."

"No, that's all right. Maybe I can drive with you to the Canadian border. There's plenty of places to cross."

"What the fuck do I want to go there for?"

"I don't know. To stay there for a while until this whole thing blows over. It might be safer."

"I'm not interested in being safe."

"It's up to you. If you're really serious we can take a crack at leaving here tomorrow." I looked out the window again. Had the snow really let up? I couldn't be certain.

"I'm serious, don't worry about that. Turn around. Let me see something." I did, and he laughed. "You look so *relieved*," he said.

14

T HE NEXT morning we ate the last two onions and
debated whether or not the snow was falling with
less force. Melissa wore one of Tracy's sweaters and
Tommy wore my gloves to protect his hands, which
had blistered at the joints. Tracy and I sat close to each
other, our knees touching. Each of us had a cup of
water. We'd melted the snow but by the time we were
through the flames on the stove were sputtering. We'd
run out of Pyrofax.

"I'm sure it's snowing less than yesterday," I said.

"I think so too," said Tracy. "But maybe we're getting used to it."

"I'm colder than before," said Melissa. "My head's
stuffed. I've got the shakes."

"Poor, poor you," said Tommy.

"I wonder if my car will start," I said. "This will be
its big test."

Tommy got up quickly. "Come here," he said to me.
"I want to show you something."

We walked to the windows above the kitchen sink. Through the storm I could see the contours of the land; hills and peaks of pure soft white; a bleached, bloodless world that, as I stared at it, terrified me.

"Where's your car?" Tommy asked.

I pointed to where I'd parked it but it wasn't there, or it wasn't visible. I looked harder and made out the outlines; the Mercedes was buried beneath a drift. I saw the tip of the radio antenna and a little patch of the back roof. Melissa's VW might have just as well dematerialized.

"It's going to be really difficult to dig that fucking car out," I said.

"Now you're catching on," said Tommy.

I felt Tracy's hands on my waist. "Look," I said, "our car's buried. What are we going to do now?"

"Awful." She shook her head.

"That does it," said Melissa. "That really does it." She leaned forward on her elbows and tugged nervously at her hair. "We're going to die here."

"Stop that," said Tracy. She moved maternally toward Melissa and said something to lift her spirits. I wasn't paying attention. I'd heard the beginning of a distant motorized hum and I held my breath to hear it better. It seemed to be getting closer.

"Quiet," I said. "Listen. I hear something coming. Do you hear?" It was louder now. "That's no car," I said. "Listen, for God's sake. Listen. It's coming from above us." I slammed my hands onto the counter. "We just might be back in luck."

"I hope they know we're here," said Tracy. "They won't see any cars."

The noise was much closer. As I suspected, but didn't dare say, it was a helicopter. I saw a glimpse of it. We could hear the blades beating against the air with a great hollow sound, incessant and joyful.

"Let's get outside and wave to them," I said.

We went to the back door, Tracy and I, with Melissa a few steps behind. We pushed but the snow had drifted flat against the door and it didn't budge. I stepped back and gave it a vicious, frantic kick. It didn't even quiver.

"It's going to pass us by," I said.

"We'll break out the windows," said Tracy.

"No." I thought for a moment and turned to Tommy. "Load your rifle. Shoot it out the window. They'll hear shots and know we're here."

During the activity of the last minute, Tommy hadn't moved. He leaned against the sink, his feet a little in front of him, his ankles crossed. "How do you know what that is up there," he said in an appallingly casual tone.

"It's a rescue squad," I said. "Isn't that obvious?"

"No, it's not."

"Get your fucking gun and shoot it." I looked out the window. A dark blue helicopter passed overhead. It lingered over the house.

"I can't do that, Virgil," Tommy said.

"Then let me. Put the clip in." I listened for a moment. The helicopter still seemed to be hovering above us, the blade slicing hard into the wind. "Fast," I said, grabbing his shoulders.

"I can't. If it's the police, it's all over for me."

"What other chance do we have?" I looked wildly at Tracy. "Do you know where the clip is?" She shook her head.

"Tommy's right," said Melissa. "It's too risky."

I looked at Tommy. It was clear he had no intention of firing any shots. The sound of the helicopter was still loud but not so loud as before. You didn't have to shout to be heard. "Oh, Christ," I said, "why don't they land?"

I put my hand through the windowpane above the sink and hollered out. My voice was shredded by the wind, every word dismantled letter by letter. Wind and snow blew in. Needles of glass stuck to the side of my hand. I was bleeding.

One last chance. I raced into the living room in the

hope that a fire was burning. Surely, they would see
smoke. There was nothing in the hearth but ashes. I
tore up a book and tossed the pages into the fireplace.
Slapped my pockets for a match. Swept my hand over
the mantelpiece. Nothing. I turned around. There was
a cardboard book of matches on the couch. I grabbed
them. Two left. They looked soaked, and their bright
green heads were half off. I struck one. Fizzled. Then
ignited. I put it to the pages in the fireplace and they
curled in leisurely immolation. I listened for the helicopter. Its hum was more and more distant.

I remained hunched before the small fire, waving at
it, blowing on it, hoping to send one globe of smoke
through our chimney. Tracy came in behind me and
put her hands gently on my shoulders.

"They're gone," she said in a consoling voice, as if I
was the only one in the house who would be at all
disappointed.

That afternoon we broke up Cleveland Page's kitchen
chairs and burned them in the fireplace. Tommy was
still strong enough to crack the legs with his hands but
I used the heavy steel fireplace poker to break them
down. We boiled snow and cleaned the cuts on my
hand. Tommy nailed a cabinet door over the window
I'd broken. Tracy remained on relatively good terms
with Tommy and Melissa though, judging from the
way she winced as I picked the glass out of my hand,
she was softening toward me again.

Tommy continued to solicit my understanding, as
well as to solidify Tracy's apparently wavering support
of his choice not to fire the gun. "There's sure to be an
all-points out on me. I stand to spend a lot of time in
jail if I'm caught. Who do you people think was in that
helicopter? A minister and a farmer? Wake up, why
don't you? That was the law. They take one look at me
and that's it. We're going to get out of here. Just not
with the police. All right? Virgil?"

"You will regret this," I said. "I promise you." Tommy shrugged it off; Melissa memorized it.

"I know what I'm doing," he said.

"There was no chance of anyone in that helicopter knowing who you were," I said. "It was a simple rescue operation. It happens every winter, I'll bet."

"We didn't have to tell them who you are," said Tracy, in a tone so friendly and reasonable I didn't catch on immediately that she was working my side of the street. My first impulse was to dispute what she said but then I smiled at her.

"They might have had a picture of me," Tommy said.

"Are you ready for this?" I asked Tracy.

"They very well might have," he said.

"No one has a picture of you, Tommy," I said. "Who are you? You're utterly small-time. You're an ex-con who did a little time on a petty charge, kissed ass in jail to get out, and now you've been annoying people with your absurd broadcasts. Do you know how people react to your little interruptions? What do you think? That they race out of their apartments screaming? It's a complete nothing. Nobody cares. It's a fucking joke."

"*You* think it's a joke," said Melissa. "That's just because you're so middle-class you think everything's a joke."

"And you are a parasite," I said. "Your family has two hundred times as much money as mine and you live off the government. You use public money to buy three-hundred-dollar valises." I wasn't very fussy about what I said; I spoke from the molten inspiration of sheer hatred. "Who are you to call me anything? Who knows *who* you are? All you are is the pills you take."

"I told you he hated me," Melissa said to Tommy, in a bright vindicated voice.

"Keep off his back, then," said Tracy. "You're always on him and it pisses me off."

* * *

Later that day, I reminded everyone that this was the day we had planned to dig out the Mercedes and try to drive to Tommy's car. Tracy was skeptical about the possibility of doing this but I think she was willing to try. Tommy laughed off the suggestion and when I pressed it, he flatly refused.

I scarcely slept that night. I kept my senses poised for the return of that aerial hum. Tracy complained of sharp pains in her stomach. I had them too. It was hunger, we both knew, but we didn't want to say. The first two days, we'd fantasized and joked about food but now that all we had was garlic, we didn't want to talk about it any longer.

The springs in the next room were quiet. I rolled over and took Tracy in my arms.

"Virgil?" she whispered.

"Yes?"

"Do you think we're going to get out of here?"

"Yes." I waited for her to consider this. "That is," I added, "if we . . ."

"No, please. I don't want to hear what you think we have to do. I just want to know what you think will happen."

"I think we'll get out."

"It's just a matter of time, then, isn't it?"

"That's right."

"This is my moment to feel desperate."

"We'll be all right," I said.

"I think so, too. But being here was a lot easier before. When I liked them more."

"I should have killed him when he let that helicopter go by."

We were silent for a few moments. From the next room came a long, orgasmic groan, and then another. What were they doing? Even oral sex would have made a little bit of bed noise. Tracy remained silent and I had a sick feeling that she'd fallen asleep, or was faking sleep.

Finally, she said, "This isn't working out the way I hoped. I feel like a failure. Everything is so awful."

"We'll carry on," I said, my voice suddenly thickening.

"I know we will. We always will."

15

I'VE BEEN required to describe the next day in scrutinized detail a number of times and I still can't get it solidly right. I have no idea what time it was when I got up. There was light from the outside, but you can't tell time from blizzard light: it's weak, distant, and always the same until it disappears. I was alone when I awakened. There are days, even in the midst of a reasonably running life, when you wake up and give your life a great kick in the chops: doors are for slamming, you throw yourself onto chairs, on the off chance you might break one, shoes are stamped into, ties are yanked from the rack with that brisk snap you use to start an outboard motor. That was roughly the mood I was in. I have admitted as much.

I heard voices downstairs. My stomach seemed to have caved in at the sides and there was a steady, hollow pain in its center. I tried to remember what it was like to be warm and after a poor start I imagined *exactly* what it felt like: the thoughtless luxury of seventy-degree air circulating around your skin, of breathing the stuff in, not being able to see the shape and substance of your exhale, stepping out of the shower with your hair slicked back and sitting naked in the kitchen taking big noisy bites out of a Granny Smith apple.

I switched my socks around. I was wearing three pair now but my feet still ached with cold. I tied my shoes and had a little trouble manipulating my fingers. Not a great deal of trouble, but there *was* stiffness. There's no question about that. I tried to make a fist but couldn't, no matter how hard I tried. There was an eighth of an inch between my fingernails and my hand. I have demonstrated this in court.

After some effort, my shoes were tied. I sat up and almost passed out from the redistribution of blood. My impulse was to stay upstairs. The thought of facing the others, even Tracy, unnerved me a little. I had lost the ability to anticipate what was going to happen next, and the world, or life, or time, or whatever it is we are living in the midst of, this somewhere wrapped in the center of a somewhere else—all of it loomed before my faltering imagination. My ears ached, from their outer rims straight through the ducts that led to the brain.

When I came down, Tommy was in the armchair and Tracy and Melissa sat on the couch. The conversation stopped and all looked at me as I shuffled down the stairs. They were trying to gauge how foul my mood was. It was embarrassing to be noticed that way so I smiled and said good morning. A great fruitcake smile and something Melissa was later to make a point of mentioning to the police.

"Well," said Tommy, "well well well well. Have you cheered up?"

"I'm beyond mood," I said.

"Do you want some water?" Tracy asked, pointing to the cast-iron pot next to the fireplace.

I went over and took a drink. It was tepid and tasted of the iron; it seemed to add to my emptiness.

"I think it's time to break up some more furniture," said Tommy.

"What now?" I said, looking at Tracy.

"Nothing nice," she said.

"You two choose," said Tommy with a shrug. "It's up to you."

"Thanks," I said.

"Probably if we took this couch apart, there'd be enough fuel for a day," Tracy said. "We could burn the stuffing and not have to waste any more books."

"My grandmother had a couch like this," said Melissa.

"No," I said. "It's too good." I thought for a moment. "How about that dresser in the guest room. It's cheap pine. Relatively unadorned."

"He *would* take something from our room," Melissa said.

"Melissa . . ." said Tracy.

"All right. No hassles," said Tommy. "I'll do it. I need the exercise."

"I'll come, too," I said. "I may as well execute my own furniture."

We went upstairs and looked over the chest of drawers: it was empty except for an old issue of *Life* with a photograph of Grace Kelly on the cover. The insides of the drawers were lined with thin paper with pictures of quills and inkwells.

Tommy kicked its side. "Shouldn't be difficult taking it apart," he said.

"I'm going to go down and get that poker."

"No," he said, "why bother? We can do it with our hands and a couple kicks."

"I'll do it my own way," I said, turning on my heel.

I went down for the fireplace poker. Tracy and Melissa were talking on the couch. They looked at me as I picked up the poker. There was the sound of collapsing wood from upstairs.

"Don't bother, man," Tommy called. "It's already falling apart."

I didn't pay any attention. I tightened my grip on the poker and went back upstairs, feeling its heft as I walked. Solid steel, with a sharp point, it weighed a dense ten pounds.

Tommy had kicked the side of the dresser and some of the wood had caved in. He had then abandoned this section and taken out the drawers. He stomped out the bottom of one of them and then pulled the sides apart.

"Look," he said, "it's like a model airplane."

"Is that how you spent your youth? Breaking people's model planes?"

"My own."

I put my foot into one of the drawers and, swinging the poker like a golf club, knocked down the sides. I was delighted that my method took less effort than his. And the edges of the boards I'd loosened were neater. He pulled out the last of the drawers and crudely dismantled it, jabbing himself with one of the needle-like nails that had once sealed it. Operating in the realm of sheer competitive rancor, I pointed to the dot of blood that rose through his glove and I grinned.

He went to the side of the dresser and resumed kicking at it. He had his back to his target and kicked like a mule. The wood withstood the first blow, cracked at the second, and collapsed on the third. Now there were two excavations but it seemed to me we were no closer than before to being able to use it for fuel.

"Turn it over on its top," I said, grabbing a side. "I'll begin by knocking off the legs."

"We can just pull them apart," he said. "Moves the blood around."

"Come on," I said, "turn it over."

"What you're doing is taking all the fun away. Fuck the white man's technology. Let's use our hands."

I wasn't so sunk in myself that I missed his attempt at friendliness but there was no cell in my body that was in any way susceptible to him. "Look. It's my chest of drawers. We'll do it my way."

"Oink oink," he said.

The dresser was on its head now, its pale stubby legs pointing straight up. I smacked the poker against one of the legs and it came partly off, dangling from the frame like a child's loose tooth.

"You see?"

The poker felt like a thin cool train in the tunnel of my paired fists. My hands were stiff and I couldn't get a proper grip but I was determined to destroy that dresser myself. Tommy stood near me as I circled the dresser, trying to decide where to strike next. I remember noticing that he wasn't a safe distance away but, then, he never was. Still, it occurred to me to ask him to step back. "Give me a little room," I said.

"You're only going to break that poker," he said, his arms folded in front of him.

"This poker is ten times stronger than the wood."

"You're wrong about that."

I held the poker as if it were a baseball bat. I took a couple of half swings for practice. I wanted my next swing to be perfect. I didn't want to take an impetuous swipe and hit nothing but air and I didn't want to graze my target.

That's as far as I can go in certainty. The most important thing is something I can never know. Just as I was about to begin my swing, Tommy said, "Wait," but I truly don't know if he moved toward me when he said that or if he'd been standing within my swing's arc all along. I have turned this over in my mind a thousand times. I have tried to sneak up on it, take my memory by surprise and so learn the secret, but all that I can safely say is that the poker hit him on the side of the head. It made a dull, sick sound, like an old cucumber being broken in two. The damn thing hit him on the side of the head and its hooked point took a bite out of his forehead.

He fell to one knee. He didn't utter a sound. He

buried his face in his hands. Then he sat on the floor; his spine was curved in an unnatural U shape.

I thought to myself: I've killed him. I had an impulse to leave the room and this has caused me frequent bouts of shame, even though I've been told it's not an unusual reaction.

"Are you all right?" I said. I couldn't believe the voice I heard: it sounded as if I were apologizing for jostling somebody.

His hands fell from his face and landed limply in his lap. His chin was down on his chest and there was a ring of somber red blood on his forehead.

A little chink of time is missing here. I was now at his side. I don't remember moving toward him. My hands were hovering about his shoulders. I was afraid to touch him. The circle of blood grew larger, the borders indistinct. A bubble of the stuff emerged from his nose; it was suspended for a moment and then burst. He let out a long moan—the first sound since he'd been struck—and fell back. He was conscious enough to put out his elbows to break the fall but not strong enough for it to do any good. I saw he was going to hit the floor and I made a grab for him but it was too late.

He was expressionless. His eyelids fluttered, desperate and horrifying, like trapped moths. Threads of blood went through his hair. I said his name. He didn't answer; he probably didn't hear.

I called out for Tracy. "Come up here, Tracy, quick." Thank God she didn't question me. She was up in a moment, with Melissa.

I stood to one side of Tommy's body as Tracy and Melissa came into the room. They stopped short when they saw him. Melissa made a tight, choked cry and came quickly forward. I put up my hand to slow her down.

"I hit him with the poker," I said. "I think he's knocked out or something."

Melissa was down on one knee. She stroked his

silky hair. His eyes were closed now. "Tommy?" she said. "Are you okay?"

I looked at his chest. It rose and fell, rose and fell. He's breathing, I thought, thank God he's breathing.

"We've got to prop him up a little," said Tracy: her voice sounded quick, a little out of control, like a dime skipping over ice.

Suddenly, the room began to move away. Sweat poured off me; I swallowed back a little worm of vomit. How I wanted to sit on the edge of the bed, with my hands over my eyes.

I grabbed for the pillows. Melissa was weeping now; I took her place at Tommy's side. Tracy and I took him by the shoulders and lifted him slowly. His head hung back. I put my hand at the back of his neck and Tracy slipped the pillows beneath him. He seemed so still, so quiet. But then, just as his head was about to touch the pillows, his body was gripped by a long wrenching cough. His lips were blown apart by the force of it and a fan of blood sprayed out. He seemed to be coming to. He moaned softly. I don't know if anyone could have understood what he was trying to say but I couldn't even listen. Maybe he was calling for his mother, or Melissa, or someone else who loved him, or maybe he was saying something disjointed and incomprehensible as sleepers sometimes do, but I suspected he was cursing me.

"What should we do?" cried Melissa.

Tracy and I were silent. Tommy's eyes struggled to open again but soon the trembling stopped and he was still. There was simply nothing in our power to do. We couldn't even make him comfortable. We were afraid to move him, afraid to touch him. I tore the sheet off the bed and dabbed at the blood on the side of his head. It appeared to be stopping on its own. His face was pale, the lightest imaginable shade of blue. His breathing was slowing down.

"What should we do?" said Melissa, on her knees, staring at Tommy. "We're not doing anything."

I thought she was about to shake him, as if all he needed were bringing to. As soon as her hands moved toward him, I impulsively grabbed them. As I touched her hands she went completely out of her mind.

Melissa begged to be relieved of the sight of me so I went downstairs and sat on the couch. A small dark pink fire burned in the hearth. I was too terrified to think.

I went into the dining room. Its one window revealed a shifting curtain of snow. Then to the kitchen. I paced around, looked out the window, opened the refrigerator. Then I went down to the basement.

My heart was pounding. The concrete floor felt like mud beneath my feet. Every time I blinked I saw a flash of Tommy falling to his knees. Just to his knees. I picked up an oar and slammed it against the worktable, exploding trays of screws and nails. Finally, I rested my head against the hot water heater and waited for my nerves to unfurl enough so I might weep.

When I got back to the front room, I could hear Tracy coming down the stairs. I pressed the heels of my hands against my face, hoping to hide the fact that I'd been crying: I was obscurely afraid that any evidence of remorse would be interpreted as a plea for forgiveness.

"Well, how is he?" I asked.

She stood in front of the dying fire, her body shaking. One of her hands had a little smear of blood on it. I looked at mine: nothing.

"He's not coming to," she said.

"Jesus," I said. I tried to formulate my next question.

"He feels so cold, Virgil."

"I think I should go up."

"What are we going to do? I feel so stupid."

"I don't know. I don't know what to do."

"What happened up there, Virgil?"

There was something in her tone that horrified me —she seemed somewhat incredulous.

"It was an accident," I said. "He moved toward me just as I was swinging the poker."

"I guess he's in a coma. I don't know if we're supposed to keep him warm, or try to give him water. I don't know."

"If he's unconscious he'd probably choke on anything we gave him," I said.

Tracy put her head on the mantel and let out a small cry. Her eyes were open and the sharp points of light from the fire were reflected in them. I took her hand and pressed it to my lips. The faint heat of the fire touched one half of our bodies, emphasizing the chill on the unheated halves. I didn't know what to say to her; I didn't know what she felt about being touched by me. All I wanted was to hold on to her.

"I think he's going to die," she said. "He's going to die right here and there's nothing we can do about it."

"We have to get to town," I said.

I waited downstairs while Tracy told Melissa we were going to try to make it to Gardner Point, or anywhere we could to find someone to help us. I didn't know what our chances of making it to town were but I knew that after dark it would be hopeless, and I figured it to be about noon. By four, the sky would be asphalt. Still, there was no reason to trust that anything would happen in any particular order: perhaps the sun would sink at noon, maybe it would set for days. I didn't know exactly what had happened to my life but my unyielding heart was beginning to accept the horrifying proposition that *anything* could happen.

My nose was running, my head felt petrified. I lay back on the couch and the upholstery scratched my unshaven face. Beneath my clothes I itched. My bones ached. Encased in the chill that dominated me was a small hot pulse of fever.

I don't think I believed for a minute that we would make it to town. It just didn't seem possible that we could walk miles through the snow. And even if we did miraculously arrive at some safe haven I didn't think anything would save Tommy's life.

Finally, Tracy came down.

"Melissa wants to stay here," she said.

"I suppose that's the best thing," I said, standing up. I felt disgraced to have been seen lying down. "Well," I said, "are you ready? Are you up for it?"

"I think we'd better hurry," said Tracy, not moving. She looked sick and terrified. She had her boots on. The zipper was broken on the left one: halfway up there was a stretched oblong space where her jeans had burst through.

"How does he seem?" I asked.

"I don't know. He's out of it."

"Is he bleeding?"

She shook her head. She was looking in my direction but not really *at* me.

"There's no good reason why we both have to go," I said. "If two can make it then one can. And if one can't then two couldn't."

"What?" she said.

"I'll go alone," I said.

We argued for a minute but I could see from the start that she would agree. Her eyes were bright with fever; when she took a deep breath you could hear little clicks and burrs. "If you can only get to the road," she said.

"There's bound to be people up and around by now," I said.

"Do you think you can get the car started?"

"I don't know." I was about to say that Tommy had said he could get it going but I didn't dare say his name.

I put on boots, two sweaters, my coat, two scarves, and tied a shirt around my face to protect it. I waddled to the back of the house, flexing my arms, trying to move my blood, feeling stupid and incompetent. I didn't think I'd get very far but I felt compelled to try. Tracy and I kicked at the back door until enough snow had moved for me to slip out. Just as I felt that first layer of bitter freezing wind, beating against me like the wings of a huge bird, I turned around to nod good-bye to Tracy and saw that Melissa was in the kitchen. She'd come to see me off and I waited for a moment, in case she wanted to say something. But all she did was stare, with all of her hatred and all of her pleading.

I moved away from the house; the door closed behind me; my heart seemed to contract with sheer dread. It was not the sort of reckless gesture I was equipped to make; had I merely been asked to parachute from an airplane I could have bullied my legs into propelling me out of the plane. But now I had to gather all my will and bravery for each step—there was always time to turn back and no such thing as a point of no return. I was in snow up to my thighs. I could hardly move. The snow soaked through my pants and then through my boots. I hoped that soon I would reach a point after which I could become no colder but as I stood in the gathered tons of untouched snow, in the dim light that seeped from the low-slung sky, with the wind coming from every direction, my body's temperature seemed to halve with every heartbeat. I did not so much walk as throw myself forward. I fell. I sank into the stuff, took a mouthful of it. I was still a good ten yards from my car and the closer I got to it the more obvious it became that I'd be lucky to even get *in*, much less start it. And even if it were to start, where could it go?

Still, it was a destination and I threw myself toward that car. I wondered if I was being watched from the house, but I couldn't see a face in any window. I couldn't see anything.

My clothes were soaked. Snow was packed in my

ears. It clung to my hair, my eyelashes. It fell down my back and soaked through my sweaters.

I wondered how Tommy had made the walk from his car to the house. I remembered how he had exploded into our house, how the cold had poured off him in waves, how he had grabbed me to keep from falling. I'd held him, my grip was certain. Yet when it was time to grab again I missed. I'd closed my fingers on air as he fell backward; his head bounced a little as it hit the floor.

I finally made it to the frozen Mercedes. Using my arms, I pushed snow off the windshield. Continents of snow broke off; thick white spray caught the wind and flew into my face. My coat was solidly white. Snow dropped into my gloves and the cold on the heel of my hand felt like teeth, digging deeper and deeper. I cleared one-half of the windshield. There was no sight of glass, just an opaque layer of bumpy ice. I plunged my hands through the snow on the side of the car, feeling for the door handle. I stood thigh deep in a convulsion of white. Slowly, I began to feel less cold— it meant I was beginning to numb over, but I was grateful. After some undeterminable amount of time, I'd pushed away enough snow to see the door handle. I shoved my thick clumsy hand into it, pressed the button and pulled. Frozen. I pulled harder. I felt a sharp hot pain, like a guitar string being tightened around my chest. One more, I promised myself. The door opened a quarter inch. I pulled again and there was room to crawl in.

I sat at the wheel. The light in the car was a thick, undifferentiated gray. It was a relief to be out of the snow but there was something crushing about being in that car; it was a cave, a trap, a church on the moon. I pulled off my gloves so I could dig the car keys out of my pocket. My hands were bright white, like hands held in front of a thousand-watt bulb. I moaned miserably as I shoved my fingers into my pants, gritted my aching teeth as I fished for the keys. Got them. Pushed them into the ignition. Took a deep breath. I put my hands on the steering wheel to steady myself. The clouds of exhaust from my nose and mouth were only wisps now, and I realized that the difference between my body's temperature and the air's had been narrowed. I stared ahead of me as the dull opaque shine of the icy windshield grew slowly darker, as new snow replaced what I'd brushed away. What if I were to be frozen in that car? The fantasy of suffocation sucked the air from my lungs: I saw spots, my head pounded.

I stamped my foot on the gas pedal and turned the ignition. If the motor made a slight noise, I couldn't hear it over the wind. I tried a couple of times but it was useless and senseless: what if the motor started? Then what? Where would I go? I'd somehow operated on the assumption that I could generate enough power to blast out of the snow, to get the car going a hundred miles per, and shoot out across our estate like an arrow.

But the car could not make it and neither could I. I switched off the ignition and rested my head on the steering wheel. I knew I could not go another step away from the house. It simply was not in me and I didn't see how it could possibly do any good. If there were any real possibility of my making it to town, or even making it as far as the public road—then what? What would I have done? If there had been one chance in fifty, one in twenty, or even one in ten, would I have taken it? I couldn't go further away from the house but I couldn't face going back, either. I didn't want to just sit there while Tommy slowly died. I didn't want him to hang on for hours and hours and then die. And then have it be implicitly understood that had I gotten help he could have been saved. I didn't want to be any more a part of his death than I already was. I kicked my way out of the car thinking that the best thing, if I was not to go insane, would be if Tommy were already dead by the time I got back.

16

FOR A WHILE, the house felt warm. I'd half collapsed a few feet from the door but Tracy, who'd been watching all along, pulled me in. I sat exhausted on the kitchen floor as she helped me strip out of my soaking clothes.

"I couldn't make it," I said, after a period of gasping speechlessness. "I couldn't see. It would have been suicide."

"I know. I was praying you'd turn around." She looked up at me. She was crying.

"How is he?"

"I can't tell."

"But he's alive?"

"Yes."

"Well, thank God." I didn't know what I meant: I overheard myself, trying to gather clues from what I said.

"The car wouldn't start," I said. Tracy pulled my

socks off and rubbed my feet. "I'm not that bad," I said. "I can get up."

"You better relax."

"It's warm in here. My face itches."

"Maybe I should go outside. I'd like to feel warm."

"Even if I'd started it there was no place to go."

"I know."

"Where's Melissa?"

"I'm here," she said, standing in the entrance to the kitchen. She hugged herself tightly; her lips were blue, her hair berserk. "Would you please come upstairs? Something's wrong." Her voice was thin, but essentially calm.

I was in my underwear, though Tracy had thrown a blanket around me. The house no longer felt warm and bumps the size of marbles began to rise from my skin. "What's wrong?" I asked, though I was certain Tommy had taken a silent turn for the worse.

She answered furiously: "I don't know."

Tracy was at her side in a moment. "Come on," she said. "Let's go."

Before they left, Melissa looked at me and said, "Did you decide not to try?"

A few minutes later I went upstairs to Tommy's room. I don't know what I expected to see. That long narrow body covered with a sheet? Or did I think I'd see him sitting on the edge of the bed, dabbing at his wound with a wad of cotton, smiling and shaking his head? All I can fully remember is that when I walked up the stairs I saw a long pale cloud of breath floating from me and I was glad that I was finally warming up.

Tommy had come to, but only barely. His eyes were half open and he'd bent his right leg a little. Melissa hovered over him, her hair tucked behind her ear, which was turned toward him, for she expected him to say something. Tracy touched his wound, which had begun to run again, with the edge of a pillowcase. Slowly, Tommy lowered his right leg until it was flat on the floor again. Then he began to bend it again but this time he could only raise it an inch or two before it fell, flat and lifeless. I couldn't tell if his body was shaking or if its image was trembling on the surface of my hot, wet eyes. I blinked and looked away: the room was lethally stationary.

"He wants you out of here," said Melissa. "Get out. You don't belong here. Get out."

I backed out of the room. At the time, I thought that Tommy had murmured his request to Melissa but now I no longer know.

I found hard, cold, but dry clothes, dressed, and went downstairs. The sun was sinking fast, though I really couldn't be certain. It was definitely growing darker but such things as sunsets had been one of the facts of my former life. Now, for all I knew, the light diminished because the earth had swung out of its orbit: there was nothing I could be certain of. Well, it's getting dark. My voice boomed in my ears: was I talking to myself?

All of us were sick. I coughed so hard it felt as if I were being stabbed. Earlier that day, Tracy said she'd been sneezing so wildly she was afraid her eyes would pop out. When had she said that?

I sat on the couch, suddenly longing for someone to talk to. My mind moved quickly from one thing to the next, like a sewing machine running at a thousand times its normal speed. I needed something to do. I got up and kicked the wood into the fireplace. Then I ripped up a paperback book and dropped the pages into the hearth. I felt the world retreating from me, like scenery being moved on little caster wheels. When it was gone, what would there be?

There are some people who seem to know a great deal about dying and death, but I was not one of them. Most of the death in my life had been notional. My mother's imaginary funeral: a waxen angel surrounded by flowers, the minister biting his lip at her grave and me sobbing, running past the flashing tombstones. Or

Earl: the times I'd come home from school and, not hearing him at the keys, thinking he was dead, that I would find him at the piano, slumped over, a revolver smoking on the highest octave. In the subject of real, unalterable death, however, I was a novice, a child. I'd been to my grandfather's funeral but they'd kept the coffin closed. In Amsterdam I saw, from a block's distance, an old man run down by a streetcar but by the time I reached the spot there was a crowd around him. I couldn't see. Didn't want to. I had looked at the newsreels of Asians we'd murdered, the bodies in ditches, fathers holding dead children, the rain slanting through the bamboo trees. I watched, like everyone. But the deaths were as distant as they were numberless.

Now death pressed its hands against the windows of my house, and I had brought it there. For the first time, death was truly with me and it seemed then that it was everything, the air we breathed, the ground we stood upon.

I knew he was going to die, but even if he didn't I had ruined him. He'd be an idiot, deaf, paralyzed. I longer for a deeper sense of his life: I wanted to know more fully what I'd done, exactly which precious, unduplicatable structure I had cracked. I looked at my hands, somehow expecting them to give evidence. I remembered the feeling when the poker hit him, how the swing stopped short, the little jolt that reverberated through my wrists, my shoulders, that instantaneous flicker of annoyance followed by a practically complete realization of what had happened, what had happened to Tommy, what I'd done.

How I yearned for company. I wanted to go upstairs but I couldn't face the possibility of being asked to leave.

I called up. "Whenever you're ready, I've got wood for a fire. Okay?" I screamed. "Okay?" There was no answer.

* * *

Tommy slipped back into a coma; his eyes closed and his body seemed brittle and vulnerable beneath the blankets we piled on him.

I went to our bedroom and waited for Tracy. She stayed with Melissa and Tommy for a while but when Melissa fell asleep Tracy came to our room. I lay in bed, shivering, with one cover over me. "Any change?" I asked, afraid to look at her directly.

"No." She got into bed and looked at the ceiling. "I'm losing track of everything," she said. "Melissa's going nuts in there. She's eaten all her pills and they haven't done anything. I'm afraid to close my eyes. Every time I even blink I feel I'm falling. I just wish she'd shut up. She's asking me questions. I don't know anything. I'm so selfish. I can't stand her anymore. I can't help it."

"You're not selfish."

"I don't know. The ground moves beneath my feet when I walk. I feel dizzy all the time."

"Me too," I said. "I do too." I took her hand. "I wish you didn't have to be with her all the time." I paused. "I mean I wish I didn't have to be completely alone so much of the time."

"There's no choice. She's bad enough. She can't face you."

"I know. But I'm down there completely alone."

"It's hard for me, too, you know."

"Probably it's harder for you than for anyone. Whatever this is going to mean to Melissa is going to take a long time to happen. She holds on to you the way I'd like to."

"Why me?"

I new the answer: because there was something competent, steady, and unflappable in Tracy and we wanted to grab it. Her hard body, even in its weakened, terrified state, radiated a kind of certainty, an eternity, or a sense of eternity. It was beautiful and it made you feel better to be near it. "Because you're great," I said.

"How are you, really," she asked, and rolled over; with the instinct of a priest, she wanted me to speak to a faceless intelligence.

"I don't know." I felt sick to my stomach. "I'm waiting, I suppose. To see what happens to Tommy. Waiting to get out of here. I'm going out of my mind, really. But not enough. It would be better to be completely insane until we got out of here, to get drunk, take LSD. Do you think I could have made it to town if I'd tried harder? Tell me the truth."

"I feel like a fool for letting you try."

I listened to the wind; it seemed to be racing around and around the house, screaming at every corner. "Thank you," I said. I held her hand more tightly. What I wanted, but didn't dare, was to pull her close to me, to press myself against her. I wanted to weep in her arms. I wanted to explode in front of her. I pressed her hand to my lips. It smelled of smoke and tasted of salt and blood.

We fell asleep. I woke for a moment, stiff with panic: I didn't have it in me to spend a sleepless night. I didn't want to be alone with my mind and all that was in its power to conjure: ghosts, faces, the image of Tommy falling to one knee. The middle of the night loomed before me like enemy territory. I begged to be asleep before I reached that bristling hostile midpoint of darkness.

I closed my eyes but instead of that thick cold blackness I'd come to expect, I saw a faint rose color, with dancing, floating bubbles of white. I opened my eyes. There, above me, hanging from a chain, was the tulip-shaped light bulb, long gray, but now bright yellow. I stared at it uncomprehendingly until I realized what it meant: the electricity was on again.

I went downstairs and turned the lights on, every one of them. I wanted that house to blaze in the night, in case anyone passed overhead. My breath flowed silver as I leaned over the long-sleeping lamps.

I looked out the window. Moonlight. That pale copper disc sailed across the low sky, brighter than the sun had been in days. The snow was still falling but it was coming softly now, you could see through it, far into our land, past the cars, into the thickness of trees. I knew the storm was ending. The whole area was recovering from it. The road crews were out. Tomorrow, some of the stores might open again.

I went upstairs and awakened Tracy. "The lights are on," I whispered in her ear.

She opened her eyes and then covered them.

"And the snow's almost stopped," I said. My voice sounded stupidly happy. "The moon's out," I whispered.

She nodded.

I sat next to her and took her in my arms. Clearly, there was to be no celebration.

"What do we do now?" she said.

"I've got all the lights on. If someone sees them . . ."

"Do you think that'll happen?"

"Maybe if I can find the clip to Tommy's gun. I'll fire it. Maybe someone will hear it."

"Do you think it's too late?"

"I don't know."

"I mean for Tommy."

"I know what you mean. I don't know."

"Well, it's not too late for us, is it?" She got out of bed. Her legs were weak and she stumbled. She sat on the edge of the bed and dropped her head into her hands.

"I think you should go and ask Melissa where the clip is," I said.

"Okay." She got up slowly. She'd become a little afraid of Melissa. I think she couldn't bear to be with her, knowing Melissa thought that I'd deliberately struck Tommy.

I waited while Tracy spoke to Melissa. I wondered if

the local hospital was properly equipped. I went to the window and scraped a portion of frost away. The moon was lower, the sky a little paler. There were two or three distant stars. I felt a nearly overwhelming desire to weep but I couldn't permit it. I stood with my head against the icy glass, my hands balled into fists so tight that when I tried to open them I had to go slowly.

Finally, Tracy stood in the doorway, her face bright red. She said my name and then waited for me to turn around. "Tommy's dead," she said.

As she said it, I could hear Melissa weeping in the other room.

By dawn, the snow had stopped completely. There was even a sunrise of sorts: a violet and red smear in the east that colored the ocean of snow around us.

I was downstairs, trying to read one of Cleveland Page's old mysteries. The heat was on again, but it could not warm the house. Tracy and Melissa were in what had been my bedroom. Tommy was alone.

I went upstairs to make my apologies to his staring remains. I stood over him, my heart beating in my throat. He looked no different from the way he had when he was in the coma. I put my fingers beneath his nostrils and waited for a feather touch of breath, but of course none came. The covers were off him now. His sweater was bunched at the chest, where Melissa had clutched at it.

I heard a high, sharp scream coming from the other bedroom and quickly straightened up. It was Melissa. "I can't stand it," she shrieked. She called on God, she called for Tommy, she said things that only an expert in wild human misery could interpret. I wanted to burst in and comfort her—I wanted to lay just one finger on her shoulder—but I didn't dare.

I knocked on the door. I just wanted to find out if she knew where the clip was. The door wasn't properly closed and it swung open. Tracy sat on the edge of the bed. The lights were out but there was some sun and the window blazed opaquely. Melissa was sobbing, choking. She lay face down on the bed while Tracy smoothed her hair. Melissa looked up at me. Her hands were on her face and when she removed them I saw long translucent welts.

"I'm sorry," I said.

"You killed him," said Melissa. She sounded calmer than she looked.

I shook my head. I didn't want to intrude on her grief with my own unstable testimony. All I wanted was the clip.

"Get out of here. Please."

"Melissa, it was an accident," Tracy said.

"It was no accident," she said. "You know it."

"If I can find the clip to the rifle, maybe I can attract some attention," I said, already backing out of the room.

"Get out of here," she said, her voice shaking. She grabbed at Tracy's shoulder. "Please. Make him leave. I can't stand it."

I searched the house. It was good to have something to do. I first looked in Tommy's room, but couldn't find it. Then the bathroom, and living room, the dining room, the kitchen. It took a long time and I wanted it to. The limits of the task calmed me. Finally, I went to the cellar and turned on the light. I found the clip in the second place I looked. It was stuffed into some rags and shoved under the icy hot water heater.

I went to Tommy's room, grabbed the gun, and put the clip in. Tracy heard me and came in to see how I was.

"You found it," she said.

"In the cellar. This is our telephone." I raised the rifle.

"Be careful of that," she said, shrinking back.

"Don't worry. I'm careful. Christ."

The door to the other bedroom opened and Melissa emerged. She peered in at us and then, taking a deep

breath for courage, came in. Mucus glazed her upper
lip; her hot blue eyes seemed covered by spun sugar.

"What are you doing with his gun?" she asked,
glancing at Tommy's body and then quickly away from
it.

"I'm going to get us out of here."

"Where?"

"Into town. There's a chance."

"Oh." She nodded, staring at the gun. "May I see
that?"

"What for?"

"I'd like to. It was his." She extended her hand.

She wants to kill me, I thought. "Why?" I said. "So
you can kill me?"

"I've never hurt anyone in my whole life," Melissa
said. "I don't hurt people." She stepped quickly forward and grabbed for the gun. I pulled it back and she
reached for it again, catching my sleeve. "It's his gun,"
she said.

"Will you please take her in hand?" I said to Tracy.

"Come on, let's go down and get a fire going,"
Tracy said to Melissa.

Melissa stepped back for a moment and then, just
as I relaxed a little, she pounced on me. Her small
reddened hand wrapped around the thin barrel and
she squeezed it so hard the cracks in her hand turned
dead white. My bowels turned to water. It was not
difficult to imagine the gun accidentally firing, or Melissa folding to the bloody floor, her corpse crossing
Tommy's. Was the safety on? I grabbed for the barrel
of the gun and pulled. I fully expected to be twice as
strong as she but her grip was fierce and as I yanked
the gun I could not unloosen it: I pulled her closer to
me. We sent gusts of foul empty breath into each
other's faces. She bit her lower lip and closed her eyes
and pulled. I drew her close to me and told her to let
go of it. Tracy screamed at her to let go. But her eyes
were closed, her face blank, and she had no intention
of relinquishing it, of ever relinquishing anything. I

strengthened the grip of my left hand and released the right to hit her across the face. I only wanted to bring her to her senses, or to shock her into letting go. She didn't appear to respond at all to the blow. I hit her again, and a third time, a fourth, this time with my hand half closed. Finally, she let go, cried out in pain, frustration, and grief, and raced out of the room. My hand felt as if it were on fire. I stared at it, opened and closed it. How hard had I hit her? I looked up. Tracy was still there.

"I had to do that," I said.

I waited in the kitchen for a sign from the sky. Once I heard a faint hum but I couldn't see anything flying from either side of the house. Still the hum persisted. I covered my ears and it was louder.

The sun moved lower and dark blue shadows slid across the snow. It would be unendurable to spend another night in that house.

I couldn't wait any longer. I forced the back door open and fired the gun into the air. I fired three times. Waited. Fired twice and then one more time. I had no idea how many shots I had and I was terrified of running out.

I waited for an answer.

Tracy and Melissa were upstairs. I thought about telling them that I'd fired the shots but, of course, they had heard them.

The sun sank lower, dragging the temperature with it.

I have no idea how much time went by. It seemed like days. At one point, I looked out and it was dark. The house was bright, icy and glaring.

I sat down. I felt somehow compelled to make some sense out of everything that had happened. My hand still hurt from hitting Melissa. I could still hear the shots I'd fired into the air. And whenever I closed my eyes I would see Tommy, falling. But I didn't want to think about any of that. Instead, I thought about a

pensione I had stayed in in Rome, with a laundry-
decked courtyard. I'd bought a bottle of Ritalin and
read H. G. Wells. That had been delightful. It was also
to that pensione that I'd brought the first and only girl
I'd ever picked up out of nowhere, an American girl
named Diane, who'd told me she'd been molested in
Turkey and hoped that whatever happened between us
would help put that behind her.

Finally, I heard a distant hum. This was it. It was
exactly the sound I'd heard when the helicopter came
over before. I wasn't surprised. I would have been surprised had it not come. This was only fair.

I continued to stare out, waiting for the sight of the
helicopter. There. Maybe a mile off. It was close to the
ground, its propeller a black blur. It had a searchlight
in the cockpit, an enormous golden globe that poured
out an almost edible stream of light. Should I fire a
shot to let them know we're here? No longer necessary. Every light in the house was on. I pointed the gun
down and fired six shots into a drift. The spotlight
lifted until it shone directly on the house. My eyes
were wet. I shielded them from the glare and soon
after that I held my ears against the roar of the motor
and the incessant, joyful beating of the blades as the
helicopter hovered dreamily before me and then set
down a hundred feet from the house.

Two men in orange snowsuits jumped out and simply
took control of our spluttering, fragmented lives.
There was no time for questions, no time for tears or
accusations, not a moment for anyone to fall down and
thank God they'd been saved. We were immediately
overpowered by their direct functional energy. We
were told to move quickly, to take whatever we could
carry with us. Tracy ran upstairs to pack a bag. The
younger of the two men in orange looked at his watch
while the older stamped the snow off his big shiny
boots.

"Does anyone need help getting out to the helicopter?" asked the younger of the two. "We've got a medic with us."

"There's a dead person here," said Melissa, in a cold offhand fashion.

"There was an accident," I explained. I leaned toward the open door; the beating of the propeller pulled at me.

"It was no accident," said Melissa.

"All right, let's go," said the older of the two. He had a full beard and blinked rapidly as he spoke. Then, to his friend, he said, "Goddamned storm. That's three dead so far."

"So far," said his friend.

The bearded man pulled a flashlight out of his side pocket and blinked it three times toward the helicopter. A few moments later, the medic, dressed in white with a green cross on his armband, came in holding a folded-up stretcher.

"I'll help bring him down," I said.

"Just take us to him," said the fellow with the beard.

I brought them upstairs. We lifted Tommy onto the stretcher and then strapped him in. I tried to help but the two of them were far more adept than I was. I managed to cinch the belt around Tommy's unmoving chest, but that was the extent of my usefulness.

Tracy and Melissa followed the men outside when we got back downstairs. As I closed the door to leave, I thought I might turn off the lights but it seemed a terribly wrong thing to do. The two men in orange moved efficiently through the snow, and it was all I could do to keep pace. The spinning helicopter blade whipped snow into our faces and a little flurry was beginning to fall. Tommy was covered with a blanket but I could still see the impression of his lifeless face, the long nose that created a gentle rise in the stiff wool covering, the sudden, heart-stopping hollow of his eyes. I caught my breath and looked up. The moon floated uncertainly above as the clouds that were soon to obscure it began to glide across its distant face.

The helicopter had been designed for medical emergencies. Although the two men from the rescue squad still held the stretcher, I grabbed a side and tried to help them carry Tommy up the ridged metal ramp that led to the helicopter's sliding door. Inside, it smelled like a hospital. There were oxygen, two cots, bottles of clear fluid medicine.

There were seats built into the sides and I sat next to Tracy. The medic gave us each a small thermos bottle of broth and then went back to Melissa, who needed him more. He fed her brandy out of a spoon. She was staring, she seemed to be jut staring into space, but how I dreaded that electric gaze falling on me.

The pitch of the motor rose an octave, and then another. The blade whipped up more snow. The helicopter quivered. Everything quivered. We were airborne. Then, suddenly, a cross-current caught us. The helicopter shook and buzzed and didn't seem to be gaining altitude. It gave a sudden bump and Tracy gasped; she grabbed hold of me but quickly let go. It was far too overpoweringly noisy to speak.

Finally, we began to rise steadily and my only clear thought was that I was being rescued too soon. I felt a sudden surge of panic. There was something in that house that I'd left undone, something I was leaving behind that I couldn't afford to be without. Somewhere I had misplaced the sense of what I'd done. Maybe I'd never had it, but I was certain I was leaving without it. Suddenly, it didn't seem like being rescued at all. It was an interruption. I felt as if I were being abducted from my fate. And where could anyone possibly take me where I'd be safe?

I turned in my seat and looked out of the side of the helicopter. With the lights on, Preservation Hall looked warm, inviting. Its bright golden windows seemed to offer solace to the wilderness. Tommy's body was on the floor, up near the front of the helicopter. The two fellows in orange were talking to each other. How could they hear over the noise? Melissa was crying now. The medic tried to give her more brandy but she wouldn't swallow it. She was trying to tell him something and I think it was about me. Tracy had her boots off and rubbed her toes. The only light in the helicopter was from the small electric heaters on the floor. I turned again for a last glimpse of the house but we'd made a change in our direction and it was no longer visible. Replacing it was the night, intersected by the snow, millions of dotted lines.

FOUR

17

WE LANDED on the snowy lawn of a ranch-style hospital called Bailey Memorial Hospital and, against our wishes, we were carried in on stretchers. Tracy and Melissa were taken in first and then they came back for Tommy and me. There were spotlights at the entrance of the hospital, the kind that some people in the suburbs will put on their lawns. These lights pointed to a large wooden thermometer that stood in the snow. There was a red line painted halfway up the thermometer, endng at a line that corresponded to the figure $35,000. The top of the sign was covered by snow but I figured the display must have been part of a fund-raising campaign.

As I was carried into the hospital—past the emergency room, through the bright, cluttered lobby, with the ceiling racing past me—I saw two orderlies taking Tracy down a corridor to the left, while I was taken to a room down the right corridor. It was a small yellow room, with a hot unshielded bulb in the overhead light. I was carefully placed in what felt like the most comfortable bed in existence. As I touched that bed, I knew I was physically out of Preservation Hall.

The hospital was busy and while the staff seemed cheerful, if you listened you could tell that most of them were in a kind of frenzy. I was in a room that had been built as a private chamber but they'd squeezed two beds into it, with no more than six inches separating them. I shared the room with an old man who glared at everyone, as if to prove he'd been rescued against his will. Later I was told by a nurse that he was an "actual hermit." He'd been there for several hours before I was brought in and since there was nothing particularly wrong with him he was restive. When I was put into bed, he snarled at the orderlies that he wanted to go home. One of the orderlies, a young Indian boy who wore a thin turquoise bracelet, said, "You can't even get to that old trailer and you know it. You know you can't leave until Dr. Martin looks you over. Same as last year."

"So where is that loony bastard?" said the hermit, flashing his yellow teeth.

"He'll be around. We got some messed-up people here."

I didn't have it in me to make detailed inquiries about Tracy. I was told she was in the left wing of the hospital, where most of the women were being treated. I was given a paper gown and a pair of paper slippers but what I found I wanted even more than food was a bath. They told me I'd have to wait for that but the nurse who brought in a tray of food also brought me a metal bowl of steamy water, a little wrapped cake of soap, a mirror, and a razor.

I ate the tasteless food and got as clean as I could. Then I lay back, coughing, aching, and slowly coming back to life. I was seized with a quick fit of yearning to see Tracy, to know how she was, but I was slipping away. I touched my shaved cheek to the pillow and was instantly asleep.

I slept deeply and dreamed ceaselessly, but the dreams could barely stir me. I dreamed that my father and Melissa visited me in a small room, where I sat with a cat on my knee. I dreamed that I'd been given several parking tickets. I woke in the middle of the night to see two orderlies and a doctor gently place an old, enormous man on the bed next to mine. The hermit was gone. This case looked more serious. The man's hands and face were bandaged and he was moaning. I tried to sit up. I felt feverish, yet insulated from my discomfort by the luxury of a bed and warmth. I woke again later, this time from a dream of Tommy sitting in our New York apartment with a glass of snow in his hands. It was still night. The man in the next bed slept calmly, his great stomach swelling with every breath.

I was up near dawn the next morning. Feeling naked and absurd in my paper gown and slippers, I shuffled down the hall to go to the bathroom where I used the sink to wash more of my body. I looked in the mirror. I'd lost about ten pounds and had cut my chin to ribbons while shaving. There were little spots of blood around the collar of my gown.

The hospital corridors were quiet. From a distance I heard kitchen noises and two women laughing. A nurse sat in a folding chair; she seemed to be dozing. Everything seemed so remarkably clean! The cool marble floor, the bright white walls, the very shoes and stockings on the sleeping nurse's outstretched legs. I walked past her, hoping to find Tracy. I went to the center of the floor I was on and entered the corridor they had taken her down. I peeked into the first room I found: two women, both sleeping, one with a bottle of plasma hanging over her. Good: the women's section. I peered into the next room: three women. Two were sleeping and one was on her side, her eyes tightly closed, receiving an injection from a nurse. I closed the door quickly. When I turned around, I faced another nurse, a small woman with copper-colored hair wrapped in pigtails around her perfectly round head.

"I'm looking for my wife," I said, wondering if she thought I was a trouble-maker.

"We don't allow—" she began to say.

"We were both brought here by helicopter yesterday. I haven't seen her since." My voice sounded stricken.

"That's all right. Which one is she?"

"Tracy Morgan."

"Okay. I'll tell her you tried to visit. I'm sure she'll be glad to know." The small woman took my arm with her freckled, incredibly strong hand and led me away. "But we don't want to wake anyone. We'll let everyone sleep to their little heart's content. Okay?"

A little later, I was examined by Dr. Martin, a fortyish man with one of those stand-up bristling haircuts and the beginnings of jowls. He looked as if he'd once played football; not only was he huge but his hands and chin were covered with little white scars and his nose traveled toward you in such an idiosyncratic route that you knew it had been broken a dozen times. He sat on the edge of my bed and seemed half asleep. He listened to my heart and my breathing, looked into my eyes and ears, took my temperature and asked me how I felt. I asked him if I could visit my wife and he said of course I could but he didn't know exactly when and he didn't even know where she was. "She's in the other wing, right?" he said, as if that were in a different country. Then he got up, told me I had a slight fever and said he'd try to get back in a short while to see how I was holding.

In the middle of the morning, Tracy came into my room. She wore a robe she'd brought along with her and paper slippers; she looked shining clean, and smelled of cheap pink soap.

"Are you all right?" she said, sitting on the edge of my bed.

"I tried to see you."

"I know. The nurse told me." She took my hand and held it. I sat up and swallowed; there was a metallic taste in my mouth and I felt inexpressibly nervous about breathing in her face.

"Are you feeling all right?" I asked.

"Okay. You?"

"I'm okay. How's your room?"

"It's okay. Do you know where Melissa is?"

"No." There was silence. I heard the squeaking wheels of a cart rolling by in the hall. "I guess we can leave anytime," I said.

"This afternoon." Her voice broke and she turned away from me. "Are you really feeling all right?" she asked, looking at my neighbor in the next bed, who still slept soundly.

"I miss you. I don't know. I don't think I quite know where I am yet."

"I don't either," said Tracy. She gripped my hand and raised it to her cheek. I felt something wet and warm fall onto my wrist and it was only then that I fully realized Tracy hadn't come to visit. She'd come to mourn.

I held her close and she burrowed into me. Her tears soaked through the side of my paper gown. She barely made a sound but her body shook and writhed. A queasy coldness spread through me. I feared there was only one real mourner in that bed and I was merely a survivor. Aren't we all born with equal shares of sorrow? Where, then, was mine? Tracy's poured out of her naturally; after a few moments at my side, she seemed not so much to weep for Tommy, or for Tommy and Melissa, or even for the four of us and the shambles we'd made of our lives in that house. She seemed transported by her grief until she was every person who had ever lived weeping for every other person who had ever lived. And where was mine? Just at the time when I should have been baptizing myself in sorrow for what had happened, what I'd done, I found myself staring in terror at the ceiling, sick with the insufficiency of what I felt. Even with Tracy's hand clutching me, and her hot tears burning at my side, my sense of what had happened to us remained elusive. I could not touch it. It floated within me. It hovered maddeningly over what I can only call my mortal soul, but it had no place to land.

Melissa, in virtual solitary confinement, wasn't taken seriously by the hospital staff. It was assumed that everything she said was forced through the prism of madness and her constant demand to see the police was met with only squeamish tolerance. But she persisted; she even grabbed a nurse and spat her request into that terrified woman's face—further convincing them that she was mad. But when the police finally showed up and told the hospital administrators that they wanted to talk to the people who knew something about the circumstances of Tommy's death, it was to Melissa that the police were escorted and it was in that room, which Melissa shared with no one, that room with its dizzy odor of grief and persecution, that Melissa told the police that I had murdered Tom Douglas.

The guys in the rescue helicopter were half insensate with exhaustion and all they'd been interested in was getting us out and continuing on their rounds. When I dared think about it, I realized that the unquestioning acceptance of Tommy's death by the hospital personnel was not a promise of continued immunity, and while I did not think this directly, I don't think I wanted the matter to be simply dropped: there was no comfort in that. I felt that the law was working its way toward me and that that could only be for the best. I wanted to have my story questioned, scrutinized with the kind of acrimonious manner I could not quite summon from myself. I wanted to be forced into a corner so I might come out swinging. I wanted to describe how the blow had been landed and I wanted someone who reeked of cigar smoke to lean toward me and say, "Now, just how is that possible?

You must have known where he was standing. There is no way you could not have known." Did I have an answer for that? I wasn't certain but I had to trust that somewhere within me, the answer ran through my befuddled memory, like a vein of crystal in a stone. "You must have been quite upset," my ghostly interrogator would say and I could say that indeed I was. "Then you liked him?" What does that have to do with it? "Then you didn't like him?" I did, I didn't, I didn't, I did. It's not the point. It doesn't matter. "I wouldn't be so sure." Look, something incredible happened, something fierce and unexplainable. I burst into someone's life and wrecked it; I cracked the shell that separates us from Nothing. "But you wished he'd die, isn't that true?" Only to relieve his suffering. "Not true." You don't know. No one knows even what they themselves wish; our desires come at us from behind, dressed in outrageous disguises.

The cop who came to see me was Lieutenant Munt, a man in his late thirties, dressed in gray. He had flat, reddish eyes, like a Weimaraner, and a belly that looked perilous and unnatural on his small-boned frame. He wore a thick gray wool tie clipped to his shirt with a silver clasp in the shape of a sailfish. With him was a younger cop, dressed in uniform, who carried a stenographer's pad.

"Hello there. Mr. Morgan?" said Munt. He had a drifting, reedy voice: he reminded me of my Uncle Duncan, my father's only brother, who sold vitamins in Baltimore.

Two orderlies zipped in and rolled out my slumbering neighbor, closing the door behind them.

Ah hah! my blood said.

"Hello," I said. I knew then for certain that the police were involved but it was, of course, no surprise.

Munt pulled a folding chair close to the bed and sat with a long ironic sigh.

"I don't mean to trouble you, Mr. Morgan. But I have to ask you a few questions?" He was one of those people who give statements the interrogative inflection. I've never trusted people who speak that way. Especially when they accompany their lilting, patience-begging tones with a flash of the badge. He shoved his wallet back into his checkered jacket and leaned back.

"Can you please tell me how Tom Douglas received his injury?"

I told him in as few words as possible. Before I even knew what I was doing my manner took on all of the clipped, officious charm that a couple years in business had taught me: I spoke in the voice of premature success and I suspected immediately that Munt was going to fall for it. It was embarrassing and disappointing, just as it had been every time I'd pulled it off in New York.

As I spoke, the younger cop leaned against the wall and scribbled in his pad.

"And this boy, what was he to you? Just a friend?"

"My father married his mother a few weeks ago."

"Ah," he said, nodding demurely, as if I'd brought up a matter of considerable delicacy. "Then you didn't know who he was?"

"What do you mean?"

"He was in a great deal of trouble."

I paused for a moment. "I knew that," I said.

"I would like to be very blunt with you, Mr. Morgan. Miss Cavanaugh? She made a statement regarding Mr. Douglas's death that was different from what you've told us. Of course, she's very upset and—"

"She said I did it on purpose, isn't that it?"

"That's what *she* said. What she'll say tomorrow is anybody's guess. But there are some matters that we're obligated to clear up?"

"Are you arresting me?"

"No. We just need to get a clear picture. The chances are this is just routine. But we have to investigate."

"I want to get back to New York."

"Of course you do. This has been some ordeal. But we will have to contact you."

"In other words, I'm free to go?"

"That's up to the doctors, not us."

"I want to cooperate with you, but I'm not going to answer any more questions without a lawyer." I sounded like a little punk who's just been busted in a whorehouse: my voice was rich with the misuse of privilege, smooth in the certainty that I was recognized as the sort of person cops can't push around. I had hoped for a chance to defend myself and had gotten it, but not as I'd planned. I wasn't answering questions, I was merely repelling the questioner. I knew this but I couldn't stop. It was not my nature to let that man probe. My jaw snapped shut; my eyes sought the middle distance, but even as I, in effect, dismissed him I felt the same useless yearnings for another kind of life that a bomber pilot might feel the moment he has unleashed a five-megaton load: how do you stop them from falling? how do you climb fast enough and high enough so you won't hear them explode?

I stood in a phone booth in the corridor and for the fifth time since entering the hospital I tried to call Earl and Lillian in New York. I later found that Melissa had gotten the news to them immediately and that they'd checked into a nearby hotel for the night: Lillian didn't want to be in familiar surroundings.

Finally, after Munt left my room for Tracy's (though I didn't know this was his destination), I found them at home. My father answered the phone.

"Hello, Dad?"

"Yes." He sounded as if he didn't recognize me; his voice did not color at all.

"It's Virgil."

"How are you, Virgil?"

"I've been calling you since yesterday."

"Are you still in Maine?"

"I am." I waited for him to help me out. Finally,

stupidly, helplessly, I said, "Have you heard anything?"

"I have, Virgil."

"We were snowed in for a few days. There was an accident."

"I told you I heard."

Whatever, in my frequent rehearsals, I'd planned to say next was lost to me. I stood in the phone booth, breathing into the receiver, watching my breath cloud and evaporate on the mouthpiece. "I don't know what to say," I said.

"There is nothing to say," said Earl. "The boy is dead. Nothing could be simpler. The boy is dead."

"How is Lillian?"

"How do you think?"

I took a deep breath. "May I speak to her?"

"Please, Virgil. What are you thinking about?"

"I feel I should speak to her."

"Why? What good is that going to do?"

"I don't know."

"You see?"

"I'm not trying to do good."

"Yes," he said, "you've made that clear." Silence. I wanted to hang up on him but I didn't have the moral capital to spend on such a gesture.

"I'll be in New York tomorrow," I said. "I'll come over."

"They're not keeping you up there?"

I let it pass. "No. We'll be back soon."

"Are they going to arrest you?"

"No."

After a silence, he said, "Good. I'm glad of that, at least."

18

WE SPENT one more full day in the hospital and then flew back to New York. We arrived at three in the afternoon and took a cab directly to Lillian and Earl's. I kept the shopping bag filled with our belongings on my lap and the sun shone through the side window of the taxi, casting a bar of golden light before us. On the top of the bag was a square of paper on which Lieutenant Munt had written his telephone number: I was to call him if I remembered anything more about what had happened in the house.

As the cab spun through the Midtown Tunnel Tracy took my hand and gave it a good hard squeeze. I felt my color come back and realized I'd gone a little faint. I turned toward her. The inside of my head seemed to rotate a second behind the outside; I had one of those colds that make you feel that there's another, vile person inside you. I tried to give Tracy a reassuring smile but the gesture was botched and a stupid, embarrassed grin spread across my face.

"I still don't know what I'm going to say."

"You're not supposed to," said Tracy.

I imagined myself falling to my knees before Lillian, or asking her to hold a knife while I ran up to its hilt. I was tempted by the *idea* of offering my life in exchange for the life I'd accidentally ended, but a modern man's heart is ruled democratically and the judgment of the majority was: What would the point of that be? No, there was no real question of making broad gestures; I was not even completely convinced that I should see Lillian at all. Why not wait? I wasn't wanted. But when I'd told Tracy that Lillian and Earl's was to be our first stop she only nodded, as if nothing could be more appropriate, or obvious, and so I was locked into it. And it did correspond to my own obscure sense of manly conduct. There was still a danger that if we went back to our apartment I would backslide into being, once again, a flush youngster with a view of the park. I didn't yet trust myself to grieve on my own; I still felt it was necessary to take another step deeper into what had happened, what I'd done.

Lillian lived in the kind of new high-rise building that begins to deteriorate even before the air conditioners are put in. It was made of shiny gray bricks and it rose up in a design as regular and repetitive as a chant. There were names for a hundred tenants. I found Lillian's, 8-D, pressed the buzzer, and moved toward the milk-white intercom.

"Who?" my father's voice barked out. It popped out at me like one of those gag snakes you stuff into cans.

"It's Tracy and me," I said. A few moments shook by and then we were buzzed in.

We held hands in the automatic elevator. When we got to the eighth floor I took Tracy into my arms and kissed her. I'd meant it to be gentle. I ended up pressing so strongly that I practically pushed her teeth down her throat.

We walked down the cinderblock corridor, in that

weak underwater light. Apartment 8-D was directly ahead of us and as we approached it, Earl opened the door and waited for us. If we'd wanted to do it up right we could have made it a *High Noon* scene, with the out-of-town killer at one end of the corridor and the beleaguered lawman leaning in the doorway, but as soon as I saw him I lowered my eyes and kept them down until we were right next to each other.

"Hello, Dad," I said.

"Hello, Virgil. Hello, Tracy." He wore a burgundy silk robe over his bare chest and a pair of gray trousers. His hair was wet and combed straight back. He smelled of cooking and there was gray stubble over his unshaven face. His goatee, after a quarter of a century of rule, had been removed from his chin.

"We came directly from the airport," I said.

He nodded and looked quickly over his shoulder, down the small hallway, leading to the front of his new apartment. I peered past him. The windows faced west. I saw the cold flat surfaces of office buildings in the shadow of the setting sun. The apartment itself was in shadows: a lamp dropped a yellow ring of light onto the carpet but the light neither glowed nor spread.

"How are you two?" Earl said, in a sharp, nervous voice.

"Let us in and find out," said Tracy, with an annoyed smile. She stepped forward and Earl moved aside.

"Wait here," he said, as he closed the door behind us. "I'll tell her you're here."

We were left in the narrow foyer. There was a Navaho rug and sepia-toned photos of American Indians on the wall. On a little table stood a black stoneware vase filled with cattails. I heard something jingling and an old red-eyed little dog, round as a roast, came hobbling toward us, sniffing with cautious, proprietary curiosity. I took a deep breath and closed my eyes: all I could think of was the soft, naked, utterly astonished skin on my father's chin.

Earl was back to lead us to the front of the house. The living room was perfectly square and the rigid, childish geometry startled me in a way. Lillian sat at a small antique-looking table at the left of the living room's large single window. Sharing the room with the table and chair was a small turquoise couch and Earl's piano. There was no room for anything else; there was scarcely room to walk.

Lillian wore a black blouse, tight in the sleeves, and flowing gray trousers. Before her was a large art book open to the middle; it appeared to be Miró reproductions but I couldn't be certain. There was a bottle of red vermouth open and two glasses, one upside down, the other half filled. There was an almost empty pack of cigarets in a leather case; one cigaret smoked in a small glass ashtray that must have just been emptied.

"Sit down," said Earl, waving us toward the couch. "Drop your bag anywhere. Your coats."

Lillian seemed to be staring at me but she turned abruptly away, probably to rein in her passions, and when she faced me again her features were dull and impenetrable.

As Tracy and I sat down on the couch, Lillian rose and went to the window. A long sweeping ray from the setting sun moved through her untamed hair. She moved slowly; her long thin hands clasped each other in fierce, silent grief.

"I'll make some coffee," said Earl, backing out of the room, as craven as I probably would have been in his place.

Lillian wandered to the piano bench. The silence in the room was almost unendurable. Finally, just when I was about to blurt out some token of regret, Lillian said, "Are you out on bail?" She leaned back and her elbow hit the piano keys. We all jolted in our seats.

"No," I said.

My father came in with four cups trembling on a flat wooden tray. He set it down and was gone. He kept his face in the shadows; I couldn't see his eyes.

"We wanted to be here..." said Tracy, her voice trailing off.

I thought to myself: I wish I could make my voice sound like that: soft and involving—the music of the undefended heart.

Lillian nodded and turned away. I followed her eyes; she was looking for the bottle of vermouth.

"Can I get you anything?" I said. I sound like a waiter, I thought.

"Melissa is coming to be with us," Lillian said.

I wondered if she meant we should leave. I was ready to go at the slightest provocation. There was nothing I could say to her. I couldn't touch her, I didn't have the right to ask forgiveness. The fantasies I had had in the taxi—of offering my life for Tommy's —turned out to be the only real gesture open to me, and, of course, I could not make it. But what else would do?

Earl came in with a pot of coffee and a carton of skimmed milk. We all prepared our cups. Earl sat next to Lillian on the piano bench. He seemed to be staring into the dark heavy air of the apartment but as I followed his eyes I saw he was looking at an oil painting of a 1930s Paris street scene.

I could not even feel grief in front of them. Everything seemed an indulgence.

"Is there anything you want to know?" Tracy said. "About what happened?" She rested her coffee cup on her knee, where it was as still as a photograph.

"He was nothing to you," said Lillian. She was looking at me.

"That's not true," I said. I thought to myself: the woman's son is dead, don't argue with her. I looked at Earl for a little help and almost laughed out loud it was such an unlikely notion. "I didn't kill him, Lillian," I said. I'd meant my voice to be steady—a hero's voice —but it sounded matter-of-fact.

"Please," said Lillian, "don't." She waved her hand between my face and her eyes, as if I were a message she wished to rub off a chalkboard. Then her hand dropped into her lap. "Even your father doesn't believe that."

"Lillian," said Earl, his face coloring.

The room was silent again. I listened to the traffic eight floors below. A siren whooped past—a fire engine, a police car, an ambulance, some vehicle on its way to someone else's personal disaster. The thought of living in a world of grief may have been ordinary enough but it held within it the root of madness: it made me suspect that the world had been invented for no decent reason. Another siren yelped by, and then another. Somewhere nearby a calamity deepened: people were leaping from a burning building, or crawling from the wreckage of an overturned bus, or someone had finally crossed over and was spraying Second Avenue with bullets, firing blindly from a hotel window.

I looked at Tracy, at Lillian, and then at Earl, almost ill with the certainty that they knew better than I what was passing through that room, what the depths of our lives were, what connected us, what was driving us apart.

"When is he being buried?" I asked.

"Tomorrow," said Earl.

"I'd like to be there," I said.

Lillian stood up. Her eyes looked cruel, feral. She went to the window and pulled the curtain closed. Then she touched a wall switch and the overhead lights went on. Brightened, the room seemed smaller and infinitely sadder. The old dog, aroused by the sudden movements, waddled across the living room and stood before Lillian, its stumpy tail vibrating nervously.

"I have always hated the police," she said. "Even as a girl. I have always despised them. The fascist bastards." She shook her head, remembering. "The way they hounded my son. But now I want them to put you in jail. How did you come here? Why aren't you in jail? I don't understand." She turned away and covered her eyes. When she spoke again, it was through tears. "I don't understand how you can just be free to go where you choose, after a thing like that. Why did you come here? What did you expect from me? I don't understand you."

"We wanted to be here," said Tracy.

I shifted in my seat and Tracy placed her hand on my wrist, thinking I was about to bolt.

"What happened to you happened to us, too," said Tracy. "I know it isn't the same. . . ." It sounded as if a bubble burst in her throat; she lowered her eyes. "You have to trust us."

Lillian turned around to face us, her cheeks streaked with tears. "I don't want to. I don't want to see you."

I looked at my father.

"She's very upset, Virgil," he said.

Lillian looked at him, her expression a combination of fatigue and horror. "How can you say something like that?"

"I think we'd better go," said Tracy.

I nodded, though my instincts were running several beats behind the events and a part of me was still prepared to ask Lillian where Tommy was being buried, to ask repeatedly, to somehow get that information.

Tracy got her coat and I followed her. We went down the narrow hall, with my father following behind. He opened the door for us.

"Where's the funeral?" I asked.

He shrugged and smiled helplessly. "It's not worth it," he said. "I'll talk to you later." He made it sound as if we shared the secret meaning of it all.

We parted with confused, half-hearted nods and then Tracy and I stood in the cinderblock corridor. We didn't move for at least a minute, as if we expected them to ask us in again.

There was nothing we could do with what we felt. We sat with it, as one might sit with a dying friend. We looked out at the park and didn't say very much;

we waited for the first half of the day to recede. In the midst of this Mario, who'd come to water our plants, burst in. He was delighted to see us and dragged us down to his apartment for supper. He fed us well and got us drunk on wine. He showed us a videotape of his talking to a skinny redheaded woman who decorated her toenails while Mario rambled about his theories on art, totalitarianism, Hitler, and black holes in the universe.

"This is the fool I dream about when she is not around, which is nearly always because I bore her so terribly," Mario told us, drumming his index finger against the TV screen.

He was easy on us. He could tell, I'm certain, that we weren't well and when we avoided one of his questions about our stay in Maine he asked no more. After we'd eaten and Mario was pouring cognac, the distress that had been beating steadily behind Tracy's eyes spilled over and she lowered her head for a few moments, as if to rest. Mario's hand shook as he poured her drink and it seemed he struggled to keep himself from kissing her hair. She lifted her head soon after that and said she was all right. He nodded. "Of course you are. We know that. Everyone knows that. But do you?"

He was such a perfect friend that we were probably wrong for taking solace in his hospitality and not telling him what we'd been through. I came close, at one point, but then told myself that, in his own way, he knew as much about us as he cared to. Besides, I didn't know what I could say, and still keep my composure.

The next day was Tommy's funeral. We called the National Association for the Rights of Prisoners but there was no answer. Had they gone to bury him or was it too early for them to open? We wanted to call Melissa but her number wasn't listed. We checked the *Times* and, near the back, there was a two-inch story, which reported his death as if it had just happened.

A young paroled convict named Thomas Douglas, who was known for a week during the past Christmas season as the Phantom Broadcaster, was killed. Police in Gardner Point, Maine, report that the body of Mr. Douglas, 23 years old, was recovered by state rescue teams after one of the worst storms in central Maine's history. Mr. Douglas appeared to be a victim of a household accident during the blizzard. Circumstances leading to the death are currently under investigation.

Mr. Douglas, a former student at Yale University, came into the local spotlight as the Phantom Broadcaster. Using sophisticated electronic equipment . . .

"There's nothing in here about where he's being buried," I said, giving the paper to Tracy.

"We can take a cab to Melissa's."

I tried to pour some more coffee into her cup but she covered it with her hand. A few drops spilled over the high veins on the back of her hand.

"I'm sorry," I said. Trembling, I wiped her hand with a napkin.

"I think I'll go to work, Virgil. I don't want to stay around the house."

"We can stay here and read our mail. If you want to, we can rent a car."

"What for?"

My idea was to drive to a couple of randomly chosen cemeteries, with the hope of picking the right one. But there were thousands of acres of dead people around town; it was a deranged idea. "I don't know," I said. She let it pass.

"Maybe we should both go in to work," she said.

"What's the point? It's not going to take my mind off it."

"I know that," she said, with an edge in her voice. "I don't want it taken off your mind. Jesus, Virgil."

I finally did go to work. I was welcomed back by Bob Halpin and a few of my workmates. Halpin talked to me about my upcoming trip west; I didn't want to tell him just then that I couldn't go, that I was needed by the police as they investigated a death. I smiled, shrugged. My elusiveness annoyed him.

That evening when I came home Tracy was in the bedroom with the door closed. I made myself supper and ate while reading the magazines that had been delivered in our absence. Our cat paced around my legs. Halfway through the meal, the house phone rang and the doorman said my father was in the lobby.

I asked him to be sent up and I went to our bedroom, where Tracy lay in an old blue flannel bathrobe, her eyes closed, a magazine opened on her stomach. With the only light in the room coming from a tensor lamp on her side of the room she looked like an illustration of an occult text on the treatment of depression.

"Who was that?" she asked.

"Earl."

She opened her eyes. "Here?"

"He's on his way up. Should I tell him you're asleep?"

"No," she said, swinging her legs out of bed. "If I sleep now I'll be up all night."

"I'll stay up with you."

"No, I'm going to work tomorrow."

My father rapped at the front door and I walked down the long foyer to let him in. He wore a bronze ski jacket over a black suit, dark blue shirt and a black tie. His eyes were red, the tips of his ears were pale, and there was a small sore on his naked chin.

"Can I come in?" he said. I nodded and stepped aside. "I'm just coming from that damn funeral," he said. He smelled of liquor; just being near him made me ache for a drink. "Not directly from the funeral, of course." His eyes momentarily engaged mine and he took a clumsy step backward.

He followed me into the living room and sank heavily onto the couch. Tracy came in from washing her face, the tips of her hair shining and wet. He greeted her with a wave and a desultory attempt to rise.

"You both may as well know it," he said. "Lil's blaming me for what happened. We're all in the same boat, now."

"I'm not surprised," I said.

"No, of course not," he said, his voice settling onto its familiar edge. "All I am to you is an object of ridicule. That's clear to me. It was clear to Lillian, too, in case you're interested. I don't need people who don't believe in me."

"What happened at the funeral?" asked Tracy.

"The funeral. The funeral. It wasn't really a funeral, you understand. There was no Tommy there, just a cheap plaster container of his ashes. There's something degrading about cremation. Please, don't allow that for me. I want to be placed in the ground. I don't want people worrying about how much space I take up. I'm not going to apologize for my own death."

"Where was it?" asked Tracy.

"Way out in the Bronx, with the sound of traffic and the wind blowing and the sky hanging so low you could feel it touch the back of your neck. That Reverend Healey was there, mumbling some bloodless, liberal, washed-out homilies. Quite a few people, though. I will say that. Fifty, maybe more. Some of the boy's friends. Everyone Lillian ever knew. She really keeps people in her life. I don't know how she does it. People love her forever.

"Every single person there was crying. That wind would keep your tears stuck to your face. I cried, too. I'm not even sure why but once I started I couldn't stop. I didn't want to stop. I didn't want Lillian to think she was suffering alone. I reached over to hold her hand but she moved it away from me. I thought maybe it was an accident or a reflex. So I reached again and this time she stepped away from me.

"After the thing was over, we walked back to the cars. We drove up there with her cousin and there were six of us jammed into that old junk. But I wasn't going to let it pass. I think that's what went wrong in my first marriage: I let too much pass. So I asked her what was wrong and right in front of everyone she tells me it was my idea—which maybe it was—to send Tommy up to Maine. But that doesn't make it my fault. Not at all, goddamnit. It only means—" He stopped himself short and glared at us as if we'd been eavesdropping. "What the hell. It's all ignorance. The woman is hysterical. You've got to feel sorry for her, in a way." He fell silent.

"What happened to your beard?" I asked, after a long silence.

He touched his chin and winced. "It gave Lil a rash." He shook his head and his eyes went suddenly bleary. He got up quickly and went to the windows. It was dark in the park but you could see a few people walking through the circles of light dropped by the streetlamps. I looked at Earl with true helplessness. The only decent thing to do, it seemed to me, was to go to him, to wrap my arms around him, to tell him I was on his side, even though I had no idea what that meant and, what's more, I knew he could not want me as an ally.

"I'd like to spend the night here," he said, turning around. "I don't have any place to go."

We ate in: a scrawny chicken, a cucumber salad, and a bottle of astringent Burgundy that no one wanted to finish. Dinner conversation moved along the footpath of familiar banalities: had a stranger observed us he might have guessed Earl was an out-of-town uncle visiting a couple whose marriage was agreeably fading. We didn't say one personal thing and so locked were we into our individual senses of what the evening held that when we passed salt and pepper we seemed to take particular care lest we accidentally touch.

It was the first night in ten years I'd spent under the same roof as my father and I must have been more dismayed than I let on, for as Tracy and I prepared for bed I tried to take off my shirt after unfastening only one button and I popped the other five. Earl was on the couch, as he'd so often been when we'd roomed together. Why didn't my father sleep in a bed? I could not imagine him comfortable, not even when he was asleep: there was always a lamp to peer down at him, a window left open to early morning frost and the rumble of passing trucks, or a tone arm stuck in the wounded groove of an old record, playing the same four-note phrase, torturing his unconscious while he clung to his fragile sleep. He was a frequent insomniac, and I had inherited his sleeplessness, but at least my pacing was done in a peaceful room and when I lay in bed and stared at the dim presences of the room's objects it was in a huge, firm bed with pressed, clean sheets. There was never anything between Earl and suffering. Was it that he'd bravely decided to do without the things that temper the blows of misfortune, or didn't he know such protection existed? Or how he could gain it if it did?

I wondered if his marriage to Lillian would survive. The possibility of his reverting to his bachelor ways—this time without his beard—frightened me and I felt sick for having helped damage what had probably been his only source of comfort in years. It was not easy for even a calm man to concoct a new life at sixty. I felt the beginnings of pity, of remorse, but they were washed away by a surge of hatred. Hatred for Earl, for Lillian, for all those lives that pressed so heavily on my own. I had not been able to figure out the first thing—what had really happened at Preservation Hall—and now I was required to watch and somehow feel something as the consequences of that obscured act spun out.

Someone was knocking at our front door. I started at the sound while Tracy, acres away at the extreme left side of our bed, turned on her back but continued to sleep. She had developed terrifying capacities for quickly entered and staunchly maintained fits of unconsciousness. The knocking continued, loud and cheerful. I stepped out of bed, slipped into my robe, and went to answer it. In order to get to the door, I had to pass through the living room, where Earl loomed, beneath one red and one yellow blanket, his big shoulders bulging beneath his white undershirt, his feet, with their hard yellowish bottoms, resting on the arm of the couch. Next to him was a bottle of vodka and a box of crackers; the table lamp near his head was on bright and he leafed through a book about medieval musical instruments Tracy had designed.

"Who is it?" he asked.

"I have no idea." I pointed to the phone. "Did the doorman ring up?"

Earl reached down for the vodka and took a small sip. He shook his head.

By the time I opened the door, Mario was walking back toward the elevators. He turned around. "I'm waking you?"

"Not really. I was just lying down listening to my blood."

He nodded. "I thought I would visit. I did not miss you when you were gone but now you're back I'm enormously glad. And I am starved. All I have downstairs are bouillon cubes. You and Tracy ate everything last night."

"Come in, then. Tracy's asleep."

"What has happened to you? It's eleven o'clock."

"Country hours. My father's here." I closed the door and we walked into the living room. Earl was trying to put on his trousers while keeping himself covered by the blankets. He writhed and kicked, while greeting us with a quick smile. I looked on in dim amazement; I'd forgotten his pathological modesty, even though I shared a version of it. Finally, he stood up to zipper his fly and faced us in his undershirt, his proper black trousers, and bare feet.

Mario turned to me. "I am truly sorry. Your whole household is in slumber and I come banging at the door."

"No, it's fine. I have insomnia and Earl was reading."

"We meet again," Earl said to Mario, extending his hand. "Care to join me?" he said, pointing to the half-empty vodka bottle.

"Prime choice," said Mario. "Liquor is yet another commodity of which I am out." He bent down to scoop up the bottle.

"What's wrong, Mario? Are you bankrupt?" I asked.

"Always at the middle of the month."

"I should be so bankrupt," I said. For some moronic reason I chose that moment to make a loud, odious laughing noise. "We all know you're a secret millionaire." I glanced momentarily at Earl. It was how I had played with my friends when I dared to bring them home: peals of exclusionary laughter. And the vicious habit, unchallenged and unexamined, remained.

We went to the kitchen. I made cheese, onion, and tomato sandwiches. Earl and Mario sat at the table, smoking Mario's black cigarets.

"Do you know someone named Crandall Popkoff?" Earl asked Mario. "From LA?"

"Popkoff? Why, yes. The man who runs the new composers series."

"That's right! You know him?"

"A little."

"He's got my 'Absurdium Continuum.' Do you remember?"

"Of course."

"I sent it to him. Rather my wife did. As I under-

stand it, the Los Angeles Chamber Music Society pre-
mieres works of undiscovered composers."

"Yes. Quite often."

"It's a good place to be featured, isn't it?"

"I should think so."

"Well, I got a letter from him. He said he wanted to
hold on to my piece for a week or so more. I suppose
that could be extremely hopeful."

"I don't know."

"You didn't tell me about this," I said, putting the
plate of sandwiches on the table.

"In your case, I wait until it's a sure thing," Earl
said.

"It sounds wonderful," I said, turning away. My
eyes felt a few degrees warmer than the rest of my
body.

"It would be a good thing," Earl said, in a soft
voice.

"Much of what they premiere ends up on a record-
ing," said Mario.

"I know. I know. It's a real opening. A genuine beginning."

"Where's the vodka?" I said. "We'll drink to your
luck."

"Right this way," said Mario, pushing it toward me.

I went to the cabinet for three wine glasses. I put
my fingers on the expensive crystal but shied away and
chose some simple glasses we'd picked up for a couple
bucks each. I filled each glass. "To music," I said.

Mario and I took large gulps but Earl downed his at
once.

"You don't think for one minute that it'll happen,
do you?" he said.

"Me?" I said. "I don't know. How can I know?
Sure. You're due."

"Due. You see?" He turned to Mario. "Implied in
that—due—is the assumption I've been waiting
around for it."

"I'm sorry," Mario lied, finishing his drink, "my English is not for nuances."

"Well," said Earl with a wave, "it's too complicated to explain." He poured some more vodka into his glass. "It's the story of a man whose life did not take shape."

"Mario has his own family nightmares," I said. "He doesn't need ours."

"I do," said Mario, refilling his glass and taking a sandwich. "My entire family history is upset, including the history of my life. One sister dead, a wife who is now active in the lesbian movement, a daughter who looks in the mirror all day."

"Virgil has always thought of me as a failure," said Earl.

I finished my drink and quickly poured another. "Christ," I said.

"Virgil has the morals of a hunter," said Mario.

"But exactly," said Earl, thinking he'd found a supporter.

"He admires the arrow that hits the mark. He is very sane and very accurate. He is what American people call a winner."

"He knows how to get what he wants," said Earl.

"I'm going to throw both of you out of here if you don't stop talking about me," I said in a voice far more cheerful than I was.

Mario smiled at me and raised a finger. "One more thing," he said. Then, turning back to Earl, "He is loved by his friends, you must know that. Because he is a good friend to have. He's—"

"He may be a good friend but he is a very hard son," said Earl, finishing his drink with another quick toss, as if in the process of establishing an alibi for anything he might say. Was it my imagination or was he starting to mimic Mario's accent? "He always wants you to prove yourself. He does not care about intentions. He is not impressed by effort."

"I'm going to slander you in front of all your

friends," I said, my voice still not quite free of good humor.

"Oh, shut up," said Earl. "You love it. You love being talked about."

"You're embarrassing me."

He leaned toward me. "Grow up, Virgil. You're—what are you? Twenty-six? Twenty-seven? It's time you stopped being embarrassed by me."

"You're right," I said. I slammed my hand against the tabletop. The noise was sharp and severe and it seemed an overture to an opera of filial rancor, but I had nothing I cared to say so I was forced to glare at Earl for a moment with cryptic fury.

Mario poured the last of the vodka into his glass. "All finished," he said, laying the bottle on its side and steadying it with his fingers so it would not roll.

"I've had too much," said Earl, placing his huge pale hand on his stomach. His biceps looked permanently flexed.

"I'll see if there's more in the liquor cabinet." I stood up and momentarily felt faint. I grabbed a sandwich, hoping to absorb some of the liquor.

"Wonderful," said Mario, when I returned. "Real Russian vodka. You see," he said to Earl, "yet another wonderful thing about knowing Virgil is he has good *things*."

"You notice he started us off on the domestic," said Earl.

"That was just a test. To see if we can drink. We have passed and this," he said, taking the bottle from me and unscrewing the cap, "is our reward. Smell." He pushed the bottle under Earl's nose.

Earl shrugged.

"Potato dreams," said Mario. He filled our glasses. He glanced at the sandwiches. "I'm not interested in those sandwiches anymore."

"I'm getting a headache," said Earl. "I've been to a funeral today and I've been drinking ever since."

"Alcohol was invented for taking after funerals," said Mario, quickly.

Earl picked up the bottle of vodka. "At least there's not much in here. I've got to be at work tomorrow."

Mario raised his glass. "I am humbled."

"I was at the funeral of my stepson," said Earl. "You met him after my recital. Tom Douglas."

"Of course," said Mario. "I remember him." He took a sip of his drink and closed his eyes. "He's gone to a better world."

"Yes," said Earl, "the world of worms."

Despite my drunkenness, my heart was slamming against my chest.

"I'm being blamed," said Earl.

"Death brings out the worst and the most good," said Mario.

"Because I sent him up to you," said Earl, pointing at me for an instant and then letting his hand drop to the table. He tipped over the vodka bottle but Mario caught it before any spilled.

"You should never have done it," I said.

"A boy was in trouble. I thought you would want to help."

"You're lying. You wanted him out of the way. You did what was convenient, stupidly, stupidly convenient." I was drunk, but not nearly enough. I felt there was a lot I could say but every thought and every impulse was accompanied by a terrible, dispiriting desire to let it pass.

"You two are making me homesick," said Mario. "In the Nicolosi family all deaths are followed by months of accusations." He finished his drink. "Let's wake Tracy. She has a good effect."

I shook my head.

"No? Then let us be very quiet and go into the bedroom and watch her while she sleeps."

"I'm fucked," said Earl, shaking his head. "This time I'm ruined."

"You don't even like her," I said.

"How do you know? How can you possibly know? She is a *good* person."

"You cannot possibly be talking about Tracy," said Mario. "Tracy is not a good person. She is a miracle. She is the reason for everything. So intelligent, so kind, so beautiful, and so skinny."

"Maybe I should call her," Earl said. He stood up and swayed.

"By all means," said Mario.

He sat down. "No. She doesn't want me. It's too late. She's sleeping. I'm too drunk. I'll say the wrong thing."

"Saying the wrong thing is always very charming to women," said Mario. "You remember, I met her. The recital. Wait. Not a word. I'm going to remember her name. Rosa. No, of course not. Gail?"

"Lillian," said Earl.

Mario laughed loudly. "Why is that funny?" he asked, looking at Earl and me and smiling. "Why does that make me laugh?"

We finished the Russian vodka. Earl made continual attempts to talk about Lillian but Mario, operating on the radar of simple good taste and compassion, managed to interrupt him, misunderstand him, or simply ignore him. The vodka had ushered me to the very edge of perception: on one side was a grotesque, gesturing image of my father and on the other was a solid wall of dark blue sand.

It seemed as if Earl had been sitting there for months and that he would never leave. I felt that special breed of terror and sorrow I felt in his presence. Had I ever told him that my shunning him as I did was unconnected to my love? I loved him, there was no question of that. Even if I had never quite known it before, I knew it now. He had done me more wrong than I thought he was capable of yet I could not pull away. I had never wanted to see him but I'd loved him. He was the only family I had—mother vanished, grandparents dead, uncles and cousin—forget it, relatives on the moon. A Christmas card, a surprise meeting at Penn Station, an invitation to a wedding in Baltimore. Strangers. But who needed them? Earl was family enough. He was a patriarch in his own right: he should have had a thousand children. We could have founded a school of philosophy, or our own disease.

There was something I wanted to tell him, but I wasn't certain what it was. I needed one, maybe two more drinks; there were still habits of reserve. I was drunk enough to say things I might regret but I was not yet past caring.

I wanted to tell him that in order to move through life some of us latch onto a belief in the eventual outcome of things and we lack, perhaps, the faith to question this belief. If we do, we will fall, like those cartoon heroes who step out of a window and walk blissfully through thin air until they happen to glance down: then comes the scrambling, the bug-eyed panic, the eventual ka-boom. I was walking on air and Earl was always by my side, tapping me on the shoulder, howling his warning, look down, look at what you're doing, you arrogant, stupid thing. I threw myself forward with the one flimsy notion that tied my life together: time unfolded with incomprehensible, yet somehow benevolent logic. Earl was there to tell me that the general path was downward, that time was a hammer beating you on the head, that those who tried hardest and wanted most deeply often got a two-room apartment and an appalling pension for their pains.

Rage was my only friend. I would always rather slam the door in my father's face than admit that what he wanted in his life was attainable had he been good enough, calm enough, smart enough. But then whose fault was it? The world's? The world that had treated me as its blessed son? No, that tragic sense of life was not mine, no more than it could be that of a farmer whose fields are fertile, whose most casually planted seeds spring into oceans of corn, of wheat, of rye, of every imaginable thing. Then what could be wrong?

Why was Earl coming up empty-handed, time and again?

Just as Melissa and Lillian wanted to keep Tommy alive by dragging me through courts of law, I kept Earl mine by despising him. The moment his ambitions stopped setting my teeth on edge, pity—soft, helpless pity—would reign. I would rather my father be a villain, a buffoon, an assassin than one of those poor creatures spit out by eternity's imperfect machinery. As much as being raised by him left me enthralled with Chance and Luck, I didn't want my father to be a victim of those eerie, impersonal forces, forces which I never entirely believed existed. I chose to turn away from him and so allowed him to remain a star in my life. I made him hateful, and so he retained an aura of gallantry and potency in my imagination. And by turning away I also allowed myself the freedom to do whatever I pleased, with no serious second thoughts about hurting his feelings or challenging his enormous pride.

But I needed one more drink. My hands were shaking with sheer joy and anticipation. I had seized the notion of making a speech to my father, of explaining our lives together. It was the apology I'd searched for all my life: there would be no embrace, no reunion, just clarification. The necessary distance between us would not be disturbed.

I got up. "We seem to be out of fuel," I said, pointing to the second empty bottle.

"I'm at my limit," said Earl, through a yawn.

"Nonsense. It's early." I went into the dining room and opened the liquor cabinet. Vodka? No vodka. Gin? No. No Scotch either. We'd brought it up to Preservation Hall and drunk it. There was some apricot liqueur but that was out of the question. Tomorrow I would go to the liquor store and drop a C note. But tonight. What were we going to do about tonight? Finally, I chose a small bottle of Cointreau which had been lingering around the house for a year. I grabbed it by its short, sticky neck.

Mario was already standing up, tucking his lemon-yellow silk shirt into his gray trousers. Earl's head was cradled in his arms on the table; he appeared to be sleeping.

"No need to leave," I said, hoping to awaken my father.

"I never act from need, only desire," said Mario.

"I was just getting going," I said, holding up the Cointreau.

"Your father is asleep. He has passed out."

"I see that. I wanted to say something to him."

"These things are never said. I do not think they are meant to be."

"I wanted him to hear it."

"Your stepbrother died in your house in Maine?"

"That's right."

"Tonight as I fall asleep I will think about why you have not told me this. I am not insulted. It is your kind of delicacy."

"I can't talk about it."

"Don't be sorry. I think it delights me. Now you are my one true American. You have a terrible secret. The picture is complete."

"I've got more than one."

"No. The rest are illusions." He grabbed for a sandwich. "Walk me to the door."

I felt awash in the odd passions of friendship. "Thanks, Mario," I said.

"Nonsense. It is I who should thank you. Someday soon I will leave this city, this country, which is now already a thing of the past. And it is you who I will remember, far more than anything else. You are better than Radio City Music Hall."

I came back to the kitchen. Earl was snoring softly and I thought again of waking him. Tentatively, I moved my hand toward the back of his neck and that part of me that was ripe for drama and hungered blindly for miraculous change called out for me to touch him with real love, to bend over and kiss his long, thick hair. But of course it was impossible. It took more than the pinings of the drunken heart to change who I was, what I had made of myself. I made the move toward him, an inch, two inches, I came that close.

The next morning, Tracy's alarm clock fired off at nine o'clock. She staggered into our bathroom and took some aspirin. After she swallowed them she splashed water in her face, great handfuls of warm water that dripped onto her throat and her breasts. I joined her in the bathroom and put my arms around her from behind.

"You look terrible," she said.

"Hangover."

"From that crummy wine?"

"Mario and Earl and I drank vodka last night. A lot of it."

"Really?" She turned around. There were purple circles beneath her eyes. Her breath was warm and smelled old. "I didn't hear anything."

Without any warning, she burst into tears, only this time it seemed as if she were crying from exhaustion. I tried to comfort her, but we were now living in different dimensions. I patted her, held her, said her name into her ear.

"I hate this, Virgil," she said. "I just want it to stop."

We dressed and went into the living room. Earl was dressed and sitting on the couch. He flipped through the morning *Times* and listened to the radio, which was on a rock and roll station. "So you're finally up," he said, glancing at his watch. "Look, I came here without much notice. I wonder if you've got an extra toothbrush and razor around. I'd like to get as much of yesterday off me as I can." He smiled and got up. "I talked to Lil this morning. She's expecting me home."

"Sure," I said, "go right in."

"I've got another favor to ask. Would one of you

call my school and tell them I'm out of town, or something? I feel bad. I've been rehearsing these two Puerto Rican kids in a piano and violin duet and now I won't be there for the assembly. But I want to spend this day with Lil. Ask for Mr. Gertz."

"What's the number," asked Tracy. "I sound very sincere on the phone."

"You'd sound sincere anywhere," he said in a gratuitously smarmy voice.

Tracy made the call and I went to make coffee. A few minutes went by and Earl came into the kitchen, reeking of my aftershave lotion.

"Whew," he said, looking around the kitchen. "The scene of the crime. You hung over?"

"Completely."

"Not me. One of the few indignities I'm immune to." He laughed. He was in terrific spirits.

You're lucky, I was about to say, but I didn't want to start anything. "French coffee all right?" I poured in some shiny black beans to grind.

"You're damn right it is. You should see what Lillian likes to drink. Maxim freeze-dried coffee. Sometimes it annoys me, sometimes it's endearing. I've always loved coffee. Good, fresh, really strong brew."

Tracy came in. "I said you'd be there next Monday."

"Good idea! You talk to Gertz?"

"Sure. It was cool."

"He's a real treacherous prick, that one," said Earl, high on the energy of his reunion with Lillian.

I put out cups and saucers.

"Look at these cups," said Earl, sitting down. "Each one's a work of art. Here's one with hunting dogs. Yours has a little English country scene. What's yours got, Virgil? Rabbits? They look like Dürer's rabbits. Beautiful. That's the nicest one."

19

SOMEHOW, the word despair has been used up by our language, but there is no better word to describe Tracy's state in those days, the weeks following our return to New York. She fell asleep with nerve-knotting speed and slept not only in bed, but on chairs, on the couch, in the car, at her desk at work. Often she had nightmares which she leapt out of with a small gasp but which she would not describe. She claimed not to recall them and this was such an ambiguous lie that I couldn't challenge it—was she withholding the secrets of her monstrous dreams or was she merely protecting my conscience from them? After these frightening, secret dreams she would slip out of bed on the pretext of going for a glass of water, or a glass of sherry to coat her nerves: my clearest memory of her in those long, formless nights was the feel of the sheets on her side of the bed when she'd left it, those warm wrinkles, the occasional dark hair, that faint musky scent. Often, she wouldn't return and I'd find her the next morning, curled on the couch, a blanket wrapped around her body as tight as a cigar.

It was downhill, but it was not all downhill. There were times when our love managed to free itself from the awful circumstances it, along with us, had fallen into: times when we necked with the aching, furtive passion of young cousins; a brief moment in a restaurant when I passed Tracy a little pewter peppermill and our fingers touched; the time I called her at her office at the perfect moment and her voice sounded quick, eager, and free. They were moments, really, only instants. But I would think: it's passing, it's going away, just as I had when I saw the moon the night in Preservation Hall, after the blizzard.

When I thought about it honestly, I realized she was drifting away from me. We were drifting away from each other. I was sinking, and she was sinking, but it seemed as if we were being swallowed up by different species of anguish. Tracy mourned Tommy and suffered from the memory of her own fear—fear of the storm, fear of Tommy. For one who had waited to be dismantled by apocalyptic events, the sharply remembered desire for it all to end was a plague. Mostly, however, she suffered from a deepened knowledge of death, and from having sat with someone as he left forever the only world she knew or believed in. It was what I suffered, too, and maybe it should have brought us together, but the fact was that I had swung the poker. In every way, I stood at the very center of that death and my reckoning was both slower and more vast than Tracy's. What she basically had to accept was what had happened; I had to face who I was.

Our lives did not stand still. Tracy and Gary Fish landed an important new account and there was a kind of perverse excitement there. I was called by a clerk from the Eastportsmouth police station, to make certain I was reachable at the number I'd given them. A day later, in the evening, Tracy's parents called us to say they'd be in New York the next day.

All of these events pulled our lives forward and they were blessings, in a way. They gave us safe topics to talk about. We still could not speak about those frozen, berserk days in Preservation Hall, though, of course, it was *all* we talked about: it was what we meant when we said, "How are you feeling today?" Even when it became clear that we were drifting from each other, we could not speak about it. We waited for our lives to resolve behind our own backs; we played the outside chance that one of our elliptical, practically Aesopian conversations would miraculously find its way to the pained and neglected cores of our lives. What we needed was to talk about everything that had happened to us, everything that was steadily, sickeningly separating us, but we had neither the habit nor the vocabulary. The only thing I still had any trust in was my luck and it wasn't something I could talk about; what Tracy looked to were experiences so powerful that she might be transformed by them, made larger, less coolly certain, and, it turned out, that was not something she could talk about, either. I longed for a dark church, stinking of paraffin and incense, where we could prostrate ourselves and be granted release from the awesome, tedious burdens of our personalities. How sick we were of our personalities, especially when we came to suspect they were all we had.

But we could talk about the police and we could have scary fantasies of what might happen if I were faced with some hostile motor-mouth D.A., and we could talk about how we'd get up to Maine and how I'd better make plans about getting a lawyer. When we knew Tracy's parents were coming up we talked about the best way to tell them what had happened in Maine. Though Tracy had already told them over the phone, we knew we'd have to go through it again and without exactly mentioning what we wouldn't say, or couldn't say, we tried to delineate what we would reveal. It wasn't that we felt we had secrets but there was only so much we could go through in public and for two people who found conversation, even with one another, to be a form of public exposure, it was impossible to seriously conceive explaining anything important to the most benignly concerned outsiders.

Deborah Keating was in town to attend a conference on diabetes held at the Hotel St. Moritz. Ordinarily, Roger Keating didn't attend these conferences but he wanted to be around to see Tracy—the sound of her voice had truly shaken him. The Keatings believed, passionately, in personal autonomy and felt that the best you could do for people was the least. Still, they could not resist offering a steadying hand when the life of one of their children was in crisis. There was something a little awesome about their apparent indifference once you knew that their distracted, blithe manner was the velvet glove that covered the iron fist of their sheer, instinctual determination.

They had a small room overlooking the southern flank of Central Park, where the horse and buggy drivers waited for customers and gossiped with each other. Their room smelled of flowers. There was an open can of Planter's Peanuts, little bottles of grapefruit juice, a stack of paperback mysteries. On the coffee table lay brochures from the diabetes conference, theater tickets, travelers' cheques, and Xerox copies of restaurant reviews from the *Times*. The room, in fact, was a mess and when Tracy and I walked in seeing that self-confident clutter buoyed my spirits. Roger called room service for roast beef and beer and, for a moment, it seemed that we were just going to mark time. Tracy was being hugged by her mother, quizzed about the scent that lay in the folds of her neck—"Musk? I don't believe that's musk. It's what they *call* musk but it cannot actually be"—and Roger, his long legs crossed, his hands smoothing the lilac silk on the arms of the tiny, feminine chair he perched on, looked as sleepy and ready to be entertained as he had the first time Tracy introduced us.

But the mood changed in a heartbeat. As soon as space was cleared for Tracy and me to be seated, Deborah wanted to know *exactly* what had happened and all of the subtle strategy Tracy and I had devised seemed to deliquesce: we gawked at each other like a pair of dummies. You go first, no you go, no *you* go. Finally, I told a version of those days at Preservation Hall that was so stoic, and so brief, it was probably designed to be misunderstood.

Still, it seemed to suffice and when I was finished Deborah crossed her slender legs, folded her bone-white hands, and said, "What I fail to understand is why the police are causing you any inconvenience whatsoever."

"They obviously think there's some question about what *really* happened," I said. My decent spirits had lasted thirty seconds; now I was merely trying to control myself.

"What a bother," said Deborah. Her voice was like Tracy's; high, clear, only hers seemed faintly piercing. She had a habit of giving a little shudder after she spoke and this was meant to stand for all of the things she'd charitably deleted. Her black and silver hair was swept back. She wore gray trousers and a blazer, a yellow silk shirt and a string of pearls. "Well no matter," she said. "I happen to have a very close friend who is a lawyer in Maine. I'm going to call her this afternoon and she'll make certain this doesn't get out of hand. You're going to love Kathryn Perl and believe me she'll make mincemeat of those people."

I shrugged.

"There was no doubt about that, Virgil," she said. "Roger and I know Maine and we have a very clear idea of how things work there. Believe me, there's nothing to worry about."

Roger Keating nodded. He was sixty but his hair was coal-black, as were his long spiky eyebrows.

"Kathryn Perl has the spirit of Antigone," he said. "We have nothing to fear."

"It's only going to be routine," said Tracy.

"If there's a full investigation you're going to have to testify," I said to Tracy.

"I know that."

"But do you know what you'll say?"

"Virgil . . ." Her voice sounded hurt.

"I'm just asking. I never had the impression that you were altogether convinced I was blameless."

"I'm going to call Kathryn right this second," said Deborah. "She's such a homebody, I know I'll find her in." She made no move toward the phone. "I suspect she's rather expensive, comparatively. She's used to living well."

"As long as she's good," said Tracy.

"I'm not sure I want to be represented by some rich Wasp country gentlewoman," I said.

"What would you like?" asked Deborah with a smile. "A Pakistani?"

"You're not going to do better than Kathryn," said Roger.

"I don't even know this woman," I said. "I was thinking of just talking with this old friend of my father's, Sid Pollizar."

"Is he in Maine?" asked Deborah.

"No. Union Square," I said.

"What makes you think he can practice in Maine?" said Tracy.

"I can just consult with him." I got up and went to the windows. It was growing dark. A carriage started off through the park, with steam pouring from every inch of the horse. Where was old Sid Pollizar now that I needed him? I remembered his butterscotch candies, the aroma of his pipe that lingered on the front of his soft white shirts, the slick brilliance of his manicured nails. A bachelor, a joker, he had been my favorite of the visitors who came to my father's apartment in Brooklyn Heights. What had become of him? Were he and Earl still close? Would he take the case or had he been turned against me? Recently or long ago? "Look kid," he used to say to me, "if you ever get in trouble and I mean serious trouble, when your ass is grass and the whole world is a lawn mower, don't forget old Sid when it's court time. At least I'll make sure they don't hang you." Then he would laugh, his sweet candied breath touching my face like a hand.

We left the hotel; the good-byes were tentative, muffled. Tracy and I stood as far from each other as the elevator would permit. She got into a cab and I went home on foot, taking the park route. It was dark and as I walked the persistent dispiriting drizzle turned to snow. The park was empty as far as I could see. Every now and then a cab would hiss past me, the headlights bending like elbows in the dark. I took off my gloves and stuffed them into my jacket pockets and then I unzipped my jacket. The cold was wet and feeble; it could not penetrate me, could not drag me back to that blizzard in Maine.

Two young black kids pedaled by me on ten-speed bikes. They glanced my way and looked a little unnerved to see someone walking alone, his jacket open, his arms swinging at his sides. I think I radiated my willingness to have my life interrupted. Was it just my imagination or did those kids start moving faster once they noticed me? I had an impulse to call out but I didn't know what to say. I realized, suddenly, that in a way I was invulnerable: I was like one of those crazed men who shout on street corners, begging for someone to slap their face or step on their foot, while an orbit of impenetrable moral fastidiousness forms around them —for it seems that at a certain point in one's search for retribution no one will help you, no one will even acknowledge how acutely you long for it. I could have walked through that park naked; I could have called those boys niggers; I could have shit in the bushes and no one would have said a word to me.

"You look half frozen," Tracy said when I walked in. She sat at her desk, doing a paste-up of a book about boxing. She was dressed in a robe and slippers and I could tell by the bright redness of her skin she'd recently taken a scalding shower. She turned on her swivel stool. "Do you want me to make some tea?"

I shook my head. It seemed somehow indecent that I should walk into a scene of domestic splendor, no matter how muted it might be. I realized then what the price is for defending your *way* of life: as soon as you do it becomes a confection—arbitrary, unsatisfactory, and stupid.

"I don't want anything," I said, dropping my jacket onto the couch and sitting down. What I wanted was a drink but I didn't want it quite yet.

"My mother called," Tracy said.

"So?"

"She wanted to know whether or not to go ahead and call that lawyer."

"What'd you say?"

"I asked her to give me the number."

"I'm not going to call her. If it goes to trial I'll conduct my own defense." Of course, I didn't mean it but my voice sounded so earnest that even I was almost convinced.

"Oh come on," she said, not quite daring to let it pass.

"Whatever I do is my business. I don't want your parents' lawyer. You call them and tell them to keep out of this. They have no idea what's involved. They are so fucking dry and confident. How do they know what's best? How do they know what I want? I can't stand the way they treat this. They act as if I've got this minute problem. As if my hair was mussed and this lawyer is a comb they can pull out of their back pocket."

"I think you're being very selfish."

"Oh?"

"You don't know beans about the law. What if you get yourself into trouble?"

"I am in trouble. Right now."

"I mean real trouble, Virgil."

"I *am* in real trouble. And I don't want some clever bitch to get me out of it."

"Stop it."

"Screw off. I know what I'm doing."

"I want you to talk to Kathryn Perl, or to some other decent lawyer. I don't want you in jail."

"If I go, I go."

"Do you want to take Tommy's place behind bars? Is that it?"

"Spare me your analysis, please."

"I just want to know. Tell me what you're doing. You seem suicidal. You're scaring me, Virgil. And you're making me hate you."

"You're being very stupid," I said. "I want you to stop trying to make things better."

"I'm going to call Kathryn Perl myself. If you don't."

"You'd better not," I said. "I mean it. I'll smash you if you do."

"Smash me then," she said, leaving the room.

20

WHEN I learned, the next day, that Kathryn Perl was in New York to visit her brother I was furious, shocked; in the days when my luck was steady and good, when luck was what seemed to keep my life running, it would not have bothered me. It did not even bother me that Tracy had gone ahead and contacted the woman. That didn't surprise me at all. But when I learned that Kathryn Perl was in town, was, in fact, six blocks away and willing to see me, I felt plotted against. Innocence proved is simpler than innocence felt and what terrified me was if I achieved the first too quickly I might never reach the second.

I was tired of squabbling, so when Tracy announced Kathryn's availability I just swallowed my objections and followed her over. By noon, we were in Kathryn's brother's apartment. His name was Cabot Rollins and though it wasn't possible to say what he suffered from it was clear that he was sick and that his sister was with him because he might not be alive for long. He greeted

us in a purple silk robe. Veins stood up from his bare
ghostly legs and he smelled of medicine and bed. He
was a tall man, in his fifties, but his shoulders were
hunched and misshapen. He walked with a limp and
cracked his knuckles nervously as he saw us into the
interior of his long, dark apartment. "You must excuse
me," he said, in a gentle elegant voice, "but I have
nothing to offer you."

I looked at him, not quite understanding.

"That's all right," said Kathryn, in a windswept,
upper-class voice, "we're going out for a fast lunch."

"That's a very good idea," said Cabot. "That's what
I would do." He smiled genially. I wondered if he was
glad we were leaving or if he'd gotten the knack of
enjoying other people's pleasures.

We went downtown to a restaurant on Twenty-
eighth Street because that was where Kathryn used to
eat when she practiced law in New York. Kathryn Perl
was a woman so independent, so capable, and so aloof
that, by comparison, Tracy and her mother were passive and frivolous. She had short bullet-gray hair and
two deep lines on either side of her thin, weathered
face. She was one of those people who force you to
walk at their pace and you always end up saying less
than you planned because your breath is running
short. You knew, just by looking at her, that she was
the undisputed champion of her own life, that she lived
in a beautiful house, owned four dresses, two for
court, one for visiting, and one that seemed a little
odd—something red, or something with lace sleeves
—that expressed the blind, whimsical taste of the solitary. Today, she wore her visiting dress, dark brown
with a black belt and sleeves that touched the elbow.
She wore eyeglasses on a silver chain around her neck,
but she never put them on and it seemed she was judging physical reality as unworthy of a closer look.
Kathryn Perl would put on her glasses when she fell in
love again and stare at whoever it was, giving her heart
an extra ten seconds to flee.

Ordinarily, she was the sort of person who'd fill me with admiration and there was a time when I'd have been eagerly memorizing her gestures. But I'd had enough of self-assured people and Kathryn's cool, impervious bearing repelled me in a way. In the taxi, we were all silent, while Kathryn looked out the window, remembering this corner, that pharmacy. "It changes less than people think it does," she said at one point, evidently referring to New York.

The restaurant she took us to was muted and undistinguished and I wondered how it survived. It was only after we'd sat in that rectangular blue room, with the large tables covered with faded white linen, and eaten the broiled fish and boiled potatoes, that I realized the very amorphousness of the place constituted a kind of inverted flamboyance. While we ate, Kathryn had me describe what had happened in Preservation Hall.

"Well basically what happened," I said, "was I clobbered someone on the head and he died." I wanted her to know what sort of client I'd be.

"That's not exactly how I heard the story," said Kathryn, not blinking.

"Well if *you* know what happened..." I said, ending with a somewhat obnoxious shrug.

"You're making me crazy, Virgil," said Tracy. She grabbed for her napkin and I could tell she wanted to throw it on the table and storm out of there, but her hand remained on her lap.

"Who told you the story?" I said to Kathryn.

"Deborah."

"I thought you told them to keep out of this," I said to Tracy.

"I did."

"Let me make something clear, Virgil," said Kathryn. "No one's pushing you into anything whatsoever. I think you might be acting a little dishonestly. After all, you did come to see me. So you do realize you're in need of some assistance."

"I'm sorry," I said. "The whole thing is working its

way through me in a way I don't really understand. Something's trying to turn in me but it doesn't have any place to go."

I saw a flicker of understanding and even of sympathy in Kathryn's small blue eyes; when I glanced at Tracy, she looked softened, too, and her hand smoothed out her napkin.

"You're going to have to describe to me exactly what happened. If I'm going to assist you—"

"Look, I don't know how to make this clear," I said. "But if I'm guilty I don't want any help and if I'm innocent I don't see why I should need it. At least not from someone like you. You're too good. I know it. You could get me off even if I was guilty."

"But I wouldn't want to," she said.

"If I don't know whether or not I'm guilty, how can you?"

Still, I told her what happened and for the first time Tracy learned that when I sat in the car after Tommy was hit I wished he would die. "I never wanted him there, neither of them. From the moment I heard Melissa Cavanaugh's car coming down our road, getting them out of our way was the most important thing. Even when Tommy came in half frozen. Even as I watched him stagger through out kitchen with icicles in his nose. I just wanted them out."

"Of course, that has very little to do with the case at hand," said Kathryn. "No one can blame you for how you feel. Especially in those circumstances. You wanted to be with your wife. Anyone would resent the intrusion. That's only natural."

"Not with me. It's beyond that. There was a part of me that would have done anything to get them out."

"I wanted them out, too, Virgil," said Tracy, putting her hand on my arm. I realized I was talking far too loudly.

I pushed a small potato around my plate—a white stoneware dish half an inch thick. If I'd have closed my eyes I know I would have seen Melissa's VW bouncing down the access road to our house, its exhaust rising in the wind and mixing with the snow that was already falling: that cream-colored car, that pale gray smoke, and everything else supernaturally white. I pressed the edge of my heavy silver fork into the boiled potato until it split and then I separated the halves and split them again.

"If someone else was invaded by Tommy and Melissa," I said, "and they wanted to get rid of them it would be more understandable. I can't explain it. In me, it seems different. There's always been a kind of person I couldn't be around, people who seemed like jinxes to me."

"It has nothing to do with the law," said Kathryn.

I turned to Tracy. "I don't want to get away with anything. If I do then I'm lost."

She took my hand. "I love you, Virgil," she said.

I thought a moment, waiting for her words to sink into me, wondering what they would touch. But they touched nothing; they seemed to be absorbed by my hunger for solitude and retribution. I came close to saying, "I don't care," but I'd already trotted out enough of my life's disorder in front of Kathryn. I pressed Tracy's hand to my lips, quickly, clumsily, shutting myself up until I could respond to her. "Thank you," I said. "Thank you."

The grand jury was due to convene in Eastportsmouth in March. In the meanwhile, the police investigated Tommy's death. I wasn't arrested; there was no probable-cause hearing; whatever they were doing was leisurely, roundabout. I thought about the man who interviewed me in the hospital, Lieutenant Munt, and, though I still expected the case to be tried, I had to admit that Munt treated me as if I were unquestionably innocent. If Tommy had killed me, I couldn't help thinking, it would have been a different matter. But in the view of the law, Tommy was a criminal and I was a citizen and as the days passed I wondered if I would ever hear from the police in Maine again—would that act simply evaporate? The year before, I went to the motor vehicles department to renew my registration, knowing that I hadn't paid the one parking ticket I'd gotten that year and assuming that when they ran my number through the computer this would register. However, my record came out spotless and I was instantly issued new registration. I still had a library book I'd taken out two years ago and I never received notification about that, either. So there was a kind of immunity, a creepy species of exemption from the law I was sometimes granted. This business with the police in Maine was, of course, different: this wasn't a parking ticket or a book of short stories, this was a man's life, his one and only life, yet sometimes it seemed nothing was going to be done about it.

I was sick with curiosity about what was going on up there and it was partly for that reason I finally told Kathryn Perl I wanted her to help me. I figured she would be my source of information. Nothing was proceeding as I expected. I waited to be questioned, interrupted, examined, arraigned, but I was merely left to float in the still, cold waters of my normal life. I called Kathryn in Bath, Maine, two days after our lunch and she told me that she'd already put in a call to Lieutenant Munt, whom she happened to know rather well, but he hadn't gotten back to her. I asked her to let me know as soon as she knew anything. She informed me what she'd be costing me, which I found out later, when I mentioned it to someone, was rather a lot for a country lawyer.

At the office, Bob Halpin asked to speak to me. He brought me into his glass and chrome office and closed the door. He said I'd been looking "gray and nervous" and wondered if there was something wrong that I cared to talk about. As soon as he said this, I wanted to quit. Along with my luck and my marriage, the job seemed to sit on top of my heart like boulders on top of a volcano—remove them and it might erupt.

"As a matter of fact," I said, stretching out, "a great deal is wrong. I killed someone."

Halpin smiled uncertainly. His confusion shamed me, made me feel like a wise-guy.

"I was involved in an accident," I said. "I told you we were stuck in that storm. It was during that."

"You should have said something, Virgil," Halpin said. "I'll give you all the time you need."

"I am going to need time. I have to go back to Maine soon. I'll probably have to stand trial. I can't do the job here anymore."

"Take all the time you need," he said, placing his hands on his desk, palms up. It struck me at that moment that Bob and I could have been friends; somewhere within our association, buried in the functional formality, was a germ of easy, nourishing human companionship. But it had never happened and now it seemed it never would. That had been my choice. Bob was the man who paid me, who dragged me to cocktail parties with people twice my age, who sent me to South Carolina as a talisman, and made it possible for me to support a wholly fanciful style of life with the smallest bit of effort. I had never thought about him outside of all that, nor had I ever known what to make of anything he said. It had never occurred to me that he had struggled for anything in his life. In a year, if someone were to ask me to describe him all I could say was what he did and that he wore orthopedic shoes.

"I'm going to quit, Bob," I said. "I hope it doesn't screw things up too much. But I can't hold this job anymore."

"There's no need, Virgil. Take a leave of absence. Take a month, six months."

I shook my head. "Thank you," I said. "But it's over. I used it up. I want to do something else."

"What?"

"I don't know. Pump gas. Short-order cook." I smiled. He knew as well as I did how ignorant I was of real work. "Anything. Or nothing. I just can't do this anymore."

He regarded me for a few moments. He was skilled at negotiations and had a kind of radar that detected not only how committed someone was to a point of view but how far they would go to see it through. Finally, he nodded. He stood up. I stood up. He walked around his desk and we shook hands and came damn close to embracing. It was a moment's friendship that warmed me but at the same time it rubbed my face in the two years we had spent—people seem suddenly so accessible when you're saying good-bye.

That day, as I cleaned out my desk at the office, the secretary brought me a letter from Deborah Keating.

All my life I have disapproved of those mothers who watched like hawks over their brood, and especially those whose vigilance continued after their children were grown. I have always believed—passionately—in Tracy's right to privacy and it is only after much "soul searching" that I write to you and confess how terribly terribly worried I am about her.

We have never run the kind of family in which confiding came easily. I suppose all of us were far, far too capable of taking care of ourselves and we assumed—rightly, I still believe—that every one of us could manage quite well. Still, I am worried. I don't want you to ever ever tell her I've written you. It's too late in the game to change the habits of Tracy's and my regard for each other.

I have made it my business to call her frequently, especially now that you are forced to go through this legal obscenity. She seems terminally unhappy, Virgil. Her voice is so faint, her attention wanders. I feel always that I've just awakened her. I know that the horrible accident you had up in that cabin of yours has wounded Tracy deeply and I suppose there is something noble about her ability to mourn so, even for a boy who not only was a stranger but an intruder, and a potentially dangerous intruder at that. But there is a degree and kind of mourning that changes us, changes us forever, and I think it is wrong and unfair for Tracy to be allowed to sink into that.

I write to you because sometimes when you live day in and day out with someone you can lose track of things and, to be honest with you, the chance that you might not notice this change in Tracy has been disturbing me (and Roger, too) of late. My own feeling is that she should see someone. Whatever mechanism you evidently possess that has allowed you to make sense of what has happened to you, Tracy is without and there is no reason why she shouldn't receive professional help. As I've said, this suggestion cannot come from me. But if you do decide to recommend to Tracy that she see someone, I wish you would have her consult with my old friend Dr. Janet Fisher, though how you can manage this without betraying the fact of this letter is something I'll leave to you and all your remarkable cleverness. . . .

When Tracy got home that evening I showed her the letter. "Do I really seem so awful?" she asked, folding the letter into fourths, eighths, sixteenths, noticing what she'd done and then smoothing it out, smiling, embarrassed.

"Not awful. But very low."

"Do you think I should see a doctor?"

"I don't know. Not really. You're mourning, still. I think it's right. Anyway, it's what you've always wanted. You're being changed, transformed." I smiled at her. After leaving Halpin Associates, I'd gone to an empty bar that reeked of the previous night and read the afternoon paper over a quartet of Scotches, stopping just when I was about to cross into drunkenness, like a man freezing in his tracks in a turnstile. I'd had half a pot of coffee since coming home but still my nerves were blurred and I couldn't quite keep track of what my face did: that smile really hurt Tracy's feelings.

"I quit my job today," I said. As I said it I realized that I meant, in some obscure muddled way, to convey the sense that soon I would be leaving her as well and the way her face paled when I told her my news made me suspect that, on some level, Tracy knew this too.

"Why can't we go through this together?" she said.

There is something we call a conscience and I had never been totally without one. Like most, my sins had been ones of omission and I didn't have the heart to directly inflict harm. But the small tender spine of morality snaps easily when you are desperate. I knew I was hurting Tracy. I knew that I loved her and knew she loved me. I could feel my hand grabbing meanly at her heart as if that tender muscle were my own, as if our parts had been scrambled, bewitched, and it was no longer possible to determine who was who. But none of that mattered, or it did not matter enough. I needed to operate without restraint. I wanted to rid my life of everything that could be moved so I could finally face what was unbudgeable. If Tracy loved me, as she did, I couldn't be responsible for it. It was her affair. And as I looked at her and saw how she suffered for loving me, a large part of me hated her for it.

The silence in our home reminded me of my father's and my apartment when I was, at his great expense, attending a private high school in New York. Then, the pretense of a relationship had to be delicately maintained and we lived in fear of what might happen if we tried to speak. I knew I could never be sufficiently grateful for the sacrifices he made to send me to the marginal, snobby school, full of ruddy dumbbells and well-dressed neurotics. In fact, I had been generally

uncomfortable there and was made to feel slightly
needy and inferior, since most of my classmates had
parents who were either wealthy or illustrious. I stuck
it out, however, thinking that the experience, the
background, would be, in the end, good for my cause.
And Earl felt not only could I not be sufficiently grateful but that the privileges I was so haltingly accepting
were making me slowly but surely better than him—
haughtier, more assured—the very qualities he craved.

In Tracy's and my case the silence was not one of
misunderstanding. A cord had been cut, one of the
connecting links, and we waited to see if it might heal
on its own. My first unemployed day was on a Wednesday. I stayed in all day, flipping through magazines,
flipping the TV dial, waiting to flip out. When I
thought it was time for Tracy to come home, I went
out for dinner and then to the movies. When I got
back, around ten, she wasn't home. She came home
near midnight with a friend of hers from school named
Carol Marshall, who, as far as I knew, had been to
four graduate schools. Carol wasn't kidding herself nor
was she a fool: she really did have a fierce, child-like
passion to know everything. So far she'd studied math-
ematics, ethnology, French literature, and geology. She
was humorless, irritable, yet somehow exciting, the
way people are when they loyally follow their earliest
ambitions. I never had the feeling she cared much for
me; I suspected she didn't respect people who worked
in business. When Carol and Tracy walked in I had an
impulse to announce that I was no longer working and
this reflexive, degrading desire to please made me sit
up and grin with self-loathing. I finished my drink and
closed my book. By the time the two of them were
seated comfortably I was saying good night. I'll never
see Carol Marshall again, I thought, as I closed the
bedroom door.

Thursday, the three-week mark since Tommy's
death, was yet another day we could not, or did not,
speak. I stayed in bed, faking sleep. When Tracy got

up for work I waited there, reliving the moment when the poker struck Tommy: had he stepped into my swing's orbit or had he been too close all along? I could not decide and the harder I tried to visualize precisely what had happened, the less important it seemed. What could I possibly prove like that? Even if he had stepped closer to me as I swung, couldn't I have stopped it? And even if it could be proved that I was technically blameless within the scope of that instant, what about everything that led up to it? What about his chiding me for using the poker? What about my suggesting we break that particular chest of drawers? Had it been something else, had one detail changed, then Tommy would be alive. Yet it was not even the dresser, nor the poker that had, finally, done it, or so it seemed to me. Tommy's presence had triggered in me a kind of fear, and it had been this, this thing within me, that had killed him.

Finally, Tracy left and I got out of bed. I went to the kitchen to have coffee and there was a note waiting for me.

Virgil, I knew you weren't really sleeping when I got up but I couldn't say anything. You have gone so far from me, I really hate you for it sometimes, hate you for cutting me out, for putting me away from you, for wanting, for even imagining us to be finished with each other. You won't use me for anything except a stick to beat yourself on the head with and I won't do it so there doesn't seem to be anything left, nothing left to us at all. I don't know how much I can stand of this. I don't want to pull a scene. I hate threats. But you're driving me away. Don't do this to me. You're such a fool, such a complete fucking fool. I don't know why I let you do this, to yourself, to me. Here I am writing this note and I know you're fully awake in the bedroom. I should go in and say it to your face but I know

that as soon as I walked in you'd close your eyes
and pretend to be sleeping. I want to kick you.
Please. Stop this. When you said good night to
me last night I shivered. I don't know your voice.
I don't know you. You frighten me and that isn't
fair. You should never do that.

Late that morning, just when I was thinking of calling Tracy and meeting her for lunch, I got a call from
Kathryn Perl.

"It looks like the D.A. wants to bring it to grand
jury," she said. "I just got through with Munt and with
Prashear, the D.A."

"When?" I asked. My hands were ice.

"I'm not certain. I think we can still stop it. Maybe
if they talk to you and Tracy. This Cavanaugh girl is
the only witness they have so far, and she's not much.
Anyhow, I want you to know there's not even any talk
about homicide. It's going to be a question of manslaughter, accidental. It remains to be seen how anxious they are to get that kind of indictment, especially
against someone who can muster a decent defense.
Those manslaughter indictments get convictions
maybe one time out of twenty. They might decide the
whole thing's a waste of time. Anyhow, that's what I'm
trying to convince them of."

"When do they want to talk to me?" I said.

"No hurry. But you might have to come up at the
end of the month. I'm going to try and arrange it so
you can simply write a statement and not have to make
the trip."

"I'd just as soon say it in person."

"Fine. But I'd rather you not."

"Well, what else is going on?"

"With what?"

"I don't know. What do the cops say? I feel so removed from this whole thing."

"Try and relax. No one thinks this is much of a case.
The boy was a fugitive. That Cavanaugh girl didn't
even see it. I honestly think there's very little we have
to worry about and you can ask anyone who knows me
that my opinions generally run to the pessimistic."

"I feel very out of place down here," I said.

"Just sit tight. It's the best place for you."

I could not sit tight. A part of my life, perhaps my very life, was being settled in Maine and while I had no idea what I could do about it, I wanted somehow to be closer to the process, just as some men want to watch their children being born, even if they can't help in any way, even if their presence is only an obstruction: it's an enormous event and they must be there.

When Tracy came home, I told her I was going up to Maine. "I've got to talk with Kathryn. I'll pick up our car and whatever else we left up there."

"I'll come with you."

"No. I'm going to leave tomorrow."

"I'll take off."

"No. There's no reason. I've got a reservation on a morning flight." I knew she wanted to go and, again, I knew I was hurting her by refusing. I think I knew exactly what I was doing.

"I don't want you leaving without me, Virgil."

"But that's what I'm going to do." I felt, momentarily, like a third person, watching two people I loved drift apart.

I felt that way for perhaps an instant, for just as I was trying to arrange my face into a composed smile, Tracy slapped me.

"Asshole," she said, her face going red. Her gold band caught me on the side of the upper lip. I touched it and there was blood.

I stared at her, expecting her either to take another swing or to burst into tears, but she just stood there and her eyes were as dry as smoke.

"I can't live with you anymore," she said.

"Good," I said. "You shouldn't. I'm sick to fucking death of you dragging your sensitivity around like a little wagon. *I'm* the one who's taking it on the chin. Let's not forget that."

"I'm not forgetting. *You're* forgetting. You're forgetting *me*."

"Look, you're right. We shouldn't live together. I shouldn't live with anyone."

"I guess you shouldn't." I could feel her giving up on me; it was what I wanted but as I felt it happening I wanted to moan.

"So how do you think we should run it?" I said. I felt the mitigating heat of distant tears but they would never make their journey in time. They'd be shed after she was gone.

"Run what?"

"Who moves out."

"I don't want this place. It was yours before you met me. I'll move out."

"Where will you go?"

"I'll stay with Gary."

"Great. Perfect."

"I'm glad you're pleased."

"You were never proud of me, were you?"

"That's not true. What a dumb thing to say."

"Yes it is. It's completely true. The way you used to talk about how lucky I was. That was really your way of saying I got things I didn't deserve."

"I married you, for God's sake. I've never loved anyone the way I loved you. I'd be loving you right now, if you'd let me."

"No. Not true. You always wanted me to be different. You had big plans for my moral education. You didn't seem to ever approve of what I'd made of myself. Not that you minded living off it."

That was it. I knew it as soon as I'd said it. She stepped back, shaking her head. "Really, Virgil, you can be so incredibly ugly," she said, and the anger and love were out of her eyes, replaced by condescension, pity, and what looked like absolute good-bye.

My plane left LaGuardia at eight o'clock and I was in Eastportsmouth by eleven. There was still plenty of snow on the ground as the red and yellow ten-seater touched down. I'd been one of two passengers. The other traveler was a little girl with dark olive skin who couldn't have been more than twelve. She read a movie magazine with a picture of Robert Redford on the cover and as she read she chain-smoked Pall Malls. At one point, she seemed to consider engaging me in conversation but one look in my direction discouraged her.

After we landed, I carried my overnight bag into the Quonset hut that stood to the left of the landing strip and from there I called a taxi. While I waited I had a hot chocolate from a vending machine and listened to the two fellows who worked there talk about removing the propeller from someone's plane because the owner hadn't paid his landing and storage fees.

The cab was driven by an old man wearing a checkered coat and yellow rubber boots that came up to his knees. I told him I wanted to hire him for a good part of the day, first to take me to the police station in Eastportsmouth and then past Gardner Point to my house. He asked where exactly my house was and when I told him it was the old Page Place he glanced at me in the rearview mirror. I wondered if he was an old friend of Cleveland Page or had he heard about the killing that had taken place? Chances were that the killing was widespread gossip in those relatively peaceful parts. I settled into the back seat as we made the short trip to the police station. It was beginning to snow.

The police station in Eastportsmouth looked like a drive-in bank. The stones were off-white and rough-textured, the shape was rectangular, and there were thin strips of windows placed here and there as a sort of embarrassed nod to design. My taxi pulled in next to a squad car; the driver gunned the motor and then switched off the ignition.

"I won't be very long," I said.

The old man nodded. I'd offered him forty dollars for the trip and it didn't seem to matter too much to him how long I took.

"Do you want me to get you something?" I said, pointing to a variety store across the street. "A paper or a magazine?"

"Nope," he said. He opened his glove compartment and took out a Bible.

Eastportsmouth was the county seat and had a population of nearly 20,000, so, unlike some of the state's smaller towns, the life of Eastportsmouth remained normally vigorous, even in the winter's dead center. Traffic moved along the streets and, in the middle of town, with its white churches and rows of stores, hundreds of cars were vertically parked, each one facing an oversized parking meter. I'd lost track of the fact that the state was filled with people leading regular lives; I had reduced it to the sketchily painted backdrop for the opera in which I sang lead.

If Tracy or anyone I knew had suddenly appeared to ask me what I was doing standing before the bright glass doors of that police station, I don't know what I could have answered. But I was still obscurely confident that the purpose of the visit would reveal itself— that blind urge to fly north had to be connected to some greater purpose.

The front desk of the station was manned by an officer about my age. He sat on a high three-legged stool filling out an official report. The light in the station was wholly artificial, a sick brightness. The floors were blue linoleum and there were shabby plastic chairs along the cinderblock walls, all of them unoccupied. The young cop didn't look up as I approached him.

"Excuse me," I said.

As soon as he heard my voice, he put his pen down and smiled at me. One of his front teeth was silver. He was skinny and unkempt and you sensed that in his innocent adolescence he had covered his arms with tattoos.

"I'd like to talk to Lieutenant Munt," I said. "Is he in?"

As I said this, I heard voices approaching us and I turned to see Munt himself, pushing his way through a door that led to an inner corridor, accompanied by a woman wearing a bright orange coat and a beehive hair-do.

"Lieutenant Munt!" I said, moving toward him, my heart slamming.

Munt's lined, bumpy face registered nothing but then his reddish eyes lit up a little and he nodded with considerable enthusiasm. "Mr. Morgan," he said. "How are you?"

"Okay, okay," I said. We shook hands.

"This is my wife," he said, introducing me to the woman. She looked annoyed. She had a small face and her ears came almost to a point: she looked like a large disagreeable elf. I wondered briefly why she was displeased and thought for a moment that she knew that the law's full force had only grazed me. Then I realized that, more likely, she had come to meet her husband for lunch and now I was threatening to delay them.

"What brings you to town?" asked Munt, in his soft, endlessly questioning voice. Again, the sound of it reminded me of my Uncle Duncan, but whereas the first time the memory had been comforting this time it gave me a chill.

"I'm going back to our place to get the car. We had to leave it behind."

"Well, you won't have any trouble. All the plowing's done. We haven't had much snow since the storm." He buttoned his overcoat as he spoke and glanced reassuringly at his wife.

"I'd like to ask you a question," I said, knowing I had only a few more moments. "What's going on with—" Suddenly, I lacked the vocabulary. It was as if my will and my confusion, generally immune to each other in separate mental orbits, had crossed paths, one eclipsing the other.

"Nothing's going on, Mr. Morgan. Fact is, I just got through talking to your lawyer." He smiled. "You picked yourself a dandy."

"What do you mean nothing's going on?"

"Well, we were going to have you and your wife come up to make statements? Now it looks like we don't have to do that. We can do the whole thing through Kathryn. You know, I was always sure you were telling the truth. It figured to be an accident. But we had that girl accusing you? We had to look into it. But the girl was no good. She didn't make any sense. And there was no one else who had anything to say? The D.A. gave the case to his assistant, the assistant didn't want it. It was an accident."

"You mean the case is closed?"

"Not really. No. Might still go to grand jury next month. But it doesn't look that way." He looked at his watch and then glanced again at his wife, who had turned away from us and stared into space. "If I were you I wouldn't worry about this."

"I'm a little surprised, that's all," I said. I'd meant it to be a provocative thing to say, almost like a slip of the tongue, but Munt didn't appear to notice. If I'd grabbed him, shaken his shoulders, and screamed out a confession, maybe that would have pumped blood into a case that seemed to be dying right before me. But, unable to do that, I just swayed from my right foot to my left, staring at him uncomprehendingly, and delaying his lunch.

"I'm going to have to rush off?" Munt said.

I nodded. "Okay." I thought of asking if I might wait for him but I just continued to nod and when he offered his hand to shake good-bye I grabbed it clumsily and pumped it up and down. I felt the warmth of his flesh; the hard ridge of his wedding ring. Dimly, woozily, I thought to myself: another human being.

It was a ride of some thirty-five miles to the house Tracy and I had named Preservation Hall. The driver kept his Bible next to him on the seat and I looked out the window as we passed icy farms and big frozen clumps of forest. We passed a beaten-up old trailer, in front of which stood an old car, its wheels off, the axles mounted on milk crates. A collie appeared and chased after us, but soon it gave up and its disappointed bark slowly faded away. Before leaving Eastportsmouth, I asked the driver to get some jumpers in case my car's battery was dead. He told me that would cost extra and so I suspected he didn't like me very much. The jumpers were next to me on the back seat and I drummed my fingernails on the long metal clips.

"What's your name?" I said, leaning toward the front.

The driver started, as if I'd awakened him. "Bill Foster," he said.

"Hello," I said. "My name's Virgil Morgan." We passed another farm; two boys on snowmobiles were scooting around in quick, large circles.

He nodded. I waited for him to say something, anything. It just seemed obscene that we would ride all the way in silence. I seemed to be in the middle of a life of missed opportunities. If my heart did not drag me up here to see Munt, maybe it was for a message from Bill Foster. I looked at the back of his old, dark neck. I saw how the barbered white hairs touched the edge of his coat collar. He smelled of hair tonic. It seemed, in fact, to be the brand I used when I was ten or so: Wildroot Cream Oil, the aroma of sheer, guileless yearning. Finally, my silence embarrassed him and he said, "I used to own Mr. Lumber, just outside of Eastportsmouth."

I nodded and sank back into the back seat. "Do many people take cabs around here?" I said. I just couldn't think of anything better to say.

He explained to me that his job was part-time, just something to help meet expenses. The car was his own and every once in a while the taxi service called him with a fare. "When I sold Mr. Lumber," he said, "I thought I could relax. But I don't like staying at home, 'specially now that I'm on my own. I like to get out."

We turned off the highway at the junction. He seemed to know exactly where I was going. Part of my arrangement with Evan Tarwater had been that he would see to clearing the access road after storms and I had trusted this arrangement implicitly. But now, as we approached the old Page spread, I feared that the road was still invisible beneath the snow and we wouldn't be able to get near the house and my car.

The road had been plowed and we rolled over it, beneath the towering snow-brilliant trees. Loose snow fanned out beneath our tires and all the land that I had somehow managed to own passed by. It reflected on the windshield, swelled and trembled.

"It's about a half mile in," I said.

"This your place?" he asked.

"I bought it."

"It's a good piece of land, if you like to look at land. You won't grow anything on it."

"I know. We were thinking of a garden, that's all."

"Oh, a garden won't be any trouble. But you know all these trees won't be worth much as timber. You may as well keep them standing, if you ask me."

"I never thought we'd sell them."

"I knew Cleveland Page."

"He was a carpenter, wasn't he?"

"He was a lot of things. Carpenter, fisherman. I think he was a musician once, when he was young and living in Burlington. I think that man played piano in a whorehouse." Foster looked up at the rearview mirror and smiled. The car wheels bit off edges of the narrow road. "When his wife died he used to say to me, 'Wait till it happens to you, Bill.' But I've never had the loneliness that man had. And I don't have a daughter to look after me. What I've got is friends, hobbies, and this book." He tapped the Bible.

We turned a bend in the road and I saw the small stone cottage, its windows bright with sun. We passed the lake, still frozen, still stocked with trout. The plowed snow was pressed into slopes on either side of the road; it must have taken a full day to clear it. I didn't know if the door to the house would be locked but I had the key with me. I turned it over in my hand; it was the color of brass, it was the color of that fireplace poker.

We pulled up next to the house and I got out of the car. Melissa's VW was gone. I saw tracks in the snow where it had been backed up and turned around. I touched the treadmarks in the snow, wondering if she'd just removed her car. They were frozen solid.

A strong gust of wind came whistling out of the west, lifting powder from the roof of the house. I glanced back at the taxi. Bill Foster was reading his Bible.

The area of land where the cars had been parked was plowed and salted. The ice had been chipped off my windshield. Snow still coated the back of the car but it had been removed from the hood. Apparently, someone had checked the motor, the battery.

I was only wearing a leather coat, a thin sweater, and business shoes, and I was freezing.

I went to the door of the house and found it was locked. The windows were still icy, though not so thickly covered. I peered in. The floors were swept and though it appeared that less was in the house, everything seemed neatly placed. I put the key in the door to see if it unlocked. It did, but I did not open it. I went to the back of the house. The kitchen windows had been replaced. Little smears of putty joined the new glass to the windowframes. I stepped back and looked up to where we'd made our bedroom. The window there had also been replaced. So much had been done that it was difficult to fully feel that this was my house.

But it was, and I could not enter it. I paced around it like a virgin burglar, devaluing every object I'd come to take. Who needed those clothes, the quilt, the tape recorder? And as I delayed my entrance I became more and more incapable of it, until I could not have gone in at gunpoint.

I went to my car, wondering if I'd be as incapable of entering it as I was the house. But the terror did not spread; it remained fixed in one place. I climbed into the freezing Mercedes and dug through my pockets for the keys, my heart slamming against my chest. The motor turned over on the third attempt. I gunned it a couple of times and put it in neutral.

I walked over to the taxi and paid Bill Foster. "Looks like the car's in good shape," I said. "I'm on my own from here."

He looked at his watch. "All right," he said. "Which way you going?"

"I'm going south," I said.

"Well, I'll stick with you till we hit the highway. Make sure that car of yours keeps running."

We got back on the access road and I followed Foster off the land. I wished mightily that he'd move faster. I was ringing the curtain down on a blissful *idea* of my life and I didn't want to prolong it for another moment. When we reached the highway, he pulled off the side of the road and he waved at me when I passed. I waved energetically, realizing, when it was too late, that the thing to do would have been to stop and shake hands. I watched his car in the rearview mirror, turning onto the highway and heading north toward Eastportsmouth. I slammed my hand against the steering wheel.

I moved south on Route 1 and thought about suicide. Cars passed me, going north, and it would have been easy, or so it seemed, to steer my Mercedes into their lane and so end my life. The thought was so intoxicating, so horrifying, that I tendered it for minutes before I realized that my car was so heavy that the chances were I would inflict more harm on my northbound accomplice than on myself. Then what about steering into a diesel truck or off the edge of a mountain? No, no, it wouldn't work: by the time I got to the alternatives, the appeal of the act had already faded. And it *was* an act, I knew that, and the knowledge ground me deeper into my shame. I could not kill myself, I didn't even want to. If what I feared was to spend another day as exactly the person I was, it was no more or less than what I fully deserved. My life was a hook, and as I kept my car in its proper lane, I really did not want to wriggle off of it.

My unhappiness inhabited me as if it were another person and it had the power to pull memories from me, as if from an open file: here, look at this, and now this. I thought of my father, and every recollection was bound in bad faith. I remembered my humiliation over his impromptu concert at the Keatings' and then I could practically hear the sound of his voice, the buzz of the public school piano as he led me and my classmates in song. If I could have sung along I would have known then more than I knew right now about disappointment and earnest small tragedy, and I would have known a great deal more about grace. But I chose to flee and it was as a fugitive that I'd learned most of my terrible habits. I hid from the image of Earl swaying in a honey-colored classroom, from his nights on the couch and his Left Bank breakfasts, from his loneliness and from my fear that he'd never get half of what he so unfailingly desired. I'd shrunk from the very whiskers on his chin and now I knew that it was too late: not only were they gone but he was gone, too. He had found someone who was not humiliated by his struggle and he was right to choose her, to choose loyalty over capricious blood. Once Earl had told me I was lucky to have been born in an age when oral sex was "freely bestowed" and I'd felt like throttling him. Why? At the time he seemed so goddamned intrusive and needy, but I was already eighteen and I could have known that, once more, I was being offered a chance to embrace everything in life from which I was in hiding. I should have thrown my head back and laughed. I should have put my arms around the old fucker. But I could not do it. There was a space between us, as invisible and powerful as a magnetic field. I knew exactly when and how far to step back and I was an expert in looking the other way. I had learned early in life that, if I wanted it to, what happened to me could be substantially different—that is to say, better—than what happened to those around me, no matter how many of them there were, no matter how closely they crowded, no matter how I loved them. And this notion, this lunatic, pragmatic notion, had protected me and moved

me through what had until recently been a life without
interruptions.

Now it seemed that the beast that had guarded my
heart for so many years was turning, turning slowly,
had already turned and was tearing at me with all of its
awful strength.

21

I GOT BACK to New York around midnight. I had
stopped in a Howard Johnson's around New Lon-
don, Connecticut, and broken a long, unconscious
fast. I'd tried to call Tracy but there'd been no answer.
Now, passing through the Bronx with the radio on
loud, I both hoped and dreaded that she wouldn't be
home when I arrived. The news came on; there was an
immense fire in the part of the Bronx I was passing
through at that very moment. I searched the black,
starless sky for the glow of flames but saw nothing.

Fifteen minutes later, I was standing in the living
room of my apartment. I took a deep breath. I
couldn't even smell her; she must have left hours before. She'd spared me the country and western touch
of the Good-bye Note: there was merely a slip of
paper next to the phone with a number written on it.

I sat on the couch and poured myself a huge,
splashing drink. I did not weep but my body was alive
with a hideous tenderness. I grabbed the phone and

dialed the number Tracy had left. Someone picked up on the second ring.

"Hello?"

It was Gary Fish, sounding whimpier and more ecstatic than I'd ever heard him.

"Hello? Hello?" he persisted, tempting me to believe that he really *was* too stupid to know who sat in dead silent hatred on the other end. Carefully, I hung the phone up.

I stalked into the bedroom. The bed was perfectly made, like a bed in a hotel. I went to the closet and checked for her suitcase, knowing full well it would be gone. The closet, however, still looked essentially filled. Her clothes still hung from the front tier, freely fraternizing with mine, and there was something about their inanimate commingling that nearly bent me over with grief. Her shoes were scattered on the closet floor; a summer dress had slipped from its hanger and now lay there like a silk puddle. I touched her things. I could instantly remember a dozen places each article of clothing had been worn. I could see her stepping out of them as well, preparing for bed, using that brown velvet dress as a mat in the chilly bathroom as she stooped, as graceful as Narcissus, and inserted her diaphragm.

I emerged from the closet and fell onto the bed. It was not yet quite actual that I was without her. Sudden grief is largely a matter of imagination: you know what this is going to mean. I knew I was going to know, but that was as far as I could take it. I was asleep in less than a minute.

I awakened a couple of hours later, with only my hot, clammy clothes to remind me of whatever dreams I might have had. I stripped and turned off the lights, secure, almost tranquil in that tunnel vision madness you get when your actions are run by an infinitesimal portion of your brain. But as soon as I lay down again, as soon as my skin touched the chilly sheets, I experienced an odd, passive horror. I could feel myself waking up. I forced my eyes to remain shut but it was useless. The realization that I was alone, that Tracy had finally given up on me now blazed within me. I felt myself speeding toward my own solitude, unable to stop, wanting only something to occupy my mind. But I had nothing to grab hold of, no tree that I climbed as a child, no bird I saw in flight, everything was far too personal for me to bear it, and the only music I could hear was the increasingly violent pounding of blood in my ears.

I was awakened at nine the next morning by Kathryn Perl's telephone call.

"What in the world were you trying to accomplish yesterday?" she said, without a hello.

I had to think for a moment. "I was trying to sink my own ship."

"It certainly seemed that way. Please, Virgil, I mean it. Don't do my job for me. You can make things very difficult."

"According to Munt, the case doesn't seem to be going very well."

"Is Munt working for you now? Do you realize how close I was to having them drop this whole matter? Well, you took care of that. It looked like you and Tracy wouldn't even have to come up. Now I don't see how I'm going to stop them from calling you."

"That's not so bad," I said, waking up. The bed seemed to consist of vast expanses of empty space; the section of mattress I covered was like a warm current in an otherwise icy ocean.

"I don't like it. And I don't like having my work undermined. I know how nervous you are but you have to trust me. I don't want this going to grand jury; if it does then we might have a trial. I don't think you realize what an unpleasant ordeal that can be. Do you follow me? There are so many damn variables in any case, Virgil. You're a fool to go crashing around when you don't know what you're doing."

"I just don't like feeling so cut off from the whole thing."

"Yes, I know. You said that. And you see what it got you. All right. Now, when's the best time for you and Tracy to come up and make your statements?"

"It doesn't matter to me. Tracy and I aren't living together."

She was silent. I figured her reaction was that that was bad for the case.

"When did *this* happen?" she asked.

"Recently. I'm sure she won't say anything bad."

"Of course not."

"A wife can't testify against a husband anyhow. Isn't that so?"

"She can't testify to secrets of the marriage."

The phrase made me want to hang up the phone.

"Well," I said, my voice drifting, "that's a pretty broad term."

There was a silence from the other end of the line that surprised me. I had naturally expected Kathryn's voice to be there as soon as I stopped talking but I could hear nothing but the soft, furry hum of the long-distance wires.

Finally, Kathryn said, "You worry me, Virgil. You have from the very start of this. I don't claim to know you very well but I want you to understand something. If you want to come to terms with whatever part you may have had in that boy dying then you'd better make sure you stay out of jail. Don't think you're going to find a judge and jury who're going to do it for you. What might or might not happen in court will have nothing to do with what you finally make of all this. If you want to reckon with this then for God's sake reckon with it. But in the meanwhile, if you want me to have anything to do with this, let me do my job."

*   *   *

I had never been particularly graceful but a new, dulling kind of clumsiness invaded me, now that I was without Tracy. I bumped into things, doorways, tables, stupid things. I couldn't make my bed properly: the seams on the bedspread moved like ripples in a stream. My timing was off. I got jostled in crowds, pinched by elevator doors and I took too long to say things. Without Tracy, without a job, without even my father to surprise me, my phone rarely rang and except for a brief visit from Mario, who came by to borrow a little money, not one person entered my apartment for an entire week. Bob Halpin rang me up one day to suggest we have lunch and to ask me about a file they were searching the office for. I had no idea where the file might be and my refusal to meet him was, I think, a little curt. I suspected he didn't really want to see me, that what he really wanted was the missing file, that perhaps he was accusing me of stealing it, or, at best, making an empty gesture to blunt the coldly functional nature of his call.

Because I had quit my job, I had no severance pay and no unemployment insurance. I was far from destitute but some simple calculation revealed that soon I'd be out of money—a month, two months, three months, it depended on how I lived. I accepted this eventuality with no difficulty and even looked forward to it: who knew? maybe it would change my life. I could then sell Preservation Hall and find some honest work, two things I could not yet bring myself to do. I needed certain practical realities to hold a gun to my head. The house I would be well rid of. But then, of course, I'd be rich again and wouldn't need to work. Then I wouldn't sell the house. But then looking for a job would seem like a *project* and what I needed was an emergency. Then give the house away? Give it back to Tarwater, or maybe Bill Foster? Or perhaps donate it to the National Association for the Rights of Prisoners? The rapturous indulgence of such an idea . . .

No, I'd give it to Tracy, let her worry about it. We hadn't spoken to each other since the night before I went to Maine and I welcomed a safe way to break the silence. It was nine in the evening when I finally decided to call her. I was dressed in a bathrobe, unshaven, and was watching TV. I turned the sound down and dialed Fish's number, deliberately not considering anything I might say. I threw myself into it in the same spirit I had used to coerce myself off a diving board when I was twelve: if you don't do it then you're nothing forever.

Fish picked up on the third ring. "Hello?" To my enormous relief he sounded less buoyant than he had the first time I'd called.

My mind filled with hot white light; it really did feel as if my brain was being fried. I could think of nothing to say.

"Hello?" Fish persisted, sounding weary and annoyed.

"Who is it, Gary?" Tracy said, from the background.

Hearing her voice was like being stepped on. I quickly hung up the phone. Idiot, I thought, now what? I grabbed the phone again but did not lift it from its cradle.

A few moments later, the phone began to ring. I let it go four or five times and then picked it up. "Hello?"

"What that you, Virgil?" Tracy. My heart jumped like a fox.

"What?"

"Calling here."

"No."

"Oh." She waited—but for what? Then she hung up.

The next day was sunny and cold, with a few ripples of white cloud in the sky: small-town weather. I wandered through Central Park and sat on a bench for a while, eavesdropping on some elderly women talking about their sons. At one point, I almost leaped up because I thought I saw Tracy walking toward me, with a St. Bernard on a leash, but it turned out to be a stranger, a girl much younger than Tracy and not looking very much like her. But it had shaken me, deeply. It reminded me of the time Earl had come home, when we lived in Chicago, and said he saw someone in the drugstore who looked like his disappeared wife, my vanished mother. Those optical illusions of separation.

Gary Fish lived in a brownstone on West Sixty-fourth Street and as I walked through the park I neared his house. It was still early in the morning and I felt there was a chance of finding Tracy home. I had no idea what I wanted to say to her, or even if I'd actually go through with it. Still, I ostensibly had ulterior motives and these protected me: I could always say I'd come to talk about selling the house in Maine, or to scold her for ringing me up last night, or to request that she begin moving things out of my apartment. That last one sounded a little foolish: I'd say I was planning to move out and give her notice. The falsehood appealed to me and as I shuffled toward Sixty-fourth Street I decided that, perhaps that very day, I'd give the apartment's management company notice. I didn't belong in such a place and, besides, soon I wouldn't be able to afford it.

Gary Fish lived in an old, pretty building; it had a bright red door with stone gargoyles carved above it. There were three buzzers on the outside of the building: McDougal, F. Saliem, and Gary Fish. No Tracy Morgan. I peered into the small entranceway and saw her name wasn't on the mailboxes either. Relieved, I pressed Fish's button.

"Who is it?" he said through the intercom.

Twice already the sound of his voice had inspired silence in me but this time I couldn't allow it. "It's me," I said. "It's Virgil. Is Tracy there?"

There was a silence. "Umm, just a sec, okay?"

The connection broke and the intercom was dead. I

leaned against the locked door until I heard footsteps coming down the steps but couldn't see anyone. There was a steep polished wooden staircase with a gleaming banister that coiled upward like a cobra from a basket. I could tell that the footsteps weren't Tracy's, and as I stared through the front door's watery glass I saw first Fish's ox-blood loafers, then his gray and blue checked trousers, and then his whole angular self, zipping up his short leather jacket, tucking in his yellow silk scarf. He made it all the way down the stairs and to the locked door without acknowledging my stare; it wasn't until his hand was on the doorknob that he nodded his head, and his full bee-stung lips made a rapid smile.

He opened the door, stepped outside, and closed it hard behind him. "She's not here, Virgil," he said.

"Where is she?"

"She had to leave early. Appointments."

"You still letting her do all the work?"

He felt no pressure to answer. He turned away and prepared to sneeze but the sneeze eluded him. As I recognized my pleasure in his minor frustration I also realized that I was not likely to conduct myself with monumental dignity.

"Is she at the office?" I said. Fish smelled of coffee. I'd probably interrupted his breakfast. I wondered who made the coffee. Did Tracy make a pot before going to work and then leave it warming for when Fish got up? Christ.

"Can we take a little walk?" he said. "I'd like to talk to you."

We walked down Sixty-fourth Street, toward the park. Gary moved with a slight limp and I guessed he'd had one of those skiing accidents that usually kept him out of the office a few days a year. He rubbed his long bony hands together as we walked; he wore a gold ring with a lion's head on his index finger.

"How've you been?" he said, without looking over.

"I've lost track. How about you?"

He shrugged. "Fighting a cold."

"What'd you want to talk to me about?"

We were on Central Park West now, leaning on the low wall that separated the sidewalk from the park.

"Don't see Tracy for a while, Virgil," he said, finally engaging my eyes, but only for a moment.

"Why the hell not?" I regretted my response immediately. This was nothing I should even discuss with Fish. It was none of his business yet I persisted as if he might conceivably understand it better than I. "It doesn't concern you," I said, as much to myself as to him.

"Oh, yes it does," Gary said. "After all, I'm the one who stayed up with her when she was completely unglued. I'm sorry, but it *does* concern me."

It was clear he spoke with the hazy propriety of unrequited love.

"It's only fair that you let her put her life together," he said. "If you really cared about Trace—"

"Trace? Who the fuck is Trace?"

"If you really cared about her you'd let her alone. You really hurt her. What do you want to do, hurt her more?"

I was still digesting his calling her Trace.

"I'm going to your office," I said. "I'll wait for her there."

"No, Virgil," he said, probably not with the conviction he'd intended. I think he knew before I did that I was liable to slug him.

I placed my hand on Fish's shoulder. "Gary, are you sleeping with my wife?"

He moved away and shook his head. "You don't have to worry about that," he said, trying to sound superior.

"Then why are you so intimately concerned with our business?"

"It's not *your* business, Virgil. Not in the way it used to be."

"I seem to remember Tracy telling me she thought you had a crush on her."

"That's ancient history."

"So then it's true?" My hand had found its way back to his shoulder. I gripped him tightly and grinned.

"Stop it, man," said Fish, twisting away from me.

"I want you to keep out of my business, Fish. I don't ever want to hear your opinions about what I should do with my wife."

"You don't own her," he said in a very moral tone. "If you cared about her then you'd listen. You've hurt her enough. You scare her, Virgil. She can't be happy with you. I'm not saying she can be happy with me, but I want her to be happy."

"Aren't you a little bit worried, Fish?"

"Worried?"

"That's right. After all, I am a dangerous man. Aren't you afraid I might punch you in the nose?"

He smiled nervously and ran his hand through his hair. "I don't think you're looking for any more trouble with the police than you already have."

I grabbed him by the jacket and pulled him close to me. "Don't count on that," I said.

He shook loose of me and I hit him straight on, though not exactly on the nose. It was more to the side but it must have hurt anyhow because I hit him hard. Just as I was doing it, a very beautifully dressed old woman walked by with her Yorkshire terrier. I glanced at her and she looked at the pavement, terrified.

Fish reeled back, touching his face, checking his fingertips for blood. There was a little.

"You dumb grubby little cocksucker," he said, in a perfectly level voice. I'd never heard him sound so dignified. "I hope you get the royal screwing you deserve."

"Come on, Fish. I want you to fight back." It felt wonderful to rage; Gary, after all, was the first person I'd spoken to in a couple days.

"Forget it," he said, continuing to back away. "All I want to do is go home and call the police. You're even stupider than I thought."

"You'd better hurry. If you go right to the station you can show them your blood. Go on, run."

His back was to me now. He made his way across the street, dodging taxi cabs with the unconscious grace of an urban matador. As soon as he was safely across the street, I had an impulse to chase after him. Push him down, walk on him. The sudden violent desire sent a rush of overheated blood to my face and in a moment I was trembling.

He'd succeeded in one thing, at least. I was in no shape to see Tracy. Just as well.

Kathryn called the next day.

"It looks like I've taken care of it," she said. "But it's no thanks to you. Why didn't you tell me a little more about the Cavanaugh girl?"

"Like what," I said. It was nine in the morning and I'd been watching TV since seven.

"You should have told me about her participation in that psychiatric program. I could tell just by looking at her that something wasn't right. We're just very lucky they let me question her."

"You questioned her? When?"

"Yesterday. I could kick you for not telling me about her history."

"I didn't think of it."

"You understand, don't you, that she was all they had. Now there's no question of Prashear bringing it to the grand jury. He's got a hopeless case. Even if he got an indictment I wouldn't treat his witness well, and he knows it."

"Because she sees a psychiatrist?"

"That's exactly right. She's been hospitalized, more than once. This is Maine, Virgil. They're not going to find a jury that would be comfortable with her testimony. Even though she was willing to go all the way. You have no idea how willing she was. But as soon as I put pressure on her she collapsed."

I felt a deep, familiar jolt of shame.

"So that's it?" I said.

"That's it, essentially. You're still going to have to come up and make formal statements, both of you."

"When?"

"Next Monday."

"Okay. Will you tell Tracy or will I? I wish you would."

"You two are still apart? Correct that, Virgil. Take it from me. I divorced Mr. Perl twenty-five years ago and I still miss him. And while you're at it, you'd better get a job, too. You owe me a lot of money."

I waited to feel relief that my case was being settled but the part of me that normally would have responded to the news was numb with shame that my lawyer—the lawyer I'd chosen, the lawyer I would pay—had been so jugular with Melissa. Kathryn was right about at least one thing—the courtroom was no place to settle my conscience. I no longer wanted to stand trial. The reckoning was something I wanted to do on my own. But there was something cheap and obscurely typical of me to be suddenly free because Melissa saw a psychiatrist. I was sick and ashamed of moving forward on the backs of others.

Fifteen minutes after talking to Kathryn I was on the subway heading downtown. I understood that it was useless and maybe even wrong for me to apologize to Melissa for what my lawyer had done to her, but I wanted to face her. I wanted her to know I wasn't hiding from her, and I wanted to know that myself. Even if she'd had a phone I wouldn't have called. I didn't want to do it by remote control. I wanted to look again into those incandescent eyes and I wanted her to be able to see me and tell me whatever she longed for me to hear.

The train let me off at Fourteenth Street and I walked east, hoping to recognize the apartment Tommy and Melissa had brought us to. As I drew closer to her part of Fourteenth Street, the neighborhood grew grimmer. The cheap food stands were already open for business. Young, comatose chefs dropped gray steaks onto smoking grills. A sharp gaseous wind came off the East River and the Con Ed smokestacks expelled galaxies of bright waste. I was the only pedestrian in sight. Most of the stores were closed and looked as if they'd never open again. The buildings were old and covered with soot and looked so soft that you felt you could put your hand through them.

I found Melissa's building by finding the bingo parlor. I remembered her saying that the bingo parlor made the block safe and I remembered her apartment was next door. There were empty beer bottles, filthy cellophane, and flattened mango pits on the stoop. The street door was open, as was the door that led to the inside corridor. I walked up the stinking staircase, waiting for something to appear familiar. There was a bicycle chained to a hot water pipe, bags overflowing with garbage, a child's huge plastic car, more garbage, and names spray-painted on the walls: *Savage Avengers, Skull Brothers, Avenue A Vampires*. Mixed into the violent graffiti was a heart with *Pablo Loves Della* written in it. It was silent in the halls, except for the menacing buzz of the faulty fluorescent light.

What I remembered from the first time I came to her apartment was the newly constructed wooden door and that an unfamiliar name—DePasquale—was written in the center of it. When I got to the third floor, I saw the lumber door but there was no name on it anymore.

I knocked. The door was so thick that I hardly made any noise, even though I rapped hard. I hit the heel of my hand against the door and waited.

"Who's there?" said a boy's voice, with a slight Spanish accent.

"Is Melissa there?" I said.

"Who?"

"Melissa Cavanaugh."

"She moved. Who are you?"

"Do you know where she is?"

"No. Go away, man. There's people sleeping."

I could hear him walking away. Was that it? I stood before the door, with my fists curled at my side. I had no idea if the boy was telling the truth. I tried to imagine forcing him to open the door—then what? He'd look at me, in my rumpled blue suit, with four days' whiskers on my face, and he'd probably think I was a ravaged ex-cop, looking to settle a score. I leaned my forehead against the door, trying to think of what to do next.

I went down to the street and found a working phone booth. I called information and asked for the number of the National Association for the Rights of Prisoners, got it, and let it ring twenty-five times before I slammed the phone down. I stood in the booth, watching the cars go by.

The only connection to Melissa I had was Lillian and Earl. I discovered I knew their number by heart. I slipped my dime into the box.

Lillian picked up on the second ring. "Martin?" she said, anxiously.

"Hello, Lillian. This is Virgil. Is my father home?"

"You," she said, amazed.

"Is Earl home or at school?"

"You kill my son and then you call my home?"

"I didn't kill your son."

"Oh, no? Then where is he? In the next room? At the A and P?"

I heard the click but it took me a moment to realize she'd hung up. I wondered who Martin was. Her lover?

P.S. 70, where Earl had been teaching music for six years since leaving Brooklyn, was just a mile and a half away, not far from where he lived before moving into Lillian's. I had never visited him there. I had never again wanted to be in a school where my father taught music. I didn't want to smell turkey-noodle soup simmering in a cafeteria, see children with hall passes, hear a principal yammering over the public-address and know that somewhere, down that corridor, or up that flight of stairs, sat my father leading the class in song—or, more likely, a fraction of the class because no matter how he shouted there were always at least a half dozen who would have nothing to do with him, who sang one song while the class sang another, who raced around the desks, who threw erasers, and who were capable of shoving Earl off the piano bench and taking over the keys, playing rock and roll until he slapped at them with a pointer.

P.S. 70 was a five-story red-brick building with protective grating on all of its windows. There was an iron fence with pointed black stakes surrounding the school, but there were no grounds to protect, only a few feet of littered asphalt. I climbed the concrete steps to the row of doors at the entrance of the building. The first door I tried was locked and so was the second; the third swung open and I walked in. A policeman and a woman who looked like a typical elderly teacher sat at a table in the giant empty lobby, right near the steps that led to the main floor. I nodded at them and followed an arrow that said *To General Office*.

The corridors were dead silent; all of the classroom doors were closed. I knew Earl wasn't on this floor; he'd once told me that his room was at the top of the building. I pushed through the double doors that led to the stairway and continued to walk up. The stairway smelled of paste, of crayons, sandwiches, and piss. The iron grilling protecting the stairwell made the landings between floors look like corners of a penitentiary. By the time I reached the fourth floor I had to stop to catch my breath; it amazed and infuriated me that my father made that climb daily.

I walked slowly down the fifth floor, looking through the window of each door I passed. In one, the lights wee out and the class watched a film, in another a tall, muscular, completely bald man paced the room while thirty children worked at old-fashioned adding machines. As I reached the end of the corridor, I heard the distant throb of a piano and I followed the sound until I stood before Room 525. I looked in.

I felt a little like Scrooge peeking at his own muddled past. There was Earl playing what sounded like the "Moonlight Sonata," his shoulders hunched, swaying in time, glancing back at the class over his shoulder. He used to tell me, "If I'm going to have to make a living locked up with those kids, I may as well try and shove a little good music in their little tin ears." When he used to pursue my class's latent appreciation of music I would keep a poker face, hating those who refused to listen but not willing to join those five or six children who seemed genuinely enraptured by the music or who would ask by name for Grieg and Mozart. It was seventeen years past but as I stood there I could feel the splinters in my old deskseat, see the buttery slats of sun coming through the windows, and practically touch the tantalizing ponytail of Linda Mackell, who sat in front of me for two years.

I moved a little back from the door to see the children in the class, half expecting, I think, to find one who looked like me: the one with glazed eyes, balled fists, the one with crimson kisses on the tops of his ears. The class, however, was not like the ones I'd known. It was a good New York mix, with blacks, Puerto Ricans, a pair of Italian twins, a Chinese girl, and a couple of ten-year-old boys who dressed the way I did when I was in college, with Levis, work shirts, and long, uncombed hair. In the grammar school I'd attended, there were no blacks, no Puerto Ricans: the cultural oddballs were the hillbillies and my father. I could tell at once that none of these kids found Earl particularly strange: no stranger than their parents, no stranger than their neighbors, no stranger, really, than people on TV. The world had changed, it had stopped trying to hold itself so foolishly upright and Earl had been waiting for it, with his beret, with his knit ties and maroon shirts, and his Gatling gun laugh. He was more at home, more assured in that class than I could ever be.

They listened while Earl played. They weren't rapt, the weren't transported, but they listened. The Chinese girl took off her glasses and rested her face in her hands. The room was drab; paint hung from the walls in large curls. The windows let in little sun and the overhead lights were not as bright as they should have been. In the front of the room were stacks of books, probably song books. The room was undecorated except for encyclopedia pictures of Beethoven, Bach, Mozart, Brahms, Schubert, Stravinsky, Bartók, Berg, and Webern. There was a music ledger drawn on the blackboard but there were no notes on it.

Earl stopped playing. "Ludwig van Beethoven," he said, as if announcing a pinch-hitter over the public-address. "Who likes it? Who hates it? Let's see some hands."

Nearly everyone in the class raised a hand.

"Are those the likes or the hates?" he said, smiling. The bell began to ring. He put up his finger and raised his shaggy eyebrows. "Ah. Now I'll never know." He stood up and clapped his hands once. "When does this class have music next?"

"Friday, Mr. M," a boy said.

"Okay. Friday."

The class filed out. I moved away from the door, suddenly furtive. I listened to hear if any of the kids said anything about Earl but I didn't hear anything; so it had been when I was his student. I simply never heard anything that was said.

The halls were filled with children changing classes or going to lunch. Most of them moved in groups of twenty or thirty, supervised by teachers, but a few roamed maverick, bedeviling those who operated under restraint. I pressed against the wall so they could pass. Suddenly, Earl emerged from the music room and closed the door behind him. He carried a brown bag with his lunch in it.

"Hello," I said, but he didn't hear me over the noise of the children, even though I was only ten feet away. "Dad," I said, louder.

He looked up. Following his glance were the eyes of a half dozen curious children.

"Virgil," he said. "What's wrong?" He kept his hand on the door.

I approached him with my hand extended. He shrugged, bobbed his leonine head and rather than using his right hand to shake my own he used it to swing open the door to his room. He used to call handshakes businessmen's gestures.

"Come on in," he said, waving me in so emphatically that I could only think he wanted as few people as possible to see us. He flicked on the lights; the room bucked and trembled as the fluorescents came back on.

"What brings you here?"

"I haven't seen you in a while. How are things with you and Lillian?"

He walked over to his desk and sat on the edge of it, his feet extended. He wore rope-soled shoes and pale orange socks. "She's all right most of the time."

"I spoke to her on the phone a little while ago." I looked around for a place to sit but the seats were far too small.

"You did?" He sounded truly alarmed.

"I was looking for you," I said.

"What'd she say?"

"Nothing. She didn't want to speak to me. She hung up."

He nodded. It was clear he thought he would have to account for my call.

"She never wants to see me again, does she?" I said.

"I told you her love for that boy was fierce. I told you that."

I nodded. "You did."

"Maybe in time."

"I don't expect you to take my side against her. I know you're in a terrible position."

"Virgil, if she walked in here—which she wouldn't, but if she did—and saw us talking, even if I told her you surprised me, that you came here from out of bloody nowhere, she'd have a tough time forgiving me. It's not that I don't keep my eye open to see if her attitude changes. But the woman is convinced you killed her son. Deliberately."

"I know."

"Well, you picked the worst time to call, that's all. Melissa called last night and told us that your lawyer is getting the police to drop the whole thing." He paused for a moment. "Not that *I'm* sorry, you understand. I knew the police weren't going to bother with the matter. But Lillian was *counting* on it."

I wanted to ask him if he was taking her side against me. I knew the answer was, at best, yes and no, and was probably simply yes. But I could not bring myself to ask him; as much as I wanted to smoke him out, I did not want to make him lie.

"I still don't know why you're here," he said.

"I wanted to know where Melissa is. I want to speak to her."

"You want to speak to *her*? You certainly can pick them."

"I feel lousy about what my lawyer did to her."

"Your lawyer is supposed to be the smartest in that whole state."

"Do you know where Melissa is?"

"She's pregnant, you know. She's carrying Tommy's kid. At least that's what she tells us. I say, who knows? I believe she's pregnant but I'm a devout Strindbergian on the question of rightful fatherhood: it will always be woman's ultimate secret."

"I went to her apartment."

"She's not there. She's not even in the city."

"Where is she?"

"Her family's got her someplace where she can have her baby in peace. You know the rich and their timely reconciliations."

My legs felt weak. I walked to the blackboard and leaned against it.

"You're going to get chalky," Earl said.

I stood up but then leaned back again. I thought for a moment I would pass out. I could picture myself on the floor. I looked at Earl and he stared back at me. His eyes were glassy with what looked like tears.

"I never thought I'd see the day when I'd feel sorry for you," he said.

"That sounds like an insult," I said, with some of my strength seeping back into my legs.

He shrugged and looked away.

"I'm not living with Tracy."

He nodded.

"I quit my job, too."

"What are you going to do?"

"I don't know."

He walked across the room and sat at the piano.

"I got a letter from Los Angeles yesterday. I'm one of ten finalists for that chamber music competition."

"When will you know?"

"I hate competition." His fingers touched the keys without pressing. "But that's not very extraordinary for a loser, is it? The thing to do is get the award and then say you don't want it."

"I hope you get it."

"I don't even like the piece I sent them. I'm working on something new. Something different for me. Do you want me to play it for you?"

"Yes." I sat at his desk.

"You'll be just the second person to hear it." His hands expanded to play the beginning chord, but then he stopped himself. "Lillian loves this," he said.

It was different from the kind of music I associated with him. The jittery rhythms had been smoothed out and though the chords were stuffed with notes they seemed remarkably agreeable, almost placid, unlike his usual chords in which the notes blindly warred. He played loudly, with his back straight and his chin abnormally high, like a Prussian officer on review. I closed my eyes and listened. I didn't know much about music, but I suddenly suspected that Earl's new piece was brilliant. Even in its raw form, with its hesitations, its halts, its repeats, and its one section in which he merely hummed a part he'd yet to satisfactorily compose, the music sounded natural, strong, and, as most lovely melodies sound to people who don't understand music, unbearably sad. I had always thought of the great composers brushing tear drops from the score as they worked and now, for the first time, I thought of my father composing in that same way. I'd never heard him play so passionately. The floor buzzed with the reverberations of his piece; the sound must have carried to every room in the school. His piece reminded me of Debussy, of Ravel, of Satie, Scriabin: it was the first time his music made me think of other music, rather than of sinks piled with dirty dishes. It was music! It was an incredible thing: my father was making music.

Abruptly, he stopped playing. His hands rested on the keys but the sound seemed to linger in the room, as if waiting to be dismissed.

"That was beautiful," I said.

His eyes were closed. He shrugged.

"I think it's your most beautiful piece," I said. I stood up. I wanted to throw my arms around him, and I felt a little surge of gloom because I knew I never would.

"If it's so brilliant then why hasn't anyone heard of me?" Earl said, stopping me in my tracks with a hard stare.

"I don't know. It's very hard to understand why things happen the way they do."

"Oh, shut up. You don't know anything about it."

He stood up suddenly. The piano bench toppled over and fell dully to the floor.

"Does it have a name?" I asked.

"What?"

"What you just played."

He shook his head. "I can't stand naming them anymore. When I name them I see them published, I see them on concert programs, on record labels." He touched the keys—a high discordant chord. "I get so fucking angry. You just don't know."

I nodded. I wanted to say that I *did* know, but I wasn't sure if I was supposed to and I wasn't even certain that I did.

"I hated your music when I was growing up," I said. "I hated your playing in front of my friends. I hated how much you wanted something that you didn't have."

"I know you did. But you know how these things work, don't you? You'll get over it. You'll need to make a certain kind of judgment about your own life and part of that will be elevating me. But when that happens, if I'm still alive—"

"It's happening."

"Well, I just want you to know that you can't expect to all of a sudden become a part of my life."

"I don't expect that."

"Because that just can't be. You understand that?"

"I do understand."

"I've got to protect what I have. That's why I sent Lillian's boy up north. It had nothing to do with you. I hope you understand that. But he was killing everything between Lillian and me. It's not as if we've been married for thirty years. And it's not as if I'm an easy man to live with. I've got to have this one thing, at least. I think I deserve it."

"I think I'll go home now," I said.

"Okay." His eyes looked glassy again and I knew he wanted to touch me.

"Are you going to grow your beard back?"

He touched his chin. "Who knows?" He moved his fingers along the route his whiskers used to grow.

"I better go," I said, coaxing myself out of the room.

I put my hand out for a moment. He didn't respond and I withdrew it. I couldn't help thinking this was the last time we'd ever see each other.

"I'd like to kiss you good-bye," I said.

"Ah," he said, leaning back, "very continental."

"Look," I said, stepping back. My heart and mind were halfway down the hall. "I'm ruining your lunch."

"I don't care." He touched the piano keys. What I wanted him to do was play the theme song of my timid youth but he ran a chromatic scale. Then he stopped and righted the piano bench.

"Good-bye," I said.

"Wait a second, Virgil. I want you to see something."

He picked up the piano bench and held it at chest level for a moment. Then, with a long, violent grunt, he flung it across the width of the room. It crashed into the wall and fell onto the children's desks. In the stillness of the room it sounded as if a mine had collapsed.

"That's how I feel sometimes," he said. "And it's also a bit of advice."

My hands were shaking. My face felt stiff and I realized I was grinning from ear to ear. I stared at the bench. "Thank you," I said, with a hot rush of feeling. I heard footsteps running down the corridor.

"You'd better go," said Earl. "Fast. I'll know what to say."

I let myself out of his room. Two teachers were running toward me. The youngest was my age and he carried a small baseball bat.

"It's nothing to worry about," I said, moving past them. I walked quickly away, still shaking, still grinning, as they burst into Earl's room.

"What the hell happened here?" one of them cried, but by that time I was on the steps, going down.

* * *

I took a West Side train uptown and emerged two blocks from Tracy's office. I caught my reflection in a store window and nearly decided to go home, shave, and change my clothes before going to see her, but I had no confidence that I'd be able to maintain my hold on my soaring spirits. I was finally ready to tell her that I loved her and that I wanted us to live together and I didn't want to waste another moment.

The lobby of her building was unattended. The floor directory was half empty. Businesses were going under. Dust was pyramiding in the corners. And I'd never felt so confident in my life. I punched the UP button of the elevator and it opened immediately. Slowly, the elevator rose to the sixth floor while I looked in the ceiling mirror and tried vainly to smooth down my hair a little. I probably stank as well. No matter.

Just as I had in the beginning of our love affair, I charged into Tracy's office. The frosted glass door said *Morgan and Fish*. I threw it open. It hit a coat rack. I faced Gary Fish, who held a telephone to his ear, his feet on the desk. He went pale when he saw me.

I raised my hands in what I hoped looked like a peaceful gesture.

He clapped his hand over the phone. He had a yellow and violet bruise on the side of his face and a half moon of dried blood on his nostril.

"What do you want?"

"Is Tracy here?"

"No."

"No?"

Their offices consisted of two rooms. Through a door directly behind Fish was another, larger room, where most of the company's physical work was done.

"I'll look in back."

"She's not there," said Fish.

In the back room there were three drafting tables, one with a light on above it. It was the table Tracy most often worked at. I went to it. She was pasting up a book about yoga for elderly people. There was a pack of cinnamon-flavored gum on the top of the table. On a small note pad, written in her hand, was a reminder: *Friday lunch with Courtney.* I looked at my watch. It was just noon.

Back in the front office, Fish stood next to his desk, with his hands behind his back. I suspected he held some kind of weapon, in case I were to attack him again.

"Please, Gary," I said. "I have to talk to Tracy. She's having lunch with someone named Courtney. Do you have any idea—'"

"I have no idea," he cut in.

"Where does she usually go for lunch?"

"She doesn't *usually* go anywhere. She goes where she wants."

"I'll wait here until she comes back, then."

"She's not coming back. We close at noon on Fridays."

"Is she going back to your house?"

He looked at me strangely. Perhaps he sensed my need of him at that moment and it pleased him. Or maybe he tendered the secret knowledge of a pistol he held hidden behind his back and this gave him gruesome confidence.

"I don't know where she's going, Virgil. And I don't know what you want with her or if she wants to see you. I don't know anything about anything that's between you. She's staying at my house when she wants to, for as long as she wants to."

"When she wants to? You mean she's staying someplace else, too?"

"I'm not going to be involved."

"I've got to see her."

"From what I understand you two will be in Maine to talk to the police. You can see her then."

"No," I said, backing toward the door. I had no

idea where I was heading, but I needed to move. "I want to see her today. Now."

The elevator was waiting for me. A minute later—a long minute—I was on Broadway. Across the street was a Chinese restaurant Tracy and I had eaten in a few times. I stared at it for a moment, remembering her sitting at a small table, near a paper light shade, a bowl of cold Chinese noodles before her, a pair of gleaming black chopsticks in her hand. I loved to watch her eat.

I raced across the street, vaulting over the divider, dodging a bus, and, slowing myself down a little, taking deep, calming breaths, I walked into Li Tung. I was greeted by a Chinese in a dark suit, cradling a dozen menus in his arm.

"One? Two? How many?" he said. The restaurant was half empty.

"Just looking," I said, and moved past him. I began checking the tables, one at a time. I knew the chances were slim indeed that I'd find her but I didn't want to discover I was in the wrong place all at once. And if I were to find her, I wanted to give myself time to think of what to say, and what I'd do if this mysterious "Courtney" wasn't a client at all, but her lover. Slowly, I revolved around the restaurant, until I'd checked each of the thirty tables. I felt like screaming: she wasn't there.

Back on the street, I tried to remember the places she liked to lunch, though now I realized that her appointment might have taken her to the East Side, or the Village, or anywhere at all. Still, I had to trust my luck and I finally thought of some of the restaurants in the vicinity which she preferred. The first one was a vegetarian restaurant two blocks away but she was not there. I tried a Cuban restaurant but no luck. I tried a Jewish dairy restaurant and, last on my list of possibilities, a Japanese macrobiotic restaurant where, a year before, Tracy had pried from the chef his recipe for salad dressing.

I didn't know where to go next. I was on Broadway, in the Eighties, not terribly far from my apartment and I thought of walking home. A cab sped by and I thought I saw Tracy sitting in the back seat. I watched it for a moment, waiting for the illusion to pass, but it persisted and I chased after the cab. I went pounding down the pavement after it, and it didn't stop for a traffic light until Ninety-second Street, where I saw that it wasn't Tracy at all. However, unlike the girl walking the dog through the park, this woman actually looked like Tracy and after I backed away from the cab she smiled at me, an act which I interpreted as a kind of benediction.

On the corner of Broadway and Ninetieth Street was a new Italian restaurant. It had a glassed-in section which extended onto the sidewalk where a dozen small tables were set for lunch. Hanging plants and stained glass mobiles obscured the view in. I gave the place an inspection through the window and I saw Tracy sipping on a glass of something. In front of her was an un-touched sandwich and further in front of her was the man who I assumed was Courtney. He was a tall silver-haired man, wearing a forceful checkered suit. He looked like someone's father from out of town. I watched them from the street, my heart exploding with joy, relief, and fear. This was clearly a business lunch. Courtney, good Courtney. Courtney the Stout-hearted was smiling shyly and then—bliss!—he produced a brochure from his breast pocket. Of course, there was a chance that the folder described the Caribbean hotel to which they planned to run away, but more likely it was connected to whatever it was he wanted Morgan and Fish to do. Tracy took the brochure from him, looked it over, nodded, and placed it on the table. I loved watching her move. I could have stayed peering into the window for an hour had I not yearned so to speak to her.

It was noisy inside and it smelled of garlic and beer. The tables were packed close and I had to snake my way toward Tracy. When I was halfway to her, she looked in my direction and her face went red with amazing speed, as if a lever had been thrown. Her emotion was so apparent that Courtney turned in his chair to see what she was reacting to.

"Tracy," I said, praying that she'd say nothing to stop me.

She picked up her glass and sipped delicately. It was a way she had of composing herself; she slowed everything down, like a yogi in the first stages of meditation.

"Hello, Virgil," she said, as if I were someone she'd met long ago at a dance. The deep flush had left her face and now she looked merely healthy. She'd changed; she'd gained a little weight, she was wearing lipstick. I glanced down. She wore beige nylons and shiny black shoes. A moment's panic: who *was* this?

"I've been looking all over for you," I said. "It's just insane luck that I saw you. I was passing by." I gestured vaguely. "I looked in."

She nodded.

Say something, goddamnit. Aren't you glad?

"You must be Courtney," I said to her lunch partner. "I'm sorry to crash in like this, but"—I noticed his wedding ring—"you know how these things can be." I stood straighter, suddenly conscious of how wrecked I must look. "I'm Virgil Morgan," I said, extending my hand.

"George Courtney," he said, half rising from his chair.

"Oh, so *George* is your first name. I thought Courtney— Well." I realized I was grinning. Perhaps I'd been grinning since leaving Earl, leaving with his unexpected gift—this new lightness I felt and my ability to act foolishly.

"What do you want, Virgil?" Tracy said.

It was wonderful to hear her voice.

"I want to see you. I need to talk to you."

"Now?"

I thought for a moment and then nodded.

"Why don't you take my seat for a few moments?" Courtney said, getting up. "I have to use the phone." Quickly, without any smiles of self-congratulation, he slipped between the tables and was gone.

Alone with Tracy now, I suddenly felt less brave.

"Is it all right if I sit down?"

"You're fucking up a business lunch." She lifted her hands as if to cover her face but she stopped midgesture.

"Well how are you?" I said.

"Is that what you wanted to know?"

"I want to know everything."

"I'm all right." There was a silence. "You?"

"I don't know." I was beginning to panic. We could conceivably waste all of our time talking about nothing. "Tracy?"

She looked more closely at me.

"I miss you," I said.

"What am I supposed to do with that? I mean— Well, what difference does it make? I miss you, too. Okay?"

"It makes a lot of difference." I looked down. I stared at Courtney's abandoned lunch: a veal chop, a little logjam of chopped green beans, a boiled potato. "Is the food good here?" I asked.

"I don't know. He likes it."

"Tracy—"

"You threw me out of your life, Virgil. Today, that hurts more than ever. I'd really like to slug you."

"I miss you so horribly."

"You miss what our life used to be."

"No. You."

"Maybe I shouldn't have let you force me out. I thought that once the bottom dropped out of our life I'd find something enduring. But I was completely wrong, wasn't I? I let everything drift out to sea. Including you."

"I'd like us to try and live together again. We don't

have to pick it up from where it broke. We can begin right now and just make it up as we go along."

She shook her head. I chose to take it as a sign of uncertainty.

"Please, Tracy."

"We're being horrible to George. You'd better get up so he can have his seat back."

"I don't care about his fucking veal chop."

"Well *I* do."

I stood up. "Can I see you after you're finished here?"

"I've got an appointment."

"After that?"

"I'll be late."

"Why are you doing this?"

"I'm only telling the truth. I've been very busy." She paused; her features softened momentarily. "It's better for me."

"Can I tell you, then?"

"Look, Virgil. I've got a book to paste up. I'll be working all weekend. Monday's shot."

"Can I call you anyhow?"

"Gary had the number changed. We were getting strange calls. I don't know the new one."

I felt Courtney moving up behind me. I turned around. He smiled shyly.

"Walk with me outside?" I said to Tracy. I knew it would be difficult for her to refuse. Despite Courtney's sympathetic smile and his soft gray eyes, I suspected he knew nothing of the troubles between Tracy and me and it wasn't her way to confide in him.

"Okay," she said, standing. "I'll say good-bye to you."

Out on the street, she extended her hand to me.

"I'll see you," she said.

"When?"

"Are you worried about what kind of statement I'm going to make for the police? Is that it?"

"That's not it at all."

"You don't have to worry. I would never say anything to get you in trouble. I never thought it was your fault, anyhow."

"You didn't?"

"I've got to go back in."

"Tracy."

"I'm sorry, Virgil. I'm sorry you can't accept what's happened to us."

"I can't. I'm glad I can't." I moved closer to her.

"You smell like a pig," she said, but she did not move back.

I put my arms on her shoulders. I waited for a tremor of resistance. And then I kissed her. She did not throw herself into my arms but her hand touched the side of my face.

Suddenly, she broke the kiss. "Don't do this to me."

I reached for her but she was already moving away.

"Tracy." Her back was to me.

"Please," she said, smoothing the back of her hair.

I watched her through the glass, threading her way back to her table. I thought I might simply stand on the pavement and watch her and evidently she sensed my capacity for poor behavior because she picked up her sandwich and drink and Courtney picked up his plate and together they walked to the restaurant's invisible interior.

My face burned with shame.

Alone in my apartment I threw myself into preparing my statement for the police with the blind devotion of the truly unhinged. I brooded about it as I paced. I finished what liquor I had left and then I finished all my food, down to the capers. I tried to mentally compose what I'd say but I couldn't keep it in suspension. I tried to take notes but the physical act of writing depressed and exhausted me and each time I lifted the pen from the page thoughts of Tracy would rush into my mind and I would be lost in them.

Finally, after looking all over the apartment for it and then remembering I'd failed to bring it back from Maine, I ran out and bought a cassette recorder and some blank tape. I sat on the edge of the couch and wrapped my hand around the tiny microphone as if it might take flight, and talking slowly, with the kind of nerve-racking enunciation some people are left with after they outdodge a speech impediment, I began to prepare for Monday in earnest.

"I didn't do it," I began. No, that was terrible. "It is impossible to say what happened the afternoon—" No, that would be like begging for a full investigation. And what I wanted was to return fully to my life, with all of my concentration and my new-found energy.

I made a dozen tries, listened to each one, and then erased it. I didn't lose patience. When thoughts of Tracy intruded I placed them aside, thinking that constructing my statement was part of my way back to her. By evening, I had something I could accept.

"I hit Tom Douglas on the head with a fireplace poker while he, Melissa Cavanaugh, Tracy Morgan, and I were trapped in a house owned by my wife and me. The house is near Gardner Point, Maine, and we were trapped because of the great blizzard that came to the area on or around January first.

"We were without heat and water so it was necessary to break up furniture to burn in the fireplace. On my recommendation, we chose, at a certain point, to break up a pine dresser that was in the room used by Tom Douglas and Melissa Cavanaugh. To make this task simpler, I brought up a fireplace poker which I planned to use as a tool. Tom Douglas thought this was a poor idea and urged me to do it by hand. I refused. He stood near me with his arms folded. I took a couple of practice swings at the dresser. During these practice swings I had no idea Tom Douglas was standing within the range

of my swing and he said nothing to warn me that the poker was coming close to him.

"The question that has tortured me personally was whether or not he moved forward when I was in the middle of my swing and now I can say that, in all probability, this is what happened. He said, 'Wait,' and I believe he was going to try and tell me not to hit the dresser, or perhaps he was going to say something else. He was unpredictable. At any rate, he stepped forward and I couldn't stop my swing. He was hit on the side of the head and he never fully regained consciousness.

"This is what happened. It may or may not be pertinent to the investigation, but I want to mention that there had been friction between Mr. Douglas and myself. He had come without warning, without invitation, without either my wife or I really knowing him, and he was in serious trouble with the police. There was considerable bad feeling between us, especially after a rescue helicopter passed over the house and Mr. Douglas impeded my efforts to signal it. I am willing to testify in detail about the nature and extent of the friction between us but here I want to reaffirm that this friction had nothing to do with his death, which was an accident. This is not to say that I take no responsibility for what happened, but this is a personal responsibility, a spiritual one. I am not a criminal."

I played this tape over and over. I must have listened to it three dozen times. When the batteries began to run down and my serious, controlled voice began dragging drunkenly, I used the plug. I took it with me to the bathroom where I shaved for the first time in days and then I turned up the volume as far as it would go so I could listen while I showered. I listened until I believed every word, until I no longer had an impulse to add ambiguities, to ruffle the tone of it so my role might appear more open to questions. I wanted to believe that voice, that reasonable, honest voice, and finally, when it was practically midnight, I did.

I don't know if it's possible to know exactly what our responsibility is for the lives we touch. There is too much that happens in even the simplest life for any real accounting. There were wars I did little to stop, the eyes of suicidal strangers which I could not engage. Half the world was in ruin while I shopped for neckties. But I had to begin with the events I could touch, the ones I could participate in. There was, I knew, a great deal I could have done differently while Tommy and Melissa were with us and most of the bad choices I made were the bad choices I'd always made. *That* was a responsibility I could hold. It was mine and I saw, finally, that Kathryn was right: it was nothing any court could make me feel. As far as the law was concerned, I was innocent.

I could publicly proclaim my innocence while keeping my thumb on the pulse of my secret knowledge and still not feel that I was lying. I didn't do it, even though I did, but as far as the world was concerned, as far as I had to face the judgment of others, I had nothing to defend. For the first time since Tommy fell to the floor, and really for the first time in my life, I didn't feel like a fugitive. For the first time I did not tender the dreadful suspicion that I was somehow a moral inferior.

I wanted her to be walking through the door. I thought of our meeting in the afternoon and raged at myself for not making myself clearer. I thought of myself as someone who was all alone in the world but I just could not believe that it was true. I was someone who was *almost* completely alone. Almost. I had a fool's antic confidence that Tracy still loved me.

I waited for her to call but the silence peeled my nerves. I called Information for Fish's new number but it was unlisted.

I turned on the radio. Tracy loved the radio, especially when she was working. I turned the dial slowly, listening to each station and trying to decide which one she'd most likely be listening to. Maybe she was sleeping, or maybe she was making love with someone I'd never heard of. But I chose to believe she was sitting chastely at Fish's, working on a design for a book and listening to the radio. She liked talk shows, especially on noncommercial radio. I tuned in a show hosted by two men from a humane society. They described the mistreatment of animals in the movies. The station broadcasted on a weak frequency and continually drifted into the rush of static on either side of it. I crouched before the radio, kept my hand on the tuner, and listened. They talked about trip wires and cockfights. Tracy conceivably listened to the same station, the same words, while she pasted up a book and sipped cold coffee. She might know that I was listening too. Something would be said, some phrase, a tone of voice, and it would remind her of me. She'd wonder if I was home. She'd think about our trip up to Maine. Perhaps she'd vow to give me more time there, not to run away, not to make it so hard. We'd make our statements and drive out to Preservation Hall to look at it before selling it and there we would make love, in that haunted house, right in the place in which our lives had blown up in our faces.

The station was taking calls from listeners now. A woman called and added some films to the list of ventures which had mistreated animals in the making. I wrote the number down and stalked across the room to dial in. My heart was slamming with excitement. It was the perfect way to reach her. I would push my love through the electronic net. I would be undeniable.

The first time I dialed, the line was busy. I hung up, counted to twenty, and dialed again.

The program host answered with the station's call letters.

I knew I had only a few seconds. As soon as my purpose was clear, the connection would be broken.

"Hello, Tracy," I said. "I'm thinking of you." My voice reverberated across the room. "If you are—" He had hung up on me.

I resumed my post before the radio. The announcer asked his listeners to "show some care" and warned them that the FCC had many times attempted to revoke the station's license. Then another call came in. It was a man who used to be a stunt rider in Hollywood in the twenties. He sounded very old and very angry.

I would give her fifteen minutes to respond to my message. I prayed that she'd heard me, that she was now stuffing her toothbrush and diaphragm into her purse. But maybe she needed to be asked again, or perhaps she was just now turning on the radio.

I waited. The stunt rider was raging, correcting points of facts, challenging innuendos. I didn't know whether or not I agreed with the old man but I loved his fury. I felt suddenly, rapturously connected to everyone in the world who slammed a fist onto a table and said, "No. Now you listen to *me*." I felt my heart and will connected to nationalists crawling through jungles with makeshift weapons, secret Christians praying in basements, and my own father throwing his piano bench across a decaying classroom. I was a revolutionary ready to seize power in my life. I'd often wondered where people found the daring to engage in all-out struggle, but now, finally, I saw there were fights that simply obliterated all thoughts of consequence. You had to be a fanatic; you had to feel a truly desperate hunger to *know*. I was ready to risk everything, ready to fight. I thought of Tracy, remembered her hand as it touched my cheek as we kissed outside of that restaurant. We'd lived with each other for so long and so rarely touched on the mysteries between us, yet it was her I wanted, her I loved, and heeding the heart's thundering wisdom, I knew that whatever I would eventually come to know of myself, finding my way back to her, back to us, was next. With every moment, my certainty grew stronger. I wanted Tracy to hear me, to know me. I would not take maybe for an answer. If I couldn't reach her through the radio station then I'd try something else. I looked at my watch. Soon I'd call the station again. What would I say? It hardly mattered. I probably wouldn't have time to do more than bellow her name.

About the Author

SCOTT SPENCER is the author of three other novels:
LAST NIGHT AT THE BRAIN THIEVES'
BALL, ENDLESS LOVE, and WAKING THE
DEAD. He was born in Washington, D.C., in 1945,
grew up in Chicago, and graduated from the University of Wisconsin. He lives in Rhinebeck, New
York, with his wife and two children.